Return of the RUNEBOUND PROFESSOR 4

ACTUS

aethonbooks.com

RETURN OF THE RUNEBOUND PROFESSOR 4
©2024 ACTUS

Also in series

Return of the Runebound Professor

Return of the Runebound Professor 2

Return of the Runebound Professor 3

Return of the Runebound Professor 4

Check out the entire series here! (Tap or scan)

The Story So far

In Book 3 of Return of the Runebound Professor, Noah pissed off a bunch of people. The summary could probably be left there and be largely accurate, but I do imagine that would make it somewhat useless.

To get more specific, Noah pissed off a few criminals and freed a girl by the name of Alexandra from the grips of a mind mage.

He also managed to piss off the Torrin family — or at least, the portion of it that he didn't care all that much about. He, along with Moxie and Lee, were having a great summer right up until Evergreen decided that Moxie had overstepped her bounds and had to return to the family estate to be executed.

Noah wasn't much a fan of that.

Thus, upon arrival, the gang took it into their own hands to orchestrate the downfall of Evergreen. And, as usual, Noah got himself killed in the process.

That should have been that, but their troubles were far from over. While Noah was out getting an oversized grimoire for himself, he found a magical book of Linwick records claiming that Father was supposedly dead.

On top of that, Noah's antics drew the attention of the head of the Linwick family, Jalen. While he has been trying to enjoy the last of his summer break together with Lee and Moxie, Jalen has sent Karina, as well as a number of assassins, after him.

They're probably going to have to find a way to deal with that —
but first, the group has a Great Monster to kill.

Chapter One

Silver moonlight shone down on the mountainside, illuminating a forest in its glow. Noah and Moxie crept behind Lee as she led them through the foliage. Their target, a Great Monster, drew nearer with every step. They'd spent more than enough time figuring out their plan—now it was time to act.

Noah held his violin and bow, prepared to start playing as soon as they came into contact with the Great Monster. One of the most glaring drawbacks of casting Formations with music was quickly becoming evident.

He couldn't prepare them beforehand. It was one thing to know what song he was going to play, and he was *fairly* certain it would work, but he'd still have to actually play it. That meant Moxie and Lee would have to hold the snake off until he finished.

"We're close," Lee whispered. "I smell it next to us."

They all came to a stop. Wind whistled through the trees around them, rustling the branches and nipping at their exposed skin. Noah strained his ears, trying to see if he could pick up any traces of the Great Monster.

He couldn't. It just felt like they were standing in the middle of a sparse forest on a mountainside. The only things he could hear other than the wind and plants were the faint noises of insects hiding in the darkness.

"Is it sleeping?" Moxie's voice was a hushed whisper. "How close are we?"

"Close enough that we shouldn't get closer," Lee replied. "If it's changing its shape, then we could get too close and get squished when it transforms. It's here somewhere."

That's a lot of 'closes' in one sentence.

Lee sniffed at the air again, then turned slightly to her left and squinted into the trees. Noah followed her gaze, calling on his tremorsense to see if he could pick up anything out of the ordinary.

There was a good amount of motion in the forest around them, but largely by small, inconsequential creatures. The environment was definitely a lot more diverse than the Scorched Acres had been, probably because it wasn't artificially created, but there was still no sign of anything that could have resembled a Great Monster.

"It's probably more than twenty feet away," Noah said. "I don't feel—"

A crunch echoed through the forest. A tree pitched forward and crashed to the ground like an executioner's axe, sending up a cloud of fragmented wood and dirt. Several more trees followed it as a roaring hiss echoed through the dark forest.

The head of a massive snake burst out above the treeline, its fangs flashing silver in the moonlight.

"Found it," Lee said.

"Thank you," Noah said dryly. "So did I. Let's go with the plan."

Lee blurred into motion, bounding across the ground. The ground around Moxie came alive with vines that burst from within it, rapidly growing in size. A shadow passed over all of them as the Great Monster brought its considerable bulk crashing down.

"I got it!" Lee yelled. She launched herself into the air, rearing back and swinging her axe as she blurred. She slammed into the Great Monster like a bolt of lightning. A reverberating crash shook the forest as the force of her strike knocked the snake's head to the side—not stopping the attack, but redirecting it.

It slammed down through the trees, crushing them with a splintering crash. Moxie raised her hands into the air, and the vines beside her erupted forth, winding up beneath her feet to carry her like a wave.

Noah tore his attention away from the fight and laid his bow against the strings of his violin. The forest ground shuddered as the fight intensified, and the first note hummed out from the violin.

His hand started to move faster, the lone note slipping into a song. His eyes closed in concentration as he sank completely into his work. Power coursed through the music and swirled around his body, flooding into the Formation. Another crash shook the forest, and a cloud of dust rolled past Noah, pelting him with small fragments of sharp wood, but he didn't stop playing.

I'm not good enough to both make a Formation and dodge attacks, so Lee and Moxie will keep the Great Monster's attention until I finish.

The power gathering around Noah started to intensify as the Fragment of Renewal filled the notes of his song. He was mildly amused to note that the music he'd chosen to fit the Master Rune into was a bastardized version of Paganini's Caprice Number 5. Something about the rapid, energetic notes felt like they fit the Fragment of Renewal's power.

Noah's bow flitted across the strings at such a rapid pace that they would have caught aflame if the magic coursing through them hadn't been present. He was quite certain that the violin was aiding him somehow, intensifying the speed of his movements to inhuman levels.

The final notes of the song rang out, finally slowing to a stop. The power welling around him reached a crescendo and roared out, forming a crackling rune circle in the air above him.

He opened his eyes once more as streamers of pink mist danced around his body, rising up into the rune circle.

"Now!" Lee yelled.

Vines shot out of the ground, wrapping around the struggling Great Monster and bringing its head crashing down to the ground, causing it to quake. A furious hiss tore from the snake as it thrashed, easily tearing through the vines holding it.

Unfortunately for the Great Monster, its moment of distraction meant that there wasn't any time to get out of the way. A wave of pink mist rolled out from the Formation and passed into its mouth.

The monster's massive eyes widened in shock, and it ripped free of Moxie's bindings, hacking and hissing. Its tongue flitted out as if trying to spit out the mist, but the damage was done.

Glistening scales turned black and rotted, falling away from its body. The monster thrashed as its body rapidly liquified and sloughed away. Within seconds, the majority of the monster had melted to nothing.

Lee burst into motion. She flashed through the air, and her hand shot out just as a green blur leapt from the massive pile of goop. It was about as wide as Lee and a little more than twice her height—but that wasn't anywhere near enough to slow Lee down.

With a cry, she spun around and flung the blur straight at Moxie. Red vines covered with jagged, dripping thorns whipped out, their ends sharpened points. The Great Monster didn't even get a chance to dodge.

It slammed into the waiting spikes, impaled in half a dozen different places. Its body went limp immediately, having no life left to spend.

Noah lowered his violin as the last of the power from his Formation faded away. He let it return to his tattoo as Moxie's vines dropped the corpse of the Great Monster at her feet. She drew in a deep breath and opened her eyes, a shudder passing through her body.

"Hah! That was awesome!" Lee glared down at the dead Great Monster. "That's what you get for squishing my wylf. Did you get the Master Rune?"

"Yeah." It took Moxie a moment longer than normal to respond. "It's so... intense. It has far more energy than any of my other runes."

"I guess it helps that Master Runes come pre-filled," Noah said. "And I suppose they're truly perfect as well. What does it do?"

"It's called Earthen Muster." Moxie held a hand up, pursing her lips in concentration. Chunks of dirt flew up, pelting around her fist and forming into the rough form of a gauntlet. She flexed her fingers, then shook her hand off. The earth fell away. "And it's definitely how the snake was making the armor."

"Can you get huge?" Lee asked, her eyes going wide as she stretched her arms out to her sides. "You could squish things just by stepping on them."

"I don't think so," Moxie said with a laugh. "I think the Snake's body must have really been optimized to use this. I don't think I could get nearly that much dirt without losing control of it, but I can definitely make some armor."

"Do you have any idea what the passive is?" Noah asked.

"I think it's got something to do with pushing the dirt away from me instead of calling it over," Moxie said after a moment of thought. "I'm not completely sure yet. I'll need to test it a bit more, but I believe that's how the snake was controlling its body to make those spikes. We'll see after I can mess with it a bit more."

"Huh. Cool," Lee said. "I'm glad I didn't get it, then. Running around with a bunch of armor would just slow me down."

"I'm not so sure it'll be all that useful for me either," Moxie admitted. "You sure you don't want this, Noah?"

"Nah. Not my style."

"Then we honestly might be best off trying to auction it off or give it to one of the kids at some point. We'd probably be able to get a pretty nice amount of money for a Master Rune—enough to buy some other ones that are a lot more useful. I'd imagine Todd or Isabel could also make good use of this. I don't think it's Emily's style, but she might want it as well."

"We can definitely figure something out with it, so that sounds good to me," Noah said. He nudged the dead Great Monster at their feet. "We should skin this thing. I'd imagine its fangs and scales will earn us some good coin as well."

Lee raised her axe and sent a pointed look at the snake. "I can do it."

* * *

She did it.

Noah was actually rather impressed—he'd fully expected Lee to just hack the monster apart and pick up the broken pieces, but after one nasty chop to the head, she peeled its skin quite effectively. She then proceeded to rip its fangs out one by one before stuffing everything into Noah's bag and sending him a smug look.

"That's what it gets."

I'm not sure if I should be impressed or terrified.

"Good job," Noah said, settling for the former. "I'd say this was a pretty worthwhile venture. I only died once."

"Don't push your luck," Moxie said. "That was really quite effective, though. Formations are terrifying. I'm honestly a little anxious to see what you'll be able to do once you start making them with more than just one rune. That's where they really shine."

"Me too," Noah admitted. "Though I'd need to find a way to balance them. Since I'm only drawing on the power of one rune at the moment and using the others just to support it, the only runes that could balance each other out in power are Sunder and the Fragment of Renewal—and I don't think combining their powers is going to do much for me."

"They're kind of opposites," Lee mused. "One is for killing things with a passive that saves them, and the other is for saving things with a passive that kills them."

"Tell me about it. I'm irony incarnate," Noah grumbled. "I really want to get around to fixing my Rank 3 runes. How do we feel about hunting a few more Wylves so I can get the rest of the Sand Runes I need before heading out to find or buy some more runes?"

"We've got some time left in our vacation, so I've got no objections." Moxie shrugged. "Besides, I still need to figure out exactly what I'm going to be teaching when we get back. Maybe I'll get inspired."

"Killing things is fun," Lee said. "And I need to get some more runes myself, so that works for me."

Noah drew his flying sword and tossed it to the ground. Lee's body rippled as she turned to her crow form. She flew out of her clothes as they flopped to the ground where she'd been standing. He put them into his travel bag, and Lee settled in on top as he stepped onto the flying sword.

Moxie got on in front of him, and he sent a pulse of energy into the blade, activating it. Then they were off. As Moxie had said, there was still some time left before the school year started once more. They weren't going to waste a second of it.

Chapter Two

Time passed quickly—and enjoyably. At least, they were enjoyable for Noah's team. The monsters that were unlucky enough to fall into their path probably would have considered the time far worse had they still possessed bodies with which to think.

Over the last few weeks of the vacation, the group traveled around the areas surrounding Dawnforge, hunting for runes and monster parts. They didn't encounter anything particularly dangerous, and everyone made good progress in filling their runes with energy.

Noah managed to secure all the Rank 1 runes he'd need to put together a new set of Rank 2s that would eventually become a Rank 3 Sandstorm Rune. He also gathered enough Rank 1s to make all the Water, Earth, and Wind–based Rank 2 runes.

He steadily rotated through the new runes, filling them up before depositing them back into his grimoire. Whenever he filled enough of them, he then combined them into their Rank 2 versions—up until the point where he was just about prepared to form their Rank 3 disaster variants.

Unfortunately, they didn't find much in the way of Shadow, Lightning, or Ice–related runes. Even though they still had a few strong runes left over from Dayton's scroll that could be butchered, Noah and Lee both decided it would be better to hold off.

All the monsters they'd killed and sold had earned them a hefty profit, and they all had around ten thousand gold to spend by the end of their efforts. Noah couldn't quite bring himself to spend the coin he'd earned, recalling exactly how expensive a replacement potion to heal Todd's injury would be.

At the same time, he didn't want to spend the money on a potion now, as he had no idea if Silvertide had already helped Todd fix the issue. If he had, buying a potion would have been a massive waste.

Moxie and Lee didn't spend their money either. Moxie didn't have anything she wanted to use it on yet, and Lee just couldn't make up her mind if she wanted to buy clothes, weapons, or runes.

They also held off on trying to sell the Master Rune. There was always the chance that Isabel could use it, and since they weren't desperately wanting for coin, there was no need to rush anything.

Either way, they were all more than pleased with the results of their work during the vacation. Noah had continued to practice on both music and his Formations, and he was growing steadily more comfortable with the new form of magic. He'd only mistakenly blown himself up twice throughout the rest of the trip, which definitely deserved an award of some kind.

In the time that Noah practiced his music, Moxie and Lee had sat to the side of the camp—far enough away from Noah to avoid getting caught up in any errant explosions—and planned their lesson plans for the coming semester.

They were all quite looking forward to getting back to Arbitage. With the drama and difficulties of the vacation behind them, it felt like a new start.

And so, only a day of travel away from Arbitage, Noah found himself sitting next to Lee and Moxie beside their campfire. He leaned against his grimoire, which contained all the runes he'd gathered over the past few weeks.

"Now that the vacation is almost over, it feels too short," Lee said. "I want to run around and explore things more. But I also want to see Todd and Isabel again. Emily too. Why can't we just all leave and go travel around?"

Noah opened his mouth, then closed it again. Arbitage was really more of a tutoring program than a real school. He couldn't actually think of any good reasons why they couldn't just wander off and do what they wanted until it was time for the exams.

"We don't know what'll crop up during the school year," Moxie said. "Besides, it's not like we can't travel. We can use the transport cannon."

"Oh, yeah. That's true." Lee yawned, then shrugged. "As long as we don't go back to the Scorched Acres. They're boring now. We have to go somewhere more interesting."

"I'm sure we'll find somewhere," Noah said. "I wonder how much the kids have grown since we last saw them. I'm going to need to fix their runes, since I don't think any of them had perfect Rank 2s."

"We'll find out soon enough," Moxie said. Her gaze shifted away from Noah, and she chewed her lower lip. "I wonder if Emily's heard about what happened to Evergreen."

"Do you think she'll even care?" Lee asked.

"I'm not sure," Moxie admitted. "Part of me is worried because Emily's been raised to be the next head of the Torrin house, and that likely isn't happening anymore. On the other hand, I don't think she would have liked it in the first place. I won't have any way to know for sure until we speak."

"I don't think she'll hold anything against you, especially if she finds out just what was going on."

Moxie's gaze sharpened, and she grabbed Noah by the shoulder. "No. Don't tell her."

"Are you sure? I'd think—"

"I don't want Emily to find out that I was only mentoring her because I had to. That was true at first, but I wouldn't be coming back if I didn't actually enjoy teaching at least a little. I don't want her to think that I'm only doing this because I'm obligated to."

"If you're sure," Noah said. "It's your relationship with her, so I won't interfere. I don't think I'm one to speak on keeping secrets."

"Me neither," Lee said. "But every time I've shared my secrets, I've felt better. It works."

"That's because you shared them with *us*," Moxie pointed out. "Nobody forced Noah and I to spend time with you. It's different. If Emily finds out that everything between us has been a lie, she'll be crushed."

"We won't say anything," Noah promised. "Don't let it eat you up, though. I don't think Emily would think any worse of you either way, but we can drop the topic if you'd prefer."

"I think I would. Something happier, please. I don't want to think about Evergreen and the lasting consequences of her fingers in my life."

Noah's violin materialized in his hands, and he laid the bow against the strings. "How about a song?"

A small smile tugged at Moxie's lips. "That sounds preferable."

* * *

They reached Arbitage the next day and headed straight to Building T. Noah actually had some semblance of a plan as well—before he met back up with his students, he wanted to make some of his new Rank 3 runes— and he certainly had enough materials to work with.

Since he had a pretty good idea of what he wanted, Noah didn't expect it to take long. He'd already spent a good amount of time thinking about what intent he'd need for each of the seven Natural Disaster Runes, so he was just missing the pieces for his Ice, Fire, and Lightning Runes.

He could have done the combination before he arrived, but he'd been more focused on actually gathering and filling the runes than combining them. His Formations had also been at the forefront of his mind, but now that they were back at Arbitage, it was as good a time as any to finish putting everything together.

Noah, Moxie, and Lee arrived in front of his room. A frown shot across his lips as his tremorsense picked something up. There was motion on the other side of his door. Noah immediately held a hand up, his thoughts of runes banished.

He nodded toward the door. Moxie and Lee both lowered their stances as Noah reached out and rested his hand on the doorknob. It was conveniently unlocked. He gathered Natural Disaster's power in case someone had sent an assassin to wait for him. There wasn't any shortage of possible candidates for that.

Father, Gentil's master Wizen, someone from the Torrin family, or quite literally anyone they'd run into in recent travels—there was no shortage of people that would have been happy to see his head on a plate.

Noah pushed the door open, prepared to blast whoever was standing on the other side to kingdom come.

Sitting on his bed, frozen in shock, was Contessa. Beside her was

Karina, and standing near the desk, her shoulders hunched in shame, was Alexandra, the girl that he'd freed from Gentil's grasp.

"What the hell is going on in here?" Noah demanded. "What are you doing in my room?"

They all started speaking at once, consequently making everything they said completely indecipherable. Noah threw a glance back at Moxie and Lee to see if they were as confused as he was.

"You did say Contessa could stay in your room," Lee said.

"That was before we went to visit Evergreen," Noah exclaimed. "Why is she here now?"

Contessa started talking even louder, which made Karina and Alexandra both increase their volume to try and be heard over one another. Moxie started to snicker.

"Stop!" Noah threw his hands up, and they all snapped their mouths closed. He thrust a finger at Contessa. "You. Go first. Why are you here?"

"You said I could stay in your room," Contessa said meekly. "And I didn't have anywhere else to go. My employer is dead, and the family didn't have a use for one of Evergreen's aides. You still... you know. My head."

What is she—oh. I said I put some form of magical bomb in her brain or something, didn't I?

Noah pursed his lips. "Right. What about you, Karina? I was under the impression that we'd both completed our ends of the bargain."

"I need to bring you back to the Linwick Estate."

"No." Noah said. He turned to Alexandra. "And you?"

"Arbitage was the only academy close enough for me to reach that didn't require a massive entrance fee, and they still ended up taking just about everything I had," Alexandra said, not meeting Noah's gaze. "They said I could choose from a few teachers, and I recognized your name. I was hoping you'd be willing to teach me."

Chapter Three

N oah worked his jaw in thought. "Someone is just going around and assigning me students? I didn't realize I *could* get more."

Alexandra nodded, adjusting the sword at her side. At first, Noah thought it might have been meant to be some sort of threat, but then he realized that it was just a nervous tick. "I spoke to a woman at the administration building who gave me a list of the professors that could take on non-noble students that didn't bring funding for rune research. You were one of the only ones—and most of the others were either missing or not taking on new students at all."

Meaning that if I don't take her on, she might not be able to find a teacher at all.

Karina and Contessa exchanged a glance, both realizing that their requests had been sidelined for the time being. They were both smart enough to bide their time and wait until Noah finished with Alexandra.

"What exactly is it you came here to learn?" Noah asked. "I've still yet to actually figure out the purpose of Arbitage, if I'm being honest. I thought it was basically a babysitting program for noble kids with a side of some basic training."

"It depends on the teacher," Moxie said, finally getting over her silent laughing fit behind him. "Generally, families send their students to a specific professor because they have experience in something that the student wants. The general exams are only to ensure baseline competence. But, for someone without the backing of a family..."

She didn't have to finish the sentence. For someone without money, the school taught whatever their professor decided to teach. Arbitage didn't care about you if you weren't funding them.

"You beat Gentil," Alexandra said, clenching her fists at her sides. "And you're a teacher, aren't you? So you can teach me."

"I can't use a sword."

"I can practice the sword on my own," Alexandra said, but she did take a moment to look down at the flying sword hanging at Noah's side. "I want to learn how to fight."

Noah chewed his lower lip. Taking on a new student wasn't something that should be done impulsively. He was basically promising to be responsible for her health and safety, not just teaching her.

It didn't look like Alexandra had much choice, though. If she'd come to Arbitage and had already paid to get accepted, she was desperate.

"You can come to some of my lessons," Noah said, breaking the uncomfortable silence that had started to build up in the room. "If everything goes well and you mesh with my other students, then you can stay. If not, we'll have to figure something else out. I know the school accepted you already, but I've already got a responsibility to them that I won't sacrifice. Is that fine with you?"

Alexandra didn't respond immediately, which raised Noah's appraisal of her on the spot. She was actually thinking things through —even though there wasn't much room for her to bargain, it was still a good quality to have.

"Yes. That works. Thank you," Alexandra said. "I promise I won't let you down."

"Just focus on yourself," Noah suggested. He looked back to Karina and Contessa. "Now, would either of you care to explain why my room has transformed into a gathering hall?"

"I needed to find you." Karina nodded at Contessa. "When I came to your door, she was here. I thought she might have broken in, so I started interrogating her. It seemed like she was telling the truth, so I decided to wait with her until you got back."

"Alexandra showed up a little while ago, and I didn't think you'd have wanted to send her away," Contessa said nervously. "So I said she should stay."

That's... surprisingly not shitty of you.

"I see. And did you have any plans for what you'd do when I got back?" Noah asked. "I said you could stay here when we still had business together, but that is concluded."

"What else am I going to do?" Contessa asked. "I'm not good enough of a mage to become an adventurer. My family won't employ me because Evergreen had so much power that they're worried I'll try to sabotage them in her name, and no other family would hire me unless it's to be a spy."

"Have you considered just doing something other than being an adventurer or working for your family?" Noah asked.

Or just getting better at fighting?

"What? No." Contessa stared at Noah. "Why would I do that? I'm a Torrin."

Ah. Too proud to live a normal life but not capable of actually earning a better one. At least she's being honest.

"I see. And why is this my concern?" Noah asked. "Are you saying you want to actively work for me?"

Contessa shifted uncomfortably. "It's not that different from what I've been doing, is it?"

"Except for the part where I have to pay you."

"I don't need that much. Just some money and a room that I can occasionally use would be enough. Just a bit of gold wouldn't be that hard for you to earn with your—" Contessa cut herself off, glancing around the room and clearing her throat. "Your talents."

"And what would I get in exchange for giving you a room and money? Is there anything worthwhile you could offer me?"

"Information. Nobody cares about what I do, and I still have some of the old connections from Evergreen. I'm sure some of them would be willing to feed me information that you couldn't normally get."

Keeping tabs on the Torrins isn't exactly a bad idea, now that I think about it. Hm.

"I'm not opposed to it." Noah rubbed his forehead. He'd been hoping for a considerably more relaxing return to Arbitage. "One hundred gold a month, provided you can provide me with something interesting. You can use the room—I'll crash in Moxie's, so long as she doesn't mind."

"Works for me," Moxie said with a shrug.

Noah turned his eyes to Karina, trying not to let his weariness show on his face. "And you?"

"It's urgent that you come back with me to the Linwick Estate. I ran into the family head, and he wants to meet you." Karina's eyes flicked to the book on Noah's back. "About that."

A flash of worry passed through Noah. Someone had figured out that he'd taken the artifacts out of the catacombs. It wasn't like he'd been particularly stealthy about it with the whole collapse, but he hadn't had much choice.

But if they were really mad, Noah doubted they would have sent Karina to *ask* him to come back. They would have either sent assassins or their demands.

"He wants to meet me? Not needs to?" Noah asked.

"Is there a difference? He knows about the artifacts," Karina said, stressing the last word of the sentence to make sure Noah understood her deeper meaning. Both of his robberies had been discovered, not just one of them.

But no matter what anyone claimed, they didn't have a way to prove Noah had the Records of the Dead. At least, he was pretty sure they didn't. After all, the alarm was nowhere to be found, as the book was gone, eaten by his grimoire.

"If you mean this artifact, then all I can say is that nobody was using it," Noah said. "I don't believe there's anything further to address. I didn't take anything else."

Karina's eye twitched. "You know that isn't true."

"I don't have any idea what you're talking about. The catacombs collapsed after I messed around a bit and checked some other artifacts out. Our dear family head is welcome to come meet me at Arbitage, where we're on neutral ground."

Where he can't try to kill me without at least having to think for a second about the consequences, as minor as they may be for someone as powerful as a family head. I wonder if Karina ratted me out of her own volition or not.

Noah's eyes caught on Karina's legs—or, to be most accurate, the leg that she should have been missing. It was covered by her pant leg, but there was definitely something there that hadn't been there before.

"Nice leg," Noah said. "You managed to get a healing potion for it, then?"

"I didn't, but don't change the subject. This is important," Karina said tersely. "If you don't come with me, they're going to send assassins after us. You have to meet with him."

"Threats are not a great way to get me to agree to anything. Now that I know the head of the family is pissed enough to be sending assassins, why would I ever leave campus? As I said before, if he wants to talk, then he can come here."

Karina ground her teeth. "He won't. At least, I don't think he will. Jalen—"

"Jalen?"

"That's his name. Jalen basically dragged me off the streets of the Linwick Estate when I got there. He's strong, Vermil. High Rank 6, I think. He thought I took the artifacts at first, but when he realized I didn't, he gave me the choice between dying or coming to find you." Karina's voice steadily raised, though it never quite reached a yell. "He literally healed my leg in a blink. Don't you realize that you can't fight someone like this? Just talk to the man!"

I don't blame you for looking out for your own hide, but there's no way in hell I'm going to waltz out and let myself get squished by a new Linwick asshole.

Maybe I should have a chat with Father and see who I'm dealing with. Devil you know, eh?

"All he made you do was come find me?"

"I don't think I can risk saying much more than that, but I swear that's all he said he wanted me to do. He was going to find you himself before I got myself caught up in the mix. If you ignore his summons, I have no idea what he'll do to you—or me."

"My students?" Noah asked, his eyes narrowing.

"He didn't say anything about them. I... I don't think he'd go after them. He's a bit insane, but he felt genuine in wanting to only speak with you."

"What do you mean by not being able to risk more, then? If you really want to convince me to do anything, shouldn't you be sharing literally everything that happened?"

"For all intents and purposes, I have. That's everything that I'm allowed to share, but I swear that it's all that really matters. I can tell you that there's another part, but it's got more to do with me than you." Karina glanced over her shoulder, as if the head of the Linwick family was going to sprout from beneath Noah's bedsheets and drag her, kicking and screaming, to a pillowy death. "Can't you just trust me?"

"No."

"No," Lee added. Noah was pretty sure she'd only said it because she was bored of getting left out of the conversation.

"But—"

"Discussion over," Noah said, suddenly remembering that he'd had this entire conversation in view of Alexandra, who was looking at Noah like he'd just revealed himself to be the crime boss of a city. He adjusted his jacket and shook his head. "If you want me to meet this guy, make it worth my while. And stay away from my students. You've used up all your warnings."

Assassins or not, I'm not just going to waltz out of Arbitage and deliver myself to the Linwick Estate. Jalen is welcome to send assassins if he wants to. The worst they can do is kill me.

The blood rushed from Karina's face and she nodded her understanding.

"Alexandra, do you have a room?" Moxie asked. "Or anywhere at all to stay?"

"Yes, I'm in the student housing," Alexandra said. "I haven't looked at my room yet, though. I came straight here."

"Go head back and get some rest," Moxie said. "Meet us by the transport cannon tomorrow morning at sunrise. That'll be our first lesson of the semester."

"Understood." Alexandra straightened and gave Moxie a curt nod before darting out the door and practically sprinting down the hall.

Noah was torn between laughing and rubbing the bridge of his nose. He was pretty sure Alexandra was getting the wrong idea about him and Moxie, but it was probably a little late to go about fixing that now. He'd have to wait until class.

"Are we done here?" Noah asked. "Because, if so, I'd like to be left alone. I've got some prep work to take care of before school starts up again."

Karina looked like she wanted to argue, but she let out a heavy sigh and remained silent. That was more than enough for Noah, who stepped out of the doorway and headed toward Moxie's room. A few seconds passed in silence as Karina and Contessa sat alone in the room. Then Karina cleared her throat. "So, you get to stay?"

"Looks like it."

"And Vermil isn't going to be sleeping here?"

"Gods, I hope not. He's terrifying."

"Good, good."

They were both silent for several seconds.

"Say," Karina said, drawing the word out. "Do you think this room is big enough for two people? I might need somewhere to stay for a little while."

Chapter Four

As soon as they were through the door of Moxie's room, Noah made a beeline for her bed. A vine shot out and wrapped around his chest, yanking him to a stop before he could flop down.

Noah shot a glance over his shoulder at Moxie. "What?"

"When's the last time you had a shower?" Moxie asked. "We've been traveling for weeks. You are not getting on my bed in those dirty clothes."

"To be fair, these are pretty clean. I blew my old clothes up."

"Shower."

Noah grumbled and fished through his bag in search of a new change of clothes, only to find that he'd actually managed to go through all of them. He cleared his throat. "I appear to be out of wardrobe replacements."

"That's because you keep blowing them up," Moxie said. "What, are you asking for my clothes? I don't think they'd fit you very well."

"I've probably got something left in my room. I'll be right back."

He headed down the hall and back toward his room. When he got a chance the following morning, he'd have to go place an order with the seamstress to get some more outfits made. Not fully paying attention to his surroundings, Noah reached his door and pulled it open.

Contessa sat cross-legged on his bed, petting a white ball of fur curled up in her lap. Noah recognized Mascot's glowing red horns immediately. Contessa's head jerked up to meet his gaze. She had a small piece of jerky in her hand that was half eaten—and, judging by the small pieces of food scattered across the top of his sheets, Mascot had been the one enjoying it.

Either that, or Contessa is a really messy eater.

"I don't know where the monster came from," Contessa stammered. She made as if to stand up, then looked down at the cat and elected not to move. "It sat down on my lap, and now I don't want to get up. I'll wash the bed, I—"

"Forget it," Noah said, walking across the room to his dresser and digging through it. "Looks like he's taken a liking to you. Don't piss him off. That cat has indirectly killed a few people."

"This?" Contessa paused mid-pet, which caused Mascot to let out a threatening purr. She started to stroke his fur again and Mascot fell silent. "How? It seems so... innocent. And soft."

Noah found a change of clothes and pulled them out, tucking them under an arm. "Well, hopefully he'll stay that way. I didn't realize you liked animals. Not a plant person like the rest of your family?"

"Not everyone in the Torrin family is a plant mage," Contessa grumbled. "And I was never good with them anyway. At least animals can think. There's nothing wrong with them."

"Hey, don't let me mess up your mood." Noah shrugged. "Like what you like, it's no concern of mine. A cat-sitting service for Mascot when he's bored is pretty useful. It means he won't try to bring monsters to kill me while I'm trying to relax."

"Has... he done that before?" Contessa swallowed and sent another look at the contented cat in her lap.

"Only a few times. I've never seen him that calm before, though."

Contessa nodded thoughtfully. It was one of the first times that Noah had seen her genuinely care about something other than her own life. He wasn't particularly worried about Mascot's safety with her—the small monster could break into Father's office without a second thought, so a Rank 2 mage definitely wasn't going to put him at any risk.

"If you want to include taking care of Mascot in your contract, we can replace some of the information gathering," Noah offered. "I don't know how much of your time he's going to take up, but if he sticks around a lot, you may not be able to get much more accomplished."

Contessa's eyes shot up. "Seriously?"

There was definitely more excitement in her voice than she'd meant to let through, because her cheeks reddened in shame a moment later.

"Just keep an ear out." Noah turned to leave, then paused. He looked over his shoulder at Contessa. "Just so you know, I'm not going to hold you here. So long as you don't disrespect Moxie again and don't try to share our business anywhere, you can do what you want. You don't have to stay here. I'm sure you could find a real job somewhere else. I won't come after you for revenge or anything if you do."

A small smile pulled at one corner of Contessa's lips, but it was a moment before she responded. "I kind of figured that out. You kept threatening me, but everything I know about demons says that they almost never care about other people. I just don't know what else to do. I've lived my whole life for the Torrin family, and now they don't need me anymore."

"Do whatever you want to," Noah said. "So long as it doesn't involve being an asshole."

Contessa cringed slightly. "Yeah. Point taken."

"Good. Never too late to improve. I've been making great strides in my own personal pursuit of self-betterment."

Namely, not killing myself too often.

With that, Noah headed out and closed the door behind him. He didn't know where Karina had gone, but he wasn't particularly interested in finding out. She was probably still somewhere in the general vicinity, but the only thing on his mind now was a shower and a change of clothes—if only so he could flop on Moxie's bed.

* * *

Noah flopped on Moxie's bed. His dirty clothes—the only remaining set from the ones that Father had donated to him—lay in the corner of the room in a small pile. His shower had gone on for considerably longer than he'd planned it to, and he felt more refreshed than he had in ages.

"I should get a Bath Rune," Noah said into the soft vines making up the sheet beneath him.

"That's called a Water Rune, and you have one."

"Oh. Right. That's lamer, though." Noah rolled over. A vine grabbed a pillow from beside him and smacked him in the face with it. He grabbed the pillow, wrestling it from the vine and sticking it behind his head. "Speaking of runes—we've got more than enough money. Maybe we should look into buying the missing ones to fix your combinations, Lee."

Lee looked up at him. She finished chewing the last of the jerky they had left over from the trip, then wiped her mouth with the back of her hand. "Okay. We should save some in case Todd still needs a healing potion."

"Naturally." Noah sat up and leaned against the wall. The scratch of Moxie's quill on paper broke the silence. She was hunched over her desk, still trying to figure out the exact specifics of her lesson plan for the next day.

"Do we need to have everything figured out by tomorrow?" Lee asked. "Don't we have more time until everything officially starts?"

"There's no official start," Moxie replied without looking away from her work. "Most professors will get things kicked up this or next week, though. We'll get a letter with information on the exams for the semester soon, so we should be ready."

Noah watched her for a few moments, remaining quiet. Moxie was really putting a lot of thought into her role as a teacher, but she'd never wanted to be one in the first place. Evergreen had forced the role onto her.

I don't want to undermine her efforts, but is this really okay?

"Moxie?"

The woman glanced up, picking up on the tone of Noah's voice. "Yeah?"

"Is this really what you want to do?" Noah gestured to her desk. "Teaching, that is. I know you feel responsibility toward Emily, and that's important, but it's almost as if you're trying harder now than you were before, and that's saying a lot."

A second passed. Moxie lowered her quill, returning it to its resting place and leaning back in her chair to look up at the ceiling. "I don't know. At first, I thought I'd just want to cut free once I was free of Evergreen. Then I got free, and I realized I didn't know what else I'd want to do. It's a lot easier to just... not think about it, you know? If I throw myself at this as hard as I can, then there's less to worry about."

"That doesn't seem like the healthiest way to cope with things. I'm not sure if I'm the best person to be harping on that, given my ideal solution for most of the problems I face," Noah said. "I don't really have a good answer, but as I've said before, I'm sure Emily wouldn't hold it against you if you wanted to stop."

"I know that, but it doesn't really change anything. Now that I'm actually the one doing the teaching instead of worrying about Evergreen over my shoulder, I guess it feels a bit different. I think."

"Teaching is fun. It's stretching and hitting your friends," Lee provided. "And sometimes you learn stuff too."

I'm not sure that's the definition of teaching I'd want to go with.

"It's certainly better than a lot of other things. I have been having a bit of fun trying to figure out what I'm going to spend time teaching now that I'm the one that actually gets to decide what it'll be," Moxie said. "This year is going to be interesting, especially with a new student. She's not exactly the standard."

"Far from it," Noah agreed. "Based on how strong she was when we fought, she's a Rank 3."

"I think some of that power came from Wizen's control over her, but she's definitely at least a Rank 2, if not more. Well ahead of our current students—or at least, ahead of where they were before we left for our vacation."

"Isn't that gonna mess the tests up?" Lee asked. "She's gonna stomp all the other students."

That brought a grin to Noah's face. "Can you imagine her dropkicking Edward? I haven't thought about that little brat since we went to the Linwick Estate for the first time. I'd love to see the look on his face when he realizes that Isabel and Todd are Rank 2 already."

"We'll have to see. I don't think Arbitage is going to let someone that much stronger than everyone else screw with the results of the exams, but who knows." Moxie picked her quill up and got back to work. "Noah, do you want to handle most of tomorrow's lesson? You might as well just introduce Alexandra to your... unique form of fighting."

"Sure." Noah shrugged. "You'll just have to keep Alexandra distracted for a bit afterward while I'm using Sunder to help Todd, Isabel, and Emily. I'm not going to be sharing that around yet."

"Logically," Moxie said. "That'll be fine. I'll just sic Lee on her."

"We could stretch," Lee said, a spark of glee flashing in her eyes. "And then we could spar. It'll be fun."

For one of you.

"Sounds like a plan," Noah said. He lay back down on the bed and yawned. "Okay. I think we've dealt with just about everything we need to for today. I'm going to make my new runes now. Wake me up if anything important happens, okay?"

"Will do," Lee promised.

With that, Noah grabbed his grimoire and opened the large book up in his lap. There were some new Rank 3 runes waiting for him.

Chapter Five

The cold steel of Sliv's dagger bit into his palm as his grip tightened around it. His heart pounded like a runaway horse in his chest, and his entire body shook with excitement and tension.

A few weeks ago, he'd thought that his life was over. His runes hadn't been strong enough to pass any of the final exams for the Linwick Guard. He'd lost the majority of his fights. There had been nothing left. His future had been engulfed in flame, and all that remained was a short, brutal life of hunting monsters until one of them got the best of him.

And then, in the darkest moment of his life, there had been light. An extended hand and a thin-lipped smile had lifted him, giving him one more chance. Another shot to prove himself. A target.

The target that was currently seated just on the other side of the window from him, blissfully unaware of his presence. Sliv's fingers trembled with exertion from holding onto the side of the building— he'd spent more time than he cared to admit crawling along it and following his target, waiting for the moment to strike.

Just drive the blade into the back of his neck before he even realizes I'm here. He won't even have time to activate his Shield, and I'll be gone before anyone knows what happened.

Just one kill.

Sliv's tongue ran along his lips. Excitement pumped through his veins as he envisioned the future that was just a single stab away from him. A cushy, easy post at the Linwick Estate. He'd never have to really work again.

Sliv caught a hold of himself before he got too distracted. He could celebrate once the target was done. The windows in Arbitage had some basic Imbuements that kept people like him from breaking them too easily, but his dagger was no simple tool.

A tiny flicker of energy passed from Sliv's palm and into the pommel of the blade. It let out the faintest of hums as it activated. The hungry grin on Sliv's features stretched as he thrust the dagger for the window.

There was a loud crack—but it wasn't the window.

He was falling. Sliv's mind spun, sputtering and failing as he saw the sky opening up above him and the building pull away. His mouth opened, trying to muster noise as he mentally scrambled to figure out what had happened.

A figure dropped from the air above him, their features obscured in the darkness. Sliv never got a chance to make anything about them out. His head hit the ground with a loud crunch, and then there was nothing.

* * *

Karina dropped to the dirt beside the would-be assassin, the hammer in her hands melting away and turning into a bracelet on her wrist. She glanced over her shoulder to see if anyone had seen her, but they were on the less-populated side of the building, and there was nothing but foliage around her.

"Thank god he started with shitty assassins," Karina muttered, straightening back up and brushing her hands off as she gathered her breath. The man hadn't even noticed her coming. She had some basic stealth training, but nothing that would let her evade the notice of someone even slightly competent.

I need to get rid of this guy before—

"Whatcha doing?"

Karina spun, and guilt played out across her face so clearly that it might as well have been written in blood. Lee stood across from her, leaning against a tree. Karina was certain that she'd seen the short girl in the room just a few seconds ago.

Her mouth worked, trying to come up with an explanation. "I, ah—"

"Another guy trying to kill Vermil?" Lee asked, walking up to the body and stretching her arms above her head. "I smelled him, but he seemed so weak that I didn't even think it was worth doing anything. I didn't think he'd try to stab the window. Why didn't he just open it?"

Karina closed her mouth and swallowed. "He was an assassin. After Vermil. I told him. You heard. Jalen is going to send people after Vermil until he comes back to the Linwick Estate with me."

"If they're anything like this, I don't think we're going to have much trouble," Lee said. She nudged the crumpled body on the ground at their feet. "Who's Jalen?"

"The head of the Linwick family."

"Right. Why doesn't he just come here?"

"I'm being honest when I tell you that I can't answer that. He wants Vermil to come to him, and he's going to keep sending assassins until he does. I'd be willing to bet the next assassin will be a lot more capable than this one," Karina said, throwing her hands up. "I just want to get out of here. I don't want anything to do with this."

"Does that mean you don't want his body?"

"What? No. I meant the situation, not this exact spot in particular." Karina pulled at her hair and groaned. "Though I need to get out of here too. I just killed someone on Arbitage grounds. That's—"

Karina trailed off. Lee had picked up the assassin's body and shoved the entire thing into her mouth. Loud cracks echoed from within her as she somehow pushed the whole man down her gullet, devouring him whole—clothes and all.

"What in the Damned Plains?" Karina took a step back, her blood running cold. Lee turned to her and flashed a wide grin—blood still covering her teeth.

"Vermil isn't going back to the Linwick Estate. We aren't scared of a bunch of useless assassins," Lee said. "If Jalen wants to talk to any of us, then he can come here."

Karina blinked, and Lee was gone. A trail of ice ran down her spine and she spun, tripping over her own feet and falling to her back.

Lee had somehow moved behind her at such a speed that she hadn't even noticed her arrival.

"We aren't scared of you either," Lee said, crouching beside Karina. "Thanks for catching my meal for me, though. And don't tell anyone about this. It would go poorly."

Lee disappeared once more. It was nearly a minute before Karina gathered the courage to sit up. Even though the sun was shining and the ground beneath her was warm, her entire body felt like it had been frozen in a block of ice.

By poorly, does she mean that she'd just eat me? I don't think I'd even manage to get a word out before I was dead with the speed she was moving at. What kind of runes gives someone that much power?

There was no answer in sight, and Karina wasn't about to track Lee down to ask her. It didn't make any real difference to her situation one way or another. Bringing another party into the mix would only make things worse—her only hope was to somehow convince Vermil to meet with Jalen before the assassins ended up coming after her instead of him.

* * *

Power stormed within Noah's mindspace. Four Rank 2 True Sand Runes and three Rank 2 True Wind Runes floated before him, all full and waiting for combination. It had taken a little work to convince his grimoire to release the runes, but he'd worked out that it was willing to cooperate so long as he provided it with enough runes to consume at other times. Since he'd completely stuffed it full over the vacation, he had more than enough leeway to work with.

His plan for combining everything into a Rank 3 Sandstorm Rune was pretty much the exact same one he'd had when he'd made the Rank 2 Sandstorm Rune. The ratios already worked, and the intent was identical to what it had been before.

Noah drew in a deep breath and pulled the runes together. They pressed against each other, the pressure building in his soul as the runes struggled against his will—but he was relentless.

Power churned through his body and soul, lighting up his mind-space as the runes merged into a single point. Waves of pressure beat against him, threatening to push him back, but his other runes pressed, aiding his efforts.

Noah squeezed his eyes shut for a moment before a flash nearly blinded him. The pressure whooshed past his body, stabilizing itself. He peeked out at the newly formed rune as it floated over to sit across from Natural Disaster.

Sandstorm

It was 10 percent full, and there was no modifying word for it. The rune was simple—it was focused. Even though it had been exactly as Noah had been planning, he couldn't keep the grin from crossing his lips. He called on the power of the rune without waiting, testing out the pressure it put out.

To Noah's delight, there was no change. The Rank 3 rune's power was perfectly steady, even as he drew more and more from within it. Noah released the power and let out a laugh.

Sure, it worked for Moxie, but there was still a small part of me that thought it wouldn't do the same for me for some reason. Also, this is interesting. I thought one-word names were reserved for Master Runes, but it looks like you can achieve them just by having the right intent and combination. That means that the length of the name really does just indicate the rune's focus, and having a shorter name means having a better rune. What the hell are Master Runes, then? Sandstorm doesn't feel like one.

The answer to that didn't come, but Noah was too pleased to ruminate over it for long. He had more work to do.

Whelp. That's one down, six to go. I should take care of the easiest ones first.

Noah drew runes from within his grimoire like a starving man devouring a feast. His water-based disaster came next, and it only took him a minute to copy his exact strategy for Sandstorm to create a Tsunami Rune, made up of four Water and three Vibration Runes.

He'd considered going with Monsoon instead, but now that he was remaking his work, having both Monsoon and Cyclone felt like it was a little redundant. It was better to really spread himself out and focus on each individual element as much as possible while maintaining his disaster focus.

After Tsunami came Cyclone. He formed it even faster than the previous ones due to his increased experience with wind, and it turned out exactly how he'd wanted it to. Cyclone was followed by Earthquake, which was a mixture of four Earth and three Vibration Runes.

One of his goals in the creation of his re-designed Rank 3 runes was to increase the amount of Vibration present in them. Now that he could actually justify spending effort on music, Vibration would be invaluable. Tsunami and Earthquake were both good spots for it, and the third would be in his remade Lightning Rune. He hadn't worked out exactly how he'd do it yet, but he was certain it was possible.

Unfortunately, Noah didn't quite have enough of the Rank 2 Vibration Runes left over to make the Rank 3, but he was confident he'd be able to buy them soon enough.

He finally let his hands lower, looking out over the four new runes that floated in his mindspace—Sandstorm, Tsunami, Cyclone, and Earthquake. His final three would be Fire, Ice, and the Lightning-Vibration combination.

"Not too far from Rank 4," Noah mused to himself. "After I buy the runes for the last few and get them made, I can just go hunting for a little while and rank up shortly afterward."

His entire soul pulsated with energy. He could feel it expanding to accommodate the pressure of his new runes. Noah's fingers twitched involuntarily as his body absorbed some of the excess power.

It felt odd to have made four Rank 3 runes in the span of minutes— almost as if he hadn't earned them, even though he'd already put in all the work over the vacation and was now just reaping the rewards.

Noah's smile faded as a thought struck him.

This is what nobles do, minus the part where I actually earned all the runes myself. They can just feed people fully filled runes and force them up to really high ranks. Time and money basically aren't constraints to them.

The only thing really holding them back are functional combinations. It doesn't matter how fast you can reach Rank 5 if you can't get past it and can't use your runes properly. Maybe Isabel and Todd were actually the lucky ones.

Noah took one last look at his runes. He wasn't Rank 4 yet, but he couldn't help but feel proud. It would have been a little awkward if he'd come back to Arbitage no stronger than when he'd left—his Formations notwithstanding, as he couldn't exactly show those off in public.

As soon as class is over tomorrow, I'm going to look into finding out where we can buy a bunch of runes for Lee, the kids, and myself. Maybe I'll register myself as a Rank 3 as well. As funny as it would be to show up and have jumped straight from Rank 2 to Rank 4, I think that might cause a few issues.

That's all a problem for tomorrow, though.

For now, I'm going to brag to Lee and Moxie.

Chapter Six

"About time," Moxie said from where she sat on the bed beside Noah.

"That's it? I made four Rank 3 runes in like five minutes!" Noah exclaimed. "And the best you can say is about time?"

Moxie laughed and held her hands up in surrender. "I mean, you did have those runes for a while. I was surprised you didn't just start making the Rank 3s as they came."

"I was focused on Formations," Noah replied, "and I still needed to make sure my intent for everything was perfect. I just need to buy a few runes to finish everything off—both for myself and for Lee. Then I can get to Rank 4."

"If you get to Rank 4 before me, I'm going to be pissed," Moxie declared, smiling to show that she was only joking. The smile slipped away as her expression turned serious. "You really need to register as a Rank 3 mage, though. When you hit Rank 4, people might start to notice. I suppose you could always act as if Father was boosting your ranks because he got fed up with you being behind, but it could cause issues that you don't want."

"Yeah, I was already planning to do that," Noah said. "After our class tomorrow, probably."

"Do we have to do anything about Alexandra?" Lee's voice came from the window, and Noah nearly jumped out of his skin. He suddenly realized that Lee had somehow disappeared from where she'd been sitting.

She hung upside down, her hair framing her head on the other side of the window. Noah reached over and opened it, letting Lee slide inside before closing it behind her.

"God, Lee. You scared the life out of me," Noah said. "And if you mean her runes, I don't see how it's our problem. Arbitage let her in. I guess they don't have a strict limit on strength, but it'd be really awkward if she's at or above my rank when I'm the professor."

"Sounds good," Lee said. She hopped down from the bed and splayed out across the floor. "I'm bored."

"Have you figured out what you're going to need to fix all of your current ones so they're true Perfect Runes?"

"Yeah. I just need to find them," Lee said through a yawn. "Can we go shopping soon? I don't know where to find shadow-aligned monsters."

"I need some more Vibration Runes as well, so I'm definitely not against it. We can go after class," Noah said. "Besides, we'll know if we need money for a healing potion to fix Todd's neck injury by then."

Moxie and Lee nodded. Noah cast a glance out the window. There was still a fair amount of time left in the day—and that meant more time to practice his Formations. Testing his newly made runes would have to wait until tomorrow. He didn't want to mistakenly destroy Moxie's room.

* * *

The rest of the day passed quickly, and the next one dawned as it always did. As the sun rose above the tall buildings of Arbitage, Noah headed for the transport cannon with Moxie. Lee had gone ahead, having woken up several hours before them.

She also had the added benefit of being able to sniff out where Isabel, Todd, and Emily were. It struck Noah that there was always a possibility that they hadn't actually shown up yet, but Silvertide didn't strike him as the kind of man who was often late.

Sure enough, when he and Moxie arrived at the base of the transport cannon, there was already a small group waiting for them. Noah nearly missed a step. The students had gone through a pretty significant change since he'd last seen them.

Todd was more muscular than he'd been a few months ago, and he stood with the casual ease of a fighter. He'd never been particularly stiff, but the difference between now and his previous posture was like night and day.

Isabel, like Todd, had put on some muscle. She stood with just as much grace—if not more—and had her hair tied back into a ponytail. There was a long, thin scar running along the side of her cheek that looked like it had long since healed over.

Emily and James stood beside them, just across from Lee. Out of all of them, Emily had changed the least. She was still, unfortunately, the shortest by a wide margin, and her long silver hair hung low at her back.

She was locked in an excited conversation with James, who also looked largely the same as he had before the vacation. He still had the same vacant-eyed expression that hid a rather intelligent mind.

Todd was the first to notice Noah's approach. He paused mid-word, turning to look at him and raising a hand in greeting, a wide grin stretching across his face. Noah noted that he didn't seem to have any issue with the sudden motion.

"Teacherman!"

The other students all turned toward Noah and Moxie as they came to a stop beside the small group.

"It's been a while since I've heard that one," Noah said with a laugh. "How have you all been? Did Silvertide treat you well? I don't see him anywhere. Did he not come back to Arbitage?"

"He was great," Todd said. "Way less crazy than you. Richer, too."

Isabel smacked Todd on the shoulder. "He was a very effective teacher, but his methods were really different from yours. They're more in line with what I would have expected from a soldier."

"I'm not sure if that's meant to be a compliment or an insult. Before I get any further, though—Todd, is your injury..."

"Fixed?" Todd asked, putting a hand on the side of his neck. He flashed Noah a toothy grin. "As much as it's going to be, yeah. Silvertide spent a whole crapton of money on healing potions. He's out taking care of some personal business now."

"Upwards of fifty thousand gold," Isabel muttered, a note of awe in her voice. "Apparently, damage like that gets more set in the longer it takes to get healed. Even the best stuff we could buy wasn't a perfect fix."

"It was more than enough, though," Todd said, moving his head from side to side. "It gives a bit of a twinge every once and a while, but I can handle it."

Holy shit. He dropped fifty thousand gold? I thought we were rich, but evidently not. How much money does Silvertide have if he can afford to do that? I mean, quests paid well, but if he dropped fifty thousand that quickly, he must be absolutely loaded—or incredibly kind. Maybe a mix of the two.

"That's a relief to hear," Noah said. "It does mean nobody is going to be going easy on you during fights anymore."

Isabel snickered. "That's what I told him."

"Bah." Todd crossed his arms. "As if I need the help."

"How have the rest of you been?" Moxie asked, her eyes locked firmly on Emily. "Did your training go well?"

"Yeah, it went fine," Emily said with a casual shrug. She pushed her hair out of her face. "It wasn't anything special, but it was effective. James and I mostly just worked on some fighting techniques and hunted a few weak monsters."

"Ah. That's good." Moxie nodded sagely. "That's good."

Wow. I've never seen her this awkward. Emily seems like she's trying to do the exact same thing.

Judging by the expressions on everyone's—other than Lee's—faces, nobody was buying it. Noah nudged Moxie with the top of his shoe, and she cleared her throat.

"Either way, it's good to see you all again," Noah said. "James, I almost hesitate to ask this... but where is Revin?"

"No idea," James replied. "And to be honest, I'm happy to keep it that way. I haven't seen him since vacation started."

They all paused and glanced over their shoulders. By some miracle, Revin didn't show up at the sound of his name being bad-mouthed.

"Are we going to have a real class today?" Todd asked, rubbing his hands together with an eager smile. "Lee wouldn't say what we were doing."

"Probably stretches," Isabel said.

"Probably," Noah agreed. "Among some other things."

"Can James come with us?" Emily asked.

Noah tilted his head to the side. She'd definitely gotten closer to the shaggy-haired boy over the vacation. He wasn't keen on picking up every random student that came by, but he didn't have any reason *not* to let James tag along.

Isabel and Todd were already friendly with him, and he was already adding Alexandra to the mix.

"For today, sure," Noah said. "We'll have to figure something out in the future if you're continuously coming to class without your teacher, but I can't say I blame you."

"Thanks." James rubbed the back of his head. "I'll try to avoid getting in the way."

"You'll be fine," Noah said. "We've got one more person joining us today, actually."

"Another instructor?" Isabel asked, looking from Noah to Moxie.

"Nope. Lee, do you know where Alexandra is?" Noah asked. "I thought she'd be here by now."

"She's over there," Lee said, nodding down the road. Noah turned to look over his shoulder. Sure enough, Alexandra was heading down the path in their direction, her sword hanging at her side.

She noticeably slowed when she realized they were all looking at her, then accelerated to avoid remaining the object of attention for too long. Drawing up alongside Noah and Moxie, Alexandra inclined her head slightly.

"Sorry. I got lost."

"No harm done. Everyone, this is Alexandra," Noah said. "She's a new student."

"A new student? You?" Todd's eyebrows lifted and he crossed his arms. "What, we aren't enough for you? Don't tell me you've reverted to your old ways, Teacherman."

Isabel prodded Todd in the side, and he doubled over with a startled yelp.

"Sorry about him," Isabel said, her words polite but flat. "Todd doesn't think before words come out of his mouth. Did you choose Professor Vermil? Or were you assigned to him?"

"I chose him," Alexandra said. "He, Lee, and Moxie helped me out of an... uncomfortable situation. I just happened to see his name as one of the available professors teaching non-noble students here."

"And you *chose* Vermil?"

"She's not from Arbitage," Noah said wearily. "She doesn't know about my unfortunate reputation."

"Ah. That explains it," Emily said. "I see she's a sword-wielder. Or is that a flying sword?"

"It's for combat," Alexandra said. "I don't have Wind Magic."

"You'll all get more than enough time to get to know each other soon enough," Noah said. "Try to be nice, please. I suggest you all spend some time getting to know each other at some point today."

"So what are we going to be doing today, then?" Isabel asked. "Scorched Acres?"

"Nah. I think you've graduated from that for the time being," Noah said. "And you'd have an unfair advantage since you've fought monsters from that location before. We'll be going somewhere new so that you all start from the same spot. It'll be a better frame of reference for your abilities."

"We're leaving Arbitage?" Alexandra asked, taken aback. "I thought we would be sparring with each other."

"We'll get to that at some point, but I'd much rather see you fighting at full strength," Noah said. He nodded toward the transport cannon. "And this is a great way to do just that. We'll be going to the Windscorned Plateau. Any questions before we get moving?"

"I didn't bring appropriate equipment for fighting monsters," Alexandra said with a frown. "I'd thought we wouldn't need it yet."

"Appropriate equipment?" Noah frowned. "Like what? You've got your sword and your runes."

"A Shield. Gen—ah, I didn't have one before. The unique Imbuements I had made my body considerably more resilient than normal, but those are gone. My runes still make me harder to hurt, but they won't stop a direct attack with a sharp claw."

Isabel, Todd, and Emily all exchanged a look of mutual understanding and started to laugh. Alexandra frowned.

"What?"

"It's fine," Isabel said. "We had the same reaction. You won't need a shield."

"I won't? Why not? I thought we were fighting monsters."

"We are," Noah said. "Shields are a good tool, but if you're overly reliant on them, then they're a crutch. You won't be using one."

"You're serious?" Alexandra asked. "But..."

"Welcome to the class," Todd said with a wry grin. "You'll get used to it."

Chapter Seven

With introductions complete, Noah and Moxie herded everyone up to the top of the transport cannon. Tim was, as usual, sitting in his place, a tired expression on his face. He rose as they all emerged from the elevator and into his room.

"Vermil!" Tim raised a hand in greeting, a smile crawling across his weathered creatures. "It's been some time, lad. How have you been?"

"Busy," Noah said honestly. "It's good to be back, though. Getting things started again for the new school year."

"With some new faces, I see," Tim said, his gaze dancing over the students. "Preparing for exams already?"

"Not intentionally. I still don't know what exams are coming up," Noah admitted. "I hear we're going to find out soon. Just doing some exercises to get to know each other."

"Sharing fun facts?"

"Something like that." Noah chuckled. "Do you think you could get us sent to the Windscorned Plateau for a day?"

Tim nodded and turned his attention to the controls on the wall. A faint rumble shook the room as he adjusted the transport cannon, lining it up with a new destination before nodding to the waiting tube. "It's all set up for you, Vermil."

"I'll go first to make sure the area is clear," Moxie said, lying down in position. The transport cannon hummed to life, and, with a *whump*, she vanished in a beam of blue energy. Emily promptly walked over to lie where Moxie had been.

"Thank you. I should have asked this earlier, but how was your vacation?" Noah asked as the transport cannon sent Emily after her mentor.

"It was enjoyable. I spent most of it here, but there wasn't all that much to do, so I mostly watched the sunsets and sunrises," Tim said. He looked out a window and let out a soft sigh, a smile crossing his features. "They're really quite beautiful here. If you ever get a chance to sit down and be still for a little while, I highly recommend it."

"I've done it once or twice," Noah said, thinking back to the ruins Moxie had brought him to before they'd left Arbitage. "And it was very nice; you're right."

The transport cannon hummed and Emily vanished. One by one, the other students all got on and were launched as well. Lee was the last of the group to use it, leaving Noah and Tim alone in the room.

I remember promising that I'd find a way to fix up Tim's runes. It's not like I don't have the actual Runes to do it now… but how am I meant to fix anything without revealing Sunder's powers? Do I knock him out and fix everything while he's unconscious or something? Can you even use the Mind Meld Potion if you're unconscious? Maybe I should just leave a good rune somewhere where he can take it.

That wouldn't really fix any of the issues with his other runes immediately, but he could try to shatter the bad ones, and I could discreetly find a way to use the Fragment of Renewal on him.

"Is something amiss?" Tim asked.

Noah shook his head, realizing he'd been standing silently for a minute. "No, sorry. I just got lost in memories."

"Thinking about the sunset?"

"Yeah. It was a nice sunset." Noah lay down in the transport cannon's tube.

"Have a fun trip," Tim said.

Noah didn't get a chance to reply. Energy erupted within his body as the cannon activated, and then he was gone.

* * *

The world slammed back into its proper shape, and Noah's feet alighted on soft grass. The Windscorned Plateau was exactly as he remembered it. Steep landmasses surrounded them—some towering in the sky and others far below.

Soft grass stretched across the ground, broken up by plump blue flowers. He was still completely convinced that the flowers were probably poisonous.

The others all stood around Noah, taking in the new sights. Luckily, it didn't look like there were any monsters in the area that they'd arrived in.

Isabel and Emily were both kneeling beside one of the flowers, examining its petals.

"Don't eat that," Noah said.

They both looked up at him in confusion.

"We weren't planning to," Isabel said. "It just looked pretty. Why would we eat it?"

Noah cleared his throat. "Never mind. No reason. Welcome to the Windscorned Plateau. Assuming not too much has changed since the last time I was here, the main monster we're going to see is a Fluffant."

Moxie frowned and stepped closer to Noah, lowering her voice to whisper. "What? That's not what the Dossier said."

"I can assure you that the majority of what I fought here were Fluffants."

"What's a Fluffant?" Todd asked.

"It's a big, fluffy creature with a long trunk." Noah pointed at the flower that Isabel and Emily had been looking at. "They drink from those flowers, and they're pretty damn protective of them."

"Flower Sapper. They're called Flower Sappers," Moxie said.

"My name is better."

"Flower Sapper seems more descriptive," Emily said.

"Fluffant is cuter, though," Todd mused. "I like Teacherman's name more."

"I think it's more useful when a monster is named after an attribute," James said. "Too many are named arbitrarily, and hearing the name doesn't give you enough information about what they are."

Does it really matter if we know that they like flowers, though?" Isabel asked. "Fluffant is a good way to identify them because it shows that they're fluffy. A flower sapper could be anything."

All four of them turned to Alexandra. She blinked and shifted back slightly. "What?"

"Which name is better?" Emily asked.

"Guys, please," Noah said, rubbing the bridge of his nose. "We aren't here to debate about the name. We're here so we can see how far everyone has come over the summer and to get to know each other's abilities better."

Everyone fell silent, and he earned himself a round of begrudging nods.

"Besides," Noah added, "mine is obviously better."

That immediately ignited the argument in full. Alexandra stared at the group in disbelief as they all started yelling at each other. She turned to Noah, sending a baffled look in his direction.

He just shrugged in response.

The fact that they can just jump into an argument over something this pointless is actually good. They're comfortable with each other. I suppose that's not really a surprise, but it's good to see.

Moxie prodded Noah in the side, and he cleared his throat to get their attention again.

"Okay, okay. Enough screwing around," Noah said. "Call them what you want. Since we're focusing on your own techniques today, I'll tell you what we're up against. Fluffants are pretty much docile right up until you use magic next to them. As soon as you do, they'll try to murder you violently—and if you kill any of them, every other Fluffant in the area will come try to kill you."

"How big of an area?" Alexandra asked.

"I never actually tested that," Noah admitted. "But it seemed to be just on the specific plateau you were on, and their attention span isn't very long. As long as you don't stick around in the same spot for too long, you'll be fine. Fluffants fight mostly by charging and trying to crush you. They've also got some nasty fast trunks."

"Yeah. We've fought them before, but it was a bit ago." Todd scratched the side of his face. "Can we just attack from afar? Or do we have to get close? I'd assume we can beat them pretty easily if we just lob things at them from outside, whatever their magic-sensing range was."

"I was about to ask the same thing," Emily said.

"You're welcome to fight them however you want to," Noah said with a shrug. "I want to see how far you've come individually. If you think you can best show that at a range, then go ahead."

"I don't have any way to fight at range," Alexandra said.

"You could always throw your sword," Todd offered.

Alexandra's eyebrows tightened, and she sent him a flat look. "I'm not doing that."

"As I said, you're welcome to fight however you want," Noah said, walking past the group toward the edge of their plateau. They all fell in behind him, and Noah peered over the edge, down at the landmass below them.

There were a fair number of Fluffants milling about below—fifteen, by Noah's count. Not a single one of the monsters paid them any attention. The drop was probably several hundred feet, so Noah doubted the Fluffants had any idea of their presence.

"Range is one thing, but I don't think I can hit anything from up here," Todd said with a frown. "My magic won't make it that far."

"I might be able to hit something from here, but I'm not sure the amount of energy it would take is worth the effort." Emily closed an eye and squinted down at the monsters. She shook her head. "Yeah, it would take way too much energy to get a good shot off. If they're resistant to magic, then they probably won't go down to an attack that's lost most of its power by the time it gets to them."

"Sounds like we're fighting in close range, then." James rubbed his eyes. He looked half-asleep, which wasn't the most comforting state of mind when one was about to go fight monsters. "I could get us down there if you want."

"Is that allowed?" Alexandra asked, glancing to Noah.

Noah shrugged in response. "Go ahead. I want to see your fighting abilities, not your terrain traversal abilities. I was going to offer to bring everyone down myself, but I didn't remember James had Wind Runes."

"Hold on," Isabel said, putting a hand on James's shoulder before he could step forward. "The Fluffants are going to get aggressive the moment we use magic near them. If we kill one, then we're going to have to fight all of them, aren't we?"

"What, should we kidnap them to fight one by one?" Todd asked.

"I was more thinking sectioning parts of the plateau off," Isabel replied. "If there are big rock walls in the way of the other monsters, we should be able to take one-on-one fights a lot easier."

That's a really good idea, actually. I was fully planning on just killing all the Fluffants that weren't currently fighting someone. I'm not worried about Todd or Isabel's fighting abilities since they've both got armor. Todd and Emily also have Shields, and Alexandra is hard to hurt, so the only one I really need to keep a close eye on is James.

"I like the thought, but do you have enough energy to actually maintain it? What if the Fluffants try to break through the barrier?"

"Then we can just kill them," Todd said. "It should slow 'em down enough for us to take out the Fluffant we're fighting, and that's what matters. The barrier doesn't have to stop anything. It just has to make sure we don't get overwhelmed too quickly."

"Fine with me." James yawned. "I'm ready when you all are, then."

"What do we do?" Todd asked.

"Jump," James replied. "Together, that is. I'll slow our fall."

Noah snuck a glance at Alexandra, but she didn't seem perturbed by the suggestion. Either she trusted the others enough to believe James's promise that they wouldn't splatter against the ground or she just wasn't worried. There was a good chance the fall wouldn't hurt her in the first place, but she *had* said that her body wasn't as resilient as it had been back in Dawnforge.

"Feel free to go whenever you're ready," Noah said, drawing on Natural Disaster to channel some of his own Wind Magic. He could have pulled it from one of his newer runes, but he hadn't had a chance to play with them yet and didn't want to mistakenly over- or underestimate their power. "I'll grab Lee and Moxie if you focus on the other students, James."

And I'll have enough ready to catch the kids too, in case you don't.

James gave Noah a nod.

Then, as one, the group stepped up to the edge of the cliff and jumped.

Chapter Eight

Noah's group landed just a few seconds before the students did. He'd chosen a location as far away from the majority of the Fluffants as possible to avoid mistakenly drawing the attention of too many, but that didn't stop the nearest few from noticing him.

He gathered energy in Natural Disaster, ready to act the moment it was needed. Even as he was calling on his magic, the students all dropped around him. James had spent more energy than Noah had to slow their fall, but Noah didn't fault him for it. Slow and safe was better than fast and dead.

Two Fluffants made a beeline toward them, kicking up a small storm of dirt and grass as they accelerated. The monsters weren't going to wait around for them to get ready.

"I got one." Todd said, striding toward the charging Fluffants. Stone raced up from the ground, slithering around his arms and solidifying into armor. As before, the majority of the armor was concentrated around his arms, but Todd also formed thick leg guards and gave himself some plating across his vital organs.

He'd clearly optimized his armor during the vacation.

His teacher was Silvertide, so I'd imagine a soldier would know a lot about that sort of thing.

"Isabel, you want to get the other?" Todd asked, unperturbed by the charging monsters.

"Already on it," Isabel replied. There was a loud crack as chunks of stone ripped free of the dirt beneath her, swirling up in a pillar and slamming onto her body in rapid fire succession. It only took a little over a second for her to completely encase herself in armor.

She pressed a hand to her chest and drew it outward. A shimmering blue sword formed in her grip, and she dropped into a practiced fighting stance. Noah couldn't help but notice that Isabel had elected not to form a shield or infuse her stone armor with the blue magic.

Well, the blue energy is probably her Master Rune, so I can see why she wouldn't be using it when strangers are here. Hm. If this is hindering her progress, I might need to figure something out so she can get practice fighting at full strength.

There was no more time to think, though—the Fluffants were upon Todd and Isabel. Noah's fingers twitched at his side, power gathered to strike at the first moment.

The first Fluffant's heavy steps didn't slow in the slightest as it attempted to simply run straight through Todd. He shifted his weight and jumped to the side. There was a muffled *whump* as the move sent him sliding almost a dozen feet, well out of the monster's reach. Flames roiled up the sides of Todd's armored feet.

I think that was a controlled explosion at his feet. Damn. He's come a long way from using explosive punches.

The Fluffant skidded to a stop and spun toward him again, trumpeting in fury as it geared up to charge once more. Out of the corner of his eye, Noah saw Isabel engage the other one. She thrust a hand up, yanking a thick stone pillar at an angle. It slammed into the Fluffant and sent it staggering off course.

In the second that it was off guard, Isabel ripped more power from her runes and sent it into the ground. A rumble shook the plateau. Grass ripped and dirt bubbled back as a large wall shot up, forming a ring around the group and the two Fluffants.

That can't have been a low-energy move. She's probably filled her runes a good bit as well, then. Nice.

Todd's Fluffant charged him once more, this time attempting to slam him with its trunk. Once more, Todd dodged, giving the monster a wide berth. A grin pulled at the corners of Noah's mouth.

He's scoping out its moves instead of charging in and potentially getting surprised. Good shit, Todd.

Isabel took a different approach. As soon as her stone wall had been erected, she turned back to her opponent. Even as the Fluffant's feet pounded the ground and it bore down on her, she flicked her free hand up.

A thick, jagged spike ripped out of the ground straight in the Fluffant's path. It drove into the monster's stomach and continued onward. It let out a scream of pain and fury, thrashing desperately.

It was pointless. Isabel's rock formation wasn't some small, dainty spike. It was practically a sharpened boulder—far too wide and heavy to be broken quickly. Isabel wasn't done, though.

As soon as the Fluffant's front legs were lifted off the ground, she sprinted around to its side and flicked her sword, sending it flying for the monster's head. Its violent thrashing moved her target out of the way, and the blade bit home into a shoulder instead, sizzling as it sliced through fur.

Isabel reared back, and the sword reappeared in her hand in an instant. She flung it once again—this time striking true. The blade whistled straight through the Fluffant's ear and burrowed into its brain. As if its strings had been cut, the red-eyed creature crumpled on the spot.

"Stop playing around," Isabel called to Todd.

"I'm not playing," Todd called back as another *whump* emerged from beneath his feet and he bounded over his Fluffant's head, landing on the ground behind it with a grunt. "I'm evaluating my opponent."

"You could have killed it twice over. You only need to evaluate an opponent when you don't know what you're up against."

Todd sighed. "Killjoy."

The Fluffant roared and thundered toward him. Todd adjusted his stance, holding his ground as it grew closer. Noah tensed—at the speed the Fluffant was moving, he would only have a moment to act if Todd made a mistake. The Shield wouldn't do him much good against a physical attack if he didn't activate it in time.

Todd twisted to the side, vaulting onto his hands. The air behind his right leg wavered, and a loud crack echoed across the plateau. A burst of flame tore out from Todd's heel as it accelerated in a blur. He drove a brutal kick into the side of the Fluffant's head as it charged past him.

The crack was followed by a crunch. Stumbling, the Fluffant crashed forward and rolled over itself, sliding several feet across the grass before finally coming to a halt. It didn't move again. Its head was completely caved in.

It was resistant to magic, but not just pure blunt force. That was really clean. He made sure he understood the Fluffant's speed and reach before taking it out in one move that accounted for its strengths. Granted, if the Fluffant had been hiding any form of attack, things would have gone a lot different.

Todd—who was still in his handstand—hopped to his feet and brushed an imaginary speck of dust off his shoulder. "What do you think of that?"

"I think you were showing off," Isabel said, her helmet melting away. She scrunched her nose and shook her head. "It was a bit cool, though."

"Hah! See?"

"I shouldn't encourage you. What do you think, Professor Vermil?"

"Well done by both of you," Noah said with an approving nod. "I think these monsters might be a bit too easy for you at this point, but Silvertide clearly knew what he was doing. You've obviously been working very hard as well."

"Damn straight. Pizza party?" Todd asked.

"You don't get pizza parties for every occasion. You can have one if you crush the first exam—but we'll get to that later." Noah turned to the other three students. "Who wants to go next? It looks like the other Fluffants haven't noticed we killed these two—I suppose they use sight more than smell, which I wouldn't have guessed. It does make it easier to do this one monster at a time, though."

"I can go." James stepped forward. "Could you open the stone wall for me, Isabel?"

A section of the stone in front of James rumbled and slid back into the ground. There was a Fluffant a ways away from them, but it didn't look like the monster had noticed them yet.

I wish I knew I could just section them off when I was actively hunting these things. It would have made everything so much easier.

James formed a blade of wind in his hands and flicked it toward the

Fluffant. The attack wasn't enough to do any real harm, but as soon as it struck the monster's fur, the Fluffant spun toward him.

Its eyes flashed with fury, and it ripped its trunk out of the flower it had been feeding on, charging toward them and opening its mouth to reveal dozens of long, thin teeth in a roar.

Wind whipped through James's hair as he raised his hands, holding them before him and narrowing his eyes in concentration. The Fluffant charged through the hole Isabel had left in the wall—which closed up as soon as the monster passed it by.

It made straight for James, clearly planning to run him over.

It never got the chance.

A stream of white wind slithered out of James's palms. It twisted in on itself, forming into a javelin that carved through the air and slammed straight into the charging Fluffant's eye, boring through it.

The Fluffant crumpled to the ground, limbs flailing as it rolled to a stop in front of James. He lowered his hands and cleared his throat. "Did it."

"Bah. You just shot it," Todd said. "That didn't show anything."

"It shows I know how to fight a Fluffant."

"Fair enough," Noah said with a laugh. "And it also shows that you've got a pretty good understanding of wind. You held that attack until it was at the perfect range. Did you guess how far the Fluffant would skid as well? It stopped right in front of you."

James rubbed the back of his head at the compliment. "To be honest, I slowed it down a bit after I killed it so I wouldn't have to move."

Revin is insane, but he's no slouch. James is acting as if he's lazy, but that wasn't easy to pull off.

"It was cool," Lee said, giving James a thumbs-up.

"I'll go last if you want to go next," Alexandra offered Emily, drumming her fingers on the hilt of her sword.

Emily shrugged. "Sure. This won't take long. I was mostly practicing ranged attacks over the vacation, so I don't think it's going to be very impressive."

A section of the wall dropped away, and Emily soon caught the attention of another Fluffant. She formed an ice bow in her hands as the Fluffant approached, raising it to eye level in one smooth motion. Magic gathered in her hands, creating a shimmering arrow.

There wasn't an ounce of concern in her posture as she lined up the shot. Emily let the ice arrow fly before the Fluffant had even passed the border of the wall. It streaked out in a flash, slamming straight into the monster's skull and boring into it.

Whatever magic resistance it had did precious little against the frozen projectile. It slammed true and the Fluffant collapsed, just barely sliding past the stone wall before coming to a stop.

I'm pretty sure Emily timed that. She could have hit it earlier. There was also just enough energy in that arrow to take out the Fluffant without going into overkill territory. Simple—but very well executed.

Not exactly a lot for me to work with there, though. Whatever. They all fight differently, so I can't expect the ranged ones to get into melee when they're showing off their best moves.

"Well done," Moxie said before Noah could speak.

"Thanks." Emily released her bow and smiled, exchanging a glance with James. "It wasn't a very strong monster, though."

"We'll get there, don't you worry," Noah said with a chuckle. "For now—Alexandra, you're up."

Once again, Isabel dropped a section of the wall. Once again, a Fluffant spotted them. Alexandra drew her sword as the monster burst into a charge. Noah wasn't sure who the Fluffant was going for, as Alexandra had yet to use magic, but she was in its way regardless.

A small frown passed over Noah's features. Alexandra wasn't using any magic that he could tell. She was just holding her sword at her side, waiting for the monster to reach her. His nerves tightened as the Fluffant approached, and Alexandra remained in the same spot, still not making a single move.

She should be a good bit stronger than these things since she's either a Rank 2 or a Rank 3, but even I would still get crushed if I just stood in front of one. From what she said, she doesn't have a Shield either. What is she doing?

The Fluffant was now directly upon her, and the time to think was over. Noah nearly burst into motion, but he froze at the last second. There wasn't an ounce of concern in Alexandra's features.

Alexandra brought the blade down. It slammed into the charging Fluffant, and the monster continued straight through her. Noah's eyes widened.

Oh shit. Did she just get—

The Fluffant stumbled. Alexandra was still standing where she had been, her sword held before her. The two halves of the monster pitched in opposite directions, splattering to the ground as she turned.

Alexandra flicked the blood from her sword and slid the blade into the sheath at her side. "I did it."

Chapter Nine

"**D**amned Plains, that was awesome!" Todd exclaimed, his stone armor dropping away as he strode up to examine the dead Fluffant. "You carved it right in two!"

Alexandra shifted, wiping some of the Fluffant's blood from her face and arms. "All I did was kill it."

No, that was definitely pretty awesome. How'd she just stand there while it charged at her? That's a lot of force to bear. Even if her blade was perfectly sharp, the halves of the Fluffant were still moving quickly and should have hit her. She pushed through them without budging. I didn't see Alexandra use a Shield or anything to reinforce herself, though.

"What kind of runes let you do that?" Isabel asked, joining Todd. "Or was that just pure swordplay? I never knew you could do something like that."

"It wasn't just swordplay," Alexandra said. "It was—"

"Body Runes." Todd interrupted, looking up at Alexandra with a sparkle in his eyes. "You use Body Runes, don't you?"

Alexandra blinked. "You know them?"

"Know them? They're badass!" Todd exclaimed. "Body Runes are awesome! I mean, they're a huge risk, but they're incredible!"

Noah nudged Moxie and lowered his voice. "The hell is a Body Rune?"

"It's slang for when you completely imbue yourself with a rune to the point where it's a part of you," Moxie replied in the same tone. "Basically, you've got no energy left to pull from the rune because all of it has been imbued in your body. It goes a very long way toward making you resilient, but at a steep cost."

"That doesn't seem ideal. So you basically can't use magic, but you're super infused with it?"

"Pretty much." Moxie nodded. "It's not very common for that exact reason. Some soldiers will have a single Body Rune, but most of the time, it's better to leave at least something to work with. You can't remove Body Runes. As the name suggests, they get completely meshed with your body, and they aren't even in your soul anymore—though they still take up a spot."

Hardcore. You've got to be really committed to do that, then. And they also hard-cap your growth. Can't advance past your current rank if you've got a Body Rune. That's dark.

"How'd you know I used a Body Rune?" Alexandra asked, studying Todd as if seeing him for the first time.

"Your body was hotter than it should have been, but I didn't see you using any magic. After that, it was just a good guess. I used to know someone who used Body Runes as well, so I'm a little familiar with them."

"It was definitely an impressive kill," Noah said. "I'm surprised you were worried about a Shield if that's how you fight."

"I didn't know what we'd be fighting, and I'd rather be safe than sorry. I was only able to cut the Fluffant in half because I redirected most of the force. If it had a way to block my attack instead of charging right into it, I would have gotten crushed."

I wonder what kind of rune she uses to do that. Oddly enough, I remember her sword catching fire while we were fighting. I suppose that probably doesn't have anything to do with her Body Rune, so either it's an artifact or she was just using a different rune for that.

"Hey, Alexandra also called it a Fluffant," Lee said. "That's a majority. They're renamed."

Emily and James rolled their eyes in unison.

I wonder if Emily learned that from Moxie and then taught James, or if they're both just cut from the same cloth.

"What's next?" Alexandra asked. "Is this all we're going to do today?"

"Of course not," Noah said, tapping his chin in thought. "I just wanted a general understanding of where everyone stood after the summer. It also gave me some time to see how things stood among all of you."

"What's that meant to mean?" Todd asked. "Don't tell me we're getting even more training about how to work with others. You're the one that said we had to do this solo!"

"Not that, though it's far from off the table." Noah leaned in to whisper into Moxie's ear. "Hey, I've got a stupid idea."

"What is it?"

"You're going to give someone the Master Rune, aren't you?" Lee asked, somehow picking up their words.

"Yeah," Noah said with a grin. "We could always keep and sell it, but I think it might be better if we actually put it to use."

"How so?" Moxie asked. "I'm not against giving it away, but I thought we were going to wait for something."

"Oh, we are." Noah turned away from her and back to the students. "Right. First—Alexandra, do you mind if I ask what rank your runes are?"

"Three," Alexandra said. The other students all stared at her in shock, and she blinked. "Is something wrong?"

"You're as strong as Vermil," Todd said with a bark of laughter. "That brings back memories."

"No, I'm not." Alexandra squinted at Noah. "Not even close. We fought once, and he wiped the floor with me while he wasn't even trying to kill me."

"That was extenuating circumstances." Noah shook his head. "Never mind that. I was just curious as to how far along you were. It should be fine either way."

"Are we competing for something?" Emily asked, squinting at Noah.

"Yes." Moxie held a hand out. The stone beneath her swirled up, racing to cover her body and encase her in a layer of armor. "This."

"An Earth Rune?" Todd asked.

"An Earth Master Rune," Moxie corrected. "We got it while adventuring right before we got back to Arbitage. "One that I'd say fits several of your fighting styles. It lets you call the earth to you and form armor—I'd imagine it does more too, but I haven't really experimented with it much yet."

Todd and Isabel exchanged a shocked glance, and Alexandra's eyes nearly bulged out of her head. "You're just... giving it away? A Master Rune?"

"Well, not every Master Rune is that powerful. They're just rare. And I'm not just giving it away. You'll be earning it."

"That makes them expensive," James said, staring in disbelief. "Even a relatively useless Master Rune is going to be a few thousand gold. What's it a reward for?"

"Winning the most," Noah said. "In addition to normal classes, we'll be sparring whenever we have time. Every fight will be different. Some will be against me, and some will be against your fellow students. We'll keep track of who claims the most victories, and when the exercise is over, I'll give them the Master Rune."

"That does put Alexandra at a pretty huge advantage," Isabel said with a frown.

"She's never fought with or against any of you," Noah said. "In terms of power, Alexandra is considerably more powerful. But there are a few things to keep in mind. First—you know each other. She doesn't. Second, I never said you'd all be fighting on your own."

"We'll be in teams," Isabel realized.

"Sometimes, yes. And the objective of the training exercise isn't always going to be a direct victory."

Todd started to grin. "That sounds fun. So it's basically a bunch of games?"

"That's one way to look at it," Noah said.

"Am I allowed to participate as well?" James asked. "You aren't technically my official teacher."

"Feel free," Noah said. "More competition is better. It'll push everyone to improve."

"I'm still not sure how we're supposed to compete with a Rank 3, but sure." Emily crossed her arms. "When do we start?"

"Now." Noah glanced over to Lee. "You feeling up to help out?"

Lee tilted her head to the side. "Me? Yeah. I'm just a bit hungry."

"As expected, then. How do you feel about playing a game?"

A mischievous spark lit in her eyes. "What kind?"

"Tag," Noah replied. "For the next few hours, everyone other than

Moxie and I are going to be hunting you. Their goal will be to land a hand on you—and your job will be to avoid them. For now, you can't fight back. You can only run."

"Sounds fun. I'm in."

"Great. The first to catch Lee gets a point. Everyone else loses." Noah clapped his hands together and grinned. "Good luck."

The dirt beneath Lee erupted as she burst into motion, flashing toward the sheer rock face behind them and bounding into the air. She slammed into it, pausing for only an instant before racing straight up the wall and disappearing from view in seconds.

"You're kidding me," Emily said. "We'll never catch her. She's too fast."

Noah shrugged. "That's your problem. Do what you want—we'll be in the Windscorned Plateau for the rest of the day, and you all lose if you don't catch her by the time we get pulled back."

Emily opened her mouth, but she paused as Alexandra sprinted away from the group, following in Lee's footsteps. She jumped onto the rock face and started to climb it—not moving nearly as fast as Lee had, but still at a respectable pace.

Kind of what I expected. She's strong, and I doubt she's had anyone look out for her in recent memory if she was in with Gentil's lot. You're never going to catch Lee working on your own, though.

Todd and Isabel turned to each other.

"Do you want the rune?" Todd asked.

"Yeah, but I think you do too," Isabel replied. "We can't both have it, but don't let me catch you going easy on me. Good luck."

"You too." Todd bent his legs and his armor reformed over his body. An explosion set off beneath his feet and he was off, racing in pursuit of the other two.

James shimmered and vanished from view as he used his light magic to turn himself invisible. Emily and Isabel both took off as well, racing to catch up with everyone else. Noah watched them leave, his arms crossed.

"Should we be worried about them running into monsters?" Moxie asked.

"Nah. Lee will keep an eye on them, and we just saw that all of 'em can easily handle the Fluffants. I'm confident they'll be fine—and a little pressure is still needed to improve. But, just to be safe, we should probably follow after them. I don't want someone slipping up and getting killed."

He drew his flying sword and tossed it to the ground. Moxie stepped onto it and Noah got on behind her, wrapping his arms around her waist. Before he could send magic into the blade, Moxie leaned back and turned to give him a quick kiss on the cheek.

"That was a pretty clever way to motivate them. You're planning to make them realize they can't do this on their own—but since Isabel and Todd are in direct competition, they can't work together on this one. That means they'll have to form different partnerships if they want to win."

"Thanks," Noah said, giving her a gentle squeeze. "And now I'm going to need to figure out more interesting lesson plans if I get a kiss for the good ones."

Moxie snorted. "Don't get used to it."

Chuckling, Noah sent magic into the sword. It hummed to life and they shot off the ground in hot pursuit of Lee and the students.

"Do you think any of them actually have a chance to catch Lee?" Moxie called over the wind as it whistled past their faces.

"Probably not as things are, but that's the interesting part." Noah squinted down at the line of kids racing across the plateau below them. "Either they adapt and find a new way to approach this—or they fail. Either way, it'll help expose where they're all weak. And, more importantly, it'll be fun to watch."

Chapter Ten

Alexandra turned in a slow circle. Sweat streaked her face and her chest rose and fell with quick breaths. She'd been chasing Lee for the better part of three hours, and she hadn't even stopped once.

And, for all the effort she'd put in, her reward had been a fat nothing. In fact, she was confident that Lee was screwing with her. Every time Alexandra started to close any ground and catch up with the short girl, Lee would just turn around, grin, and then vanish in a blur of sudden speed.

She's definitely toying with me. How does she have so much energy and speed? I'd understand her being this fast if she also had low stamina, but she somehow has both. What kind of runes does she have?

Alexandra's only consolation was that nobody else was doing much better. She was well ahead of the pace of the other students, and even though Todd's use of explosions to propel himself forward actually let him move in slightly faster bursts than she did for short periods of time, he—unlike Lee—actually had a limited amount of energy to work with.

He'd fallen behind over an hour ago, unable to keep up with their speed. She'd been pretty sure that she wouldn't see him again during the exercise, but Alexandra slowed as she realized that Todd was heading straight toward her.

She glanced around her surroundings, then cursed under her

breath. Lee had turned around and led her straight back to the other students.

"Yeah, we're definitely getting screwed with," Alexandra muttered.

Out of the corner of her eye, Alexandra spotted Emily jogging in their direction. The silver-haired girl slowed, likely coming to the exact same conclusion that Alexandra just had. The three of them walked up to each other, all taking a moment to catch their breath.

"This is pathetic," Emily complained, wiping her forehead with the back of a sleeve. "I wanted to come back and show off how strong I'd gotten."

"Tell me about it," Todd said with a sigh. "But it's not like any of us can actually catch Lee. At least she isn't making us stretch."

"What's wrong with stretching?" Alexandra asked.

Emily and Todd both sent a harrowing look in her direction.

"You'll find out soon enough." Todd flopped to the ground and stretched out on the grass with a groan. "Damn, I'm sore. I don't know why I even bothered trying to chase after Lee. It's not like any of us can catch her."

"Tell me about it." Emily sat down beside him and tugged at her hair. "I don't even want the damn rune."

"You don't?" Alexandra looked at Emily in surprise. "Why not?"

"It's useless for me," Emily replied. "My fighting style is all about range and mobility. I don't have the stamina or desire to suddenly start hunkering down and taking hits."

"You could sell it, though."

Emily frowned. "I could, but why would I? Todd and Isabel can both actually use it. It would be better if they got it."

You say that, but you weren't exactly standing to the side so Todd or Isabel could win. Is this some tactic to get us to drop our guard?

"Then why are you chasing Lee?"

Emily looked over her shoulder, then craned her neck back to stare up at the sky. "I wanted to show Moxie how much stronger I got over the summer. The problem is, everyone else got stronger too, so I—"

"Kind of just feel like you're in the same spot as when you left." Todd sat up. "Same here. Not the impressing Moxie part—she's not my type."

"That's not what I meant!" Emily punched Todd in the shoulder and he cackled.

"Sorry, sorry. You're more into the sleepy-looking ones, then?"

Emily's face went red. "What are you talking about?"

"You spent all summer with James," Todd teased. "And you seemed pretty close when we got back. I guess he's got all that trauma from dealing with Revin. Trying to fix him?"

"Oh, shut up." Emily rolled her eyes.

"You aren't denying anything."

"Get your head out of the gutter, or Isabel is going to show you up and get the point for herself."

"If she does, then she deserves it," Todd said, his eyes drifting off into the distance as his smile turned more thoughtful. "I bet she'd look really badass if she had an Earth Master Rune. I'd like to see that."

What's wrong with these people? Why are they completely okay with giving up something as valuable as a Master Rune?

"I don't think Isabel would be happy if you just sat around and she won because there was no competition," Emily said. "She'd probably be pretty pissed, and she did tell you not to go easy."

"Shit," Todd said. He stood and held a hand out to Emily, pulling her up to her feet. "You're right. She'd chew me out for an hour. Okay, I'm pumped up again."

"I don't understand this at all," Alexandra said. "Aren't we supposed to be competing? Why are you being so friendly with each other while we're all at odds? Do you not care about winning at all?"

"Of course I care," Todd said. "But we're going to be seeing each other a good bit no matter who gets the Master Rune, so what's the point of being rude? Besides, you heard Emily. She doesn't want the rune."

"And you just believe her?"

"Why not?" Todd shrugged. "Are you lying, Emily?"

"Nope."

"See?" Todd shrugged. "I trust her. Speaking of which—Emily, want to partner up? There's no way either of us is going to catch Lee on our own."

"I was about to suggest the same thing." Emily held her hand out and Todd clasped it. Then, to Alexandra's surprise, Todd turned to her.

"What about you?"

"Me?"

"Yeah. You want to work with us? A Rank 3 would make this a lot easier."

"You realize that I also want the Master Rune, right?"

"Yeah, I figured. A Master Rune like that would probably work pretty well for a close-range fighter like you."

"Then why would we work with each other? You heard Vermil. Only one of us can win this exercise."

"Well, this isn't the only way to get points. He said that there would be several exercises, so all that matters is having the most points at the end. Either way, I'd rather actually get something from this instead of pointlessly chasing Lee around until we lose. And to do that, I need help."

Alexandra studied Todd. He was so different from everyone she'd met working for Gentil that every single one of her senses screamed at her to be cautious. Nobody made deals like this. Helping your enemies made no sense.

He's right, though. There's no way I'm going to catch Lee on my own.

"If we work together, how's it meant to pan out?" Alexandra asked. "Only one of us can get the point."

"As long as I actually get to do something, I don't care," Emily said.

"Flip a coin?" Todd offered.

Alexandra nearly choked. "What?"

"Winner gets the point, but that's assuming we manage to get close enough to catch Lee in the first place. We might be getting a bit ahead of ourselves."

He's screwing with me. There's no way Todd actually wants to settle something like this with a coin flip.

"Are you coming or not? We're losing time." Todd shook his hand in the air. "I won't force you if you don't want to."

Another second passed. Then she took Todd's hand, shaking it. "How are we going to catch Lee? None of us are fast enough to get near her."

Todd grinned, exchanging a glance with Emily. "There's a secret to getting her into a location."

"There is? What is it?"

"Food," Todd and Emily said in unison.

* * *

Isabel was no closer to finding Lee than when she'd first set out. She hadn't bothered wasting her energy when it became clear that Lee was actually going all out to avoid them, so she'd slowed to a walk so she could try to formulate a plan.

The most obvious way to get Lee within touching range was food. She'd tried setting some jerky out to catch Lee's attention, but after sitting in place for nearly three hours with a pile of food before her, Isabel hadn't made any progress.

And, of course, in the brief second it took Isabel to start to stand, Lee flashed by her, grabbing the entire pile and disappearing before Isabel could so much as say a word.

"Damned Plains," Isabel cursed. "My food!"

A laugh rose up from beside Isabel. The air rippled and James appeared standing beside her. "Sorry. That was pretty funny."

"Were you standing here the whole time?" Isabel asked, narrowing her eyes.

"No. Just for about thirty minutes or so. I figured you'd probably know a better way to get Lee than just chasing after her pointlessly. It became clear pretty quickly that we weren't going to catch her."

"Fat load of good that did," Isabel complained. "I thought I was being clever."

"Well, it almost worked. You just weren't fast enough to do anything when Lee got here."

"I hadn't figured that out," Isabel said dryly. "Are you hoping to sell the Master Rune if you get it?"

"I don't really want it." James scratched the back of his neck. "And even if I did, it would be a little weird if I won. I'm not even really part of your class. I'm just taking cover from Revin."

A pang of sympathy ran through Isabel, and she nodded her understanding. "I don't think any of us would hold it against you if you won it. We've all seen Revin."

"He's not terrible, but he's definitely got more than a few problems up here." James tapped his head, then glanced over his shoulder—probably to make sure Revin wasn't going to pop up behind him. "But no, I don't want the Master Rune at all. Emily wants to win, though."

"So you're planning to help her?"

"Yeah."

"Then why are you here?"

"Because Emily wouldn't want me to help her directly." James's cheeks reddened and he cleared his throat. "I don't want to make it seem like I don't think she can do it herself, but she's been talking about showing Moxie how much stronger she's gotten for practically all our vacation. This is a great way to do that."

"So you want to help her but don't want her to know you're helping," Isabel concluded, hiding a grin. "Cute. What's that got to do with me, though?"

"Emily is partnering up with Todd and Alexandra, so they might actually have a chance of catching up to Lee."

Isabel's brow furrowed in confusion. "If that's the case, why are you here? Shouldn't you be waiting invisible somewhere to try to help from the sidelines?"

"I think you misunderstood me." James adjusted his shirt and tugged at his collar. "I don't want to help Emily catch Lee. I want to help her show how far she's come—and that means giving her good opponents to face so she can really prove herself. The best story is a comeback, not someone who keeps the lead the whole way."

"You mean—"

"I want to make sure she loses the round," James said with a nod. "Which means I want to help you win."

Isabel burst into laughter. "You're more like Revin than you think."

"Egh." James shuddered. "Never say that again. Do you want my help or not?"

"Sure," Isabel replied. "How are we going to do this, though? I'm out of food."

"By getting something that takes Lee a little more time to eat," James replied, rubbing his hands together as a cold wind howled past them. He turned his gaze toward a plateau below them, where several Fluffants grazed. "Why don't we start with those?"

Chapter Eleven

"It looks like everyone came to the same conclusion," Moxie said. She and Noah stood at the top of a tall plateau, overlooking the students below them. A dozen Fluffants lay dead on the ground behind them, having made the poor decision of attacking after noticing the energy coming from Noah's sword as they'd landed. Several more hours had passed since the exam had started, and it was now well into the night.

"It was kind of a freebie," Noah said. "There's no other way to get Lee to stick around for any period of time. Hunting a bunch of Fluffants and piling them up to force Lee to stand still for just a few seconds is the best shot they're going to get."

And that was exactly what both groups were doing. They'd set out on a hunt that probably would have broken at least a few laws on depopulation on Earth, taking out every Fluffant they could and dragging the bodies into piles in an attempt to create what was functionally an offering.

"I feel a bit bad for the Fluffants," Moxie said, looking up at the sky. The sun had started to make its trek beneath the clouds, and evening was approaching at a steady pace. It wouldn't be long before the darkness was properly upon them. "And we might see some other monsters coming out soon. I'm honestly surprised we haven't seen more since there isn't a Great Monster in the Windscorned Plateau."

"I think I noticed a few bird monsters, but nothing in particular," Noah said. "Anything we should be concerned about?"

"Those are Skycutters. They're fast and large, but they aren't particularly dangerous. They eat the flowers, just like the Fluffants. I suppose they could be a bit problematic if there were enough of them, but nothing that couldn't be handled."

Noah nodded absently. Lee had managed to keep everyone in the same general area, so their vantage point let them see both groups. Todd's team had gathered quite a few more corpses than Isabel's had due to Alexandra's help.

The Rank 3 was, for lack of a better word, a menace. The Fluffants had absolutely no chance against her, and she didn't seem to expend much energy fighting them. She carved straight through their ranks, only needing a single blow to take out a monster.

It wasn't like the other students weren't effective in their work. Alexandra was just far better.

"I guess that's what happens when you get trained to be an assassin and are good enough to keep Gentil's attention," Noah mused as he watched Alexandra finish off the last few Fluffants in the herd.

"She's strong, but there isn't much variation in her fighting style," Moxie said. "And she's not comfortable around others. Only time will tell how much damage working for Gentil actually did to her."

"Can you try to get a better understanding of what we can help her with while I'm fixing the other students' runes later today?" Noah asked. "At some point, if she sticks with us and proves to be trustworthy, I'll fix hers as well. Today is too early, though."

"Yeah, I think that's a secret you should be keeping *very* close to your chest," Moxie said, her voice deadly serious. "Possibly more than your inability to die. If word of that comes out, the entire world is going to come down on us and there won't be anything we can do."

Despite Moxie's harrowing warning, Noah's chest warmed. There hadn't been any hesitation at all when she'd said *we*. Even though he was pretty sure the right move in the worst-case scenario would be for him to make it clear that he was on his own, Moxie's unspoken promise that they were in it together was comforting.

A small trail of smoke caught Noah's eye. He looked over to Todd's group as they set their pile of Fluffants on fire.

"They're cooking them. That's one way to get Lee's attention—not that she isn't already watching," Noah said. "She's probably bored out of her mind by now."

"I'd imagine so," Moxie agreed. "She's probably going to take the bait, if only to have fun. The real question is which team she'll go with first. I don't think she particularly cares if her food is cooked or not."

As it turned out, they didn't have to wait long for the answer. Even though Todd's team had the larger pile, Noah caught sight of Lee—or rather, he caught sight of the herd of Fluffants that she mowed through.

"Over there," Noah said, barely able to keep up with Lee as she blurred across the plateaus in the direction of Isabel and James. "I think she's intentionally letting herself be seen. She's really into this, huh?"

"We should do it more often," Moxie muttered. "Let's get a better view so we can hear what's happening."

They both stepped onto Noah's flying sword and zipped off toward the trap and the rapidly approaching would-be-trapee.

* * *

"I hear her coming." James turned toward the edge of the plateau. "Get ready. I'll remain hidden until the right moment if we're going to have any chance of catching her."

Isabel gave James a sharp nod, and the boy's body rippled as he bent the moonlight around himself and disappeared from sight. She walked toward the direction of the growing rumbling, standing between it and the pile of food.

Stone ripped away from the ground, slamming into place all over her body to form jagged armor. She left both of her hands open, keeping her knees bent in preparation to lunge at the first sign of motion.

Giddy laughter echoed across the empty plateau. An instant later, Lee practically flew down from the edge of a cliff face above them, slamming to the ground. Her eyes went right past Isabel and locked onto the pile of bodies behind her.

"You got me snacks!" Lee exclaimed. "How kind!"

That's right. All for you. All you have to do is let me tag you.

"Help yourself," Isabel said, her fingers twitching. "It's all yours."

"Okay! You should just watch out for that," Lee said, pointing into the air. "I brought some food of my own."

It was dumb, but something in Lee's voice made Isabel listen to her. Through the air, hurtling straight toward them, was a Fluffant. The Fluffant wasn't alone, either. There were almost a dozen other monsters, all plummeting down toward them like massive, furry droplets.

Isabel couldn't bring herself to do anything but gaze into the sky in wide-eyed disbelief.

"Move!" James yelled, shoving Isabel to the side with a powerful blast of wind. She staggered, snapping out of her reverie. The rock beneath her launched her forward and out of the way as a Fluffant slammed into the ground with a resounding crash and a splatter.

"Lee, what in the Damned Plains?" Isabel demanded, thrusting a hand into the air. The rock around her erupted like a wave, crashing down on Lee. She didn't have a chance to see how effective the attack was, though. Another Fluffant was plummeting in her direction, and standing still meant she might be in the blast radius when it landed.

Dashing to the side, more sickening thunks rang out around her. The Fluffants were so heavy that the ground shook faintly with each impact. But, unlike Isabel, Lee hadn't been idle while they'd been falling.

She had taken advantage of the students' distraction to make nearly half of their collected Fluffants disappear. Isabel had no idea what had happened to them, and she didn't even care to know.

With a yell, Isabel flicked her hands up. The lines of stone beneath the dirt surrounding the bait pile erupted, forming a cage around both Lee and the dead Fluffants.

"Now, James!" Isabel yelled, pouring magic into the bars to reinforce them.

Lee's head snapped to the side and she vaulted backward. She raised her head to the air, sniffing once before launching herself straight up. Lee latched onto the bars above her and, with a casual pull, completely ripped one of them away.

Even as Isabel struggled to regrow it, Lee slipped onto the top of the cage. James flickered into view as a burst of wind blades shot from his fingertips, but Lee hopped out of the way easily. She waggled fingers down at them.

"Nice try!"

And then she was gone, a blur in the night. James and Isabel exchanged a glance, their shoulders slumping as they took in the carnage around them.

"Damn," James muttered.

"Yeah. Damn is right," Isabel said, flopping onto her butt and trying to ignore all the dead monsters. "At least something tells me that the others aren't going to have much more luck."

* * *

"She's coming," Todd said.

Alexandra stood beside him beside the pile of charred Fluffant corpses. She sent a doubtful look back at the pile.

"You're sure *this* is going to be appetizing enough to bait Lee into a trap?"

"It's food," Todd said.

"It's a bunch of burnt monsters."

"I've seen Lee eat a squirrel. She'll bite," Todd promised. "Besides, we both heard the crashes nearby. That's definitely Lee."

"If you're sure," Alexandra said doubtfully.

Several more seconds passed. Todd shifted from foot to foot. He flexed his fingers at his sides, ignoring the excited knot of adrenaline in his stomach. There was no way Lee would pass up on this much food— but she was taking a lot longer to show up than he expected.

There's no way she wouldn't come, right? This is meant to be a training exercise. There's no way we could ever catch up to her normally, so she's got to take the bait so we actually have a chance. It's the only way this would make sense.

And still, there was nothing. Todd's confusion grew with every passing minute. He was already using a decent amount of his magical energy to keep the stone box just below the ground in shape. It had their surprise waiting within it, and losing his concentration would have... very unfortunate results.

"Do you hear that?" Alexandra asked.

Todd blinked and looked at her. "Hear what?"

"I'm not sure. It sounds like... crunching?" Alexandra's brow furrowed. She turned toward the pile and nodded at it. "From some-where over there."

Todd studied the pile. His imbued eyes were muddled by the heat coming from the monsters, but he didn't see anything odd about it. And, as hard as he tried, he couldn't hear anything.

"No," Todd said. "Nothing. Are you sure you hear something?"

"Yeah." Alexandra walked over to the pile, drawing her sword and poking at one of the corpses with it. Todd walked up with her, though his attention was split three ways already. One part of him was watching for Lee, the other was paying attention to the pile, and the third was on the stone beneath the ground.

The pile shifted. Todd flinched, taking a step back.

"Okay. I saw that."

Alexandra drove her sword into a Fluffant and heaved it to the side. In an impressive feat of strength, she dragged the monster out of the way—to reveal a very hollow interior to their pile.

Lee sat in the center of the offering, chewing on one of the Fluffant's legs. She'd already eaten almost everything inside, leaving only what was necessary to maintain structural integrity. Beside her was a hole.

"You tunneled in?" Todd asked, a mixture of awe and disbelief in his voice.

"Don't just stand there. Go!" Alexandra snapped, darting for Lee.

She was fast, but Lee was faster. Before Alexandra had even taken two steps, Lee disappeared. Todd felt a rush of wind at his back and spun to see Lee prancing past him, grabbing a Fluffant's leg and ripping it off to take with her with one smooth motion.

"Missed me!" Lee called.

"Now!" Todd yelled, releasing the power he'd been holding. The stone erupted, launching Emily into the air. She held her bow, an arrow already knocked and fully charged. She'd been holding it for the better part of ten minutes, which was no easy feat.

Even less easy was spotting Lee in a split instant while she was getting launched into the air—but Emily managed it. Twisting her body, she took aim and fired. The arrow streaked toward Lee and Todd lunged, setting off a pressure explosion within the armor at his feet.

Wind howled past him as he extended his hands, striving to brush even a single finger across Lee.

He wasn't fast enough. Lee vaulted backward, landing on her hands and avoiding his grasp. Emily's arrow slammed into the ground with a crack, and ice raced out across the dirt, but even that couldn't reach Lee as she pushed herself off her hands and landed on her feet.

"That was close," Lee said, skidding a foot back. Emily landed back on the ground with a grunt, already starting to nock an arrow. Lee gave them a wave. "Thanks for the food!"

Alexandra sprinted, her body blurring as she threw herself forward. Emily released the arrow—but Lee was gone. The arrow whistled harmlessly through the air, and Alexandra's hands caught nothing.

"Damn it." Todd let his hands drop.

"What was that?" Alexandra demanded. "How can she move like that?"

Emily's ice bow vanished and she let out a sigh. "I don't know, but I suspect if you ask, the answer is going to be stretching. I wonder if Isabel or James did any better than we did."

"Judging by the explosions we heard earlier? Probably not," Todd grumbled, crossing his arms. "This game was rigged against us from the start."

"We might have been able to do something if it was all five of us working together," Emily said. "But that would kind of have defeated the whole point of the exercise."

"Is this how all your classes are?" Alexandra asked, looking back at the pile of corpses.

"Considering we didn't even come close to death this time, nah. I'd say this one was tame," Todd said. His stomach rumbled. Both Emily and Alexandra stared at him.

"Are you seriously hungry right now?" Emily asked.

"How's it my fault? We kept talking about food," Todd said defensively. "Anyone would get hungry."

Hidden in the shadows at the far edge of the plateau, positioned on the other side of the pile of hot bodies so Todd's heat vision couldn't make her out, Lee nodded in agreement.

Chapter Twelve

Their time in the Windscorned Plateau came to an end as the morning sun rose. Both groups of students spent their last hours trying to come up with a new plan to lure Lee to them, but in the end, none of them managed to come up with anything before the transport cannon summoned them back to Arbitage.

Noah was the last to reappear in Tim's room. He blinked the last remnants of the transportation away, wiping his eyes as he rose to his feet and took a look at the small crowd gathered around him.

"Did you have a good trip?" Tim asked.

"I'd say it was educational." Noah chuckled at the glares that earned him from all the students. "Thanks again, Tim."

"Any time," Tim replied. They all stepped onto the elevator and bid the elderly operator farewell as it shook and rattled, lowering them down to the lower floor.

"So nobody won?" Todd asked.

"I didn't say that," Noah replied. "How do you know Isabel or James didn't win? I didn't see your groups meet up before we got pulled back."

"Because she's got the same look on her face that I think I've got," Todd replied as the group headed down the stairs.

"Ah. Well, you'd be right. You all lost."

"How were we supposed to win?" Alexandra asked, sending a look back at Lee, who stuck her tongue out. "Lee's way too fast. Is she seriously a Rank 3?"

"That was for you to figure out." They reached the bottom of the stairs, and Noah turned around, copying one of Moxie's specialized arched-eyebrow expressions. "Did you really think earning a Master Rune would be easy?"

That mollified all of them pretty quickly.

"Was there actually a way to win?" Isabel asked. "It felt like we weren't even close."

"There's always a way," Noah replied. "Why don't we talk about what went right and what went wrong? There were definitely some clever moves I saw."

"Baiting Lee with food?" James said, not sounding all that sure of his own words.

"Taking advantage of a weakness you know about." Noah nodded. "Sure, Lee was playing into it a bit, but that was clever. Both groups did that without much hesitation. What else?"

"Grouping up," Todd said. "We wasted a ton of time trying to catch Lee on our own. We should have grouped up earlier, but grouping up at all when you implied this was a solo event was probably a good move."

"That might have given you a chance to set up a better trap or plan things through better," Moxie put in. "But yes, it was definitely a good move. You stood no chance alone against Lee."

"Anything else?" Noah asked. Nobody spoke for a few seconds and he shrugged. "Okay. We've already started, so keep going. Tell me about the things you did wrong."

"I think we should have probably spent more time figuring out what we could do," Emily said, scrunching her nose. "I knew Todd's basic abilities, but Alexandra actually got a bit close to Lee. If I knew she was that fast, it might have been better to have her be the surprise attack rather than me."

"Knowing what your allies are capable of is definitely a big one." Noah gave Emily an approving nod. "You asked if there was a way you could have won. Do you think there is?"

"Me personally? I'm not sure. But... I'd imagine we might have had the best chance if all five of us were working together."

"You most certainly would have," Noah agreed.

"But what's the point of that?" Alexandra demanded. "We were meant to be working against each other!"

"Technically, I never said that. I just said only one person gets the point."

"That's basically the same thing." Alexandra frowned, crossing her arms. "Unless we could have split the point or something, there's no scenario where everyone is happy."

Yes, there is. It's the one where the people who don't actually need the Master Rune make the choice to give it up so one of their allies can get it, knowing that their allies will do the same for them in the future.

I don't think I can expect Alexandra to have come to that conclusion this early on, though. She'll get there. And, from what it looks like, all the other kids literally only worked in two teams because they were trying to prove something and avoid stepping on each other's toes rather than because they desperately wanted the rune.

Isabel and Todd were the only ones other than Alexandra who actually wanted it, and they just chose to work separately so neither would feel bad about winning.

"Your silence is telling me that we've missed something." Emily chewed her lower lip and shook her head. "I don't know what it is, though. Was there a trick to it?"

"Who knows." Noah shrugged, grinning at the annoyance on her features. "There will be more chances to get points in the future. There will be more prizes as well—it might be a bit early to say this, but I think this strategy will work."

"You mean you'll have *more* Master Runes for us?" Todd asked, squinting at Noah. "What, do you just have a farm of them somewhere?"

"Don't worry about where the rewards come from." Noah waved a hand dismissively. "For now, just keep your focus on improving. That's the most important part."

Every one of the students nodded, which brought him more than a measure of satisfaction. None of them were mad about their defeat. The expressions on their faces told Noah that they were all just determined to find a way to win next time, which was exactly the attitude he wanted.

"Is class over, then?" Alexandra asked. "I think I've got a lot to practice and work on before our next one."

"Yeah," Noah said.

"Before you leave, let's chat," Moxie said. "Vermil and I work pretty closely together, so even if you're in his class, I'll be working with you a lot."

Alexandra looked slightly surprised to be getting called out alone, but she just nodded and followed Moxie away.

"I'll be heading off, then," James said, watching the ladies leave before turning back to the others. "I need a shower."

Before any of them could say anything, he disappeared in a shimmer of light. Noah's tremorsense tracked James as he walked off, until the boy left his range.

"Interesting guy," Noah said.

"He's just a bit unused to big crowds," Emily said, a note of defensiveness entering her voice.

Noah chuckled. "Don't get me wrong; he seems decent enough. Anyone who has managed to withstand Revin for as long as he has can't be all that bad. He's got good timing, though. I need to speak with the three of you."

"Did we actually win something?" Todd asked, his eyes lighting up.

"No, you lost. I would have told you if you'd won. This is about something else."

Todd's expression quickly turned serious, but it was Isabel that spoke next.

"About *us?*" Isabel put extra stress on the last word, and it took Noah a moment to realize she was probably referring to how she and Todd had been blacklisted from the noble houses and their subsequent plot of revenge against the people that had killed their families.

"Not the two of you in particular. All three of you," Noah said. "We should do this somewhere private, though. Lee, could you—"

"I'll come along to make sure we aren't disturbed," Lee said, giving him a nod.

"We could go to our room?" Todd offered.

"That works," Noah said. "I'm just going to need to stop by a potion shop on the way there."

* * *

About ten minutes and three Mind Meld Potions later, the four of them stepped into Todd and Isabel's room. Lee remained outside to ensure nobody overheard their conversation.

This was the first time that Noah had seen Isabel and Todd's lodgings, and he had to admit that it felt a little odd.

They hadn't spent much effort decorating. Their room was plain, with just a single large bed in the center and a desk beside it beneath a window. They'd split the closet on the other side of the bed between themselves, and their bathroom was plain but clean.

"So what is it?" Emily asked, leaning against the wall. Based on the casual way she stood, Noah suspected this wasn't the first time she'd been in here. Clearly, they'd been spending some time together on their own.

Good. The closer they are, the better.

"The two of you already know a good bit about my secrets," Noah said, nodding to Isabel and Todd. "But not all of them."

"We'd gathered that," Isabel said. "You're just going to be telling us about yourself?"

"You don't have to sound so disappointed." Noah chuckled and shook his head. "But that's not why I brought you here, no."

"I take it that the thing you have to discuss is so dangerous or important that the only way we can learn it is through speaking in our minds?" Emily asked, her eyes lingering on the potions Noah had bought on their way over. "That seems a bit... excessive."

"Moxie is in support of it," Noah said simply.

"Oh. In that case, sure," Emily said. "Why didn't you say that first?"

Noah resisted the urge to laugh. This was meant to be a serious matter.

"I want to impress on you how important it is that we never talk about any of this," Noah said, keeping his features firm. He reached up to the grimoire and took it off his back, setting the huge book against the wall.

"Does it have something to do with that giant thing?" Todd asked as he eyed the book. "I was wondering what it was."

"I thought it was a shield," Emily admitted. "Why do you have such a big book?"

"It's my new grimoire." Noah patted the top of the book. "And that's all I'll be saying for the time being. I'm not going to make any of you swear a Rune Oath, but you'll need to promise me that you won't share anything you see or learn here with anyone—under any circumstances."

"Why?" Emily asked suspiciously. "What is it about? You didn't say if this had to do with the grimoire or not."

"Nor will I, until you agree." Noah shrugged and gestured to the door. "I won't force you to do anything, Emily. That's why I haven't made you swear a Rune Oath. This is so important that I won't even say it out loud. We'll be using a Mind Meld Potion to take things from here. If you aren't comfortable, then please feel free to leave. You can ask Moxie about this and do it later if you'd prefer."

Emily glanced from Noah to Todd and Isabel, chewing her upper lip. Several seconds passed. Noah caught Isabel and Todd exchanging a look.

"I trust you," Isabel said simply, breaking the silence and holding Noah's gaze. "I promise to keep this all secret."

"Me too," Todd added. "Imagine that. I'll drink the potion if you want me to, if only because I'm too interested to say no. I'll keep everything to myself."

Emily let out a small huff and gave Noah a nod. "Fine. I'll do it as well. I promise not to say anything."

"Thank you. I don't think any of you will regret this," Noah said. He took one of the Mind Meld Potions and held it out to Isabel. "Would you like to start?"

Isabel took the potion from him. She studied it for a moment, then popped the cork off.

"Only drink your half," Noah advised. "Then give me the potion and lie down immediately so you don't fall over. This will take us about thirty minutes, so just go ahead and sit around until then. Don't touch either of us until we wake up."

The other students nodded. Isabel tipped the glass vial back, drinking half of its contents before quickly handing it out to Noah. He took it from her and tilted it back, pouring the rest of the potion into his mouth.

Isabel lay down on the ground, and Noah propped himself up against the wall. A familiar buzzing sensation ate at the back of his mind as he opened his grimoire and rested his hand on the pages.

Then the feeling consumed him. The potion took hold and the world was plunged into darkness.

Chapter Thirteen

sabel's soul was a barren mountain. Cold wind bit at Noah's skin as his body formed upon a jagged rock. A single Rank 2 Stone Rune floated in the empty sky, too far away to reach without plummeting off the edge of the steep mountain.

But, even though there was only one Rank 2 rune before him, pressure bore down on Noah's shoulders like an anvil. It was a sensation he recognized well—the presence of a Master Rune.

He turned away from the edge of the mountain and looked up. Brilliant, glowing blue energy made up a massive rune in the air at the peak of the mountain. It was calm, but the power stored within it was intense.

Soul. What a name for a rune. I think I can see why the noble families tore Isabel's father apart to get their hands on this. I don't even want to think about what a Soul Master Rune would be capable of doing. It feels the closest to Sunder's intensity of any Master Rune I've seen, but it's still nowhere near there.

"I'm sorry I couldn't tell you before," Isabel said. Noah tore his gaze away from the Master Rune when he spotted Isabel standing on the rocky path beside him.

"What, about the Master Rune?" Noah asked.

Isabel nodded, her shoulders slumping. "You've shared so much with me and Todd, but I couldn't afford to tell you before. It was too dangerous. I—"

Noah burst into laughter. Isabel froze, staring at him in confusion.

"I'm sorry," Noah said, forcing himself back under control and clearing his throat. "You haven't done anything wrong, Isabel. I already knew you had this."

"What? You did?"

"I don't mean to be rude, but I kind of figured it out after you infused your armor with the glowing blue energy that you use for your swords. You can only call on one rune at a time, remember?"

Isabel blinked, deflating like the sail of a boat headed straight into the wind. "Oh. I thought I kept it subtle enough that nobody would pick it up. A lot of people use Stone or Earth Magic to make armor and then just leave it there. How did you know I wasn't doing that? I could have been alternating."

"You could have been," Noah agreed. "But I still suspected it, and Silvertide did too. When he came to speak with me, after he determined that I was trustworthy, he mentioned his thoughts. It's fine, Isabel. I don't fault you for not sharing the full extent of what you could do. This is a dangerous secret."

Isabel was silent for several seconds. "I guess I didn't do as good a job of hiding it as I should have. It was hard. I wanted to go all out when we practiced, but using the Master Rune was just so dangerous. But if I didn't use it, I'd have fallen behind."

"I already told you I don't fault you for it," Noah said. "If you need private lessons with just you and Todd or something like that, just let me or Moxie know. We'll accommodate you. You shouldn't have to leave something like this untouched. But, out of curiosity, what does it actually *do*?"

"I don't know the full extent of its power," Isabel admitted. "I can form its energy into shapes, like weapons or armor. They aren't really that powerful, but they're versatile. I think the passive is reinforcing my body and magic."

"Reinforcing—ah. That's how you were lifting that huge shield and armor?"

"Yeah. It made them lighter and me stronger. I suppose that means the opposite of the soul is the body. A bit odd, if you think about it."

"And yet, I think I see it." Noah tilted his head to the side thoughtfully. "Regardless, that's a powerful Master Rune. I can tell from the pressure that it's no slouch. It doesn't seem right that you feel its offensive abilities aren't that good—you might be missing something."

"I probably am. I really haven't had much chance to really test it. I've been too scared someone will realize what it is, so I've been severely limiting my use of it to forms that could be explained by a normal rune. My sword resembles something an Energy Rune could make."

"We'll look into it, but unfortunately, our time here is limited," Noah said. "We've only got thirty minutes."

"To do what?" Isabel asked.

"Fix that Rank 2 Stone Rune of yours." Noah nodded at the rune floating over the side of the mountain. "Bring it over here."

"Fix it?" Isabel's brow furrowed, but she followed Noah's instructions and held a hand out. The Stone Rune approached them, coming to a stop just beside Isabel. "You can't fix a rune, and this is the only Rank 2 I have. There's no way for me to get rid of it without seriously crippling myself. Besides, it isn't that bad. It was 15 percent full."

"It's only got Stone in it?" Noah confirmed.

Isabel nodded. "Yeah. Just stone. My intent wasn't the best when I made it, unfortunately."

"Then that's an easy fix. You won't even need a new rune."

"I'm not sure you heard anything I just said."

"You aren't the only one with secrets," Noah said simply. "Now, listen closely. There are two important things to share, and they're dangerous enough secrets that you can never mention them outside the safety of your mind."

Isabel gave him a cautious nod. "Okay."

"First, a Perfect Rune isn't what you think it is. It's less obvious with a rune that only has the same kind of energy within it, but it becomes more apparent later on. To have a real Perfect Rune, the pressure coming off it must remain the same no matter what or how much energy you're drawing from it. On top of that, your early runes should be simple. The more specific you make them, the harder it is for them to be perfect in the early stages."

Isabel looked from Noah to the rune. To her credit, she realized what he was talking about almost instantly. It took several seconds for it to properly set in, though. She drew in a sharp breath.

"Damned Plains. Are you serious? That means making a Perfect

Rune is *much* harder than I thought. The chances of getting it right are almost zero."

"Getting it right on the first try," Noah corrected.

"There aren't second tries. Nobody can afford to just take massive amounts of soul damage every single time they mess up a combination, and that's not even counting all the energy you'd be wasting shattering runes left and right."

"And that leads us to my second secret," Noah said, crossing his arms before his chest. "I can cut your rune back into its Rank 1 components."

Isabel stared at Noah. "What?"

"Exactly what I said. You aren't the only one with a Master Rune, Isabel. I think you can see why I put so much stress on this remaining a secret. As long as I'm around, you've got infinite tries to combine your runes. I can keep cutting it apart, and the only real cost to you will be a slight energy loss if you don't work fast enough."

Isabel swallowed heavily. "That's how you advanced so quickly?"

"Guilty."

"What rank are you now?" Isabel asked. "A few months ago, you were a Rank 1. Are you—"

"Just three, but I'll be Rank 4 soon enough," Noah said. "I've remade my runes more times than I can count. They're all perfect—and in the real sense of the word."

"Damned Plains," Isabel muttered. "What do I have to do? I don't think I can afford—"

Noah's eyes narrowed and he cut Isabel off with a sharp gesture before she could continue. "I didn't ask for pay, Isabel. I just told you what we'd be doing. We have a limited amount of time, and I only bought three Mind Meld Potions, so we won't have more time today. Gather yourself. I'm going to split your rune apart, and you'll have to work quickly to reform it."

Isabel slapped her cheeks with her hands and shook her head, drawing in a deep breath and letting it out slowly. She then gave Noah a firm nod. "Okay. I'm ready. I've been thinking about what I messed up since I combined my runes. I think I should be able to repair it if you can split my runes apart."

"Fantastic," Noah said. "Just focus. Remember to work fast and draw on the excess energy floating around. Take in as much of it as possible, but don't stress too much. Even if it doesn't work the first time around, we can do it again."

Isabel nodded. The determined look on her face told Noah everything he needed to know. She was ready. He stepped up to the rune, reaching out as he called on Sunder. Noah's veins turned jet black as the icy power of the Master Rune flooded through his body.

He placed his hand on the surface of the Stone Rune, feeling the power coursing within its lines.

Sunder surged from his palm, black energy carving straight through the rune in a flash. A loud crack split the still air as the rune shattered. From within it bloomed seven Rank 1 runes, swirling out in a cloud of magical power.

Noah didn't even have to tell Isabel to get started. She stepped forward without hesitation, and he moved to the side, allowing her space so she could concentrate. Isabel's eyes closed and she held her hands up, pressing her lips together.

The Runes barely had any time to enjoy their separation before she exerted her will upon them. With a shudder, seven became one once more. Energy swirled around the center of the newly forming rune like a vortex.

Noah turned away a moment before a flash lit up Isabel's mindspace. He looked back just in time to see her newly formed rune before the excess energy started to flood into it.

Ten percent full. Well done, Isabel. Only needed one more shot at it.

Only when all the excess energy had been absorbed did Isabel let her eyes open. She gazed at the new Stone Rune, her mouth hanging slightly askew.

"Not bad," Noah said. "Second time's the charm, huh?"

"Just like that?" Isabel muttered. "How can you treat it so lightly? I thought I'd be stuck with a subpar rune for a long time. I can't even believe I'm calling it subpar—it was a good rune. Most people have worse ones."

"And now you've got a better one." Noah shrugged. "The world isn't fair, Isabel. You and Todd know that more than most. Ergo, you might as well take advantage of it when you can. Just remember my other warning as well. With a single-element rune like this, you don't have to worry much about balancing energy. But when you get up to combining multiple elements, you'll need to make sure the pressure it puts off is identical no matter how you're using it."

"Trust me, I won't forget," Isabel said. She swallowed. "Do you realize that you could probably earn hundreds of thousand gold for even a single usage of this? You could literally make the most powerful mages in the empire far stronger than they already are."

Noah scrunched his nose in distaste. "Bleh. Why would I do that? I don't need the money. I've got enough right now, and the moment this power got out, I'd never be a free man again. I think I much prefer helping myself and the people I care about."

"I swear I'll never breathe a word of this," Isabel promised. "Your secret dies with me."

"I'd much rather it live with you," Noah said idly. "Either way, whenever you combine a rune and you feel like it didn't turn out as good as you hoped, let me know. Just don't do it too often, or the Mind Meld Potions will bankrupt me."

"I promise—"

Noah took Isabel by the shoulders and she blinked in surprise.

"Relax," Noah said, keeping his tone gentle. "You aren't in my debt. Don't treat me any differently than normal, please. Just keep being how you were."

"Define what point in time you're referring to." A small grin flickered across Isabel's face. "Do you mean back when you first started being a real teacher?"

"Maybe just go back to before summer," Noah suggested with a wince.

Isabel laughed. "Okay. Fine. I think I can do that. But... thank you."

"My pleasure."

Chapter Fourteen

The rest of their time from the Mind Meld Potion ran its time out and Noah woke back in Isabel and Todd's room. He sat up, pushing his grimoire to the side and blinking to adjust to the new environment.

"So? What did Vermil do?" Emily asked before Isabel had even finished sitting up herself.

Isabel didn't even reply. She just shook her head, still in partial disbelief about everything that had happened. Her reaction was enough for Todd to grab the next Mind Meld Potion without a second of hesitation.

"Let's do it. Can we do it now?" Todd asked eagerly. "I almost never see Isabel that speechless."

"Hey! I wanted to go next!"

Todd shot Emily a smug look, then glanced at Noah. "So?"

"Go ahead," Noah said with a chuckle. He tapped his hand on the top of his grimoire. If he recalled correctly, Todd's Rank 2 rune was a little more complex than just a True Stone Rune, so there would probably be some rune replacement involved in repairing it. Fortunately it was just a Rank 2, and he'd gotten more than a few assorted runes over the vacation that would hopefully be of use.

Todd tipped half the potion back into his mouth and handed it over. Noah drank the other half, keeping his hand on the grimoire as he leaned back against the wall and let himself fall into the familiar buzz of the Mind Meld Potion's effects.

He didn't have to wait long. Magic enveloped him and the world vanished in a swirl of darkness. When vision returned to Noah, he was standing on a craggy, barren landscape. Wisps of steam curled up around his body, and heat bore down on him, just hot enough to be a step beyond uncomfortable.

Todd stood directly before Noah, his fingers tapping his thigh in impatience. "I just want to let you know I've got really high hopes, so I'm gonna be disappointed if you don't basically shatter my worldview."

"Lucky me," Noah said dryly. He turned in a circle. Todd had been busy—he had several runes in his mindspace.

There was a filled Heat Rune, two Water Runes, an Ice Rune, and a Fire Rune—all at Rank 1. Noah also spotted Todd's Shattering Blows Rune floating away from the others. Its center was made up of small, short strokes, all surrounded by longer and smoother ones at the edges. "Bring that rune over."

Todd blinked but did as instructed, calling the rune to hover beside them. The pressure coming off it was definitely weaker than a Perfect Rune, but Todd had mentioned that it hadn't been perfect before.

"I know it's not the best rune, but I did what I could with what I had to work with," Todd said, looking at the rune with a small frown. "I think it turned out decent."

"You did a good job," Noah said. "This doesn't look like it was an easy rune to make. Your intent would have had to be really good, and that's not accounting for the proper combinations either. There's nothing to be ashamed of."

"Yeah. Thanks. What did we come here to talk about, though? I'm going to die of impatience if you don't tell me."

"That." Noah nodded to the rune. "We're going to be fixing it."

"What?"

"You know, I'm pretty sure Isabel said the exact same thing." Noah grinned and shook his head. "Maybe I'm a narcissist, but I'm never going to get tired of that reaction. Here's the deal—I can cut your rune apart back into its Rank 1 components, and I've got a grimoire with a bunch of runes for you to use if you need them at your side. We have thirty minutes to fix your rune until it's perfect."

"You're screwing with me." Todd took a step back and lost some of his concentration, allowing the Shattering Blows Rune to move back to its normal resting spot.

"Nope. Moxie and I also discovered that Perfect Runes aren't always actually perfect. A rune needs to exert equal amounts of pressure no matter how you use it. From what I can tell, the general public doesn't know that, and I don't think noble families do either."

Todd's eyes bored into Noah. For one of the first times since Noah had met Todd, the boy was speechless.

"Damned Plains," Todd breathed. "You're not screwing with me at all. No wonder Isabel looked like that."

"Thirty minutes," Noah reminded Todd. "We can talk more after your rune is fixed. I know this is sudden, but I think you can understand how important it is that all of this remains secret. It's at the same level of threat as Isabel's Master Rune."

Todd's features hardened and he gave Noah a firm nod. "Right. Okay. I'm with you. You—ah, won't tell anyone about—"

"Of course not. Her secret is safe with me, just as I hope mine is with you."

"Completely safe," Todd promised. He called his rune back over to him, placing his hand onto its shimmering surface. Energy crackled at his fingertips and he let out a slow breath to steady himself. "How do we do this?"

"First, think about what kept the rune from being as strong as you wanted it to be. Do you know if it was intent or rune choice?"

"A mixture of both, I think. I didn't fully understand what I was making, but the concept was trapping steam in an enclosed space to make an explosion. It's got Stone, Water, and Fire in it."

"Interesting. You might want to consider pulling the rune's focus back a bit," Noah suggested. "I've done a lot of testing with Moxie, and we found that the best way to make a powerful rune is to make sure you don't rush things too much. Shattering Blows is a little specific, so it might be best as your Rank 3 rune."

Todd shook his head. "When you say testing, do you mean you've just been putting together and chopping runes apart? Can you do it indefinitely?"

"Pretty much. There are some drawbacks in energy loss, but yes."

"Damned Plains," Todd said again. "I'll take your suggestion, then.

Do you think I should aim for Steam and Stone Runes now, then combine them into Shattering Blows at Rank 3?"

"That's probably how I'd approach it, but I can't say what the right move is for sure. The only way to find out is to test. Just keep in mind— every time I cut your rune up, you'll lose a little bit of the energy as it dissipates. The faster you work to put it back together, the less energy you lose. Just don't work too fast. Better to do it right once than wrong fifty times."

"Yeah, I'm with you. Fast but not stupid." Todd chewed his lower lip. "Okay. There's a bit of a problem."

"What is it?"

"I don't think I've got enough Fire Runes to make a good Steam Rune. I feel like Steam would be four Fire and three Water, but I only have three if I count the two that are in Shattering Blows."

"I've got a Fire Rune in my grimoire. It might not be full, but your Shattering Blows Rune has a lot of energy in it, so you can use that to fill up the Fire Rune."

Assuming the grimoire actually gives it to me. Fifty-fifty chance on that.

"Are you just made of runes or something?" Todd asked. "Do you hate money?"

"So you don't want the rune?"

Todd raised his hands into the air with a laugh. "Didn't say that. I'll take whatever you give me, Teacherman."

"Then just focus on actually making the rune," Noah said. "When you're ready, I'll pull a Fire Rune in for you to save in your soul. Then we'll get started."

"We can do the Fire Rune now. I'll keep thinking about the intent for the Steam Rune while we do that."

Noah extended his senses to his grimoire back in Todd's room, sending a mental request for a Fire Rune. For several seconds, there was nothing. Then, almost reluctantly, he felt energy prickle against his skin.

Drawing upon it, Noah dragged the Rank 1 rune from the pages of his grimoire into Todd's soul. His finger traced through the air in a practiced motion as he formed the rune. Todd watched it with a hungry look in his eyes, his fingers twitching at his sides.

As soon as the rune had been drawn out, Todd jumped into action.

He traced the pattern, drawing the power into himself permanently. It snapped into place, a small wave of pressure emanating out from it.

To Noah's surprise, the rune was fuller than he'd expected it to be. It should have been fairly empty, but for some reason, it was well over halfway full.

I never filled that rune. Why does it have energy?

Todd didn't notice Noah's confusion. He stared intently at Shattering Blows, his brow furrowed and lips pressed thin.

Did the grimoire somehow fill this? Where would the energy come— oh, shit. It put in some of the power that it took from the runes it ate, didn't it? Maybe as a peace offering? Either way, that's actually incredibly handy. I can have it chew up useless runes and distribute their energy for me without even lifting a finger.

"I'm ready," Todd said, breaking Noah's thoughts. "So you just chop this up and I take the energy, fill up the Fire Rune, and then recombine everything? And we keep doing that until it works?"

"Exactly."

"Let's do it."

Noah's veins turned jet black. He stepped forward and pressed his hand against Shattering Blows, letting Sunder's power surge forth.

Then Todd got to work.

* * *

Things did not go anywhere near as smoothly as they had for Isabel, but that was to be expected. There were a lot more moving pieces that went into Todd's Steam Rune, and that made it a lot easier to mess up.

Fortunately for Todd, he had quite a few tries to get things right. It took six separate recombining attempts and more than a little cursing as he tried to figure out what was wrong with his intent, but in the end —and just a few minutes before the Mind Meld Potion's effects wore off—Todd finally had a Steam Rune whose pressure remained perfectly constant.

Letting out a relieved sigh, Todd flopped to the ground and released his runes. Energy still crackled throughout his mindspace, but the job was done.

"How are we supposed to be able to figure this out on the first try? Your magic is completely unfair," Todd said as he let out an exhausted sigh. "Thanks, Teacherman. We need to make sure nobody ever finds out you can do this, or I don't think we'll see you again."

Noah snorted. "That would be nice, yes. Make sure not to talk about this once we leave your mindspace, but if you ever combine a rune and need to modify it, let me know. I told Isabel the same thing, but my plan is for all of you to have exclusively Perfect Runes."

"And you don't want payment for this?"

Noah glared at Todd. "Your payment is to absolutely destroy any exams you take this year."

"I think I can do that," Todd said with a weary grin. It fell away as his features turned serious, and he sat up, locking eyes with Noah. "And thank you. Not just for this. Isabel and I never had a teacher who actually cared this much about us. I won't let you down."

"You don't have to worry about letting me down," Noah said. "Just put in your all and don't do anything *too* stupid."

"How stupid we talking?"

"If you have to ask, then it's probably too stupid."

They both laughed, and a familiar tingle prickled Noah's spine. Todd noticed it too and gave him a short nod.

"Time's up, huh?"

Noah barely had time to nod before his soul was wrenched from Todd's mind and sent flying back into his own body in the room outside.

Chapter Fifteen

Noah's eyes opened to find that Todd wore the same expression that Isabel had when her Mind Meld Potion had worn off. He chuckled at the look the two of them exchanged, which only served to pique Emily's interest even more.

"What in the Damned Plains is going on in there?" Emily demanded. "Okay, I don't want to wait any longer. It's already been an hour. Can I go now?"

"Give me a second," Noah said, rubbing his eyes to try and completely wake himself up. It wasn't that the Mind Meld Potions put him to sleep, but using two twice in a row and then using Sunder so many times on Todd had drawn a decent bit of his energy.

The grimoire felt unusually warm against his palm. Noah studied its open pages, but they were blank, as they usually were. It had definitely done something to the Fire Rune, but it had been beneficial, so he couldn't really complain.

Odd. But not as odd as Azel not making an appearance. I fully expected to have to explain him to at least someone, but he didn't pop out for either Todd or Isabel. It's really been a while since I've heard from him.

It wasn't like Azel was gone—Noah could still feel the strand in his soul connecting him to the demon. The temptation to tug at it was strong, but he was pretty certain that Azel had been truthful about not being able to flat-out lie to him due to their connection. That meant the demon hadn't lied about the consequences of unraveling the strand being true death for both of them.

Not like I'm going to complain that he isn't bothering me, but I'm starting to wonder what the hell he's getting up to instead of bothering me.

Hey, Azel. You there?

For a while, there was no response. Then the back of Noah's mind prickled as a faint warmth spread throughout him, and Azel's voice echoed through his mind.

Unfortunately. What do you want, Vines?

I was bored and wondering what you were up to.

Noah nearly burst into laughter at the barrage of incredulous thoughts that struck him. Evidently, Azel wasn't much of a fan of people flipping his joke on him.

What do you actually want? Did you really call me purely to bother me? After I helped you with Evergreen?

No. I was wondering if you were doing something bad, if I'm being honest. You've been awfully quiet recently.

I have been eating well. I don't need to do anything for you to feed me, so why should I interfere?

That was actually something of a good point, and Noah paused for a moment to think about it. He'd definitely been getting up to some fairly emotional things in recent times, so Azel had more than enough food, but the idea of the demon not only knowing about restraint but showing it to this degree felt... off.

You never struck me as someone who was content with their lot in life, no matter what it was.

Do you want me to be greedy? I can be.

Again, something in Azel's threat felt wrong. It didn't have the weight that his words normally did—as if he didn't want Noah to call his bluff. That wasn't much of a bet to hedge, as Noah had absolutely no plans of calling in more trouble, and Azel was well aware of it.

Do we really have to play games like this all the time?

Yes.

Noah sighed. He ignored the looks that the students sent him.

At least tell me if whatever it is you're doing is going to put someone I care about in danger. I don't care if you're trying to cause me shit, but promise me that everyone else is being left out of it.

Azel was silent for a few seconds. Then a small sigh echoed through Noah's mind. He was probably searching for the right words that would let him answer the question without actually giving away too much by getting too close to the real truth.

I can't promise that nobody will be hurt, but I can promise that I'm not trying to hurt anyone—at the moment. My interests lie in other paths. Is that sufficient for you?

Noah copied the demon's strategy of remaining silent for a bit. He could tell Azel was telling the truth, but his answer hadn't been particularly reassuring. There were probably a fair number of ways that Azel could *accidentally* arrange for things to go very poorly. He'd left himself a pretty wide loophole by avoiding the promise.

No. Not quite. I need more.

Insufferable. Do you really think you have more patience than I do? I can sit here and play with you all day if I want to.

Don't mix my lack of patience with a lack of ability to wait, Azel. Not wanting to do something doesn't mean I can't do it. I think you know better than anyone that I've waited for things far longer than you have, and I also know you won't last nearly as long as I would without entertainment.

I am actively trying to help. How's that for you?

Noah waited for Azel to add something else, but the demon didn't elaborate, which only confused him even more. Azel was *helping*? A thought struck Noah and his brow furrowed.

Help who, Azel?

I'm done here. Call me if you're doing something interesting. If you want more answers, you'll have to live up to your threats and come wait for me out in your soul. We'll see how much time you're really willing to waste.

With that, Azel's presence pulled back. Noah ground his teeth, but Azel had caught him. He was pretty sure he *could* wait Azel out, but he had other things to do. Azel didn't. And, with the promises that Azel had given, it seemed at least somewhat likely that he wasn't actively trying to hurt someone.

It wasn't the most reassuring answer he could have gotten, but it had to do for the time being.

"Is everything okay?" Isabel asked. "You've been staring at the wall really seriously."

"Yeah. Just some things I'm working through." Noah cleared his throat and popped the stopper of the last Mind Meld Potion off, holding it out to Emily. "You're up next."

Emily snagged the potion and poured it into her mouth without a moment of hesitation. Noah took it back and removed the stopper blocking in the second half, drinking it and setting his hand back onto his grimoire as the potion's effects took hold and, for the third time that day, he was pulled into someone's soul.

* * *

Emily's soul was cold, but not overly so. A soft blanket of snow covered a beautiful forest of barren, frozen trees. They were all encased in solid blue ice that glittered faintly in the sunlight boring down on them from above.

A shimmering, frosty Rank 2 rune floated just above the trees in the distance. It felt like it was perfect—at least, as far as he could tell at the moment.

Frost Creation

Across from it was *Frozen Forest,* a Rank 2 that reminded Noah much more of the typical runes that the Torrin family had. It put off a bit less energy than the first rune did, marking it as a slightly weaker combination. Both of them were completely full, and Emily also had a filled Rank 1 Stone and Fire Rune floating in her mindspace.

"This is about my runes, isn't it?"

Noah turned to look at Emily. She stood beneath one of the glistening trees, watching him warily. He didn't blame her—they'd never really spent all that much time alone. Most of their interactions had been when Moxie was also there, so she really didn't have nearly as much proof of his character as the others did.

I really should have addressed that earlier. She's Moxie's student, but with the way we're teaching things, she's mine as well.

"Among other things," Noah said. "Could you make some chairs or something? The two of us have more to speak about than the others did."

Emily blinked, then frowned. "What do you mean? If you're about to—"

Noah raised a hand. "Please don't finish that. I didn't word the

100

sentence very aptly. I'm well aware of the reputation I once had, but I think Isabel and Todd's trust should speak for me enough to justify at least a little bit of patience."

The snow beneath Noah's feet bulged. A plain chair made of ice rose up beneath him. Emily formed herself a much more comfortable–looking one, complete with leaf padding. Suppressing a laugh, Noah sat down.

Emily was still the heir of a massive noble family, so it didn't surprise him that she was a bit bratty. And, even though the chair was ice, it wasn't as cold as it should have been.

"So?" Emily asked. "What is it, then? And if you do anything weird, I'll tell M—"

"Moxie and I are dating."

Emily choked. "What?"

"That's not the thing I actually came here to talk about." Noah cleared his throat. "But she trusts me, and I trust her. And come on— you know she cares about you. She wouldn't leave you in the care of someone she didn't trust."

"You are *not* skipping past that first part." Emily's eyes narrowed and she leaned forward. "You're a Linwick. A ratty one. How are you dating Moxie? She's a valued member of—"

"Is she?"

Emily shot to her feet, clenching her fists at her sides. "What's that meant to mean? Is she what?"

"Is she really valued by your family?" Noah asked, holding Emily's gaze without flinching.

"Of course she is! She's my teacher! Magus Evergreen chose her because of how much she trusted Moxie. This just shows how little you know about her. Why would she ever date someone like you?"

Sounds like she has no idea Evergreen is dead. Not good—not to mention she seems to actually like Evergreen. This might be a bit rough, but it needs to be done. Sorry, Moxie. I won't spill everything, but you two can't just keep avoiding this forever. The safest place to tell Emily anything is inside her own mind.

"You know, I asked her the same question." Noah chuckled and stood up. The chairs would have to wait. "And, to be honest, I don't know if this is even my place to tell you. Moxie cares more about you than you realize. Far, far more. Really, it should be her talking to you about this."

"About what?" Emily demanded. Magic swirled at her feet, kicking up the snow. "You'd better watch what you say."

"No. I don't think I will. I'm not going to spill Moxie's secrets— those are for her to share. But I'm going to give *you* an opportunity. You've got two options here. First, this conversation ends right now, and I do exactly what I did for Isabel and Todd. Then you keep on as you were, and we never mention this talk at all."

"And the other option?"

"I tell you the truth, and then you speak with Moxie and find out just how much she's done for you."

Emily matched Noah's gaze. She forced her hands to unclench. "I don't know what you're talking about."

"Then decide if you want to find out or not."

The chair behind Noah scooted forward, knocking into the back of his knees and catching him as he fell back into it.

"Talk," Emily said.

The best way to do it is just to rip the band-aid off, right?

"Evergreen was a massive piece of shit—and now she's dead. Moxie and I killed her."

Chapter Sixteen

Emily's eyes nearly popped out of her head. "What?"

"I trust you'll understand how important it is that this never leaves the safety of your mindspace," Noah said, ignoring the horrified expression on Emily's face. "If it ever gets out, Moxie is dead."

"I don't believe you." Emily's voice trembled slightly. "It's impossible. Evergreen is a Rank 6, and she loved Moxie. Moxie loved her. They were really close. You're lying. Why would she ever do that?"

"On my runes, I swear that everything I tell you while we remain in your mindspace is the truth and that I will not attempt to lie or twist the truth in any way. Do you accept?"

Emily's eyes widened, but she didn't wait for long. "Yes. I do."

Ice raced through Noah's veins as he swore the Rune Oath. It gripped his spine like the hand of the reaper and he grimaced. Emily stiffened as she felt the oath take effect.

"Repeat it," Emily demanded, rising from her chair once more. "Say it again."

"Evergreen called Moxie back to the Torrin estate over vacation to kill her," Noah said. "We went—and we killed Evergreen instead."

Emily stared at Noah intently, clearly waiting for the Rune Oath to come into effect and shatter his runes. A second passed. Her face paled and her eyes widened.

"You killed my mother."

She was your mom? Who the hell did it with—you know what, I don't want to know.

"I'm not the most compassionate person," Noah said slowly. "But Moxie was too worried about you to actually say this, so I'm doing it myself. I'd say I'm sorry, but I'm not. Evergreen was a terrible person, and she had it coming."

Emily's hands clenched. Ice gathered around her fists, swirling furiously. Noah matched her stare. He didn't know Emily that well, but he'd seen how she acted around Moxie. Between her and Evergreen, Noah was pretty sure Emily would choose Moxie.

Pretty sure.

It was a tense few seconds. The look in Emily's eyes told him that she was very strongly considering trying to kill him then and there—but that would have triggered the Rune Oath, shattering her own runes as well because of the bond. If she wanted to try anything, she'd have to wait until the oath ended at the end of their time together in her mind.

With a supreme force of will, Emily let her hands drop. The hatred and anger were joined by new emotions. Fear and confusion warred across her face. Noah actually felt for her.

She couldn't believe him, because believing him meant that her beloved mentor had killed her mother—and that her mother had tried to kill her mentor first. Noah suspected that it wasn't actually Evergreen herself that Emily mourned as much as the idea of who she could have been.

"Why?" Emily asked, struggling to find words. "How?"

"The whole story isn't mine to share," Noah said. "I'm already robbing Moxie of this discussion. What I can say is that Moxie has always had Evergreen's sword hanging above her neck. Evergreen didn't approve of how you were acting like a living being instead of a puppet during the survival exam, so she decided that Moxie had been teaching you badly."

"You're lying." Emily took a step back. "Why would she do that? She was fine with it."

"No, she wasn't. She just didn't want to cause a fuss." Noah shrugged. "I don't expect you to believe me right now, Emily. Even with the Rune Oath. You're probably trying to figure out how I'm working around it or something, right?"

"Yes, I am."

"That's up to you. I'm giving you information, not telling you how to think. Moxie was functionally a slave to your family for the majority of the time you've known her, and she didn't want to tell you because she cares about you too much. She was worried about how it would affect you."

"So why are you telling me, then?" Emily stormed up to Noah, craning her head back to glare into his eyes. "What's your angle?"

"Do you want the real answer to that?" Noah asked. He raised a hand before Emily could answer. "Think before you say anything else. I'm offering you more information than I've given anyone other than Moxie for one reason alone—I love Moxie, and this is hurting her as much as it's hurting you."

"Why would I have to think before answering that?"

"Because this information is dangerous. I've killed to protect it, and I'll kill to protect it again," Noah said softly. "Ignorance is safety. You can take my words as they are and speak to Moxie about the rest."

"But you'll tell me something she won't?"

"Yes, so long as not so much as a whisper of it ever leaves your lips."

"Why? Why would you trust me with it? What kind of trick is this? A way to make me trust you?"

Noah gave her an emotionless smile. "You have no choice but to trust me, Emily. I'm bound by Rune Oath. I already told you why I'm offering this, and it's not for your sake. It's for Moxie's. Knowing the full truth will make things make more sense."

Emily's gaze bore into Noah's features, searching his face for anything she could use. She was clearly thinking through his offer rather than just blindly accepting it. Finally, she swallowed and gave him a sharp nod. "Tell me. I want to know."

"You asked why I was willing to tell you this, right?"

Emily nodded.

"It's because I don't care about your family," Noah said simply. "I'd kill every last Torrin if I thought they posed a risk to Moxie, and I wouldn't lose an instant of sleep about it."

"Of course you wouldn't," Emily spat. "You're a Linwick."

"No, I'm afraid that's not true either."

"What? That's a lie. You're tricking the Rune Oath somehow. I know who you are. You're Vermil—"

"Also wrong," Noah said curtly. "My name is Noah. I killed Vermil months ago, a short while before you first met me."

Emily's mouth opened. Then she froze. Thoughts flashed behind her eyes. She took a step back and swallowed, understanding finally dawning on her. "You didn't know anything about Arbitage. That's why you attended the class she taught."

"Nothing about magic at all," Noah said with a nod. "I'm not from this world."

"Where are you from, then? What *are* you?"

"Honestly, I'm not so sure myself. Do you consider the place you're from the place you spent the most time in?"

Emily sent him a baffled look. "Yes."

"Then I'm from the afterlife," Noah said. "I clawed my way out of it and I'll never go back."

Emily stared at him, but there were too many pieces starting to click for her to deny it. "You're... what, then? A god? A demon?"

"Neither. I'm Noah—and I'd thank you for keeping that between us."

"Or what?" Emily challenged.

Noah tilted his head to the side. "You'll make Moxie sad. She knows as well."

Emily's features crumpled—and Noah knew he'd been correct. Emily wouldn't share anything. Not because she cared about him, but because she cared about Moxie.

"I wouldn't have said anything, but I just wanted to know what your reaction would be if I'd threatened to," Emily admitted. Her voice was softer—smaller than it had been before. "You really aren't Vermil."

"No, I'm not."

There were several seconds of silence.

"Are you really dating her?" Emily asked.

Noah almost laughed. "That's what you want to ask? Out of all the revelations I've revealed, that's what you care about?"

Emily nodded.

"Yes, I am."

She snorted. It was borderline a hysterical laugh, one born more from disbelief and shock than actual amusement. "Vermil was a piece of shit. You—no. He tried to hit on me. I couldn't believe Moxie was making me spend time with him after that. It made no sense, even though you were acting different. And if you aren't him... I guess I owe you an apology. I'm sorry for acting like such a bitch all the time."

"Apology accepted. Vermil got what was coming to him," Noah agreed. "But this isn't about Vermil. We don't have forever, Emily. The potion wears off in less than thirty minutes now. Ask your questions and ask them fast."

"You actually love Moxie?" Emily asked. "Not because of her standing in the family?"

Noah rubbed the bridge of his nose. "Moxie didn't *have* a standing in your family, Emily. She was actively looking for a way to escape them. I couldn't care less what family she's from. And, before you ask, I couldn't care less about the Linwicks either."

Somehow, that actually seemed to reassure Emily. Her tensed shoulders loosened slightly, though she was still nowhere near calm.

"Tell me about Evergreen," Emily said, swallowing. "More about her. I never knew her that well, but I never thought she was this bad. I just thought she was strict. What did she make Moxie do?"

"We're already well into the territory I shouldn't be on, but just about everything. Moxie didn't have much free will. And, even in spite of that, she still cared about you. She was looking for a way to keep teaching and spending time with you while also breaking the grip the Torrins had on her. That's how much she cared. Instead of just running and abandoning you, she stuck around."

Emily flopped back into her chair, her face nearly as pale as the ice surrounding her. She swallowed, then wiped her eyes with the back of a sleeve before they could start to water. "Is she free, now?"

Noah nodded. "Freed with Evergreen's death. The story is that a demon snuck in with Moxie, but she was unaware of it. The demon killed Evergreen, and Moxie's runes were shattered as punishment for failing to detect the demon."

"Her runes were shattered?" Emily cried out. "She's crippled?"

"No. I fixed them. It was part of her plan."

Emily stared at Noah. "What? How is that possible?"

"Put a pause on that. Ask the questions you actually care about first, and we can get to the other stuff later."

Chewing her lower lip, Emily scratched at the armrest of her chair and rocked back and forth in thought. "Evergreen was really going to kill Moxie? Just because I didn't do what she said?"

"Yes."

Emily looked down at her feet, shame covering her face. "I hate this, but it makes sense. I wondered why Moxie never took breaks and was always there. I-I thought she just really liked spending time with me. Nobody else did, but I guess she just didn't have a choice."

"Did you listen to nothing I said?" Noah snapped. Emily's eyes shot up to meet his in surprise at the anger in his tone. ,.

"I—"

"I just told you that Moxie literally chose to stay with you rather than find a way to escape. She knew her Rune Oaths would get broken regardless, but she would have done it for freedom if she didn't care about you." Noah cut Emily off and strode up to her chair, so she had no choice but to look at him. "Don't you dare start feeling pity—Moxie doesn't want it. She made her decisions. Being trapped doesn't mean you aren't in control of yourself. There's always a choice."

"But I never even noticed," Emily muttered. "She was always around me. If anyone should have noticed, it would have been me. You figured it out in a few months, didn't you?"

"Moxie was sheltering you on purpose. It was her decision to protect you from what Evergreen was doing," Noah said. "It was noble. Unfortunately, I am not. The reason I'm telling you all of this isn't so you can beat yourself up. It's so that you can know Moxie as well as you really should. You've both been caught in Evergreen's strings for too long."

Emily didn't respond to that. She probably needed some time to actually process everything he'd just told her. Unfortunately, time was not one of the resources they had much of at the moment.

"The Mind Meld Potion won't last forever," Noah said. "And, when it ends, you can't talk about anything I've revealed about Evergreen or myself. If you have more questions, I suggest you push through whatever emotions you're feeling and ask them."

"I don't even know," Emily muttered, staring down at her hands. "You're telling the truth."

"Kind of hard not to. I'm bound by the oath until we leave your mind."

That got a snort of actual amusement from Emily. "You don't sound particularly sad about any of this."

"I'm not. I told you—I don't care about the Torrins. I care about my friends, and I care about my students. That's it. You're included in that group, or we wouldn't be having this discussion. Caring about someone doesn't mean being nice to them. It means doing the right thing."

Emily sniffled. She drew a deep breath and let it out slowly, blinking furiously as her eyes watered. "Can—can you just stay here for a moment?"

Noah nodded. Emily stood and quickly walked off into the forest. She was losing time, but Noah suspected that there was no point trying to push further until she had gathered her feelings. Having her entire world turned on its head couldn't have been pleasant.

He sat back down in the chair that Emily had made for him.

And then he waited.

Ten minutes passed. They'd already spent around ten minutes speaking, so only a third of the potion's effects remained.

Snow crunched as Emily stepped out of the forest. Her eyes were red with tears—Noah was still somewhat surprised that physical changes like that happened in a mindspace, but it probably had more to do with how people subconsciously knew how their body should feel or react than a real effect.

Like how I get blinded by flashes of light when runes combine, even though I don't technically have real eyes as a soul.

"I believe you," Emily said, sitting down across from him. "But I'm still going to talk to Moxie."

"I'd expect as much."

There were several seconds of awkward silence where neither of them so much as looked at each other. Finally, Emily sighed.

"I guess I have to thank you."

"For what?"

"For telling me this," Emily said. She wiped her face with the back of her sleeve again. "Please don't make me say it again, though. Isabel and Todd will make fun of me forever."

Noah chuckled. "Fair enough. For what it's worth, I'm sorry your mother was a massive piece of shit."

Emily burst into laughter. Tears started to stream down her eyes again, and she hunched over, wiping her face furiously. "You're such an asshole."

"I'm aware."

It was another minute before Emily got a hold of herself again. She sniffled, then took a steadying breath and matched his gaze again. "Is there anything else?"

"Depends what you're asking about. There's always more, but we have one more thing I want to get accomplished before our time runs out."

"Please don't tell me Moxie is dying or something."

"What? No. Moxie's fine. It's about your runes."

"Runes—wait. You said you fixed Moxie's runes after they were shattered. How?"

"That's something else," Noah said. He turned to look at the runes floating around them. "What's important now is your runes."

"What about my runes?"

"Fixing them, of course. We have about ten minutes to go through and turn all of these perfect."

Chapter Seventeen

Perhaps it was because Emily was already off her guard, but she took the news with remarkably little surprise. She accepted the existence of Sunder easily, and it only took a minute for Noah to explain the basics of what he and Moxie had figured out about runes, their pressure, and how they should be combined to reach the optimal result.

Noah didn't have much in his grimoire that would actually be of help to Emily, as he was sorely lacking in Ice-related runes, but that turned out not to be an issue. The Rank 2 runes she had—Frost Creation and Frozen Forest—were fairly powerful and didn't seem to be far from their ideal versions. In fact, Frost Creation was almost there. When Emily tested drawing on its power, the difference in pressure was subtle. Unfortunately, it was there nonetheless.

As for Frozen Forest, the rune was a bit too general, and its concept wasn't simple enough to be a Perfect Rune, but Noah was pretty sure Emily would be able to fix it just by tweaking her intent. It wasn't like they had much time to think about it at the moment. With just minutes left in the Mind Meld Potion, the time to act was now.

We can always just get another potion if need be, but I'd rather save the money.

"Ready?" Noah asked.

"Yeah. Do it." Emily pulled Frost Creation close, which was the right move in Noah's eyes. It was already close to being perfect, so it would be a good one to start with.

Cold rivers of energy rushed through Noah's veins as Sunder pumped through him. He approached Frost Creation, holding his hand out and brushing his fingertips across the rune's glistening, silvery blue surface.

Magic poured out, and a line of black split the rune in twain. It shattered, a blue mist erupting from within it and pouring out into Emily's mindspace. Emily closed her eyes, concentration playing out across her features as seven Rank 1 runes swirled out from the remains of Frost Creation.

She was remarkably calm, almost as if she'd done something similar before. In just thirty seconds, Emily gathered the runes and pushed them back together, pouring the leaking energy straight back into them before much of it could dissipate.

Noah raised a hand just as a white flash lit up Emily's mindspace. Wind buffeted Noah's hair and a chill nipped at his skin. When the light faded and he lowered his hand, the exact same rune floated before them.

Emily wasted no time in drawing power from the newly reformed rune, testing out the pressure. Whatever she'd done had worked—the rune felt perfectly even. She grinned and lowered her hand.

"I did it."

"So you did. Think you have another in you?" Noah asked, looking to Frozen Forest. "That one might be a bit more problematic, but if you just hone in your focus to a plant or a tree or the like rather than a whole forest, I think you should be able to get it perfected."

"It's worth a try," Emily agreed with a nod, extending a hand to call the other rune over to them. "Let's do it."

And, in the few minutes they had left, they did it.

It did take three uses of Sunder, but on her third attempt, Emily finally managed to reform the Frozen Forest Rune into a Frozen Tree, like Noah had suggested. After Emily spent a moment to test it, making sure the rune's pressure was even, she flopped down in a small pile of snow and let out a relieved breath.

"Damned Plains. I did it. That was so much harder than I thought it would be."

There were only one or two minutes before the Mind Meld's

potion would run out—or at least, Noah was fairly sure how long was left. He still wasn't the best at keeping track of things.

"Well done," Noah said with an approving nod. "Especially considering we spent the first three quarters of our time talking about other things."

"Other things. That feels like an understatement," Emily said, looking up into the false sky of her mindspace. "By the way, you look really creepy when you use your power."

"What do you mean?"

"Your veins go black," Emily said, holding a hand out and making a face. "It looks like you're rotting or something. It's creepy."

"Lovely to know. I'm glad to hear."

A familiar tingle poked at the back of Noah's head. Evidently, he'd screwed up his count—but at least it hadn't been off by too much. The Mind Meld Potion was about to wear off.

"We're out of time," Noah said. "Remember—not a word of anything we talked about here. Not about me, you, Evergreen, or what we did to your runes. If you want to talk to Moxie, and you should, I'd suggest either getting a Mind Meld Potion or asking Lee to keep an eye out while you speak."

"Lee? Why?"

"She's very observant. Great at making sure you aren't disturbed."

The tingling intensified.

"I won't say anything," Emily promised. She stood up, then brushed the snow from her pants and paused for a moment. "The black veins are creepy, but if you don't think too hard about it, someone might think it was cool."

Was that a compliment?

Emily grinned at the expression on Noah's face. "Can't speak about anything that happened in here. Don't forget."

Noah didn't get a chance to respond. The Mind Meld Potion sputtered out and he was yanked from Emily's body. Darkness swallowed his vision and his eyes snapped back open in Isabel and Todd's room a second later.

"Did it work?" Todd asked, eyeing Noah as he sat straighter. He looked slightly concerned, and Isabel was wearing the same expression.

"Yes," Noah replied. "You'd better not be getting any more specific with that line of questioning, though."

"I won't, I won't," Todd said, raising his hands defensively. "It's just..."

He glanced over to Emily, who had sat up as well. Her eyes were red and her cheeks were stained with tears. She glanced from Noah to the others.

"What?" Emily asked.

I think she might have cried in the real world as well as in her soul. Oops.

Isabel tapped her cheek. "You've got something here."

Emily raised a hand to her face. She blinked, then reddened in embarrassment. "My—uh, my eyes were just a little dry. I was trying to moisten them."

That was possibly the worst excuse that Noah had ever heard, but all three of them didn't mention it any further.

Noah stood, grimacing as tingles ran through his legs and his head swam slightly. He'd been sitting in an awkward position for much too long. He snagged his grimoire and slung it over his back.

Glad it played along this time. I guess I'll need to get some more runes to feed it so it doesn't get snippy with me.

"What now?" Isabel asked.

"You tell me. Class is over. You've all got what I came here to give. I'd suggest practicing to get used to the changes. Our next class hasn't been cancelled or anything, and we won't be going easy on you."

"What about Alexandra?" Isabel asked. "Did you already..."

"No. I don't distrust Alexandra, but I don't trust her yet either. She's in a different situation than all of you. Please try to treat her kindly, though. I don't think she's had the opportunity to have many friends before."

"We will." It was Emily who spoke first. Isabel and Todd both glanced at her, and Emily blushed. "What?"

"Nothing," Todd said. "If we want to get along with her, maybe we should go swing by and hang out outside of class? She seemed like she takes competition really seriously, so I don't think she'll get along with us while we're fighting each other."

"That's a good idea," Isabel said with a nod. "Anything we should be aware of? She knew you from before, Professor. Was it in a good way or a bad way?"

"You probably shouldn't tell her I told you this, but she was wrapped up with some pretty bad people." Noah rubbed his chin. He didn't love sharing people's secrets without their consent, but it was a matter of safety, and his students deserved to know the basics.

"Bad people? Like nobles?" Todd asked.

Noah expected Emily to glare at him, but instead a flash of pain flickered across her face, and she looked to the side.

Ah, shit. Probably struck a nerve with what she just learned about Evergreen.

"Not all nobles are bad," Noah said. "Look at Moxie. And Emily."

Todd opened his mouth, then slowly closed it. "Yeah. You're right. Sorry, Emily. I was speaking without thinking."

"It's fine."

"Either way, they weren't nobles. And, either way, they're dead."

"We'll try to reach out to her," Isabel said. "Maybe we can do a little sparring. She seems really competent, and having someone difficult to hurt is pretty beneficial when you're just practicing. It would be nice to have someone I can fight without holding back so much against."

"Hey!" Todd exclaimed. "I've got armor!"

"Armor that's more meant to protect you from your own magic than anything else."

"Okay, fair point."

"Don't even look at me," Emily said. "I take one hit and I'm down for the count."

"Maybe something to work on," Noah said. "Then again, if you don't get hit, it doesn't matter. I prefer the low-defense, high-offense strategy as well."

Isabel and Todd both sent a very pointed look at Noah, clearly thinking back to the time they'd seen him get killed and come back to life. Not being able to stay dead was a pretty good motivator to not put much attention to staying alive.

"You should probably look into ways to make sure you don't get hit, though," Noah amended with a sheepish chuckle.

Emily's eyebrows tightened as she looked from Todd and Isabel to Noah. "What did I miss?"

"More secrets," Noah said honestly. "Ones that weren't very relevant to the other things we spoke about. If you really want to know, you're welcome to buy a Mind Meld Potion and ask. I'm not promising I'll answer, though."

"I can just... ask?"

"Welcome to the fold." Noah shrugged. "Don't abuse your privileges. And remember, no talking about anything out loud."

"Man, now I really want to talk about it," Todd muttered. "I wanna know what he told you, Emily."

"Get a Mind Meld Potion. I'll see you all next class," Noah said with a chuckle. With that, he turned and headed out of their room. As soon as he shut the door behind him, Lee slipped out of a shadow and fell in step beside him.

"How'd it go?" Lee asked.

"Pretty well, all things considered. Any trouble?"

Lee shook her head. "Just a few inquisitive squirrels. They were taken care of. What are we doing now?"

"I'm going to go report that I've hit Rank 3, and then I think I'd like to get some food. What do you think?"

"I'm starving. Sounds like a great idea. How long will reporting your rank-up take?"

Noah grimaced as he recalled his other experiences at the office. "I suppose we'll find out."

Chapter Eighteen

A short walk later, the two of them arrived at the office. Lee sniffed at the air as they approached the front doors, then licked her lips.

"I smell food."

"You know what? I'm not surprised."

In fact, I'm rather counting on it.

Noah pulled the door open. To his mild amusement, the secretary sat at the desk as she always did. And, as there always seemed to be, a pile of food was set out before her. The secretary didn't acknowledge them as they stepped in.

"Is this where we're getting food?" Lee asked.

"No. I'm still reporting my rank," Noah replied. He walked up to the desk and cleared his throat. As he expected, the secretary raised a single finger, not looking up from her meal. And, based on how much food was left, Noah doubted she'd be done anytime soon.

Perfect. Now, just to make sure I've got plausible deniability, I should wait a bit.

Noah leaned against the desk, tapping his foot on the ground as he let minutes pass. Lee looked from him to the food, then slowly edged closer to the table. He pretended not to notice as one of Lee's fingers slowly extended, slithering out like a small snake to snag a banana from where it rested at the base of a small pile of fruit.

With the precision of a master thief, Lee pulled the banana back to herself, one inch at a time. She wound it past plates of smoked meat and steaming bread, weaving through a veritable minefield.

The secretary's wholehearted focus on her meal proved to be more than enough cover for Lee to liberate the banana from its fate—only to stuff the whole thing into her mouth, skin, and all.

Lee caught Noah watching her and gave him a sheepish grin, the sides of the banana poking at either side of her mouth. She chewed once, then swallowed it whole, not making a single noise.

Her eyes drifted back to the table.

I'd better do something before she actually gets caught.

"I'm here to report my rank," Noah said. "It changed."

The secretary raised a finger. She wiped her greasy hands off on her shirt, then reached for a sandwich.

"I—Vermil Linwick—have reached Rank 3. I just wanted to make sure it was known so Arbitage could adjust their records and provide me with the appropriate pay."

Lee slipped a cookie off the table. The secretary took a huge bite out of her admittedly delicious-looking sandwich. She didn't once do so much as acknowledge Noah's presence, which was just fine with him.

"Well, that's that." Noah shrugged. "Shall we, Lee?"

Lee grabbed another cookie, then followed after him as he walked out of the building. She threw a glance over her shoulder before eating both cookies in one bite. "I don't think she heard you."

"That's fine. That was the plan."

"You *wanted* to be ignored?"

"Pretty much. Think about it. My rank advancement is a little fast, and if I hit Rank 4 soon, it's definitely going to raise questions. People would probably assume Father is giving me a bunch of runes for some reason. But if I can say that I reported my ranks a while ago and nobody ever recorded them. The less concrete data there is, the harder it'll be to pin exactly when I hit anything."

"Does it matter that much?"

"No clue," Noah admitted. "But I figure it's better to be safe than sorry. Doing it this way gives me a way out that I can lean on if I really need it. I doubt I will, but you never know."

Lee shrugged. "We're getting food now, right?"

Noah's stomach rumbled again and he nodded. "Yeah. Anything in particular you want? Ah—not squirrels. Not anything that's still alive, please."

Lee scrunched her nose. "You can't knock it if you haven't tried it."

"Some things are better left untried. Besides, if I start eating them, then wouldn't there be less for you?"

"Oh. That's a good point. Okay. What about that?" Lee pointed at a food cart on the other side of the square, where a small line had built up before a man selling what Noah was pretty sure were hot dogs.

He'd chosen a good spot to set up shop. There was a garden just behind him, with several tables scattered throughout it. Other students and professors sat around the garden, eating and talking.

"That works," Noah said.

It's been a while since I've had hot dogs. I get the feeling they probably aren't called that here. How'd they even get that name in the first place? They don't resemble dogs at all. They aren't made from dogs either.

One of life's great mysteries, I guess.

He and Lee stepped into the line, and they didn't have to wait long. The merchant—a bushy-eyebrowed man with a double chin—moved everyone along quickly, taking money and practically flinging the hot dogs into his customers' hands before shooing them along. They soon stood at the front.

"How many meat sticks you want?" the merchant asked.

Meat sticks? God, that's an unappetizing way to put it.

"Ah... eight?" Noah said after a moment. The merchant's eyebrows rose, but he didn't so much as flinch.

"One silver a piece."

Noah handed the man a gold coin. "Could we just get ten?"

Flashing him a gap-toothed grin, the merchant plucked several hot dogs—Noah refused to think of them as meat sticks—from his wagon and slapped them into bread buns. He poured a speckled orange sauce over the first and handed it to Noah.

Noah handed the hot dog to Lee, who slid the whole thing into her mouth and swallowed without chewing.

The merchant poured the condiment over the second hot dog and looked up as he handed it to Noah. He paused, a frown flickering over his face, as he realized that Noah no longer had the first hot dog.

His eyes widened as Noah once again forked the hot dog over to Lee, who repeated her disappearing act and ate it in one bite. The merchant readied another two hot dogs, not taking his eyes off Lee as he slid them across the table.

Like the previous two, they were devoured in less than a second. The merchant opened his mouth, then thought better of whatever it was he was going to say and settled for getting the other six hot dogs over to Noah.

Noah fed all but three of them to Lee, then gathered the remainder and inclined his head before heading off to the park with Lee at his side.

"Are they any good?" Noah asked, spotting a table in the corner of the park and changing course to head for it.

"They taste like meat. A lot of different kinds of meat, actually. I think there's some—"

"Wait!" Noah said hurriedly. "I don't think I want to know. Sometimes, the only way you can enjoy these things is by living in ignorance. I don't need to be haunted by the ghosts of whatever creatures got pushed into these things. If I find out there are squirrels in this, I don't know if I'd be able to keep going."

Lee tilted her head to the side, a thoughtful look passing over her features. Noah stuck a hot dog into her mouth.

"Don't tell me that there's a squirrel in it now just to eat mine."

Lee swallowed, then grinned. "It was a good idea, though. You gave me one."

"It was yours anyway. I'm just making you save one until we actually make it to the table." Noah rolled his eyes. "I'd have saved one for Moxie, but it'll probably be cold by the time we get back. Better to buy it as we leave."

He pulled a chair out and sat down at the table, taking a bite out of one of the two remaining hotdogs. It was actually pretty good—not exactly the flavors he remembered from back on Earth, though. The sauce the merchant had used was a lot stronger than he'd expected it to be.

Noah spotted Lee eyeing the last untouched hotdog. He held it out. "Want it?"

Lee started to nod, then paused midway through sitting down and scrunched her nose. "Hold on."

"Is something wrong?"

"No. I just need to go relieve myself," Lee replied.

Noah blinked, then shrugged. "I'll be here."

With a nod, Lee turned and strode off into the garden.

* * *

Faint tingles of magic danced across Aiden's fingertips as he watched his target from the cover of a large bush. It would only take a single bolt of concentrated wind between the man's eyes to kill him where he sat, but that almost felt too easy.

Jalen had been pretty insistent that his target was more than what met the eye. He probably had some form of Shield that would protect him from a silent, ranged attack unless it was strong enough—and a powerful attack drew attention.

Aiden watched the man happily take a bite of his meat stick, completely unaware of his presence. If he hadn't been on the job, he would have laughed.

How is someone like this drawing the attention of the family head? He knows he's being hunted, but he sits out in the open like it's just any other day. Does he have a really powerful Shield that's beyond his rank?

Even if he does, that won't stop a physical attack unless he's ready for it.

Aiden's fists clenched. There was a chance that the man *was* ready for it, though. Would anyone be stupid enough to just walk around in broad daylight when they knew they were being hunted?

No. Of course not. He must be so confident in his defenses that he doesn't even see us as a threat.

The back of Aiden's spine prickled. He released his grip on the magic, letting it fade back into his soul. His target wasn't oblivious. No wonder the previous assassin had died. He'd fallen for the very trap laid before him.

Damned Plains. I nearly died. If I attacked, I would have given my position away. Yes, that's it. I doubt he knows I'm actually here, so he wants to draw me out, so I reveal my location and he can cut me down.

That won't work. I'll reposition and strike when he doesn't actually expect it.

Aiden turned—and nearly let out a startled scream. A student-aged girl with reddish black hair leaned against the tree directly behind him, an inscrutable expression on her face. Somehow, she'd managed to sneak up on him.

"Damned Plains, girl," Aiden cursed, keeping his voice low. "What are you doing?"

"Looking at you."

The answer was so straight-forward that it caught Aiden completely off guard.

Is she proposing to me? Guess I've still got it.

Wait. No. I'm on the job. Jalen would have my head if I got distracted. I can deal with other matters once the target is dead.

"I'm flattered, but I'm afraid my current job is taking my full attention," Aiden said with an apologetic tilt of his head. "I'm currently investigating this garden for pests. I hope I didn't startle you, miss."

"Nope."

"What a relief." Aiden gave her what he believed to be a winning smile. "I'd love to get to know you another time, though."

The girl stepped toward Aiden.

Wow, she's forward.

"Oh, not that."

Aiden frowned. The back of his neck prickled, and he resisted the urge to glance over his shoulder. "Not what?"

"I wasn't saying no to being startled. I meant you weren't looking for pests."

Something cold pressed into the back of Aiden's neck. Confusion exploded through him as he tried to turn but found that his body wasn't responding to his commands any longer. His legs buckled and he fell back, hitting the dirt with a thump.

Aiden couldn't feel anything. It was like his entire body had gone numb. Something wet pressed into his back, and the sky swam above him. The girl's face wavered in the air above him, but he wasn't sure where it had come from.

"You can't be looking for the pest," the girl said. Her fingers elongated, sharpening into glistening points. "You are the pest."

He tried to scream for help, but she slapped her other hand over his mouth, muffling his words. Her palm tasted like blood. Something deep in Aiden's mind—the part that wasn't erupting in panic—told him that his body's failure to respond was because his spinal cord had been severed.

Aiden didn't have much time to process it. The girl brought her other hand down, and Aiden knew no more.

Chapter Nineteen

Lee returned to the table a minute or two after she left. She sat down across from Noah and licked her lips, her eyes darting to the half-eaten hot dog in it. Noah laughed and held it out, letting Lee snag her prize.

"Everything okay?" Noah asked. A thought struck him and he frowned. "Wait. Were you eating the wildlife again?"

"No," Lee replied, drawing the word out and immediately looking completely and utterly guilty.

"Liar." Noah laughed. "Aren't these enough? How much food can you possibly eat?"

"I got hungry. But how did you know?"

"Your breath smelled a bit like blood."

Lee paused, then sheepishly rubbed the back of her head. "Oh. Yeah, I ate a bit. It wasn't that much."

"Not someone's cat, I hope."

"Just another squirrel." Lee shrugged. "You said I could have them all."

I suppose I did say something like that. Eh. It's not hurting anybody. I can't think of a single instance where anyone actually wanted the squirrel population to be uncontrolled. They breed like rabbits.

"Fair enough." Noah finished off the rest of his hot dog and leaned back, enjoying the cold, fresh air against his skin. There wasn't anyone too close to them, so he was pretty sure they could talk freely so long as he didn't say anything too dangerous. "I guess we should probably go shopping for runes soon, huh?"

"That would be nice." Lee chewed her lower lip for a second. "I'm a bit worried, though."

"Worried? Why? You know I can just... well. You know."

"Yeah. I'm more worried about the actual rune," Lee admitted. She looked down at the table and scratched the back of her hand. "What if it changes me?"

That's right. Demons and monsters get directly affected by their runes since their bodies and souls are so closely intertwined.

"You're you," Noah said, putting his hand on top of Lee's. "No matter what your body changes to. Besides, it's just your body, right? Not your mind?"

Lee nodded, but it took her a moment to do so. "Yeah. I think so."

"You aren't sure?"

"All I know is from what I heard back in the Da—uh, back home. And I really didn't put that much thought into it at the time. It was just getting stronger, and that was never a bad thing."

"No matter what happens, it'll be fine," Noah promised. "Moxie and I will be there for you, and if the worst comes to worst, I'll just— well, you know. I'll handle it in my own special way."

"What if I get changed so much that I don't want to let you do it?"

"Then it's a good thing I've got an infinite number of attempts to make sure I can. One of 'em will work."

Lee grinned, her mood instantly shooting back to its normal state. "Okay! I'll hold you to that, though. I don't want to end up like the others I've met. They're all assholes."

Somehow, I feel like that might be a dig at you, Azel.

Azel didn't respond—not that Noah was complaining. They sat in the park for a few more minutes, just enjoying the atmosphere. Noah had fully planned to be eating for more than a minute, but the hot dogs hadn't lasted quite as long as he'd expected.

"Should we go find Moxie and bring her some food?" Noah asked. "Maybe we can go shopping afterward."

"Okay!" Lee bounced to her feet, and Noah had to hurry to keep up with her as she shot out of the park and got back in line to get more hot dogs.

At least she doesn't stay worried for long. Either that, or she's hiding it. From what I know of Lee... she's probably hiding it.

She was doing a good job of it, but not quite enough to completely trick Noah. He knew her well enough to notice a slight droop in her hair. For anyone else, that would have just been the wind or a bad hair day.

But for Lee, whose entire body was completely under her control, it was pretty much the same as hunching her shoulders and kicking a rock down the street as she walked. But, fortunately, there was always a pretty surefire way to make Lee feel at least a little better pretty quickly.

Noah bought another ten hot dogs when they reached the front of the line, feeding all but four of them to Lee. And sure enough, at least for the time being, it looked like the extra food had distracted her.

Hopefully we can buy those runes and get Lee fixed up before she has to worry about this too much longer. From what I've learned by talking with Azel, runes still affect humans like they do monsters, just to a much lesser degree since our minds are more separate from our bodies.

If that's true, something as powerful as Sunder or the Fragment of Renewal should have changed the way I approach things significantly, and I don't think they have. That should mean that Lee's safe—but I don't want to give her false promises. It's better that she just knows we'll be there to help her out should anything go wrong.

Noah remained largely lost in thoughts for the rest of the trip back to Building T. He headed up the stairs alongside Lee, stopping automatically as he reached his room. He shifted the hot dogs to one hand, awkwardly cradling them as he dug through his pocket for his room key and unlocked the door.

"Aren't we going to Moxie's room?" Lee asked, but Noah had already opened the door.

Contessa and Karina stood above a dead woman in dark clothes. There was a dagger protruding from the back of her head. They both froze, staring at Noah like deer in the headlights of an approaching truck.

"It's not what it looks like," Contessa said.

"It was an assassin," Karina added hurriedly. "I told you they'd come! Jalen is sending them. You have to believe—"

Noah grunted. "Want a hot dog?"

They both blinked.

"What?" Contessa asked warily.

"Hot dog," Noah said, holding the hot dogs cradled in his arm out.

Contessa and Karina exchanged a glance.

"You're... not mad about the corpse in your room?"

"Wouldn't be the first one."

A second passed. Contessa looked like she was trying to tell if Noah was joking or not, but she quickly gave the idea up and shrugged. She took a hot dog from Noah.

"Thanks. Why is it called a hot dog? Is there dog in it?"

"No. It's just a name. Don't worry about it."

"Are you really going to gloss over the line about this not being the first corpse here?" Karina demanded.

Contessa sent her a flat stare. "Yes."

Karina looked back to the body, then over to the hot dogs in Noah's arms. She took a hot dog.

"Sorry about the intrusion," Noah said. "I kind of forgot I wasn't in this room anymore. Was the assassin difficult to fight?"

"Rank three," Contessa said. "She wasn't very competent, though. She wasn't expecting me to be here, so we had the upper hand. Are you expecting more assassins? I don't know how many we can repel before one gets lucky. Are you sure it's wise to ignore this?"

Noah let out a sigh and pursed his lips in thought. "I don't know. I'm not really worried myself, but if it keeps happening, it might get annoying. Karina, did Jalen say if he'd give up at any point?"

"When you met with him."

"Ah. Well, I'm not going to the Linwick Estate. Can you contact him or something?"

Karina shook her head again.

"Then sucks for him. He can keep sending assassins. Can't we report this to Arbitage or something? Attacks should be illegal on neutral ground, if I'm not mistaken."

"You could," Contessa said slowly. "But that would almost certainly piss Jalen off. If you think assassins are bad, I don't want to imagine what the head of a family would do to get snubbed."

"What am I supposed to do, then?"

"Offer a different meeting location?" Contessa offered. "If he doesn't want to come to Arbitage, maybe you could offer another neutral ground. That would be seen as compromise."

"I don't think the head of a family ever *needs* to compromise," Karina muttered.

"He does if he wants to meet with me," Noah said. He sent another look at the assassin, then sighed. Having a bunch of people constantly coming for his head was just mildly annoying, but if they ever went after someone he cared about... Noah's lips pressed together as a spark of anger lit in his chest.

I'm going to need to have a talk with Jalen. If his assassins are so sloppy that they're running into people other than me, then either he just doesn't respect Arbitage's neutral ground or is an idiot. Regardless of the reason, I can't let anyone get caught up in this.

"Could you let me know the next time you run into an assassin?" Noah asked. "If possible, I'd like to try to catch them alive so I can have a talk with them."

"We can try," Contessa said. "I'm not going to kill myself trying to take them alive, if that's fine with you."

"By all means. Don't die for it, but just see what you can do," Noah said. He rubbed the bridge of his nose, then sighed. "Ask Mascot for help if he's still hanging around you. I suspect he'll be more useful than you think."

"The cat?" Karina asked, staring at Noah. "How is a cat—"

"Don't question it." Contessa put a hand on Karina's shoulder and shook her head. "You'll see."

Karina frowned, then shrugged. "Okay, if you're sure. We really need to get rid of this body, though. I don't want to get caught lugging it around."

"Can I have it?" Lee asked.

"What do you want with—"

Lee didn't wait for them to respond. She pulled the dagger out of the dead assassin and leaned over, grabbing the woman and devouring her in a single bite. Karina and Contessa both paled and averted their gazes as the sound of crunching bones filled the room.

"Don't ask," Noah said, reading the question in Contessa's eyes. "In fact, I highly suggest you forget it. You're seeing this because Lee thinks you're on our side. I don't recommend doing anything that would ever change her mind."

Lee burped. "Can I have another hotdog?"

"No, these are for Moxie. You've eaten enough. If you have your way, you'll make me spend all my money before we can go shopping." Noah shook his head, only half joking. "Sorry for the interruption, ladies. Let's go find Moxie, Lee."

As Noah turned to leave the room, he remembered something that Karina had mentioned some time ago, when they'd first met. He looked back at his former fiancée and she swallowed nervously.

"What?" Karina asked.

"I just recalled that you once spoke about an auction available only to you," Noah said. "Would that happen to have a better selection of runes than what we could find for sale normally?"

"Yes, but the one I was talking about passed," Karina said. "It was a few weeks ago."

"When's the next one?"

"It should be another two weeks."

Noah scrunched his nose in annoyance. It wasn't like two weeks was all that long, but he would have preferred something closer. He supposed they could always go shopping now and then hit the auction later, but it would have been nicer to do it in the other order.

"Actually, there might be something." Contessa cleared her throat as they all looked to her. "It's a noble auction, not a Linwick Estate–specific one. They're long-running auctions, so new things show up and get sold every day for a week or two."

"Color me interested. When does it happen?"

"It's already going on," Contessa replied. "At least it should be. I couldn't go this year because I don't have Evergreen's backing anymore, but she used to always have me visit to see if there was anything of interest."

"You need backing to get in?"

"It's a noble auction, so yes. They won't just let anyone in."

Noah's eyes drifted to Karina. "What about you?"

"I... could probably get in," Karina allowed. "I didn't know there was an auction in Arbitage, though."

"Evidently, you weren't very high up in your family," Contessa said, a flicker of her former self emerging in a small smirk. It faded away as quickly as it had come, and she looked to the side. "Not like I was either."

"Can you find out where the auction is being held? If Karina can get us in, that would be pretty useful."

Karina hesitated for a moment. Noah got the feeling she was probably thinking something along the lines of *what do I get for it,* but she ended up settling for giving him a curt nod.

"Thanks. Much appreciated," Noah said. With that, he and Lee headed out to find Moxie before their hotdogs got cold.

Chapter Twenty

"So, how did it go with Alexandra?" Noah leaned against the wall from Moxie as she polished off the last of the surviving hot dogs.

Moxie waited to finish chewing and swallowing before answering him. "About as expected. I think our read on her was pretty accurate. She's uncomfortable but wants to be better and do better. I don't think we'll have any trouble with her. Did everything work out on your side?"

Noah cleared his throat. "You might have a chat with Emily coming up in the near future, but yes. She, Todd, and Isabel have all been brought up to speed on what we know. Their runes are good."

"A talk?" Moxie's eyes narrowed. "What's that mean?"

"I'm sure she'll tell you when you speak. It wasn't too much. Just bringing her up to speed a bit." Noah suddenly found Moxie's window fascinating and directed the entirety of his attention toward it.

Moxie stood and walked up to Noah so they were nose-to-nose. She prodded him in the stomach. "What did you say?"

"I just encouraged her to have a chat with you," Noah said. Moxie prodded him again, and he let out a yelp. "Stop that!"

"You look way too shifty. Tell me exactly what you said."

"Say, Lee, are you still hungry?" Noah ducked to the side, dodging out of the way before Moxie could grab him. "I'm suddenly realizing I want food again."

"Yeah!" Lee ran over to the door and pulled it open. "Let's go!"

Noah darted out—only to have a very familiar yanking sensation grab onto his waist. For an instant, he thought he'd somehow triggered Sunder and his soul was getting pulled somewhere—but that would have been his neck instead of his waist.

It wasn't Sunder. It was a vine. Another vine shot out, whipping around Noah's ankles and snapping them together. He let out a curse as Moxie yanked him back over to her.

"Lee, help!"

"I think I'll just go get food on my own," Lee said. "Have fun, though!"

She closed the door.

Moxie's eyes glittered dangerously as she reeled Noah in like a caught fish. "Spill, or I'll make you."

Noah arched an eyebrow, but it was hard to look very intimidating from the ground. "Try me."

* * *

"Was that number four?" Jalen scratched the underside of his chin. "I lost count."

"It was the seventh assassin, Magus Jalen." The assistant tried to slide a stack of papers onto Jalen's desk while he was distracted. Jalen sent out a pulse of magic, destroying them before they could make their landing.

"Seven? Wow. That's a lot." Jalen picked at a bit of dirt that had gotten stuck under a fingernail, sticking his tongue out in concentration. "How many more did I send?"

"That was all of them, Magus Jalen."

"Really? That was fast. Weren't there a few Rank 3s among the other failed idiots?"

"Yes, Magus. They also died."

"And nobody noticed? Arbitage isn't sending complaints?"

"Not yet, Magus. But... if I may be so presumptuous, this is a poor idea. Arbitage is neutral ground. If it comes out that we're sending assassins after one of their teachers, even if he's part of our family, it will go very poorly for us."

"You may not," Jalen said. He got the piece of dirt he was digging at and flicked it away. "And I don't care. Arbitage is going to demand recompense in the form of pay. What's the point of having the bulging coffers of this family if we don't use them for what's important? They won't care that much about all the corpses I'm leaving around."

"What if the person you're sending assassins after gets killed, Magus? That would be what I'm more concerned about."

"Oh, I highly doubt it. He wouldn't have managed to gather my attention if he died that easily. I'm not actually sending anyone of relevance after him." Jalen paused, then tilted his head to the side. "I'm not, am I? I forgot."

"Every member of the Linwick family is greatly valued and—"

"Oh, can it." Jalen rolled his eyes. "I forgot your name."

"It's—"

"That wasn't an invitation to remind me." Jalen cut the assistant off. "I just don't care. You can tell me if you live to a few hundred years old, but I highly doubt it. The pressure coming off your runes is middling."

The assistant swallowed and averted his gaze. Jalen resisted the urge to let out a weary sigh. He settled for destroying another stack of papers.

This is the problem with this damn family. Back when it was still interesting, it wouldn't have mattered who I was. An insult like that would have been met with a challenge. This... wretch in front of me would have sought to prove his strength, and I would have given him advice on how to fix the garbage he's got floating around in his soul so he'd make it at least one rank higher.

But now, these cowards just stare and grovel. No annoyance. No confidence. His runes could have been perfect, and he still would have bowed and scraped instead of denying my words. If there is only blind faith, how am I supposed to trust any of these idiots to do their jobs properly? They'll just tell me what they think I want to hear while the family burns down in the background.

Jalen lost his internal battle and let out a sigh. "Just go away."

"Would you like me to send a crew to try to find out what happened to the assassins?"

"No. I'll deal with this myself."

The assistant's eyes bulged. "If you kill someone on Arbitage grounds, it could be disastrous. Magus Jalen, please reconsider. The

Linwick family cannot bear the anger of every other family for violating the neutral ground so violently."

"I'll violate what I please." Jalen paused, then grimaced. "That came out wrong. You don't mind, do you?"

"No, Magus Jalen. Not at all."

Sniveling wretch. Of course you don't.

"Good. Leave. I have... important things to ponder."

The assistant bowed and scuttled out of Jalen's room, closing the door behind him gently, as if to avoid scaring him. Jalen massaged the bridge of his nose between two fingers and muttered a curse under his breath.

"Absolutely pathetic. I'd wonder if the other families have fallen this far as well, but I don't actually care enough to find out." Jalen walked over to his window and looked out, watching the sun as it tracked through the sky.

Jalen wasn't sure how long he stood there. But when he blinked, the evening was upon him. The old family head stepped away from the window, peeling his eyes from the sky. Every passing day felt more and more like the same thing.

It makes me wonder why I do this. There's so little left for me in this empire. I should just be done with it. And yet... these little blips of interest manage to keep me here. Perhaps I just don't want to move on.

Regardless, I suppose I should stop flinging corpses at Vermil. He should have gotten the message by now. The chances of him agreeing to meet me at the Linwick Estate are likely zero. At least, I hope they are.

If he did, I'd kill him on the spot for being such a coward. I'm the one seeking him out, so he has the advantage. If he isn't a pushover, he'll send a demand that I come meet him instead.

A snort of laughter escaped Jalen before he could stop it. He shook his head, smiling to himself.

What a splendid change of pace that would be. I need to stop getting my hopes up, or I'm going to leave the boy as a bloody splatter on the dirt when he fails to live up to my expectations.

"Assistant!"

The door opened and Jalen's assistant poked his head back in. Jalen was pretty sure the man had literally been waiting outside the door to get called on, like a dog whose master didn't care all that much for it.

"Yes, Magus Jalen?"

"I've decided to wage war on the Torrin family. Would you go deliver the head of the nearest child to them so they know what's coming?"

The assistant's face paled. He opened his mouth, and Jalen called on the faintest traces of his runes. The amount of energy that leaked out wouldn't have done much more than slightly increase the pressure bearing down on a Rank 2, but it was enough of a threat for the man to nod hurriedly.

"I will do as you ask, Magus Jalen." The assistant turned, making to leave.

Why do I even bother? Idiot didn't even ask why. The smallest threat to his safety, and he's willing to plunge the empire into a war to save his own hide.

"Stop!"

The assistant turned back to Jalen. "Yes, Magus?"

"I changed my mind. Go... I don't know. Do whatever it is you normally do. Just stop standing outside my door like some addled buffoon."

"Yes, Magus Jalen." Relief filled the assistant's words as he hurried away, closing the door. Jalen listened to the man's footsteps as they pattered down the hall.

Idiot. I hope you do something fun soon, Magus Vermil. There are grave consequences for drawing my attention and then failing to hold it.

Chapter Twenty-One

"I can't believe you told her," Moxie said, craning her head back to look at Noah from her spot in his lap. "I didn't want her to know all of that, you know. I could have said it myself if I did."

"It was hurting both of you more than it was helping. There are some secrets worth keeping, but I don't think that was one of them. Emily deserves to know you as you actually are."

Moxie harrumphed and leaned back into him. "Says the person with more secrets than any of us."

"Hey, you know all of them now. If anything, all of those secrets just prove I know more about this than you do. I've got experience. Besides, didn't you feel like we got closer after I shared them with you?"

Moxie didn't respond for a few seconds. Then she let out an annoyed sigh. "Yeah, I did. That doesn't mean I have to like it, though. You could have just told me I needed to talk to Emily."

"Would you have?"

Moxie reached back and poked him in the side. "I've got you pinned. Don't try me."

"Stop! I already surrendered," Noah said with a laugh. "You're the one who asked. I know I probably shouldn't have told Emily. It wasn't my place. I just didn't want to see both of you keep dancing around this forever. I tried to avoid the specifics as much as possible."

"It was probably the right move," Moxie admitted. "But that doesn't mean I have to like it. Emily... didn't respond poorly, did she?"

"No. Not to you, at least. I think she was more torn up about failing to realize what was going on. She definitely isn't going to be mourning Evergreen's death too much."

"Good riddance," Moxie said under her breath. She paused as the door opened, and they both looked over as Lee poked her head into the room.

"You were out for a while," Noah said. "More squirrels?"

"Nope. I was just wandering around." Lee stepped into the room and closed the door behind her. She walked over to the bed and hopped in, leaning up against Noah and Moxie. "Everyone else is eating dinner together."

"You mean the students?" Noah asked.

"Yeah. It looked tasty, so I tried some."

"Was it going well?" Noah asked. "Alexandra is with them?"

"Yeah. They went to a restaurant. They did look at me a little weird, though. I think they're getting rebellious. It was rude."

Noah's brow furrowed. Something about Lee's voice told him she was very much waiting for him to ask *why* they'd given her weird looks, and he wasn't one to resist obliging.

"What did you do?"

"Nothing! I just ate some of their food."

"How much?" Moxie asked, repressing a laugh.

"Just a nibble. I'm not a savage. I tasted it after I brought it to them to make sure it was good. That's what you're meant to do to show it's good, right?"

"Wait, you brought them their food? Why? Weren't you just eating with them?"

"No, that was too boring. I decided to be their waiter instead, so I shifted into the assassin that Karina and Contessa killed in your room. It was fun!"

"You ate some of their food while in the body of an assassin pretending to be a waiter at a restaurant?"

"Wait, what happened to the waiter?" Moxie asked.

"I told him to take a break. He seemed receptive to it." Lee snickered. "It was actually really easy to just walk in there and take a uniform. I didn't even have to steal it. It just doesn't make sense why they were confused. I could have sworn I did everything right. I copied the way the waiter spoke too."

"It's probably because waiters don't taste the food before giving it to people," Moxie said gently.

"What? How do you know it's good if they don't taste it? Anyone would want to eat food that tastes good, so if you don't taste it, clearly the food is bad and nobody would want to eat it. It's a sign of respect."

Noah pictured the expressions on the students' faces and grinned. "I kind of wish I was there. You've never seen a waiter do that before, though. Why'd you suddenly decide that was how it was done?"

"It just felt right."

"Well, now you know why they gave you looks. Honestly, they probably wouldn't have been as weirded out if you'd just done it in the form that they recognize you in."

"Probably," Lee agreed. She paused for a second. "That would have made it easier to track me down after I got caught drinking all the gravy in the kitchen, though. I don't think the assassin is going to be very hirable in the future."

Noah couldn't stop himself from bursting into laughter.

"Don't encourage her!" Moxie said, but the look on her face told Noah that she was just barely avoiding laughing as well.

Their amusement was interrupted by a knock on the door.

"It's Karina and Contessa," Lee said, slipping off the bed. Moxie got off Noah and he rose to his feet, adjusting his clothes.

Lee pulled the door open to reveal Karina, midway through raising her hand to knock again. Contessa stood behind her. It wasn't much of a surprise—he'd never seen Lee's nose lie to her before.

"I did what you asked," Karina said. "Contessa and I found the auction."

"And?"

"Contessa got me in, and we can bring guests," Karina said. She did her best to keep her eyes focused mostly on Lee, who was closest to her. "We can go whenever you're ready. It's running every day this week."

"Perfect." Noah grinned, then threw a glance out the window. The evening had started, but it wasn't that far into it. Karina and Contessa had made pretty good time on finding and getting entry to the auction. "I'm surprised it went easily."

"Me too," Karina admitted. "I didn't think I'd be allowed in after what happened to my family, but I guess news somehow hasn't made it here yet. If you want to go tonight, we should probably move pretty quickly. I rushed to get back here, but they said the doors close and the auction starts in thirty minutes—nobody new will be allowed to enter for the rest of the day after that."

"That should be fine." Noah looked to Moxie. "Unless we had something planned for the rest of the night?"

She shook her head. "Better to do this now. We need to get those runes for you and Lee already."

"I couldn't agree more. I was just trying to be polite. Aren't you impressed?"

Moxie rolled her eyes, and Noah scooped his grimoire off the ground. He slung it over his back, then nodded to Contessa. "Right. Lead the way, then."

They all filed out of the room and, after locking it behind them, headed down the hall and out of Building T. Contessa moved at a brisk pace, not leaving them much room to stroll and enjoy the evening atmosphere.

"Anything we should know about this before I go bumbling things up?" Noah asked. "Because I get the feeling some fancy noble thing like this is going to end with me somehow pissing someone off and having to blast them into kingdom come."

"Please don't do that," Contessa said, glancing over to him before returning her attention to the road before her. "We'll get banned if you start using any of your runes. When we get there, we'll all be taken to changing rooms where we get into plain clothes and are given masks to conceal our identities."

"To keep people from killing each other over losing auctions?" Moxie guessed.

"Yeah. It's pretty effective, so long as you don't reveal too much about yourself by accident during the actual auction. People usually just yell threats and the like when they lose, so as long as you don't give away too much information, you'll be fine."

"Why even respond at all?" Lee asked. "If all they can do is speak, can't we ignore them?"

"You can, but it can be seen as a sign of weakness." Contessa turned down a path going alongside the gardens. "In general, it's a lot better to just match the way you're treated. Just avoid doing anything that lets people identify you."

Lee's body rippled. Her clothes ripped at the seams as she enlarged, growing three feet taller and widening until she was both taller and more muscular than Noah. Her hair shortened, and a small moustache appeared on her upper lip. Karina stared at her in a mixture of awe and horror.

"What?" Lee asked, looking down at herself. "I'm looking different."

"Don't grow any larger," Noah suggested. "Or move too suddenly. I don't know if there's an age limit on who's allowed to attend these things."

They came to a stop beside a small stone building at the end of the garden. It didn't look large enough for their group, much less an entire auction. Contessa walked up and rapped her knuckles on the door in a short pattern.

A moment later, the door ground open to reveal the small building's interior. It was completely dark and empty, with nothing but a stairwell in its center that led underground. Noah tilted his head to the side.

"How big is this event that they've got a whole secret passage building dedicated to it?"

"Oh, it's not just for the event. They also do weddings." Contessa started down the stairs, then paused. "I think they do birthdays too, but you've got to be really rich for that."

"Noted," Noah said, and they all followed her into the darkness. Behind them, the door rumbled shut.

The stairs didn't go on for as long as Noah had expected. They ended just a few minutes of walking later, leaving them in a circular room lit by warm torches. It was ringed by doors—some open and some closed and a large passage at the far side of the room presumably led into the auction proper.

"Get changed in any of the rooms that have open doors," Contessa said, already heading toward one of the rooms. "There are runed safes where you can put your belongings. Don't take anything but your money, or it'll go poorly."

"Not sure I love that." Noah frowned. "What if someone steals my shit?"

"They won't," Contessa promised. "You lock the safe with energy from your runes, and it won't open again until you release it. If anyone tried to break in, you'd have more than enough time to know—and the whole of the auction would come down on them. That's why this thing is so exclusive."

Noah scrunched his nose, then shrugged. It wasn't like anyone would be able to lift his grimoire in the first place—and if they were dumb enough to try and steal his gourd, all he had to do was kill himself, and he'd pop out right beside them.

He chose a room and headed inside. There were two sets of plain black robes hanging from the wall. One was fitted for a male, and the other for a female. Beside them was a single white mask with the number 17 on it. Noah changed into the male robes, and they adjusted the size to match his form perfectly.

Huh. That's kind of nice.

The far end of the changing room had a metal door hanging askew. Beyond it was a safe roughly the size of a small changing closet. Noah could have fit himself into it if he wanted to. He set his belongings down inside it, only holding onto his travel bag with the money in it, then studied the door for a moment.

Swirling Imbuements covered its surface, hidden from identification but still clearly present. Shrugging to himself, Noah closed the door. As soon as it shut, he felt a tiny pull coming from where his hand met the door.

I don't know how much information this thing gathers, so I'm not going to let it use anything but my worst rune. I guess that's Natural Disaster since all my other runes don't have any flaws at all.

Noah fed a slight amount of power from Natural Disaster into the door. There was a whirr and a clunk as it locked, and the lines covering it lit up a dull white.

I guess it looks secure enough.

He grabbed the mask from the wall and lifted it to his face. There wasn't anything to hold it there, but it let out a faint hum as it touched his skin, attaching to it like a second skin. He could see through it perfectly, as if nothing was there.

"Huh. That's neat," Noah said, stepping out of his changing room. Karina, Moxie, and Lee were already waiting for him.

The Imbuements on the clothes were evidently more impressive than he'd thought because they'd grown to match Lee's considerable new form.

"Ready?" Contessa asked.

They all nodded.

"Let's get moving, then. We want to get a good spot before the auction gets started."

Chapter Twenty-Two

The main corridor came to a stop before a pair of already-open stone doors. They were carved from stone, and the swirling patterns running along them looked to be nothing more than decoration, but Noah knew better.

Those are definitely hidden Imbuements.

Contessa didn't stop to appreciate their surroundings. She stepped through the doors and started down into an amphitheater beyond it. There were twenty different viewing platforms, each with small walls and completely isolated from the others.

Pathways ran out of the amphitheater in every direction, leading to doors identical to the ones they'd just come through. At the very center of the amphitheater was a large, raised dais.

A man in pure white clothing with a black, featureless mask stood at the center of the dais, his hands crossed behind his back. He wasn't the only other person in the room, though. About three-quarters of the viewing platforms were already occupied by groups of up to six people.

All of the platforms had at least one person with the inversed clothing colors—white with a black mask—standing in a corner. Karina led them over to one of the unoccupied viewing platforms, and they piled in, sitting down at an awaiting table. Noah inclined his head in greeting to the masked woman in their room, but she didn't return the gesture.

Bah. It's going to be a bunch of stiff assholes here, isn't it?

Once they'd all gotten onto the platform, the woman strode over to the back and closed the door behind them, locking it with a click. Noah's scalp prickled as a low hum washed over all of them. He stiffened.

"Don't worry," Contessa said, raising her hands. "It's to make sure nobody can overhear us when we're talking. It's just a safety measure."

"Can we trust it?"

Contessa shrugged. "I... think so? As far as I'm aware, it's trustworthy. There would be a lot of anger if anyone was somehow breaking through the Imbuements or abusing them. That's the whole point of doing the auction like this. It ensures privacy."

"Just how Arbitage ensures a neutral zone, huh?"

Contessa cleared her throat and looked out at the dais. "Yeah. Either way, everything should be getting started really soon. We made it with just a bit of time to spare. There will be a few different rounds, categorized by what they're selling today."

"Do we know what they are?" Moxie asked.

Contessa shook her head. "No. They change, but I'd assume some of it will be runes, some will be imbued items, and some will be information. I don't know what the rest will be—probably monster parts or the like."

"I didn't think about selling information at an auction, but I guess it makes sense." Noah paused, then glanced at Moxie. "You know, I completely forgot again, but did we ever get that letter from Thaddius with our money?"

"Oh, shit. I forgot to tell you." Moxie let out an embarrassed laugh. "Yeah, we got it. Nine thousand gold."

"Damn, that's a solid sale," Noah said. "We'll definitely be able to get some nice shit here, then."

Contessa turned away from the dais to look at them. Noah couldn't see her expression because of the mask, but her head tilted to the side in confusion.

"What?" Noah asked.

"How much money did you bring?" Contessa asked.

"About ten thousand each," Noah said. "Plus the money Moxie just mentioned, so around... forty thousand, I guess? A bit less."

"That's it?" Karina demanded. "Are you crazy?"

"What? What's wrong with that?" Noah asked. "Forty thousand is a huge amount of money!"

"This is a noble auction," Karina hissed. "Forty thousand isn't going to get anything good! Most of these people probably spend thousands of gold a week on travel and luxury expenses alone."

Noah's eye twitched behind his mask. "You can't be serious. Forty thousand would be enough to buy so many flying swords."

"This is an exclusive auction for members representing the noble houses. Do you really think they're measuring things by the number of flying swords they can buy?" Contessa asked, choosing her words carefully. She sent a glance at the employee in their booth, but the woman seemed unconcerned with their discussion. Evidently, she wasn't paid enough to care.

"There should be some stuff that isn't that expensive. Even auctions like this have less rare or damaged objects for sale, right?" Moxie asked. "Not everyone comes here wanting to spend enough money to buy a nice house."

"Well, yeah. There's bound to be some garbage, but I thought you came here wanting to get powerful runes, not trash. If that were the case, we might have been better served going to a normal auction or just buying things outright," Karina said. "This is overkill."

Trash runes aren't so trash when I'm the one that buys them. If I can get my hands on some poorly combined runes, as long as they aren't complete garbage, they could actually be really useful. Nice thinking, Moxie.

"Well, we're here now." Noah shrugged. "No point complaining. Might as well see what they've got. Besides, if they're buying information, can we sell?"

"I suppose you could," Karina said after a moment. She looked at Contessa. "That's normally what I've seen in other auctions. Can you do that here too??"

"Yeah, you could," Contessa said with a nod. "I wouldn't be concerned at all about your safety, but you'd need to be able to provide a way to verify that what you're selling is true. If you can't, you won't be able to sell it."

"Noted," Noah said. "Well, for now, let's just play things by ear. No point worrying when we don't even know what's for sale yet."

They all settled down to wait, but they didn't have to wait long.

Just a few minutes after they finished speaking, the lights in the amphitheater blinked out, plunging everyone into darkness. An instant later, a silver glow lit around the dais, illuminating the man standing upon it.

"I'd like to thank you all for joining us tonight," the man said, pressing one hand to his chest and stretching the other out to his side as he lowered into a bow. "For those of you who are returning, the Troupe greatly values your patronage. And, for those of you who are visiting for the first time, my name is Rin. I will be the auctioneer for tonight."

Rin raised, then crossed his arms behind his back in parade rest. Another hum washed over Noah's skin as beams of light erupted, illuminating all but five of the platforms.

"We have fifteen grand houses with us today," Rin continued. "I beg your forgiveness, but I must reiterate our rules before we can enjoy ourselves. As always, the Troupe strives to be as unintrusive as possible. Our assistants are all thoroughly bound by Rune Oath—not a word of what you say will leave their lips. In fact, they can't even hear you unless you touch them as part of the Imbuements on their mask."

That's... intense. Definitely a way to make sure that information doesn't leak, though. Can't share what you can't hear. Of course, that's assuming I actually believe this guy.

"Should you wish to bid on any item that arrives, you may simply call out your offer. Your Troupe member is only present in the scenario where you have questions or need clarification on anything. Please know that any attempts to threaten or otherwise harm a Troupe member will result in expulsion from this auction and hefty fines that will be paid in blood."

Don't screw with the employees. Got it. Hey, at least they care. Better than the shitty school administration I had back on Earth.

"Finally, please be aware that while visiting your neighbors on their viewing platforms is permitted, any altercations involving runes are not. If someone requests you leave their platform, you are requested to comply as quickly as possible. Interfering with another group's ability to place bids will be punished accordingly."

Noah's brow furrowed behind his mask. The rules about interference felt... off. They could have easily said that everyone had to stay in the locations where they started, but instead allowed anyone to walk around as they wished.

I suppose that lets you bargain or try to convince another house to give up on something without broadcasting your intentions to everyone else, but it also leaves a lot of opportunity to strongarm someone. You could easily go over to a competitor and threaten or otherwise try to figure out who they are to determine if you can afford to fight them or not.

"Furthermore, collaboration in order to acquire an item is allowed, though it will require that you identify yourself to the group you are working with. The Troupe is not responsible for anything that happens in this occurrence," Rin said, his voice echoing through the room. There was no way it was naturally that loud—it had to be magically enhanced. "We guarantee that no information of yours will ever leak at the fault of the Troupe, but this guarantee only goes so far as you maintain your secrecy. We have a running promise—if we fail to uphold any of our promises, your family will be accommodated with their choice of an item valued at a range of one million and four million gold."

Noah nearly choked on his saliva. The amount of money the Troupe was using as collateral was enough to buy so many runes that he didn't even know what he'd do with them.

I could probably boost myself and everyone else all the way up to Rank 6 with that much money. What the hell are these people doing where they can throw it around? Although... I guess money doesn't mean you can make a rune that doesn't suck. Dayton is proof of that.

"With that, it's time to get our festivities underway," Rin proclaimed. He clapped his hands together once. "The auction has begun!"

A grin slowly stretched across Noah's lips, though it was concealed by his mask. Money or not—the situation was more perfect than he could have ever asked for. Nobody knew who anyone else was, so if a group believed they were bidding against someone that had more power than they did, they had to be careful to avoid offending them. While there was theoretically no way to retaliate outside of the auction, Noah highly suspected some of the powerful houses would buy out every item someone else wanted purely just because they'd been annoyed.

The whole thing was one giant bluff competition. And, if there was one thing Noah was good at, it was bullshitting.

This is going to be fun.

Chapter Twenty-Three

A glimmer of golden magic danced across Rin's fingertips, flowing out to form a sphere above his head. He held his hands up, and, with a theatrical flick, the sphere burst like a miniature firework.

The light that exploded out of it gathered, changing color and shape to form a large potion vial. It was full of a rippling blue liquid and corked with a wax seal. The potion swirled like a three dimensional model in the air above Rin, and he waited several moments before speaking.

"We'll be starting with our miscellaneous offerings today," Rin declared. "Coming up first, starting at a mere one hundred gold, is a Waterbreath Potion from an amateur alchemist who wishes to remain anonymous. It functions for approximately one hour, though we were unable to guarantee this claim. It's a bit of a risk—but for a hundred gold, it's a steal!"

Lee licked her lips. "It's so blue. I bet it tastes like fruit."

"It probably tastes like rotten fish," Moxie said with a shake of her head. "And never buy potions from an amateur. That's a good way to turn your insides out. Stick to people who have been doing it for a while."

"One hundred," a man standing on the platform across from them called.

"One hundred and five," a woman called from the platform beside him no more than a second later.

Evidently, not everyone followed Moxie's way of thinking. Noah wasn't personally sold on the use of a water breathing, so he didn't really care who got the potion—especially for a hundred gold. It might not have been much to the nobles, but it was still a hefty chunk of money to him.

In the few seconds that Noah had spent thinking, the price of the potion had already raised to two hundred gold. Even though the two voices bidding on it were curt and professional, Noah picked up more than a small degree of animosity between them. A small frown crossed over his lips.

I don't know a ton about potions, but I feel like the price on this isn't going up because people actually want it. Is this a dick measuring contest?

"I bet it's tasty. Look how much they're fighting over it," Lee said, scrunching her nose. "Are you sure it's bad?"

"It's just two families trying to prove that they're the bigger fish in the pond," Karina said with a shake of her head. "I've seen this at almost every auction I go to, especially the ones where your identities are hidden. The loser isn't the one that doesn't get the item, though."

"It's the one that gets stuck with it, huh?" Noah chuckled. "God, that's stupid. They're trying to show they've got more money, but neither actually wants to end up with the piece of shit at the end, right?"

"Yeah, but it also shows that you're willing to fight what you want," Contessa said, reaching up to scratch at the side of her neck. "So it'll keep some families from bidding on things that you want when it's clear you plan to get them. There's a lot of nuance to this kind of thing."

"So I can see," Noah said.

I wonder how much I can screw with these people.

"Sold for 350 gold!" Rin called. The image of the potion vanished with a pop, and Noah looked back down to the stage just as the auctioneer formed another item with light—this time, it was a flying sword.

Noah already had one of those, so he wasn't particularly interested in buying it. The sword started bidding at four hundred gold, and this time, three families got into the fight over it. The actual numbers they bid didn't matter too much to Noah.

He was more interested in watching how they acted with each other. It seemed like the majority of the bids were relatively small increases over each other—likely to avoid accidentally scaring any of the other families off and mistakenly landing an unimportant item.

Several minutes passed, and Rin auctioned off half a dozen other assorted items that were of absolutely no interest to Noah. None of them seemed particularly interesting, and the vast majority seemed to be made by amateurs.

Rising to his feet, Noah walked up to their attendant and, after standing around awkwardly for a moment, put his hand on their arm.

"Excuse me?" Noah asked.

"How can I help you, sir?"

"I had a quick question about the items being offered," Noah said, ignoring the looks the rest of the group sent him. "Is there a reason they all appear to be... well, fairly unimportant?"

"There is, sir. Many families bring the products that their young masters have made or found and set them up for auction. It's a way to introduce them to the business while letting them make an allowance. The Troupe allows attending members to put any item up for auction."

"Any item?" Noah raised an eyebrow.

Can I auction my dirty underwear?

"The Troupe and all attending guests have a mutual understanding that nothing that is offered up will ever be substandard or a cause for concern, sir. If you happen to have anything you would like to auction stored in our safe lockers, please let me know."

Ah. That's another way to say don't give us shit or we'll kick you out. Fair enough. No underwear.

"Noted. Thank you," Noah said, taking his hand off the attendant and returning to his seat. In the time that he'd been gone, Rin had already moved on to sell another item and was now auctioning off what was supposedly an ancient dinner plate.

"Are you thinking of auctioning something?" Moxie asked.

"Considering it, but I'm not sure about doing it quite yet," Noah said with a thoughtful frown. He realized that Moxie couldn't see his expression and cleared his throat. "For now, let's just wait. I've got an idea, but we're going to have to do it at the right time."

Moxie shrugged, and they all settled back in to wait. Several more pieces went up and sold. The prices were steadily rising and were now starting in the low thousands, but Noah still wasn't ready to reveal anything.

Almost all the other viewing platforms had already bet on something, leaving only them and a platform to their left as the only ones that had yet to speak.

Rin clapped his hands, the sound piercing through the darkness of the amphitheater and drawing everyone's attention to him.

"We've wrapped up the sales for the miscellaneous section!" Rin called. "We'll now be moving on to the main event for tonight. Please keep in mind that, unlike the miscellaneous items, everything from here on out will not be sold in order of ascending rarity. So, if you see something you want, make sure to buy it!"

Clever. That's a good way to make sure people don't lowball the items they aren't really sure if they want. If you don't know if anything good is going to pop up later, then you'll go much harder for the one right in front of you.

Rin waited for a few moments to make sure everybody had heard him before he started talking once more. "Our next section will be one of our most interesting ones! We've got a fascinating mixture of runes coming up for you—but there's something we have to do first."

A loud hum filled the air. Rin snapped his fingers, and the sound tore through the room like a thunderclap. Light swirled around him, forming into a huge image of a man in black-clad armor.

The man raised a hand to his helm, pushing it back to reveal a dazzlingly handsome face with a wide, white-toothed smile.

"My friends!" the man boomed, his voice echoing through the amphitheater. "My name is Reed. Thank you so much for attending the auction. I come bearing a brief message on behalf of my organization, the Shadows."

Reed held his hands out, palms facing the ceiling. "We're an adventurer group that has completed over a hundred missions successfully, ranging from retrieval quests to hunting monsters up to Rank 5. We specialize in raids and fighting large targets. If you happen to be in need of any form of assistance, please keep us in mind. Remember, when it comes to your valued life or property, nobody does it like us."

The light blinked out and Reed vanished with a pop.

"That's all from our sponsors," Rin said with a chuckle. "Let's keep moving, shall we? I think we should get started right off the bat with something fascinating. I've got a Rank 5 Tortured Death Wind Rune that was found naturally formed in the wild. It's one of the more fascinating runes that I've seen come through the auction in recent times, and is estimated to have been 25 percent full upon formation. Bids will start at twenty thousand gold."

"Twenty-five thousand," a man to their right called out without an instant of hesitation.

Moxie leaned over to Noah. "What do you think?"

"Not that useful, and its starting price is too high. There's no way we'd be able to get it, even if we wanted it." Noah shook his head. "I could use the wind elements, but the rest is too different from what I'm working on right now. Besides, it just sound sinister. Not something I want in my soul."

"Twenty-five percent full isn't bad for a Rank 5, though," Karina said, eyeing Rin with a hungry look in her eyes. She shook her head and let out a sigh. "Whatever. I can't afford anything that expensive."

"Thirty thousand!" a woman on the other side of the room called.

"Thirty-three!"

"Forty!"

Several other people threw bids in, and the price soon rose to fifty thousand. The bids started to slow until only two people were fighting over the rune. After a few more minutes, the woman pulled out, and it sold for seventy-two thousand.

Okay. They still raise everything in fairly small increments relative to the price. That rune seems like it was right in the middle of the road for a Rank 5, and it still sold for a crazy amount. Fine with me, though.

"Our next rune is a Rank 4, but don't let that dissuade you! It was taken from a Stormprince Elemental. It has elements of lightning, wind, and water within it! The rune is estimated to have been about 75 percent full upon formation. The bids will start at three thousand gold."

Lightning and wind? Give the name... well, I can use both of those elements. Storm fits exactly what I need, even if I don't need any more Water Runes right now.

"That rune is a piece of shit. Seventy-five percent full is laughable," Karina said with a scoff. "It should be sold for two thousand at most. Three thousand for a worthless Rank 4? That's ridiculous."

"Three thousand!" Noah called.

Everyone stared at him.

"What are you doing?" Karina asked, staring at Noah in disbelief. "Did you hear him? It's 75 percent full! It doesn't matter if it's a Rank 4, Vermil. You'll permanently cripple yourself if you take that rune."

Noah ignored her. A second passed.

"Is nobody else going to bid?" Rin asked, his voice slightly strained. "This is quite a rare rune, you know!"

Yeah. Rare because of how shockingly trash it is.

The only response was silence. Noah could practically feel scornful gazes boring into his back, but he didn't care. Three thousand gold was a ridiculous amount, but it was a Rank 4 rune. Even if he lost most of the energy in it, it would be more than worth the cost when he split it up.

"Well then. Sold!" Rin exclaimed. "Congratulations, Number 17."

Well, that was easy.

"Where will it be?" Noah asked Contessa.

"They'll put it in your locker. But..." Contessa thought better of whatever it was she'd been about to say and shook her head. "Never mind."

Another two runes went up for sale—both Rank 3s that were fairly well combined, but neither caught Noah's attention. They both sold for around fifty thousand gold after lengthy bartering battles.

But, finally, Noah found what he was waiting for, as Rin called up a new rune.

"This one ought to draw your interest," Rin called. "This is a Rank 3 Inferno Rune. It is of borderline perfect quality, and bidding will start at ten thousand gold."

"Hey, do you guys mind if I borrow some money? I won't keep it," Noah said.

Moxie and Lee both glanced at him, then nodded as one.

"I guess. Is it really worth it for something like this, though?" Moxie asked.

"You'll see."

"Ten thousand!" A woman's voice rang out.

"Twenty thousand," Noah called.

All that greeted him was silence. Rin blinked in surprise, but he was a professional salesman and didn't let himself get caught off guard for long.

"Twenty thousand! That's a high raise by 17. Would anyone—"

"Twenty-five thousand," the man across from them called. Noah could see him standing at the edge of his viewing platform, looking straight at him.

Noah raised a hand in greeting. Then, without a trace of unease, he spoke again. "Thirty-five thousand."

"What are you doing?" Lee asked. "Do we really need that?"

A few seconds ticked by. Noah stood casually, making sure his posture didn't let on any of the stress that he felt. People were definitely watching them now.

Oh, shit. Come on. Don't bail out now. The other runes have sold for way more than—

"Forty thousand," the man called. Noah couldn't see his eyes, but he got the feeling the man was glaring daggers in his direction.

Rin looked back to Noah. Nobody else tried to place a bid, so it was just him and the other man. They'd both raised the price by such a high number that it became pretty clear that butting in now would cause more trouble than it was worth.

Noah tapped his head, then sat back down. Rin waited for a few more moments in hope that someone else would say something, but it never came.

"Sold for forty thousand to Number 28!" Rin's voice echoed.

"What was that about?" Contessa asked. "If you don't mind me asking, that is. I don't mean to—"

"It's fine. I didn't want the rune."

"You didn't? Why did you bid thirty-five thousand gold on something you don't want?"

"Because it looks like we're a big noble family," Moxie muttered, realization washing over her. "We've wasted three thousand gold on a worthless rune and then immediately jumped the price of the Inferno Rune. That made it look like we're rich, but Vermil showed we were willing to play nice when 28 made it clear he really wanted the Inferno Rune."

"And now, all we have to do is wait," Noah said, a smile spreading across his lips. "This is just getting started."

Chapter Twenty-Four

Two more runes sold without issue, but Noah's prediction came to be true just a few minutes later, when there was a knock on their door.

"There we go. Lee, do you think you could get that? You're the most intimidating out of all of us right now. Ah, I guess we should make sure not to use names as well from here on out."

Lee nodded. She rose to her feet, her current form towering far above all of them as she stomped over to the door and leaned down, pulling it open carefully to avoid damaging the handle.

A woman stood on the other side, her arms crossed behind her back. Her mask identified her with a small bird print rather than a number.

"I apologize for the intrusion," the woman said, her voice smooth and syrupy. She didn't look taken aback by Lee's size in the slightest. "Would you object to a brief discussion? I come representing Number 14, on the platform to your left."

Those are the ones that haven't bid on a single thing yet. Interesting.

"I'm always willing to entertain guests," Noah said, waving for her to come in. Lee closed the door behind the woman. "What can we do for you, Bird?"

If she objected to the nickname, she didn't show it. "Number 14 would like to inquire if there is a particular piece you are searching for in the auction today."

"Nothing in particular," Noah said with a one-shouldered shrug. "We're simply perusing and taking whatever catches our interest."

Something tells me that isn't the case for 14, though. They're worried I have enough money to compete with them on something they actually care about.

Noah was thankful for his mask because he could barely hold back the devilish grin crossing his lips.

"Ah. In that case, would you object to avoiding a particular object? Number 14 greatly desires this object for himself, and he would be very displeased if we had to pay more than we needed to for it."

She's avoiding mentioning the specific item in case I seem like I'll screw with them for no reason, and the way she worded things made it pretty clear she doesn't believe losing is actually possible—they've got a ridiculous amount of money, then. Probably a massive family, then.

"A curious proposal," Noah said. "Is there anything I would get out of it? I have no desire to antagonize your group, but I'm not going to sit around and pass up on something interesting."

"We understand, and we would obviously be willing to return the favor in kind. We will refrain from bidding on anything that you desire if you return the effort."

Hm. They know something really important is going to go up for sale, and whatever it is, it's probably really good. There's absolutely no way I could afford something like that in the first place, even if we pool everything we have.

But if they're rich... well, they should be able to spare some money pretty easily.

"I'm not sure I can agree to that quite yet. What if the object your group desires is identical to the one that catches my eye?" Noah shook his head sadly. "If you could tell me the item of interest, I would be honest and tell you truthfully if I would bid on it or not. My word."

Bird didn't speak for several moments. She was probably trying to read his body language, but Noah had absolutely no idea what he was talking about, so it was impossible to tell anything from it.

I get the feeling that all the big noble families knew this fancy thing would pop up, so she might think I'm being coy. Jokes on you, sucker. I'm fucking clueless.

"It is the Rank 6 rune, Violet Transference," Bird said, making a decision.

Noah tilted his head to the side, as if he were disappointed by her words. "Oh. Is that all? That's no concern to me. I had thought there would be something more interesting. Yes, your Number 14 is more than welcome. I will not compete."

And, exactly as Noah had hoped, Bird paused. She looked around the room, clearly trying to figure out if she could pick up any clues about their identity.

"Perhaps our alliance need not be so limited," Noah offered. "You're being kind to me, after all. I should return the favor."

Noah's words were polite, but they came off as arrogant, which was exactly his goal. He'd made Bird's request seem as if it were the equivalent of a man begging him for coin at the side of the road.

"How so, Number 17?" Bird asked, her tone bristling slightly.

"I have a rune that I was considering auctioning, but I wasn't certain if it was worth the effort. Perhaps your group would be interested in taking a look at it before anyone else?"

"I can't speak for Number 14, so I am uncertain. Would you be willing to say what the rune is?" Bird asked. Her tone remained even, but Noah caught the slight interest in her voice. It wasn't hard to look for. If he didn't care about a Rank 6 rune, it made sense that he'd probably have his sights set on something rarer.

"A Monster Rune," Noah replied simply. "One unique to a monster—something that I do not believe any human has ever been able to harvest."

Bird swallowed. "You're claiming to have a completely unique rune that has never been seen before? We'd have to verify such a thing was true before we did anything further."

"Of course," Noah said smoothly. "And the price of witnessing the rune before anyone else will be a piece of Catchpaper. I don't wish to reveal the rest of my collection to you."

"Of course. I would expect as much. I can't guarantee anything, but I will go speak with Number 14 immediately." She beat a hasty retreat and strode off into the darkness to return to her viewing platform.

Noah turned to the attendant and put his hand on her arm so she could hear him. "Would it be possible to retrieve my grimoire from my vault temporarily?"

"Of course. Is there something in it that you wish to sell?"

"An individual rune, but I'm not sure if I'll be auctioning it yet," Noah replied. "I'll contact you again if I need it."

The attendant nodded and he took his hand off her, turning back to the door. Something told him that he wouldn't have to wait long for a response—and he was right.

No more than a minute or two later, there was a knock on the door. Lee opened it to reveal Bird and a man with the number *14* on his mask. There was a piece of paper in Bird's hands.

"I have procured the Catchpaper," Bird said, holding it out to Noah. "We'd be interested in taking a look at what you have to offer."

"Splendid," Noah said, inclining his head ever so slightly. Number *14* didn't address him, and Noah returned the favor. "Please give me some time to retrieve the rune."

Lee closed the door.

Noah turned back to the attendant and put his hand on her arm. "I'd like that grimoire, please."

"Of course, sir. Please step back."

Noah obeyed her request, and the attendant pressed her palms together. She stretched them apart, and a familiar crackle of purple energy arced between them. A portal stretched open in the room, and Noah's grimoire thumped to the ground before him.

The Troupe's attendants have Space Runes? These guys definitely aren't underfunded.

He wasted no time in flipping the grimoire open, setting the paper down beside it. Selling the Monster Rune wasn't really much of a drawback to him—he could easily get another one without too much difficulty, and he wasn't so sure he wanted to test it on himself.

Anything that messed with his soul was something that—unlike death—posed a real risk to him. Fortunately, as long as he moved fast enough, having the Chitinous Spine Armor Rune in his mind for a few moments wouldn't be enough time to cause any changes.

Noah didn't care how dangerous the rune was if someone else was buying it. It was their responsibility to make sure it didn't turn them into some sort of warped monster-human hybrid. All he had to do was get it onto a piece of paper, so he didn't have to reveal his very recognizable grimoire.

"Give me the Chitinous Spine Armor Rune," Noah said. "It was part of Datyon's scroll. Wait, shit. You didn't eat it, did you?"

The book's pages fluttered. It shifted to the side of its own accord, sliding to touch the paper on the ground beside it. The scent of burning paper filled the air, and Noah looked down in surprise.

Glowing lines were swirled across the piece of Catchpaper as the Chitinous Spine Armor Rune drew itself onto it. Tiny glowing embers rose up from the paper and faded into the air.

The book can imbue runes on its own? I don't have to take them into myself first? Holy shit. This thing is insane. It also begs the question... how intelligent is it?

The Imbuement finished and the book snapped shut.

Noah picked up the paper with the Monster Rune, then tapped the attendant on the shoulder. "That will be all. Thank you."

The attendant opened her portal once more, and, after glancing through it to make sure the vault on the other side was his, Noah pushed the book through. Then he turned back to the door and nodded for Lee to open it.

"Thank you for your patience," Noah said, beckoning for Bird and Number 14 to step into their room and holding the paper out so they could see it. The smile on his face stretched even wider, until it probably had more resemblance to Azel's smirk than he would have cared to admit. "Please, take a look."

Chapter Twenty-Five

Bird took a step forward, but Number 14 pushed past her. Noah couldn't see his eyes, but he could tell from a glance that the man's gaze was solely fixed on the rune imbued into the Catchpaper before him.

It didn't take a genius to figure out what the man was thinking. He'd probably been confused at first—it wasn't like he could understand the rune, so it would have looked like a bunch of squiggles.

He's going to think the rune is fake and will want to touch it to feel the power in it. That's the easiest way to verify it's got actual magic.

Sure enough, the man brought the back of his hand up to the Catchpaper, brushing it across the rune. His arm stiffened and he pulled back, his masked face raising to look up at Noah.

"What is this?"

"I told you. A Monster Rune," Noah said, not even bothering to hide the smugness in his tone. It fit the role he wanted to play perfectly. "It's Rank 3."

"That wasn't what I meant," Number 14 said. "How is this possible? I can't read the rune. What does it do? Where did you get it?"

"Those are a lot of questions," Noah said smoothly. Down on the stage behind Noah's back, Rin was calling out information about a new rune. Noah paused for a moment to listen to the pitch, but it didn't catch his interest. "I take it that means you're interested?"

Number 14 grunted. He crossed his arms and took a step back, gathering himself—but it was too late. He'd overplayed his hand, and they both knew it. Shaking his head, Number 14 let out a chuckle. "Yes. I'm interested. I think that's plain enough. The question is not of my interest, though. It is of the quality of the goods for sale."

"An object is only as valuable as someone's desire for it," Noah countered. "And you aren't going to be finding something like this anywhere else."

"Which is precisely why I wish to know how you got it."

"And that is the exact reason why I'm sure you'll understand that I'm not sharing such information," Noah said with a shrug. "It was not easy for my group to procure this. I was unsure if I wished to sell it at all, to be frank."

"And yet you do—which means you can get more."

"Logically." Noah inclined his head, then waved the Catchpaper. "But for the time being, this is the only one on sale. It's a defensive rune called Chitinous Spine Armor. A Rank 3, as I previously mentioned."

"You can read it?" There was even more surprise in Number 14's voice.

"I am a man of many talents."

And reading this isn't one of them. That's all Lee.

Number 14 didn't respond for several seconds. He studied the rune on the paper, as if trying to memorize it. Noah was pretty sure that was a faux pas, as runes could be replicated if you knew how they looked and had enough of their matching energy to draw one, but he wasn't concerned.

If Number 14 wanted to steal the Monster Rune, he'd need to find another one with matching energy. That wasn't a problem for stealing a Fire Rune or the like, since anyone with enough gold could buy a Fire Rune.

Good luck finding another Monster Rune that matches this one any time soon.

"Okay," Number 14 admitted, his fingers twitching as if he wanted to take the paper from Noah then and there. "I am incredibly interested. I will not beat around the bush—but I will also be forthright and say that, no matter how fascinating this rune is, it is a long-term investment and will likely provide me little in the near future. As a Rank 3 with unknown quality, I would not be willing to overspend on it."

Bah. I get the feeling that you've got so much money that you don't know what to do with it. This is just damage control to save face after you spilled all the beans.

"I understand, but I obviously wouldn't be willing to part with something as rare and expensive as this for an inadequate amount. Rank 3 or not, it's still completely unique and incredibly rare. You can get a Master Rune by hunting down a Great Monster. When's the last time you saw a Monster Rune, though?"

Number 14's fingers drummed on his thigh. Bird shifted behind him. She was still scanning the room in search of anything identifiable, but nobody else was talking, and they hadn't brought anything with them other than the clothes the Troupe had provided. There was nothing to find.

"Never," Number 14 admitted, "but I have responsibilities. I cannot allow myself to spend frivolously on something that may turn out to be worthless or even detrimental. I do not know what will happen if someone uses this rune, and I suspect you are not offering any guarantees."

"I am not. It is an untested rune and should be treated as such."

"As I thought. Would you be willing to share your Trade Pact with me? I have no doubt of your ability to procure items like this, but I am hesitant to offer up much without knowing that I am buying from a reputable source."

Oh, shit. I figured that the only people that were invited to this thing would all be big-boy nobles, so the whole trade restriction thing wouldn't be a big deal. I obviously don't have anything to show there, but refusing will be suspicious, won't it?

"We'd like to avoid revealing our identities at this time," Moxie said, walking up to join Noah. "While we're not opposed to working together in the future should you find this item appealing, it's too easy for knowledge of our procurements to go public. I'm sure you understand."

Damn. Nice one, Moxie. Even I believed that for a second.

"Understandable, but I'm sure you must know that limits my willingness to overspend," Number 14 said, a smug note entering his own voice.

Noah suppressed an annoyed grumble as he realized what the other man's goal had been. He'd never suspected that Noah wasn't a big-time noble from a large family—he was just banking on their hesitance to share information to try and haggle the price down.

He knows what he's doing. Can't say I'm surprised.

"Well, if you're concerned about being unable to afford this, then I won't force you. I could always auction it with the Troupe," Noah said with a small shrug. "I'd imagine it would sell for considerably more that way, though I do prefer the idea of keeping this rune's existence a little quieter."

Noah did mean that. If he sold the rune to a single family, he doubted information on it would come out for some time, and when it did, it would be much harder to trace. Selling it at an auction would mean everyone knew of the rune's existence, and there would almost certainly be some prick that tried to figure out the identities of everyone that had attended the auction tonight.

"Up next is a set of runes!" Rin's voice echoed, interrupting Noah and Number 14's bargaining. "This one was a particularly fortunate collection that came from an overly ambitious mage that tried to challenge above his weight class and met an unfortunate end. It includes a Broken Master Rune by the name of Enveloping Dark as well as two Moonlit Shadow Runes and three Light Runes. He was Rank 4, with the majority of his runes being around 50 percent full around conception. Bidding will start at eighty thousand gold."

That sounds perfect for Lee. The Light Runes are useless, and I'm not sure what a Broken Master Rune is in comparison to a normal one, but she needed some more Shadow Runes to finish up her combination. I'd better make sure she doesn't—

Lee's head had already snapped toward the stage, betraying her desire. Noah suppressed a groan. He didn't blame her—ever since Lee had been able to come clean about who she was, she'd clearly gotten used to being herself and not worrying about what others thought. Unfortunately, when they were in the middle of a major bargain with someone who he had almost gotten the upper hand over, showing weakness was less than ideal.

"Should we pause for a moment?" Number 14 asked. "One of your party seems interested in the lot that just went up."

Fuck. We can't afford it.

"Oh, I didn't want it. It just sounded interesting," Lee said, but it was too late.

"Please, please. Go ahead," Number 14 said with a magnanimous chuckle. "I wouldn't want to stand between you and something you desire. I am a patient man."

The price of the set of runes had already raised to ninety thousand and was continuing to go up.

"I, however, am not," Noah said, thinking furiously as he tried to find a way to spin things in a way that wouldn't weaken his position. "Since you've been so honest with me thus far, I will return the favor. I am trying to hide some of my purchases today, and although one of my compatriots would indeed benefit from those runes, playing our hand too early would be less than ideal."

Number 14 tilted his head to the side, then nodded. "Ah, yes. I know the feeling. That would explain your earlier purchase of the flawed rune. Perhaps I could aid you?"

"Oh? How so?"

"I'll buy that set of runes for you and throw it in as part of the deal for this one," Number 14 said. "With handling fees, of course."

Noah nearly choked. He'd been planning to try to get fifty thousand gold for the rune, but clearly, the numbers he was thinking in were very different from the ones Number 14 had in mind. It took everything he had to keep himself from nodding so furiously that his head flew off.

I need to slow down. What if he wants me to pay him a bunch of gold on top of everything? That would be bad.

"I suppose that would be acceptable," Noah said, delaying as long as he dared. "Your kindness is appreciated. In that case, we should get down to what you are willing to pay for this rune."

Number 14 thought for a moment. The bids on the set of runes were slowing down, and the price had started to approach one hundred thousand gold.

"I will give you one hundred and fifty thousand gold, minus the cost of the set that is about to sell," Number 14 said.

Noah damn near said yes on the spot. His heart clenched as he forced himself to freeze in place and put on the air of considering the offer.

"Two hundred thousand."

"One hundred and seventy-five, but you will promise me another such rune in the future at a reasonable price, should I request it."

"How would that work? We are anonymous."

"We are," Number 14 agreed. He reached into his pocket and pulled out a small leather patch. It had a small cross embossed on its front, and it was clearly made from a single piece without any seams or cuts. "This will prove your identity to me. It is merely a unique piece of cloth with no runework or Imbuements on it. All the power will be in your hands—and I will take the risk to trust that you reach out as agreed upon."

"And how will I find you, should I agree?"

"One from my family will demonstrate the powers of the rune I purchase today," Number 14 said. "That will make it abundantly clear."

Noah didn't dare delay any longer. He simply took the patch from Number 14, exchanging it for the Monster Rune. Number 14 handed the Catchpaper over to Bird and extended his hand. Noah clasped it, and they shook.

"A pleasure doing business with you," Number 14 said. "I look forward to a *very* fruitful partnership. Bird, would you acquire the set on sale before some bumbling fool makes away with it?"

"Yes, sir," Bird said. She raised a hand to her temple. A moment later, a new bid echoed out through the dark amphitheater, this one coming from the platform right to their left.

"One hundred thousand."

There was a moment of silence. Then a woman on the other side of the room started to speak.

"One hundred—"

"One hundred ten thousand," the voice from the platform to their side echoed out

The challenge was clear, and the price had gotten high enough that even the other nobles were hesitant to bring it any higher when someone wanted it that badly. The silence lasted for a few more seconds before Rin clapped his hands.

"Sold for one hundred and ten thousand to Number 12!"

"That's my man," Number 14 said. "It was a pleasure. The attendant on my platform will transfer the remaining sixty-five thousand gold and the set of runes to your vault in the form of a treasury note. I trust that is sufficient?"

Kind of like a check? Works for me. I assume the Troupe can cash it, so I can use that money to bid.

"It is."

"Then I wish you a good day. Until we meet again." Number 14 raised a hand to his head in farewell, then strode out the door. Bird hurried after him, only pausing to gently close the door behind them.

Moxie waited until they were gone to speak again. "Damned Plains. What are you, a used flying swords salesman?"

"Hey, don't complain. We've got an extra sixty-five thousand gold to play with, and I fully plan to blow all of it on getting a few more runes for myself. I knew this was going to be fun."

Chapter Twenty-Six

Several more runes went up for sale and consequently were purchased, ranging from a few thousand gold to well over three hundred thousand. Noah tried to keep his eyes from boggling at the amounts of money that the nobles were throwing around, but it wasn't easy.

And to think Arbitage was paying me ten goddamn gold a month. God, they were scamming my ass.

Noah nudged Moxie. "Any of the runes catching your eye?"

She shook her head. "It's not a good idea to take on a ton of new runes at once, and I just completely redid my runes. I'm perfectly fine as I am. Besides, I think you and Lee need them more."

"The ones that we just got should be enough for me," Lee said. She looked out at Rin, then cleared her throat. "Do... I get the Master Rune?"

"Sure. I don't need it, and it seems like it should fit you pretty well anyway," Noah said. "In that case, I think I'll focus the rest of my purchases on me. I still need some more Ice and Fire Runes. Maybe a Vibration one as well, although the Stormprince's rune that I bought probably has that."

He didn't have to wait long. Neither Ice nor Fire Runes were particularly uncommon, and Noah had already established that he wanted a Fire-related rune when he'd bid on the nearly Perfect Inferno Rune that had gone up near the start of the auction.

After a few more other runes were sold, an above-average Scorching Flame Rune came up for sale at Rank 3. It started at five thousand gold and quickly made its way up to ten before Noah jumped the bidding price by ten thousand, up to twenty thousand. One more person made an attempt at buying it by pushing it up to twenty-one, but Noah immediately countered with a bid of twenty-five thousand.

Nobody tried bidding against him any further—the rune just wasn't worth the risk, and so he won it without any further trouble. Noah was pretty sure he'd slightly overpaid for the rune, but it fit his purposes perfectly, and he didn't want to hunt around for Fire Runes any longer.

After several more uninteresting sales, Noah's attention was once again piqued by a rune called Towering Frozen Glacier. It was a Rank 4 rune sitting at almost 40 percent full upon creation, which put it ever so slightly on the upper end of average.

That didn't stop people from bidding on it, though. Evidently, even a middling Rank 4 rune was of some use to weaker families. The price, which had started at twenty thousand, quickly rose up to thirty.

"Forty thousand," Noah called.

An instant passed, but people weren't as willing to let go of this rune as a clearly sub-standard one. Before long, a woman matched his bid.

"Forty-one thousand."

"Forty-five thousand."

This time, the pause was longer. It was the third time that Noah had basically brute-forced his way into a purchase. Even though the previous runes hadn't been all that expensive, the way he approached them was identical each time.

"Fifty thousand," the woman called, a slight trace of hesitation in her voice.

Noah glanced at Moxie.

"Do you mind if I—"

"Go ahead."

"Fifty-five thousand," Noah countered, deeply hoping his bidding opponent wouldn't try to push the price any higher. He still had forty thousand gold left over from what Number 14 had given him. With the addition of his own money and the money that they'd gotten from selling the horn, that put him at just under sixty thousand. If they went any higher, he'd have to start digging into Lee and Moxie's pockets to avoid getting outbidden.

Mercifully, nobody called out again. Noah breathed a sigh of relief as Rin clapped his hands together to signal that the item had been sold. "The Towering Frozen Glacier Rune goes to Number 17!"

"There goes our money," Lee said sadly. "It was nice being rich."

"You still have ten thousand gold," Noah pointed out. "Don't let these stuffy pricks screw your scale of money up. It's not normal to spend this much at once—but at the same time, what's the point of having money if we don't use it? With this, I should be able to reach Rank 4 without any more delays."

"Me too," Lee said, her posture straightening back up as she remembered the runes they'd just bought for her. "It's going to be cool. I can't wait to get a domain. What do you think it'll be?"

"Probably an all-devouring void," Noah said, only half-joking. "You know, I haven't actually *seen* much in the form of a domain from anyone we've fought or spent time with. Can you actually see domains?"

"Not until you're Rank 4," Moxie said. "There isn't enough runic energy inside your body to comprehend them yet, but not every Rank 4 has enough of a domain to actually see."

"I thought you always get it at Rank 4?"

"You do," Moxie said. "But that's where the quality of your runes starts to really come into play. If they're shitty or weak, your domain might be so pathetic that it's almost unnoticeable. It might even be weak enough to get overpowered by lower-rank opponents, although you'd have to have *terrible* runes for that. On the other hand, if your runes are incredibly powerful, you can manifest an easily visible domain with much less work."

"So if I see someone strolling around with a bunch of magic floating around them, I should assume they're strong."

"Astute observation," Moxie said dryly. "I've heard you get more sensitive to runic pressure when you hit Rank 4 as well, though I don't have any experience to confirm or deny that. But take Magus Allen, for example—his runes were pretty weak. He's still a Rank 4, but he barely even had a domain. That's why he was struggling fighting monsters weaker than him, and why he's teaching here instead of doing something that pays better."

"You make it sound like people don't want to be teachers."

Moxie shrugged. "I'm not sure I'd say that. There's a lot of money to be made in researching runes or mentoring the kids of wealthy families. Allen just didn't really have the liberty to choose, so he got stuck with Edward. I don't think he hates it. It lets him be snobby without actually having the power to back it up."

Noah chuckled. It had been a long time since he'd given any thought to Edward or Allen. The last time he'd seen them was when they'd first arrived at the Linwick Estate together with Brayden.

I guess we'll probably end up running into each other at some point during an exam. That'll be fun. I can't wait to see Isabel and Todd completely show up Edward. Spoiled little shit.

"You're thinking unsportsmanlike thoughts," Moxie said.

"How'd you know? I've got a mask on."

"I can tell. Also, you just confirmed it."

Noah rolled his eyes. Even though Moxie couldn't see what he was doing behind his mask, it was the thought that counted. "Whatever. I just want to reach Rank 4. I'm locking myself in my room after this is done, and I'm not leaving until I'm done."

"You gave your room to Karina and Contessa."

The two women in question suddenly found the Rank 4 rune that Rin was currently selling incredibly fascinating.

"Oh. Right," Noah said. "I guess I'm locking myself in your room."

Before Moxie could reply, a deep hum filled the amphitheater. The lights flashed, drawing everyone's attention back to Rin, who held his hands up in a grandiose movement. An image of a massive purple rune appeared in the air far above him.

"My dear attendees!" Rin called out, his voice magically enhanced to be even louder than it had been before. "We've gotten to the final rune of the night! And yes—I told you that there wasn't an order, but I'm afraid I lied just a little bit. I may have been saving the best for last. What you see before you is one of the most interesting runes that we've had for sale in recent months. I am pleased to present Violet Transference, a Rank 6 rune. It was 12 percent full upon combination. Bidding will start at five hundred thousand gold. If this beauty catches your eye

—well, I'd wish you luck, but luck won't help you. May the richest one of us win."

"One million."

Every single eye in the room turned to Number 14's platform. He'd spoken up himself for the first time that auction, and he certainly hadn't been lying about his desire to get the rune. Noah tried to comprehend just how much money had just been put down on the table, but he wasn't given much time to process it.

"One million and two hundred thousand," a man from another platform called.

"One million and three hundred thousand!"

"Holy shit," Noah muttered. "Was everyone just holding back for this thing?"

"It's a nearly perfect Rank 6 rune. That's incredible," Contessa breathed, leaning so far over the edge of their platform that Noah was almost worried she'd fall off. "I can't believe someone's actually selling it. It could completely change the fate of a family."

"Two million," Number 14 thundered, his words carving through the din like a sword. Noah's throat dried. He swallowed, his spine prickling. The leather patch that the noble had given him suddenly felt incredibly heavy in his pocket.

Who the hell did I do business with?

A woman started to speak up.

"Three million." Number 14's voice was like a massive wall rising up over all of them, not allowing even the slightest thought of passage beyond it. He was using the same strategy Noah had, but on such an incredible level that it felt impossible to comprehend.

"Do you think he wants a wife?" Karina whispered.

"Keep dreaming," Contessa muttered back.

Rin's fingers twitched on the stage, and Noah suppressed a laugh. He wasn't sure if Rin was more pleased that the rune was going to sell for that much or if he was pissed that Number 14 was cutting off the bidding before it could get any higher.

Silence ruled the amphitheater.

"Is nobody else going to bid?" Rin called. "This is a once-in-a-life-time opportunity, my dear attendees. You may never get another opportunity to acquire a rune as incredible as this."

"Three million—"

"Four million." Number 14 didn't hesitate in the slightest. It felt like he was just playing with someone else's money instead of using his own.

At least hear out what they're saying! You've made your point already. Aren't you just wasting money now?

Wasteful or not, it worked. Nobody spoke up again. Rin cleared his throat, clearly stalling for as long as possible. When it became abundantly clear that absolutely nobody was able to compete with Number 14, he clapped his hands.

"Sold! Congratulations to Number 14!"

The lights flashed, then dimmed slightly as the rune floating above Rin disappeared.

"Right now! We'll be moving on to the next and final stage of today's auction," Rin said. "I've always found this one to be the most interesting. It's time for the information sale! Need a question answered? For the right price, we'll handle it for you. Just let your attendant know. In the meantime, we'll be putting up the verified information that you've all sent us for auction. To open with, I've got the location of an area that has a high population of Rank 4 monsters that have a tendency toward Wind-based runes. The bidding price will start at five thousand gold."

Noah sat down in his chair as bids started to echo across the dark room, still slightly numb from the amount of money that Number 14 had been slinging around.

"He's got to be from one of the large families," Moxie said, her tone thoughtful. "That could be really useful."

"Or dangerous," Noah said. "But you're right. It'll be interesting to find out who he really is. He's evidently strong enough that he can share it without worrying about us finding out."

"Interesting indeed," Moxie muttered, looking out to the platform where Number 14 stood. "You think we could maybe try to use him to do something about Jalen?"

"It's a possibility. We'll find out soon enough, I guess."

"So we will," Moxie agreed.

"Do you think anyone is selling information on where the best food is in Arbitage?" Lee asked. "I'm hungry."

Chapter Twenty-Seven

The auction ground on. On the viewing platform just a few spots to the right of Noah's group, a man and a woman sat at a table, listening with half an ear each as Rin tried to convince the attendees to bid higher on the location of a Great Monster.

"You know, I can't help but feel like this might be breaking a few Rules," the masked man said. He scratched at his mask, which had the number 29 on it.

The woman, whose mask had a small star on it, snorted. "There's no point in having Rules if you don't break them."

"But—"

"It's only fair. If I spend all this time making sure that everything stays as it should, then it should be perfectly fine for me to bend things a bit when I want to."

"That's a little hypocritical, don't you think?"

"Do you want me to not be hypocritical?" The woman tilted her head to the side. "I can arrange for that, but I don't think you'd enjoy the results."

Clearing his throat, the man adjusted his shirt. "I don't believe I've broken any Rules. There's nothing for me to be concerned about."

The woman stood up and walked around the table, causing the man to stiffen. She put her hands on his shoulders and leaned forward so their faces were right beside each other. "If that were true, would you be so concerned right now?"

"I say this with the most respect I can—you're terrifying. I'd be a fool not to be concerned in your presence, even if I had never so much as thought of breaking a rule in my entire life."

"Aw, you think I'm terrifying? Thanks. I appreciate it." The woman let out a laugh as she stepped away from the man, running a finger across the back of his neck before returning to her chair and leaning back, kicking both of her feet up onto the table. "Flattery isn't going to change anything, though. Besides, this isn't hurting anyone."

"No," the man allowed, reaching up to touch the back of his neck. "I suppose it isn't. But don't you think introducing such a powerful Rank 6 rune to the area is... possibly less than ideal?"

"Are you challenging my judgment?" The woman tilted her head to the side.

"In the most polite and respectful way that I can imagine—yes. I don't think that's against the Rules, but I'd like to request you not kill me in case you decide it is."

The woman burst into laughter. "You get more fun every day. First you admit you're scared of me, and then you have the guts to actually try and stand up to me for something as unimportant as this. I'm glad I didn't pop your head like a grape when we first met. It would have been a complete waste."

"I'm relieved to hear you think so highly of me. If I'm being honest, I'm more concerned about drawing unwanted attention than I am about your Rule-breaking."

"This is my domain." She reached up to her mask and pulled it away from her face. "The others aren't going to care about something as unimportant as this. Besides, I didn't do this for no reason. It had a purpose."

Behind the mask was impossibly pale skin with lips curled up in a cocky smile. Garina set her mask down on the table, then flicked her fingers. "Go on, Ferdinand. Take the stupid thing off."

"They're meant to conceal our identities," Ferdinand said wearily, removing his own mask and setting it down beside Garina's. "I don't mean to antagonize you, but I am not optimistic that the other Apostles would leave me alive."

"Oh relax. You're under my thumb. As long as you don't break any Rules, they're not going to care in the slightest who you are. It's a moot point, though. They're not going to waste their time here when I'm already searching the area for our target." Garina paused for a moment. Her face scrunched in distaste. "Okay, one of them might be around somewhere, but he's probably not going to care about you at all."

"When it comes to my life, I can't say that I love the idea of *probably*."

"But you don't mind being under my thumb?" Garina smirked at the scowl on Ferdinand's face. "Relax. You're being a stick in the mud. Do you really think I'd have given away a Rank 6 rune at this level for no reason?"

"I'm not sure it's a wise idea to make any predictions about your actions."

"Oh, stuff it. I'm trying to lure my prey out."

Ferdinand's expression tightened and his eyes narrowed imperceptibly. "Prey?"

Neither of them had spoken much about their actual goals, but Ferdinand was fairly certain that they were both in pursuit of the exact same person. Granted, the only one that had to actually hide their goals was him. Garina could do just about whatever she wanted.

"I've always got prey," Garina said with a shrug. "Some are more important than others. Either way, nobody's found the one I'm looking for yet. Not the Apostles, and not your little church either. This is bait."

That's the first time she's directly pointed out that we're looking for the same person. That... might not be good for my safety.

"What makes you think they can afford a Rank 6 rune? What if our—"

"Our?" Garina arched an eyebrow.

Shit. I literally just took notice that she'd pointed it out. How did I slip up so badly?

"Your target. I misspoke," Ferdinand said quickly, but his back went stiff.

For several seconds, neither of them spoke. Then Garina gestured impatiently. "Then re-speak. Finish your damn sentence."

"Maybe I'm being presumptuous," Ferdinand said slowly, choosing his words as carefully as he could. "But you've never had trouble finding someone before. That means they aren't a Rank 7, so they aren't standing out from anyone else."

Garina rolled her eyes. "Yes. And?"

"Well, you obviously don't know who they are, or we wouldn't be sitting here. So you're assuming your target is from some massive family in this empire, right? Did they give you any reason to believe that?"

I'm straying too close to the dragon's den, but I can't find anyone on my own with Garina right next to me. Honestly, I don't think I want to find them anymore. Why am I even trying to help? Spending time relaxing in the nice forests of this backwater empire is a thousand times better than working. Either way, Garina definitely has some sort of plan. I should have stayed quiet.

"I—well, shit." Garina crossed her arms and leaned back in her chair. "That's really damn annoying. You might actually have a point."

"I do?"

"What a waste," Garina muttered. "I sent runes to just about every major city in the empire to see if I could draw my prey out. They've got power that a God wants! They've got to be one of the strongest mages, right?"

It didn't sound like that was a rhetorical question. Garina was actually asking his opinion.

I'm not even going to ask how she distributed those runes. I'm just glad they aren't mine. I'd have been tempted to buy one of those myself if I had the money for it.

"If they're that strong, it's possible they know people are looking for them," Ferdinand hedged. "And if I were them, I probably wouldn't want to be found. It's nice here. Peaceful. If they did choose this empire to reside in, wouldn't they try to keep a low profile?"

"Fuck," Garina said. She screwed her face up in annoyance, then thrust a finger in Ferdinand's direction. "This is why I keep you around. It's hard to think like a rat, so having one like yourself around to think in a similar manner is actually useful."

That's an odd way to say thank you. You're welcome, though.

"Maybe you should get your rune back?" Ferdinand suggested. "That's a big loss, and it's not like the money has any real worth to us. If they were runestones, it would be another thing, but I doubt they've even got those here."

Garina rolled her eyes. "I can't be bothered. Breaking cocky assholes over my knee is fun, but messing with someone who actually belongs in this empire would be like stomping on a child. It's not worth it."

Their conversation paused as a thunderous clap split the air. The auctioneer definitely knew what he was doing, constantly bringing everyone's attention back to him after the less interesting objects sold to make sure nobody missed a chance to spend their money.

"We'll be moving into some of the requests that your fellow attendees have placed with their attendants!" Rin called. "These will be ordered, as information requests are priced at flat rates rather than bids. Let's get started with our very first one!"

"Boring," Garina said, covering a yawn. "I've wasted enough time here. Say, did you make any sandwiches? I'm hungry."

"No," Ferdinand said. "You already ate them. Both of them."

"Oh, right. Why didn't you make more? You forgot to save one for yourself."

"Because the second one I made *was* meant for me," Ferdinand said, keeping his expression flat. "If you want food, you'll have to—"

"Our first information request is priced at one thousand gold! The request is simple—the location of the greatest restaurant within Arbitage grounds. If you believe you have a suitable answer, please contact your attendant. Please be aware that, when possible, information will be verified."

"Who spends gold on something like that?" Ferdinand asked. "What an—"

"That's brilliant," Garina said. "Saves me the trouble of looking myself. Why didn't I think of that?"

Ferdinand closed his mouth, thankful she'd spoken before he finished his sentence. It was only a few seconds before Rin spoke again.

"We've got some answers, and our team has evaluated and chosen the one that they believe to be the most accurate! Everyone with a matching answer was paid out an equal portion of the gold reward. Our next request is for the location that has a high concentration of Rank 3 or higher Earth-based monsters. The cap is fifteen thousand gold."

"Well, you've got a few million gold you don't need now," Ferdinand observed as Rin continued his sales pitches. "You could always put the same request that the other person did.

Garina started to nod, but before she could move toward their attendant, someone cleared their throat loudly, interrupting Rin mid-speech. Ferdinand's eyebrows raised as Rin turned, the annoyance clear in his posture.

A hulking figure stood at the edge of their viewing platform, barely contained by the clothes the Troupe had given them.

"Please keep the noise—" Rin started.

"This information isn't any good," the figure called out, their voice higher than Ferdinand had expected. They were female.

"If you have issues—"

"You told me the restaurant's name was Pillen's Fishhouse, but you didn't say where it was!" the woman exclaimed, her voice echoing through the room with nearly as much intensity as Rin's had.

"Ma'am, please turn the paper that your attendant gave you over," Rin said irritably. "It's on the other side."

There was a moment of silence. "Oh. Found it. Thanks."

Garina burst into laughter. "I wish that announcer didn't have a mask on. What do you think his face looked like? That's great. Getting his fancy auction interrupted because someone couldn't read a piece of paper... absolutely hilarious."

"And, better yet, I suppose we've found out where to get food," Ferdinand said. "As did everyone else in the amphitheater."

"Which means we should leave now," Garina said. "Every other idiot will be wasting time in here until the auction ends, but you've already pointed out that I've completely wasted both my time and energy. Let's go. The food at this place better be incredible, or I'm going to burn it to the ground."

Garina strode past Ferdinand and hurried to catch up with her. He wasn't sure if she was joking or not, but he strongly hoped he wouldn't have to find out.

Besides, some food would be nice. I'm starving. We haven't really spent much time in a town before now, though. I hope Garina can behave herself and avoid destroying anything too important.

Chapter Twenty-Eight

R in's voice echoed out through the amphitheater, fading into the distance behind Noah. The auction wasn't quite at a close yet, but he was out of gold, and nobody else had enough gold to afford any more purchases.

It's a good idea to leave early, regardless of money. No matter what the Troupe claims about safety and our identities being concealed, I'd rather be out early than try to maneuver my way around the other people leaving.

The large double doors were still cracked open, so they were able to slip out of the amphitheater and set off down the hall leading back into the dressing room. Lee led their party, her long strides taking her considerably farther than the rest of them. She kept turning corners, then pausing and twitching impatiently for the others to catch up.

Noah kept his senses peeled for anyone that might have been watching them, but at least as far as he was aware, there didn't seem to be any problems. They reached the dressing room and broke off into their respective rooms to retrieve their clothes and goods.

As soon as Noah's hand touched the imbued door, the energy within it shimmered and faded. The door swung open, revealing his belongings along with a few new additions. There was a bundle of Catchpaper protected by two thin pieces of leather lying on the ground, just in front of his grimoire.

And poking out the top of the grimoire was a tiny triangle of paper.

Noah's eyes narrowed. He shifted the bundle of paper to the side and picked his grimoire up. Even as he flipped it open, the little triangle of paper vanished into its depths—he could almost imagine a slurping noise as the book slurped what had likely been his runes up like a noodle.

"Figures," Noah muttered, flipping the book open. Its pages were blank, but he'd expected that. "I hope you didn't eat any of Lee's runes. We're going to need those soon. Actually, I'm going to need mine soon as well. Don't get too attached."

The book closed itself on his hand. Noah cursed, yanking his hand free and shaking it off. It hadn't hurt so much as stung, but he still glared at the grimoire. The eye on its cover rippled, blinking up at him before fading back into the leather.

"Brat." Noah changed into his normal clothes and gathered the rest of his belongings. When he was done, he flipped through the leather-wrapped bundle of Catchpaper. Luckily, it looked that whoever had sold Lee's runes had wrapped them for safety, and that had kept his grimoire from eating any more.

Noah tucked the bundle into his travel bag and slung his grimoire over his shoulder, striding back out into the main room. The others had all already finished and were waiting in a small group in the corner. Lee had returned to her normal form and size.

"Sorry. Technical difficulties," Noah said. "I've got your runes, Lee. Do you want them now?"

"Can you hold onto them until we can actually fix stuff?" Lee asked. "I'm not very good at keeping things that aren't already inside my body. I lose them. Or eat them."

"Consider it done. In that case, I want to—"

"Get food!" Lee exclaimed, thrusting a finger up. "We're going to Pillen's Fishhouse. I paid a lot of gold for that information, so we can't waste it."

Yeah. And then you shared it with literally everyone in the auction house before we could stop you. Besides, I want to upgrade my runes...

"We can go some other—"

Lee's eyes bored into Noah's, large and watery. Her lip trembled—and he could swear that her eyes were actually growing larger. Lee was changing the shape of her face to better mimic the pleading eyes of a small, starving puppy.

"Oh, goddamn it. Fine," Noah grumbled.

Lee's face snapped back to normal and she beamed. "Great!"

"I think you just got played," Moxie said as they all followed Lee up the stairs.

"The jokes on her. I don't have any money," Noah said with a grin. "She's going to have to pay for my meal."

"You know, didn't we have a bet about having to cook a meal that got interrupted by... well, a lot of shit?" Moxie cast a glance in Karina and Contessa's direction, clearly not wanting to say too much in their presence.

"Huh. Yeah, we did," Noah said. "As I recall, I'm pretty sure we all lost. We should get around to doing that. It's been a while since I've cooked anything, but it could be fun. Just make sure Lee isn't the one that chooses the ingredients when we get around to it."

They continued up the stairs, soon emerging from the small house and stepping back into the starry night.

Lee held up the piece of paper that she'd bought at the auction, squinting at the back before lowering it and glancing around. She pointed down the path. "That way."

"Do you still need our help?" Karina asked, shifting her weight from foot to foot. "Because, if not, I'd like to go to bed."

"As would I," Contessa said. "I need to get some food for Mascot as well. I don't know if he's eaten today."

"Yeah, sure. Thanks for your help getting us in, ladies." Noah started to nod, then paused. "Wait, Mascot eats?"

"Yeah. You didn't know?" Contessa frowned. "He eats a lot."

"Huh. I guess he always just hunted for food... or something? I didn't think he needed to eat."

Why does a manifestation of my rune need food? Or does it just find eating fun? I wouldn't put it past the little bugger.

Contessa and Karina both broke away while Noah was lost in thought, setting off for Building T at a brisk pace. Lee grabbed Noah and Moxie's hands.

"Come on! Let's go. I'm hungry."

For a moment, it felt like a child pulling their parents through a theme park toward her favorite ride. That feeling immediately vanished when Lee nearly yanked Noah off his feet. He started off with her, reminded that Lee was more than capable of sprinting the entire way over to the restaurant while waving him and Moxie over her head like kites.

"Where'd you put the directions?" Noah asked as Lee led them down the road. "I thought you needed them."

"Memorized 'em," Lee replied, taking a turn down the road and accelerating. She licked her lips. "How many fish do you think I can buy with nine thousand gold?"

"I think you should probably save some for a later date," Noah suggested. "If you spend it all now, then you won't have any money to buy food with later."

"That seems like a problem for me to deal with later," Lee said, scrunching her nose. "I want to eat now."

"By the way—Lee, why did you call out to the announcer about the restaurant?" Noah asked. "You easily could have found it just by asking an attendant or just by smelling it out, no?"

Lee slowed, nearly coming to a stop as she turned to look back at Noah.

"Yeah. I probably could have."

"Then—"

"But, this way, lots of people will be able to find out about it and enjoy the food." Lee shrugged. "Why would I try to hide that? It's not like I can't eat if they can, and most of them probably wouldn't spend money on buying something like a restaurant name."

Lee set back off, moving faster than she had been before and forcing the others to jog to keep up. Noah mulled over her words, but he didn't have much time to think. Lee jerked to a halt and Noah nearly tripped over her. He managed to catch himself at the last second, stepping past Lee to avoid bulldozing her.

They stood next to a long, single-story building made of wood. A rickety sign hung from the top of the open door, so old and faded that Noah had to squint to make anything out. He was fairly sure there had once been a fish and some words carved on it, but now all that remained was a vague, ovular outline.

The building was one strong breeze away from falling over. There weren't any windows—just holes in the wall to see out of. They'd been placed just above head height, so he couldn't see inside through them.

"This is it," Lee said.

"It looks... interesting," Moxie said diplomatically.

I think we might have gotten scammed.

"It smells good." Lee pushed the door, and it opened with a loud squeak to reveal the interior of the restaurant.

It was made up of a single, large room with an open door to what Noah suspected to be a kitchen on the back wall. The room had several long tables running along its middle, each large enough to seat a dozen people.

There were a few smaller tables sized for six at the sides of the room, but there weren't any smaller ones. And, to Noah's surprise, almost every single table was full. The room was bustling. Low chatter buzzed in the air, far quieter than it should have been.

A swirling pattern on the wood to his side caught Noah's eye. He peered closer at it, but he already knew what he was going to find. It was an Imbuement. And, now that he'd seen the first swirl, it wasn't hard to locate the other patterns covering the walls and ground.

This whole place is imbued like a fortress. Holy shit.

A man with a thick mop of black hair wearing a blood-splattered white apron strode up to them, and Noah nearly reached for his magic to defend himself. There was such an intense scowl on the man's face that he looked like he was an inch from trying to run them through.

"How many?" The man spoke with a strong accent that Noah couldn't place, and it wasn't helped by the fish bone he was using as a toothpick.

"Three," Lee said. "We want food."

"We don't seat three. You fine sharing a table?"

"Don't care," Lee said. "Just give me food. I smell it in your kitchen."

A corner of the man's mouth quirked up in what was possibly the smallest smile ever recorded in human history. He nodded over to one of the smaller, six-person tables where a man and a woman already sat. "Good. That's the only damn thing you're going to get. Go sit down over there. Those two just arrived, so you won't have to sit and watch them eat while you wait for your own meal."

"Thanks!" Lee said. She strode through the room, slipping by waiters—all of whom seemed to wear a splattered apron. Noah wasn't sure if the blood was part of the uniform or if they all just liked brutally murdering the fish they worked with, but he decided not to ask.

They approached the table. Noah almost missed a step as he got a closer look at the two people at their table. The woman's skin was so pale that it was practically pure white, which only made her dark red, almost black lips stand out even sharper. Long, black hair framed her face and hung low at her back. She had a spiked choker around her throat, and the spikes looked like they were real. The woman's features were beautiful, but in the most unsettling way that Noah could use the word. Haunting might have been more accurate.

The man across from her only made the woman stand out even more. If she was a freezing winter, then he was the warm summer. His face was plain and kind, clean shaven of any hair. While his cheeks weren't exactly round, they certainly weren't chiseled either.

For a moment, Noah felt like the man seemed familiar, but he couldn't place anything about him. Lee sat down on the long bench beside the woman, not even bothering to introduce herself.

"What are you doing?" the woman asked, her eyes sharp as she turned to glare at Lee.

"I am sitting. This is our table," Lee replied. She spotted a menu lying between the man and the woman and snagged it.

"What is a d—"

"Garina, please," the man said hurriedly, holding his hands up. "This is a group restaurant. They seat people together. Look at the other tables."

"I did not ask to be seated next to others. You try my patience, Ferd."

"Ferd? Why are you—ah, never mind. This is just how it works here. We could always go somewhere else if you'd prefer?" the man offered, giving Garina a placating smile. Noah didn't miss the flicker of worry that passed through his expression.

For a moment, Garina didn't respond. Her lips pressed thin and she shrugged. "Fine. If this is how it's done, then I suppose I would be remiss in being standoffish. What a pain."

Nice lady.

Noah took the spot beside Lee, and Moxie sat down beside him. Lee's eyes darted over to the menu between Garina and Ferd. Noah was pretty sure that Garina was studying it, but for some reason she hadn't picked it up.

Lee didn't notice—or, more likely, she didn't care. She reached over, snagging the menu and bringing it over to herself. One of Garina's eyes followed the menu's path. Noah cleared his throat.

"Nice to meet you. I'm Vermil. The little one is Lee, and this is Moxie."

"A pleasure to make your acquaintance," Ferd said with an easygoing smile. "Garina and I are... traveling through the empire. We heard that this location was interesting, so we decided to make a stop. Please excuse my companion's harsh tone. She means nothing by—"

There was a thump, and Ferd grunted. Noah was pretty sure Garina had just kicked him under the table. Moxie sent Noah an amused look, and he gave her a small shrug in response.

Looks like we got a table next to some weirdos. The guy seems nice enough at least. As long as we don't interact with them too much, it should be fine.

"So, what are you going to order?" Ferd asked Garina, clearly trying to keep her attention on him.

"There was a dish called the Weeping Sawtooth. It sounded fun, so I'll get that."

That sounds like a weapon.

"I was going to go with a plain sunfish. It seems like a good spot to start," Ferd said.

"Nice and plain," Garina said, a small grin pulling at her lips. "What a coincidence. Just like you."

"I am sure I will enjoy it regardless. Appreciating the finer things in life is one of Her greatest teachings. We must enjoy—"

"Is She here?" Garina asked, leaning forward and arching an eyebrow.

Ferd cleared his throat. "No."

"In that case, the only woman whose teachings you should be concerned about are mine." Garina flashed him a grin, and Noah caught a flash of pointed, sharklike teeth.

Ah, fantastic. Definitely weirdos. Whatever. I don't care. It looks like they're occupied with each other, so as long as—

"Whoa," Lee said, staring straight at Garina. "Your teeth are really pointy. How do you avoid biting your tongue?"

Goddamn it.

Chapter Twenty-Nine

"My teeth?" Garina blinked, tilting her head to the side. Noah wasn't sure if she was completely baffled or an inch from losing her cool.

"Yeah. Mine are sharp too, see?" Lee opened her mouth and pulled her cheek to the side to give Garina a better look at her palate. "But yours are way sharper. You've got to bite your mouth all the time."

"Lee, don't bother her too much please," Noah said. "She's trying to eat dinner, just like us."

"You don't have pointy teeth. You don't understand," Lee said. "I used to bite myself all the time until I made mine shorter, but hers are really big. Like a monster's."

Ferd shifted uncomfortably on the other side of the table. Noah prepared to draw on his magic—he didn't know what rank Garina was, but he didn't want to find out.

But to his surprise, instead of the fury that Noah had expected, a grin passed over Garina's lips. "You like my teeth?"

"Yeah," Lee said with a nod.

"They weren't easy to get," Garina said, pulling her own cheek to the side so Lee could get a better look into her own mouth. She continued speaking with her hand in her mouth, muffling her words. "I grew them myself, using materials I gathered from one of my greatest enemies. It took years of refining before they were worth using."

"Wow," Lee said. And then—to Noah's horror—Lee reached up and tugged at one of Garina's teeth. "They feel really strong. Have you ever bitten your tongue with them?"

Garina burst into laughter. Luckily, Lee removed her hand in time to avoid getting it chomped. Noah and Ferd exchanged a completely baffled look, and Garina slapped Lee on the back.

"I'm very aware of my entire body," Garina said, speaking through her laughter. "I haven't bit myself in a very, very long time. I've bitten a few other people, though. And I've never had someone stick their hand in my mouth voluntarily, and that's saying a lot. There aren't many things I haven't experienced yet."

"Oh. Well, you're welcome," Lee said.

"You're welcome?" Garina, who had only just started to get herself under control, started to laugh again. "Look at the arrogance on this little thing! She's got more balls than the entirety of your church, Ferd."

Ferdinand's eye twitched, but the smile remained on his face. "She does not know what we do. Ignorance can be a shield."

"I love it when you get scared," Garina said, flashing a deeply unsettling smile in Ferd's direction. "Perhaps coming to this little back-water location was worth it after all. I don't get amusement like this often."

Lee handed the menu over to Noah, but at this point, he was more interested in the two others at their table than he was in ordering food. He gave it a quick glance, then picked out a dish at random and gave the menu to Moxie.

"You said you were traveling through the area, right?" Noah asked, hoping to steer the conversation away from Garina's teeth. She seemed fine with it for the time being, but encouraging Lee to poke at other people's teeth sounded like a great way to wake up one day with her hand in his mouth. "What for?"

"I'm trying to find someone who stole something important," Garina replied, cracking her neck. A chill ran down Noah's spine. He wasn't sure what it was about her, but his senses were *not* a fan of Garina. She, for lack of a better word, scared him.

"What of you?" Ferd asked. "Are you a local?"

"I'm a professor here," Noah said. He nodded to Moxie. "As is Moxie. Lee is an assistant professor."

"She seems... young for a professor. All of you do," Ferd said. "I mean no offense, of course."

"Who cares about how young they are?" Garina asked. "Look at the little one. She's bold, and she actually respects the other two. That means they're stronger than she is."

"Not everyone you respect has to be stronger than you are," Ferd said.

"That's an excuse the weak give to justify their subservience," Garina said with a scoff. "The weak respect the strong because they fear them. That's the way of the world. I could see passing fancy for someone weaker—but if someone weak claims to respect someone strong for any reason other than their strength, it's a lie."

"I don't think that's true," Lee said.

Garina looked down at her, a frown crossing her lips. "Oh? What do you think, then? What reason do you have to respect anyone if they're weak?"

"Well, I don't know about weak or not, but I don't really consider that. I'm always going to be better at some things than others. Vermil has more magic than me, but I'm faster than him. That doesn't mean I respect him less or more."

"That's because your power likely balances out in other ways," Garina said with a dismissive wave. "Relationships are transactional. The only reason to respect someone is because you get something from them."

"No."

Garina's frown deepened. "No? Are you implying I'm wrong?"

"Yep."

"Garina, perhaps we should move on from this topic," Ferd said, a note of worry entering his voice. "We don't need to start an argument."

"Shut up," Garina said, her eyes locked with Lee's. "Go on, then. Tell me what I'm wrong about. What have I missed?"

"You do things for other people because you love them," Lee said, crossing her arms and not backing down in the slightest. "Not because you know they'll do something in return."

Garina snorted in derision. "Because you love them? So—what, if you knew that someone you *loved* was never going to return the effort you spent on them, you'd keep doing it?"

"Yeah. That's what love is."

"That's just weakness."

Lee shook her head. "You're wrong. I used to think the same thing, but that isn't true. Loving people means you're strong. The weak thing is to claim that you only respect strong people. Strong people can be assholes, and assholes don't deserve respect."

Garina's face was like a block of ice. Noah wanted to grab Lee and redirect her attention to the menu, but it was clear that interfering now would only make things worse.

With every word that comes out of Garina's mouth, I'm becoming more convinced that she's a really high rank. That attitude paired with the way she's talking about everything being backwater... shit. Is she from outside the Empire?

"Enlighten me, then. How does giving yourself liabilities prove strength?" Garina asked.

"Because you need to be strong enough to protect them, and if you aren't, you push yourself harder until you can. If you only respect out of fear, then you don't actually have any friends. You must be really lonely."

Ferd looked like he wanted to say something, but the tension between Lee and Garina was so intense that the words died on his lips before they could ever take life. Out of the corner of his eye, Noah saw Moxie rolling a seed between her fingers, ready to call on her magic if the situation got worse.

"And what about when the people you claim to love betray you?" Garina challenged. "What happens when someone stronger shows up and you can't protect them? What you describe is weakness."

"And it sounds like you're just alone," Lee replied. "What happens when you find someone too strong to defeat on your own?"

"That can't happen if you *are* the strongest person."

"There's always someone stronger," Lee said. "And even if you were that strong, what's the point? It sounds boring and lonely. What do you do, just keep practicing to make sure nobody ever gets as strong as you? I bet the weak people that are actually hanging out with each other would have more fun."

Before Garina could respond, rescue arrived in the form of a waiter. The man who had seated them approached their table, completely and blissfully unaware of the argument going down on one of the benches.

"Orders?" he asked, his gruff voice making it clear that he wasn't looking to spend much time speaking.

"I want whatever you think tastes the best," Lee said, her eyes lighting up as she lost interest in her argument with Garina. "Surprise me, but make it big, please."

"Done," the waiter said. "Next?"

Garina looked at Lee in disbelief—likely trying to get over the cognitive whiplash. Lee had gone from ready to fight to cheerful in a split instant. After a moment, she let out a huff.

"Give me the Weeping Sawtooth," Garina said, still watching Lee.

The rest of the table put their orders in as well, and the waiter departed as quickly as he arrived. Mercifully, neither Lee nor Garina said anything else. The table remained silent for several minutes, the tension surrounding everyone so dense that it could have been cut with a knife.

Their waiter emerged from the kitchen a short time later, bearing five plates in his arms in an impressive juggling act. He slid them across the table and departed in the same motion. The food looked and smelled delicious.

Well—most of it did. Noah and Moxie both had some sort of breaded fish before them, and it was absolutely glistening with just the right amount of grease. It was served with a small, colorful salad and a speckled white sauce that looked remarkably similar to tartar sauce on Earth.

Lee had received a massive pile of beautifully cooked fish, each one seasoned and prepared in a different way. Across from her, Ferd had a single, large fish. It looked tasty, but it was, as Garina had pointed out, rather plain.

The dish that Noah's eyes were fixed on wasn't his or Lee's or Ferd's, though. It was Garina's. It was a large, bulbous fish with spines jutting out of it in every direction. While its flesh looked cooked to perfection, there were so many spikes on the thing that it felt like eating it would have been a massive chore.

"I think I prefer my plain fish," Ferd said, breaking their silence.

Garina glared at Ferd. "Coward."

"But a happy one," Ferd replied, cutting a slice of his meal away and taking a bite. His eyebrows rose as he chewed and swallowed.

"That's actually quite spectacular. Some of the best cooking I've had in a long time."

That was all it took for Noah and Moxie to dig in. The faster they ate, the sooner they could get Lee away from Garina without causing too much of a scene.

And, on Lee's part, she wasted absolutely no time in devouring the top three fish of her pile in rapid-fire succession. They vanished down her gullet in an impressive disappearing act.

"This is incredible," Lee said, licking her lips. She paused as she lifted the next small fish to her mouth, then held it out to Noah. "Do you want to try?"

"Sure," Noah said, taking it from her. Lee handed another one to Moxie, who gave her an appreciative nod as she claimed it.

Noah had to admit that Lee must have won the waiter or the chef over because her meal was definitely better than his, and that was saying quite a bit.

"You're right. That was delicious," Noah said. "Want some of mine?"

He cut a piece of his fish off pre-emptively—there were certain precautions that one had to take with Lee when sharing food if one wanted to keep any for themselves.

"Thanks!" Lee tossed the piece into her mouth and paused for a moment. "Mine was better."

"Yeah," Noah admitted wryly. "They're both great, though."

Out of the corner of his eye, Noah spotted Garina poking at her fish. She was clearly trying to find the proper way to eat it. Something about the scene almost made Noah laugh. He was completely confident she was at least Rank 5, if not considerably higher, so she definitely could have eaten the whole thing and not blinked an eye if she wanted to, but that probably wouldn't have been particularly enjoyable.

For all that talk of being strong, it's nice to actually sit down and relax sometimes. Hard to do that when your meal is actively fighting back. I guess that lives up to her ideals, though. Having the power that lets you eat the spiky fish is more important than enjoying eating it, eh?

"Your fish looks spiky," Lee said through a mouthful of fish.

"Yes," Garina said curtly. "It is."

Lee pushed her own plate—still piled high with fish—over to Garina. She then snagged the taller woman's plate and dragged it over to herself.

"There," Lee said. "You look hungry, so you can have mine."

Chapter Thirty

Garina stared at Lee in shock, but Lee was far more preoccupied with the new meal she'd claimed for herself. She studied the spiny fish for a few seconds, then raised the whole thing to her mouth and took a bite—from the spines.

Loud cracking noises came from her mouth as she chewed. A moment later, she swallowed. "Mm. Crunchy. That's good."

She didn't give Garina any time to ask for her meal back. Within just a few seconds, Lee had mowed through the majority of the spikey fish, leaving Garina with nothing but the food Lee had given her.

After one last glance at Lee, Garina snagged one of the much-easier-to-eat fishes from Lee's plate and popped the whole thing into her mouth. And, even in spite of her cold features, a look of delight spread across her features.

"This is actually pretty good," Garina allowed.

Disaster seemingly averted, everyone dug into their meals in full. Lee, as usual, was the first to finish, but the others didn't take much longer. The food was fantastic, and before long, all of their plates had been polished clean.

Lee let out a curse and rubbed at her mouth.

"I bit my tongue," Lee said, scrunching her nose in annoyance. "I don't get how you haven't bitten yourself while we were talking. These teeth are too long."

"Did you… copy my teeth?" Garina asked in disbelief.

"Yeah. I told you they looked cool, didn't I?" Lee asked, giving Garina an open-mouthed smile. "They're not very functional, though. Why'd you make them so big? Was it just because they looked cool?"

Garina looked down at her own empty plate, then cleared her throat. "I'd never make a decision for such a petty reason. My only concern is accomplishing my goals, not how I look while doing it."

Lee shrugged. "Okay. Thanks for the fish. It tasted good."

Garina's brow furrowed. "I don't understand you at all."

"Thanks."

"That wasn't a compliment," Garina said. "Your order was clearly better than mine. Why did you swap our plates, then thank me for giving you the worse one?"

"Because it looked like you didn't like the spikey thing, and I knew I'd like it just as much as the stuff I ordered, so more people would be happy if we swapped."

"We have nothing between us. Beyond that—we're clearly directly opposed. Your view of life is stupid and infantile. What's the point of doing something like that?" Garina demanded. "We have no reason to help each other."

"I don't need a reason. It's fun to make people happy, and it's not like I got any sadder because of it." Lee shrugged. "And you liked my fish more than yours, right? So I was right. Thus, you were wrong, not me."

"Are you saying that my acceptance of your fish is equivalent to losing our argument?"

"Yep."

"That has absolutely nothing to do with it, though!"

"You're the one who took the fish," Lee said with a snicker. "I didn't give it to you because I'm scared of you. How do you justify that?"

Garina opened her mouth, then closed it as her brow furrowed in abject confusion. Noah didn't blame her. Half the time, he didn't understand Lee either.

The waiter returned to their table, and everyone paid for their meals. The prices were high, but Lee didn't even blink at having to pay for his food. Everyone's food had run around fifty gold, which was obscenely expensive for a single meal—but Noah couldn't help but feel that it had been worth it.

"Okay. Nice meeting you," Lee said. "I want to sleep now. Can we go back?"

"Sure," Noah said with a relieved laugh. It looked like they were somehow going to make it out of this without a fight. "It's been a pleasure. I hope the two of you find the thing you're looking for."

"Thanks," Ferd said, raising a hand in farewell as Noah's group left.

He and Garina remained at the table in silence until the waiter came to kick them out and make room for the next customers.

* * *

"Why did you shorten my name?" Ferdinand asked.

Garina shrugged. "I don't want people spreading word about you. Could end up bringing more of the rats from your church over here to bother me. Much easier to handle things if nobody knows what happened to you."

It was a threat, but for Garina, it felt oddly hollow. A small frown creased Ferdinand's face.

"You seem... off," Ferdinand said hesitantly, half-wondering why he was even bothering to speak. Garina hadn't once spoken about herself, nor had he broached personal topics on his own end. Their ability to travel together was built entirely on *not* understanding each other.

The moment Garina knows for a fact that I came here with intention to break one of the Rules, I'm dead. I've already stumbled too many times, so the wisest thing to do would just be to remain silent.

So why am I talking?

"What's that meant to mean?" Garina asked, coming to a stop at a stone bench beside a park they were walking by. They'd left the restaurant a few minutes ago and had just been continuing in silence ever since. Garina stared into the twisting foliage, partially turned away from him.

It's not like I can just say nothing now. That would only annoy her even more.

"You're less... you," Ferdinand said.

"What, do you want me to kill someone?" Garina asked with a snort. "Or maybe threaten you?"

"I'm not saying it would make me feel more comfortable, but I suppose it would seem more normal. Please refrain from killing someone that doesn't need it, though."

"I'm the damn Gatekeeper," Garina said, turning to fully face Ferdinand. She looked more frustrated than he'd ever seen her. "Do you really think that I'd go around killing random people that I protect? Is that actually what you believe I stand for?"

"I don't know," Ferdinand replied honestly. "I don't know you that well, Garina. I know the woman that you're meant to be, and the rumors do not entirely line up with who you seem to be, but that does not mean I know you completely. Just because I don't *think* you'd do something does not mean you are incapable of it—and, on the contrary, I suspect that stating you are unable to do something would likely cause you to do that very thing."

Garina let out a bark of laughter. "Honest to a tee. I suppose I should have expected that."

As if anything we've shared is truly honest.

"What did you think of the little demon girl?" Garina asked, abruptly changing the subject. "For a Rank 3, she was awfully cocky. Had quite the mouth on her. It must have been quite the experience for you—the Church of Repose despises demons, does it not?"

"It was... odd," Ferdinand said, inclining his head in agreement. "She is like no demon that I have ever met. She was genuine, but the Church would likely be at odds with her should she reach Rank 7 and leave this empire. I did not expect to find someone with such fervent views out here."

"Neither did I." Garina sat down and crossed one of her legs over the other. Ferdinand stood awkwardly beside her for a few moments, then slowly sat down on the bench beside her. A few moments passed before Garina spoke again. "You didn't say if you believed what she said, though."

"I think she is naïve. I do not agree with your view on power, as it stands in direct opposition to the Church. Repose says that—"

"Oh, damn your god," Garina snapped. "Give me your answer."

"I think she is admirable," Ferdinand said, a small grin flitting across his lips. "I never had such strong views on anything. I joined the Church because one of their mages came to my village when I was young, saving it from a powerful monster."

"That seems like a pretty clear view to me," Garina said. "You joined looking for power."

Ferdinand laughed. "No. I joined because it was safe. I knew that my home had survived the first attack, but the Church would not always be present—and so I went with them. I studied not because I cared for magic, but because I wanted to live."

"So you don't believe in their teachings at all?" Garina crossed her arms. "You've sure done a lot of preaching for someone who doesn't care."

"Another thing I took on. I do not *disagree* with the Church of Repose," Ferdinand replied, still not sure why he was giving Garina as much information as he was. "I think they do good in the world. They gave me powerful runes and have ensured that I do not want for much, so I have done my work dutifully, for the most part. On the other hand, Lee actually believed what she said. I find that respectable."

"So do you agree with her or not?" Garina demanded. "Stop skirting the damn question."

"She said a lot of things," Ferdinand said carefully. "I did not agree with all of them, but I did with some. I think that power is a means to an end rather than an ultimate goal, and the pursuit of it is not fulfilling. I do not feel as strongly as she did about love, though. Perhaps I would if I had established any meaningful connections within the Church, but alas, that never happened."

Garina leaned back, looking up into the night sky. "You disagree that power is the only thing we need, then."

"I do. I do not think power makes people respect you. It makes them fear you."

"There's nothing wrong with being feared. It's no different than being awed, which is what the avatar of your church does."

"It is," Ferdinand allowed. "And I'd imagine both paths are equally as lonesome."

"You're suddenly really philosophical. Did you decide that you weren't scared of me anymore?"

"I think anyone who isn't scared of you is a fool," Ferdinand said with a dry laugh. "But I have spent enough time in your presence to believe that you would not kill me for no reason. Perhaps you will prove me wrong."

Garina grunted. Ferdinand snuck a glance at her out of the corner of his eye, and he was surprised to find that she was studying the ground, a small frown on her lips and her expression downcast.

"I'm not sure if it means much, but I find your company rather enjoyable when you aren't trying to kill me," Ferdinand said. "It would have been boring traveling alone."

Garina looked up at him, a flash of surprise crossing her face before she snuffed it out. "Very funny. Softening me up isn't going to work, though. I prefer it when my men are scared."

"Then I suspect you rarely have issues in that department."

"Flatterer," Garina said, rolling her eyes. Her stomach rumbled, and she cleared her throat as Ferdinand gave her an aghast look.

"You're still hungry?"

"Got a problem with that?"

"No. It was just a question." Ferdinand reached into his bag and pulled out a wrapped package, revealing a sandwich within it. The sandwich had gotten rather squished, but it still looked mostly as it should. He held it out. "Here."

Garina eyed the sandwich, then took it from his hands. "You said you were out."

"I lied."

"Do you have any more?" Garina's tone made it clear that lying again was going to be disadvantageous for Ferdinand's continued health.

"I'm afraid not. That's it. I'll make more tomorrow."

Garina grunted. She took a bite out of the sandwich, and the two sat in silence for a few more seconds. Ferdinand busied himself studying the garden. It wasn't the most beautiful garden he'd ever seen —the Church had a grand one that would have put anything in the Arbalest Empire to shame.

No, the garden in front of him was fairly plain. In some ways, it was almost ugly. The vines were sharp and thorny, and there were far too few flowers. Even the scents were weak—and yet, it was still enjoyable.

Garina touched Ferdinand on the shoulder, and he nearly leapt out of his skin in surprise. He looked down to find that she was holding out one half of his sandwich. Blinking in disbelief, he took it.

"Don't get used to it." Garina's eyes were firmly fixed on the garden before them. "And make more next time."

"I'll keep that in mind."

Chapter Thirty-One

No sooner than Noah stepped through the door of Moxie's room did he dart for her bed, practically jumping into it. Moxie just let out a defeated sigh as he pulled his grimoire open, flipping it to a blank page in preparation to start reworking his runes.

"Let me know if something important happens," Noah said. "I'm probably going to be distracted for a little while."

"Will do," Lee promised, already ruffling through his travel bag in search of either food or her runes—and Noah suspected it was the former.

The book evidently sensed Noah's intentions because the runes he'd bought in the auction appeared on the pages before him. Energy pulsed off the paper as Noah brushed his hands along it, tingling against his skin. He took care to avoid directly touching the Rank 4 runes yet—they would give him a nasty sting, and he wanted to handle them with Sunder immediately when the time came.

The runes were complex, but he'd gotten used to memorizing them. Within a minute, he'd committed the patterns to memory.

Moxie sat down beside Noah as he closed his eyes and leaned back, leaving one of his hands on top of the grimoire. Darkness bloomed as he slipped into his mindspace, and the familiar pressure of his runes greeted him.

"Time to give you lot a makeover," Noah said, mostly to himself. It wasn't like his runes could hear him. At least, he strongly hoped they couldn't.

It would have some deeply concerning results if they could.

Noah forced himself to pay attention to the actual task at hand. He'd purchased three runes for himself in the auction—the one from the Stormprince Elemental, a Towering Frozen Glacier at Rank 4, and a Scorching Flame at Rank 3.

At the moment, he needed three new Disaster Runes. He already knew what they'd be—Thunderstorm, Blizzard, and something related to fire. Pyroclastic Resonance had proved to be invaluable, but with the extra experience he had under his belt, it also felt limited.

I'm pretty sure the majority of the runes I need for Thunderstorm will come from the Stormprince Elemental's rune, and the same for Blizzard. Those are both Rank 4 runes, so they'll be more of a pain to do. That leaves me with the fire-based one to start with.

Well, nothing screams a fire disaster like a volcano. That or lava, but I think lava is more of a hot rock than an actual disaster. It's the volcano that causes it, so that's what I'll go with.

Noah sent a mental request to the grimoire, then raised a finger and started to draw. Energy poured down his arm, turning into a glowing orange light at his fingertip. Stroke by stroke, Noah brought Scorching Flame into being within his mindspace.

Before long, a new rune was crackling beside his others. Whoever had sold it hadn't been skimping—the rune was over three quarters of the way full. Something told Noah it had probably been even more full before his grimoire had gotten its grubby mouth on it, but he didn't mind a little energy loss in exchange for how useful the artifact was.

He gazed upon his new Rank 3 rune, which had several glorious seconds of existence, standing proud beside its brethren, before Sunder carved through it like an executioner's axe.

Power poured out of the shattered rune, and seven Fire Runes swirled away from its center in a wave of orange energy.

The Rank 2 runes were all pure Fire Runes, and it only took a moment to confirm that five of the seven were perfect.

Well, there's definitely a big benefit to going almost entirely with a single element. If you ignore the side effect of destabilizing your soul and eventually becoming completely crippled and unable to advance further, not bad at all.

Noah worked quickly, grabbing two left-over Earth Runes they'd gotten while hunting and the last of his Vibration Runes, swapping out three of the Fire Runes for them.

They weren't all full, but cannibalizing some of the energy left over from Scorching Flame energy was more than enough to top everything else off. Without much hesitation, Noah's intent slammed down on the seven runes, forcing them together.

He squeezed his eyes shut for a moment before a flash filled his mindspace. When they opened once more, a huge grin stretched across Noah's face. Before him floated a Volcano Rune at Rank 3, a perfect 10 percent full.

Noah gathered all the excess energy left over from Scorching Flame, pushing it into Volcano and taking it up to just under halfway full. He'd lost a fair amount of energy by filling up his Earth and Vibration Runes, but overall, it had been a pretty effective combination.

After putting the new rune through several tests to make sure that it was truly perfect, Noah finally released Volcano and let it float over to join his other runes.

One more down, two to go.

The last two runes he had to modify were both already Rank 4, which meant there would be a whole lot more energy to work with. Noah was confident his soul would have room to hold the excess power once he Sundered them, but he'd have to be fast if he wanted to avoid losing too much of it.

I could always wait and try to reach Rank 4 a little slower, but fuck that. I've been waiting for too long. I'm reaching Rank 4 today, and screw how much energy ends up getting wasted in the process.

Towering Frozen Glacier is up first. Once I Sunder it, I need to grab the Ice Rune with the least complexity to it as fast as possible and then split that one up, fixing it with the Ice Runes that I've got left over from my previous attempt at a Blizzard Rune. Hopefully I have enough. If I do, then I can reform the new Blizzard Rune and imbue all the extra stuff back into the grimoire. If I don't, I split another rune and use the constituents from that to patch up anything I'm missing.

Noah rubbed his hands together, steadying himself. He prepared to open his eyes to look at the grimoire, then immediately realized there was a slight problem. The rune he needed to Sunder was currently on his artifact, and he didn't want to start chopping the artifact up.

Lee was able to briefly handle a Rank 4 in her soul. I guess I'll have to do the same. As long as I'm fast, it should be fine.

That wasn't the most reassuring strategy, but Noah wasn't too concerned about soul damage when he had the Fragment of Renewal to call on. He extended his senses and called on the grimoire, drawing the Towering Frozen Glacier Rune from within it.

Moving as fast as he dared, Noah drew the Rank 4 rune in his mindspace. Almost immediately, pressure slammed into him like a stormfront. He gritted his teeth, calling on his other runes to repress the power driving into him like a violent gale.

Sunder and the Fragment of Renewal were the tipping point, and to Noah's surprise, he actually felt Towering Frozen Glacier give before their might. The rune snapped into being in Noah's mind with a brilliant crash.

Cracks spiderwebbed out across the floor of his soul, spilling glowing white light out. Noah wasted no time in grabbing Sunder and carving the Rank 4 rune apart. A sigh of relief slipped from his lips as it shattered.

Energy slammed into him like a tidal wave, but Noah was ready for it. Even as the Rank 3 components of the rune appeared, his eyes landed on an Encroaching Ice Rune that looked like it would fit his purposes perfectly.

He Sundered it, then scanned over the runes that bloomed from within it. It had three Rank 2 True Ice Runes with perfect pressure, but the other components weren't as good. Noah Sundered a second Encroaching Ice Rune, ripping two more True Ice Runes from it and adding them together with the three from the first Rank 3 rune he'd split. Noah then pulled two Wind Runes from the grimoire and tossed them into the mix.

His soul was starting to feel the pressure of all the runes he had floating around in it, but it wasn't quite full yet—and Noah didn't plan to spend even a second wasting time looking at anything other than his task at hand.

Noah reformed the runes into Blizzard, but the result that emerged was only 15 percent full. He'd been slightly distracted by the rush, and his intent or combination hadn't been perfect. Repressing a curse, Noah Sundered it once more. He swapped another one of the Ice

Runes out for one of the extra Wind Runes he had, then reformed Blizzard.

This time, he was rewarded with a rune that was 10 percent full. He didn't even have time to grin. There was too much power that was just fading away with every second that he let slip by.

Noah shoved the Blizzard Rune full of energy, shooting it all the way up to completely full before pouring the excess power into Volcano.

The conversion rate between the Fire-based rune and the Ice-based rune was so horrible that he barely managed to fill it before the last of the power faded away. For some reason, it seemed considerably harder to fill the higher-ranked runes.

Are the runes actively resisting getting filled in the way I'm doing it? That's interesting. I don't think it's a problem for right now, but it's definitely something I should mention to Moxie. The more I understand about runes, the more I realize just how little everyone really knows about them—myself included.

Difficulties or not, Noah now had one more Rank 3 rune in his soul, bringing him up to a total of six of the seven full Rank 3s that he needed for Natural Disaster. The original, imperfect Natural Disaster took up the final active slot in his mind. He also had five Rank 3 runes left over from Towering Freezing Glacier filling up his mindspace—not to mention the remains of the Encroaching Ice Runes he'd just ripped up. All of it went straight into his grimoire. He didn't have space to keep them sitting around when he still had one more Rank 4 rune to draw in and chop apart.

He then spent some time testing Blizzard, making sure that it had been perfectly formed and didn't have any flaws that he'd somehow missed. Excitement built like water behind a dam as he realized that he'd made yet another truly Perfect Rune.

I can't keep calling them truly perfect. That's too much of a mouthful. Flawless works better. I've got six Flawless Runes. Just one more until I can make my Rank 4.

His heart slammed in his chest, beating faster with every second that passed. The rate at which he was advancing was nothing short of terrifying. It was exactly what the noble families did for their prized members, but he didn't have any of the errors that riddled the higher-ranked runes.

And beyond that, I actually understand how all of these runes work. Even though I haven't used the Rank 3s myself, I've had versions of all of them and have fought with all the powers I'm working with. That means my intent should be much stronger than that of most random nobles who are just fed runes.

That didn't stop Noah from suspecting that he'd definitely need some time to acclimate to the Rank 4 Natural Disaster when he formed it, but that was a problem for his future self to worry about.

Right now, he was only one more rune away from reaching the major milestone that many mages never surpassed. Biting back a grin, Noah sent his senses back out to his grimoire.

No matter what happened, he was determined to make sure his eyes didn't open again until he'd formed Natural Disaster as a Rank 4 rune. For almost every other mage, Rank 4 was a bottleneck.

It was a challenge to strive for most of their lives to reach, and even when they made it, their foundations were weakened by sub-par runes.

To Noah, it wasn't a challenge.

It was an inevitability.

Chapter Thirty-Two

An urgent knock rang out against the door. Moxie pulled her eyes up from Noah's grimoire, her brow furrowing.

"Who wants something this late at night?"

"It's Karina," Lee said. She didn't even stop rooting through his bag. Moxie had no idea what she was looking for, but Lee had gone through the contents of the bag twice and still had nothing to show for it.

Moxie's nose scrunched in annoyance. The amount of energy Noah had been going through was fascinating, and she'd leeched more than a little of it as it slipped out of his body. Normally, that would have been fairly rude, but she couldn't help herself.

He was going through so much power that he was wasting enough to practically form a whole extra rune. Liberating just a bit of that to fill up her own supplies, especially when it would be wasted otherwise, wasn't going to hurt anyone.

"What does she want now?" Moxie asked, slipping out of bed and walking over to the door. "Is it just Karina?"

"Yeah," Lee said. "She smells nervous."

There was another knock on the door. Moxie pulled it open as Karina raised her hand to knock a third time. Karina flinched, then quickly took a step back and adjusted her shirt.

"What is it?" Moxie asked. "Is something wrong?"

"Yes," Karina said. Her eyes darted around the room behind Moxie. "I'm the first one here, right?"

"First one? What are you talking about? Nobody else has shown up," Moxie said. Something soft brushed her leg and she looked down to see Mascot rubbing up against her.

"No assassins?" Karina asked.

Moxie threw a glance over her shoulder at the window, just to make sure nobody was staring through it at them. She shook her head. "No. Come in. What's going on?"

Karina hurried to obey, pulling the door shut behind her and locking it. She nervously adjusted her shirt again, then skittered over to the bed beside Noah to pull the curtains shut.

"Mascot did something," Karina said. "I went to write a letter to Jalen like Vermil asked, but while I was making it, he grabbed the letter and stole it."

"That sounds about right for him, actually," Moxie said, looking down at the white cat that was still doing its best to interlock itself between her feet, causing her to trip over it. "Why is that a concern? Didn't he just ask to meet Jalen somewhere neutral?"

"Yes, and that's what I was writing," Karina said. A wave of energy emanated out from Noah and crackled through the room, setting Moxie's hair on end. She and Karina both drew in sharp breaths.

"Damned Plains, what is he doing?" Karina asked, staring at Noah in disbelief, her fear forgotten.

"Don't worry about it," Moxie said. "What were you saying about Jalen? What does he have to do with this? Did he say he was going to send more assassins or something?"

It took Karina a moment to pull her eyes away from Vermil. She shook her head, snapping out of the daze as the weight of the situation settled back on her shoulders. Karina reached into a pocket and pulled out a crumpled note.

"I only had the request written without any of the niceties. It was a draft!" Karina exclaimed, squeezing the note in her palm. She was breathing so quickly that Moxie suspected the woman was about to start hyperventilating. Moxie grabbed her shoulders.

"Relax! Breath slowly and tell me what's going on. You wrote a rude letter or something?"

Karina drew in a slow breath and let it out through her nose. She swallowed, then shook her head. "No. It wasn't rude. It was basically just a demand that he come meet at a different neutral ground, but Mascot grabbed it before I could do anything else. It was just a draft!"

"You said that," Moxie snapped, her patience wearing thin as the stress started to build in her as well. Karina was far too stressed for any sort of minor issue, and she was starting to get an inkling of what might have happened. "What did Mascot do with the letter?"

"He delivered it," Karina said weakly. She held the note out to Moxie, who uncrumpled it. There was only a single sentence written on it, but it was enough to make her blood run cold.

If that's how we're playing, then I'll oblige and pay you a visit myself. See you soon, Vermil.

"Damned Plains. Jalen is coming personally?" Moxie asked, looking back to Karina. "And he thinks Noah wrote him—what, a challenge?"

Karina gave her a weak nod. "Contessa ran to try and find someone strong enough to keep Jalen from killing all of us. We need to get one of Arbitage's Enforcers. They're the only ones that are strong enough to make him actually stop before he does anything."

"Does Jalen not care about the neutral ground bit at all?" Moxie asked.

"With all the assassins he's sent? I don't think so. I'm telling you, he's insane," Karina said. "We need to run. Jalen will kill all of us without a second of hesitation. I—"

Another wave of energy, even stronger than the last, roared off Noah's body. It was so intense that Moxie staggered as the power flowed through her. It felt like a miniature storm had passed through her body.

"What in the Damned Plains is that?" Karina breathed. She shook her head urgently before anyone could respond. "No. Never mind. We need to run! And we need to do something about your cat—I swear it's trying to kill us."

Moxie wasn't sure she could argue. Mascot certainly had a penchant for pulling them into situations where their lives were threatened. She glared at the furball, which let out a rumbling purr in response a moment before vanishing in a small puff of smoke.

"I think Mascot left us to deal with the aftermath of his prank." Lee rose to her feet and stuffed the rest of Noah's belongings back into his bag, keeping a strip of jerky for herself. "Jalen is Rank 6. I don't think we can fight that. Not again."

"We definitely can't," Moxie said, spinning to wake Noah up. "Contessa has the right idea. We need to get an Enforcer immediately. We can't put up a fight against a Rank 6 with a vendetta."

Moxie managed to take a single step before a wall of force slammed into her—not from Noah, but from behind.

She stumbled, just barely managing to spin back to face the doorway. Karina had already fallen to the floor, pinned down by the immense pressure pushing its way into the room. Moxie's skin went as pale as a sheet of Catchpaper. Lee's eyes widened and she took a step back, just barely managing to keep herself upright beside Moxie.

A middle-aged man stepped through the doorway, his arms clasped behind his back. His graying hair was combed back over his head, and his eyebrows as sharp as his features. The goatee on his lip would have looked ridiculous if it wasn't for the immense amount of power coiling off him.

This can't be happening. We just dealt with Evergreen. Why is Jalen here? He's the actual head of the Linwick family! He shouldn't give a shit about some random insulting letter he got! Doesn't he have anything better to do with his time?

Even though he wore nothing but plain purple robes trimmed with faint golden threads, the man exuded the presence of a king. His eyes were like empty pools leading into an endless ocean, and they were focused directly on Moxie. She could barely breathe through the pressure driving into her from every angle.

The difference between Evergreen and Jalen is incredible. I don't know if her domain was just weaker than his or if she didn't think we were worth using it on.

Somehow, Noah hadn't noticed Jalen's approach. He was so wrapped up in his work that he didn't even twitch when Jalen entered the room.

"Karina," Jalen said, looking down at the prone woman, a displeased expression flickering across his face.

"I didn't mean for it to get sent," Karina wheezed, her hands trembling as she tried and failed to push herself upright. "A cat stole it."

"I presume that would be the same cat that took a shit on my paperwork when it arrived to give me your letter?" Jalen asked, his lips pursed in distaste. "It certainly sent quite the message."

"I swear I didn't plan for it," Karina wheezed. "Please, just—"

Jalen clicked his tongue and shook his head. "No excuses, Karina. You sent the letter. I don't care how you sent it. Regardless, it was pretty clear that you weren't the one who actually wanted to write it in the first place, though. You were just the pen—the hand that wrote it was Vermil, and you simply acted on his behest."

Jalen's gaze flicked past Lee and Moxie as it rose to Noah, who still sat on the bed, completely unaware of the Rank 6 mage in their room. Jalen's eyebrows tightened.

"Who apparently does not even care enough that I have arrived to give me the time of day. I see he's put the artifact he stole to good use, but where in the Damned Plains is the other book?"

Moxie called on her runes, reinforcing herself against Jalen's domain. She could still move within it, but the less information she gave away, the more chance she had to do... well, something.

She exchanged a glance with Lee, who inclined her head slightly. They were both able to move, but Moxie couldn't see how they could possibly do anything against him, even if they were able to move.

Calling out to Noah might just make Jalen attack and kill him on the spot. That wasn't exactly a permanent drawback, but it wouldn't help the rest of them, and Noah still wouldn't be able to use magic for a while after his death.

Despair washed over Moxie.

Shit. Noah needs time to set up a Formation—and even if we had it, we couldn't go against Jalen. This can't be it. There has to be something we can do!

Lee flicked her eyes toward the window. Escape wasn't a bad idea, but Moxie didn't believe for a second that they could actually outrun Jalen. She thought desperately, trying to think of literally any way to keep them all alive.

"We're on neutral ground," Karina stammered. "Magus Jalen, you can't do anything here. It's not the same thing as assassins, and this wasn't the deal. I—"

"You called me here," Jalen reminded. "And with the way you worded that message, I could hardly refuse. I'm starting to get annoyed, though. It's quite rude to summon someone and then proceed to ignore them."

A crackle of purple energy ran along Jalen's fingertips.

Pressure slammed into Moxie for the second time—but not from Jalen. Noah's eyes snapped open. The world seemed to slow down as energy swirled in the air around them. Despite their situation, Moxie's eyes widened in disbelief.

Noah had reached Rank 4. The power rolling over her from his domain was immense—far stronger than any Rank 4's domain ever should have been. It wasn't anything compared to Jalen's, but the fact that she could feel it at all while so close to the Rank 6 mage should have been impossible.

It only took Noah an instant to take in the situation in the room around him. His eyes narrowed and he raised his eyes to match Jalen's gaze.

He snapped his grimoire shut and rose to his feet as his features tightened in anger—not affected by Jalen's domain in the slightest. "Who the hell are you, and what are you doing in our damn room?"

Chapter Thirty-Three

A short while before Jalen arrived, while Noah was still within the confines of his mindspace, he stared at the final Rank 3 rune before him.

Thunderstorm had been, surprisingly, one of the easiest runes to make. Perhaps it was his affinity toward noise, or maybe it was just because he'd been thinking about it a lot, but it ended up coming together on his first attempt.

Before making it, Noah had finally Sundered his original Natural Disaster. It felt odd to destroy the rune that had been with him for so long, but it no longer had a place in what he needed. Still, Noah couldn't help himself from breaking it down all the way to its Rank 1 components to get a Rank 1 Vibration Rune to fit into his new Thunderstorm Rune. Once the surgery was done, Noah deposited the rest of the rune's pieces into his grimoire and moved on to the penultimate step of his ascension to Rank 4.

The pieces of the Stormprince Elemental's rune hadn't been great, but the majority of the issue was in a horribly made Rank 3 Shattered Lightning Flash Rune. After Noah had discarded the faulty rune into his grimoire, it had been a relatively simple matter to take apart a few of the other Rank 3 runes, finding and making the Rank 2 Vibration Runes and Lightning Runes that he needed for Thunderstorm.

Noah didn't want to think about the amount of energy he wasted in the making and filling of the final rune, but he was on a roll and didn't plan on stopping. The last dregs of energy swirled into Thunderstorm, filling it completely. It floated back, joining the seven other runes swirling in Noah's mindspace.

Sandstorm
Tsunami
Cyclone
Earthquake
Volcano
Blizzard
Thunderstorm

Pressure rolled off them, bearing down on Noah from every direction. It wasn't an uncomfortable feeling. It felt like he was wrapped up tightly in a safe blanket of his own power.

Far above, Sunder, the Fragment of Renewal, and Combustion awaited him. Their power was still on a completely different level. While Combustion was only a little stronger than his new Rank 3 runes, the other two Master Runes were like immense mountains that threatened to crush him beneath their weight.

Noah drew in a deep breath and let it out slowly. Every single one of his Rank 3 runes was full. They were ready.

He was ready.

Moxie said that reaching Rank 4 was a bottleneck. I'd imagine a large portion of that is going to be because imperfect runes only get more imperfect when they get combined together. But everything in my soul is flawless.

At the very least, that should help. I guess there's only one way to find out for sure, though. And hey—if it doesn't work, I can always Sunder it and try again. There's no end of the road for my runes. There are only temporary inconveniences. No matter how badly I screw up, I can just rip everything apart and try again.

Noah raised his hands, calling all seven of his Rank 3 runes to float before him. It almost felt sacrilegious to combine runes that he'd literally never used in a fight, but he'd used their powers.

Instead of knowing exactly all the things they could do, Noah knew all the things that they lacked. He knew the drawbacks of his magic and all the mistakes and misinterpretations he'd made about runes.

And, as far as he was concerned, nobody truly learned by doing everything right. Failure was the essence of improvement. Every single mistake had reinforced his understanding. It had changed and improved his intent.

The runes shuddered as they drew close. Energy crackled at their edges, hissing and popping as Noah began to bring them closer and closer together. The hair on his arms stood on end and his back prickled.

Noah's lips peeled back in a mixture of concentration and excitement as he pushed the runes even closer together. His intent was as clear as a cloudless day and as razor-sharp as a blade.

Static electricity gathered around Noah's head, and his hair rose of its own volition. His mindspace trembled beneath his feet, the cracks of white light blurring as he pushed even harder to bring the runes together.

The trembling intensified into a full-on earthquake. Magic pounded —not just around Noah but within him as well. His veins felt like molten rock was pumping through them, and jagged blades drove into his heart.

Noah was used to pain, though. His intent didn't falter. A wordless roar escaped his lips as he pushed even harder. Compared to the infinite nothingness of the line that was oblivion, pain was nothing.

Pressure continued to build around Noah. For a moment, Noah thought it would never stop. He felt Sunder and the Fragment of Renewal activate—for once, pushing back against the other runes in his favor instead of the other way around.

A loud snap tore through Noah's mindspace. There was an instant of silence as all the pressure that had been building up abruptly vanished, sucked up into the epicenter of his soul. Noah used that moment to throw himself to the ground, putting his hands over his head and squeezing his eyes shut.

The world exploded like a bomb had gone off. A wall of pressure slammed into him, tearing past his body and spreading out through his mindspace. It was followed by a roar of energy that flooded everywhere, pouring into every part of Noah's body.

Rivers of ice swirled through Noah, but he couldn't even draw in a breath of surprise. The shock of the power was so intense that he couldn't move. Mercifully, the feeling only lasted for a few moments before control returned to him.

Every single part of Noah's body tingled. He pressed his trembling hands against the dark ground, pushing himself back and rising to his feet. His skin felt different. His body felt different—or perhaps it was the world around him that was off.

Just as Noah had once been able to tell exactly where his finger was, he could feel the runic energy rolling off his body and filling his mindspace. It was another part of him, just like an extra limb. A lot of extra limbs.

And, as Noah finally looked up, he laid eyes upon his newly formed Rank 4 rune. Quiet power surrounded it. The lines that made it up were straight and plain, entirely devoid of fanciful design. There was no energy racing along its edges, nor did it look impressive in any way. It was probably the plainest rune that Noah had ever seen.

And yet, the regal force that enveloped it left him absolutely no question as to what stood before him. A Rank 4 rune, perfectly formed at 10 percent full, met his gaze and stood proud.

Noah didn't let himself celebrate yet. He extended his senses to the rune, drawing on its power. It flowed easily and naturally. Rubbing his thumb and pointer finger together, Noah used the tiny amount of friction to summon a crackle of lightning. It arced to life effortlessly.

He ran Natural Disaster through several more tests, calling on its power in a variety of different ways to test out each of the forms of energy within it. Each one responded without hesitation or restraint, and the pressure rolling off the rune remained constant.

It was flawless. All the work and modifications that had gone into making everything that had come before Natural Disaster had finally paid off. Finally, Noah allowed himself to start laughing.

"I did it! A Rank 4 Flawless Rune!" Noah's laughter intensified, rolling out through his mindspace and disappearing into the darkness around him. All the excess power from the combination filled him with temporary strength and confidence, only intensifying his delight.

Noah rubbed his hands together, drawing in a deep breath to gather himself. Luckily, there wasn't anyone who could see him cackling like a madman. He let the breath out slowly, then cleared his throat, keeping the delight bottled up in his chest.

It was time to show Lee and Moxie what he'd done.

With a thought, Noah pulled himself out of his mindspace and returned to the real world. His eyes cracked open, excess energy still pouring out of him, and he froze in place. There were people in their room that shouldn't have been there.

Karina lay on the ground, desperately trying to push herself upright. Moxie and Lee were both locked in place, their faces deadly serious as they looked at the man that stood before them, energy washing off his body in waves. If it hadn't been for all the extra magic from his combination surrounding him, Noah suspected he would have been trembling with exertion.

The look on the man's face was the casual arrogance that only came with immense delusion or power—and Noah got the sinking feeling that it was the latter. The man's eyes were firmly locked on his, and he met them without backing down.

He snapped his grimoire shut and rose to his feet as his features tightened in anger. "Who the hell are you, and what are you doing in our damn room?"

"You must be Magus Vermil," the man said, his eyes flicking from Noah to the grimoire at his side.

This guy knows who I am? Who the hell—

Noah paused mid-thought as he caught another glimpse of Karina's face. It wasn't exactly terror in the way that one would regard a random assailant. It was a mixture of fear and resignation, as if nothing she did mattered and her life was out of her hands. Noah's stomach dropped.

"Magus Jalen?"

"Indeed. I almost got offended," Jalen said, his eyes narrowing just enough for Noah to notice it. "If we've been playing for this long and you didn't even know who I was, I'd think that I wasn't even an opponent of note to you."

"Well, I was under the impression you were unwilling to meet me in Arbitage. You can't blame me for being surprised," Noah said, recovering his verbal footing. Jalen was talking, which meant he wanted something. There were a whole lot of somethings that Noah could imagine Jalen wanted, but the first step was figuring out exactly which one it was.

"I am not some child to be summoned at your beck and call. People come to *me*," Jalen said. "Anyone with half a brain does, at least. A little fear is never remiss when dealing with someone far superior. So, I can say with complete honesty that I was quite surprised when you sent me a letter demanding my appearance and had a cat shit on my desk. Surprised enough to show up. So here I am, Magus Vermil—just as you demanded."

What the hell did Karina write in that letter?

"I think the exact meaning of my words may have been warped in translation," Noah said, clearing his throat. "But now that you're here —could you stop sending assassins after me? It's kind of annoying."

"Annoying?" Jalen let out a bark of laughter. "I'll tell you what was annoying. Finding enough idiots that were actually incompetent enough to waste on something like this. The Linwicks have surprisingly few people that absolutely nobody cares about. Everyone has at least one connection that makes disappearing them somewhat bothersome."

A ripple of power rolled out from Jalen. Everyone in the room stumbled and fell to the ground as the magic slammed them down, but as it hit the supercharged energy still surrounding Noah, it dissipated harmlessly.

Jalen's brow twitched, and Noah did his best to keep a straight face. He was certain Jalen wasn't using anywhere near his full power, but he hadn't even flinched. That had to be at least somewhat surprising.

At least, I think it should be. I don't know how much a Rank 4 can normally stand up to a Rank 6, but I'd imagine the odds would be pretty stacked against me.

"Let's cut through the bullshit," Jalen said. "Where are the Records of the Deceased, Vermil? I want to know what you did with it."

Yeah, that's not happening. That book is never seeing the light of day again.

"I've got no idea what you're talking about." Noah's voice was perfectly smooth and collected, trained by months of practicing his bullshitting skills at Arbitage. "If you mean the book I saw in the cata-combs—I didn't take it with me. It started screaming and I left it in the collapsed cave."

I can't even try to deny that I was in the catacombs. My grimoire is literally on my lap. But... add in a little truth to the lie, and boom. It feels a lot more reasonable.

Jalen's eyes bored into Noah's. "You... left it? Do you think I'm an idiot?"

I certainly hope you are.

"Of course not, Magus Jalen," Noah said. "But I'm not dumb enough to lug such a massive book with me when it was clearly a trap."

Jalen looked down at the grimoire, which was easily twice as large as the Records of the Deceased had been. He looked back up at Noah. The two of them stared at each other, straight-faced.

"You're awful cocky for a Rank—wait. Rank 4?" Jalen's brow furrowed. "Why do you have a domain? You shouldn't be a Rank 4."

Whoops. Talk about bad timing.

"I just reached it recently and haven't had a chance to report my advancement yet," Noah said.

"You're registered as a Rank 2 with Arbitage as of just a short while ago. I've looked into you." Jalen's eyes narrowed into slits, and he took a step forward, causing both Moxie and Lee to get pressed even further back by the pressure rolling off him. "And—bullshit. You didn't just hit Rank 4. The amount of energy your domain has is indicative of at least four or five runes. How does a Rank 2 go all the way up to halfway through Rank 4 that quickly?"

Is my Flawless Rune that much stronger? Or is he feeling all the excess power that was released during my combination? Maybe a mix of the two?

It wasn't the time to celebrate how successful his combination had been, though. Jalen's eyes promised trouble, and the situation was rapidly deteriorating.

"I reported my advancement to the office, but I don't think they recorded it. The secretary was eating. I've just gotten a few lucky breaks as of late."

Jalen didn't look like he was buying it. The power coming off him intensified even further, pushing against Noah's newly made domain. He started to feel the world press down on his shoulders as the gravity increased, but Noah held firm.

He'd met people like Jalen before. Men that only respected power and considered all else a sign of weakness. Doing anything even remotely subservient would only make things worse for him. All he had to do was match Jalen's energy and divert questions until an opportunity presented itself.

And, of course, that was when a tiny white paw stepped out of thin air above Jalen. It was followed by the rest of a cat, which promptly did what Noah could only describe as a flying, drive-by hairball.

Mascot hacked a ball of unidentified matter up straight onto the top of Jalen's head, then disappeared in another puff of smoke. The room stared in mute horror as the ball rolled off Jalen's head and thudded to the floor.

Jalen's eye twitched.

He snapped his fingers, and Noah felt the true power of a Rank 6 for the first time. Evergreen had been nothing in comparison to the immense might that Jalen wielded. All of them were slammed to the ground, only spared from getting squashed by Jalen's restraint. A wave of purple energy ripped out of his hand, moving so quickly that Noah only managed to pick up a flash of light before it swallowed him and the world vanished in spinning lights.

Chapter Thirty-Four

Noah found himself lying on wooden floor. He rolled over and shot to his feet, his heart slamming in his chest as he went to draw on Natural Disaster and prepare for a fight—only to find Jalen standing on the other side of a desk stacked high with paper, his hands crossed behind his back and eyes transfixed on Noah.

"What did you do?" Noah asked, stumbling over his words. The world felt off, as if he were in a spot where he shouldn't have been.

"I took us back to the Linwick Estate," Jalen replied. "Not on neutral ground anymore, are we? I believe that means I can do what I want."

"I'm pretty sure kidnapping someone is against the spirit of neutral ground," Noah said. He kept his tone even, although it was definitely shakier than it had been a moment ago.

Brayden had talked about how difficult it was to do long-range teleportations. Jalen had done one so fast that he'd barely even blinked, and he didn't even look slightly winded.

"You steal from the Linwick family. You make light of my threats, then flaunt your neutral ground in my face as you send a letter to a man who has the power to snuff your life out like a worthless candle. And when given a chance to explain your actions—you mock me?"

Noah's hand brushed across his side. His gourd wasn't there. If he died, he'd return to Arbitage.

That might be for the best, because the only idea I've still got left is to actually make an impression on Jalen. He already knows I robbed the Linwicks blind, but he doesn't actually seem like he wants to kill me, or he'd have already done it.

"I wouldn't say I'm mocking you," Noah said, choosing his words carefully. "You're the one that's been coming after me. All I've done is try to avoid trouble and happen to be in possession of a cat that has a general distaste for authority figures."

"You *stole* from the Linwick Estate!" Jalen said, his voice raising as anger flared behind his eyes.

"Yeah, well, if you didn't want someone to steal your shit, you should have guarded it better," Noah snapped. "What the hell is the point of having a catacombs that is so easily accessible with borderline no real defenses on anything? And good god—why would you collapse the damn thing? You've just gone and destroyed all your other shit. If there's anyone to be pissed at, it should be whoever built that shitty thing. You're blaming the mouse for eating a piece of cheese that the chef left out overnight."

As soon as Noah closed his mouth, he realized that he might have said just a little too much. Jalen's face had gone completely flat, his back stiff. Noah matched Jalen's gaze, baring his teeth in clear challenge.

When he kills me, I'll claim I used some form of magic to duplicate my body and am actually far stronger than I appear. If it worked on Father, it should work on Jalen as well. This guy won't take no for an answer, so I'll have to play things differently. Hopefully, this keeps this guy distracted long enough for me to get strong enough to find a new way to deal with him.

Jalen shifted, and Noah prepared to get blasted to bits. He wasn't unused to dying by any stretch of the imagination, but it still wasn't a particularly pleasant experience.

What he wasn't prepared for was a small huff to slip from Jalen's nose. He blinked in surprise as Jalen's stern expression twitched, then cracked. The head of the Linwick family doubled over, roaring with laughter to the point where he was wheezing for air.

"Unbelievable," Jalen said through his laughter. "Absolutely phenomenal. What a performance. Like a cornered gerbil."

Noah stared in disbelief as Jalen fell back into crazed laughter, tears of mirth streaming down his face.

He's completely insane.

It was nearly a minute before Jalen managed to gather himself. Still chuckling, he wiped the tears from his face and shook his head before striding across the room. Noah tensed as Jalen reached him, but all the man did was slap a hand on his shoulder. "The sheer audacity you have. This is what the family lacks."

"I—what?"

Jalen snorted, clearly just a tiny push away from doubling over in another fit of laughter. He managed to contain himself and turned back to the table, flicking his hand. A wave of purple energy rolled out, tearing through the papers and making them fold in on themselves, before ripping them apart so thoroughly that nothing remained.

"Sit," Jalen said, dropping into his chair and kicking his legs back onto the now-clean desk.

Completely baffled, Noah walked over to the desk and pulled the chair out, sitting across from Jalen.

"What, did you think I'd kill you? Why would I do that?" Jalen chortled as a purple portal wound open before one of his hands. He reached inside, pulling out a sealed bottle and putting it on the table. He procured two glasses, then set them down beside the bottle. "You were right, after all."

"I... was?"

"The catacombs aren't defended at all. They're a game, and one that you played and won," Jalen said, cracking the seal off the bottle and pouring an orange liquid into the glasses. "I still want to know how you got the damn records out, though."

Noah watched Jalen warily. The man's personality had changed so suddenly that he wasn't sure which one was real. Jalen pushed one of the glasses over to Noah, then took a sip from his own.

"Go on. It won't kill you," Jalen said.

Even if it did, Noah wouldn't have been all that bothered. He took the glass and raised it to his lips, taking a small sip. Noah nearly spit the liquid out. He'd been expecting some form of alcohol or fancy drink, but it was neither.

"It's orange juice. Good for your health," Jalen said, taking another sip from his glass. "I don't enjoy the taste of alcohol much. Got boring after a few hundred years. Just like everything else. I'm on a bit of a citrus binge at the moment, though. And—let me tell you—my skin has never looked better."

Yeah. He's insane.

The orange juice did taste pretty good, though. Noah took another sip. At this point, he had absolutely no idea what Jalen wanted. It was possible the whole thing was just meant to trick him into revealing what he'd done with the Records of the Deceased, but that wasn't happening. He couldn't have given it back if he'd wanted to.

"Are you really a member of the Linwick family?" Jalen asked.

Noah's back stiffened and he fought to keep his expression neutral. "Of course I am. I'm part of Father's—"

"Bah." Jalen scrunched his nose in distaste and drained the rest of his glass before pouring himself more. "I don't give a shit about that. All the inter-family politics are the biggest pain in the ass that I've ever gotten dragged into. Everyone trying to get more resources. All the little games. Worthless. You just don't seem like any of the other bumbling fools I've met in recent years."

Is that a compliment? I think it is, but it's kind of hard to tell. What the hell is going on?

"I'm not sure I follow," Noah said.

Jalen rubbed the bridge of his nose. "That's what I'm talking about. You don't even *understand* the problem. Watch this."

He reached under his desk and pressed something. No more than a few seconds later, the door slammed open, and an elderly man hustled into the room.

"How can I serve you, Magus Jalen?"

"I'm bored," Jalen said. "Can you go find some travelers near the Linwick Estate and arrest them so I can have someone to interrogate?"

"Of course, Magus. I will—"

"Stop," Jalen said irritably as the man turned for the door. "You annoyed me. I changed my mind. Go... I don't know. Donate your life savings to the orphanage."

The man's face paled. He opened his mouth, but before he could speak, a ripple of purple energy rolled off Jalen's body. Pressure washed past Noah, somehow missing him entirely, but the man in the doorway stumbled.

"I will do as you ask, Magus." The man dropped to the ground, pressing his forehead against it. "Thank you for sparing my life."

He scrambled to his feet and closed the door. Noah could hear the patter of his feet on the floor as he sprinted away, and Jalen sent Noah an exasperated look.

"Do you see? No backbone. Nothing. Just an empty shell, desperate to live with no desires beyond that. Isn't it pathetic?"

"Yeah," Noah admitted. "It is."

"That's what I deal with," Jalen said, polishing off his second glass of orange juice. He glanced at Noah's glass, which Noah was surprised to find that he'd actually finished. "More?"

"Hm. I'm actually good, but if you're willing to give me some of that to go, I've got a friend that would love it."

Jalen held his hands out to his sides. "And this is exactly what I mean."

Noah blinked. "What is?"

"You didn't do what I said," Jalen said. "If I'd asked that coward in the doorway if he wanted anything, he would have said yes even if a single sip would have made him burst. But not only did you refuse, you actually asked me for something else. It isn't just you, either. The people in your room had just as much resilience, if not quite as much lip."

He reached into the air as he spoke, pulling out an identical bottle to the one sitting on the table, and set it down in front of Noah. That was definitely a good sign. People didn't give gifts to people that they were about to kill.

At least they generally don't. Father might be an exception.

"I want to know why," Jalen said. "Were you dropped on your head as a child? Do you lack fear?"

"I think I'm just too tired to give a shit," Noah said honestly.

Jalen roared with laughter, rocking back and nearly falling off his chair. "Too tired to—you can't be older than... what, a hundred?"

"I'm twenty-six," Noah said, guesstimating Vermil's age.

"Same thing." Jalen waved dismissively. He lowered himself safely and leaned forward, resting his forearms on the table. "It's been so long since I've had a chance to speak with someone this plainly. Not even the other family heads will do it. They're all so caught up in their worthless machinations that they forgot the reason for living is to have fun."

"You're welcome, I guess?"

Jalen cackled. He rose to his feet, shaking his head in mirth. "This is too much. Perhaps you have a death wish. Either way, I don't care. I wouldn't waste a source of entertainment as good as this."

Noah craned his neck to follow Jalen as he walked across the room and grabbed a beautiful tapestry hanging on the wall, throwing it to the ground as if it were used tissue paper to reveal a large, circular board with colorful patterns on it.

Jalen grabbed a small box that hung beneath it, then walked over to Noah and set it down on the table. It was full of metal darts. Noah slowly looked back at Jalen.

"What's this?"

"Darts," Jalen replied. "Want to play?"

Oh, what the hell. Might as well.

Noah picked up one of the darts and reared back, flinging it at the circle. It hurtled through the air—missing the board completely and slamming into the very expensive-looking wall beside it.

"You're terrible," Jalen informed Noah, grabbing a dart for himself. "Let me show you how a master does it."

He flung the dart, and it hit the wall beside where Noah's dart had landed, missing just as badly as Noah had.

"You don't seem to be much better."

"Do you know how long it's been since I last had a chance to play?" Jalen asked, glaring at Noah as he grabbed another dart. "I've forgotten more about darts than you've ever known."

"First person to land ten anywhere on the board wins?" Noah suggested.

"You are going to suffer a humiliating defeat, Vermil. Prepare to suffer." Jalen threw the dart and it hit the rim of the board with a clang, clattering to the ground without sticking.

"Damn it," Jalen said. "That one didn't count. It was a warm-up throw."

Noah couldn't keep himself from laughing. "Fine. Let's play."

Chapter Thirty-Five

"What in the Damned Plains do we do?" Karina asked, looking more exhausted than anything else as she stared at the space where Noah and Jalen had been. "Even if Contessa comes back with an Enforcer, it'll be too late."

Moxie's eyes flicked across her room, landing on the gourd resting on her bed. She kept herself from breathing a sigh of relief.

As long as that's here, Noah is fine.

"Nothing," Moxie replied. "He'll be okay. We need to be more concerned with what comes next."

"He'll be—what? Are you insane? That was Jalen," Karina hissed. "He's a Rank 6. Vermil isn't going to be able to fight him."

"I think Moxie is right," Lee said. She walked over to the door and pulled it open. "Just go back to bed. Don't worry about it."

"But..."

"It's fine." Moxie shook her head. "Besides, there's quite literally nothing we can do. Like you said, that's the head of the Linwick family. He's way too powerful to try to fight against. All we can do is weather the storm."

And all I can do is get you out of my room so Noah's body doesn't reform stark naked while you're staring at him. That would be pretty difficult to explain.

"Aren't you concerned at all?" Karina asked.

"No. He'll be fine."

"It's okay. He'll be back soon," Lee said, giving Karina a thumbs-up. "If you're worried about him, you can come by in the morning. Not too early, though. I want to sleep in."

Karina blinked, looking from Lee to Moxie in complete befuddlement. She opened her mouth, then closed it again and let out a sigh. "I —okay. I guess. It's not like there's anything we can do. We can't do anything against Jalen. Maybe ignoring the problem will solve it."

She turned woodenly, heading back to her temporary lodgings in Noah's room. Lee closed the door and turned to exchange a look with Moxie. Moxie's false bravado evaporated, and she started to pace around the room, tugging at her hair.

"This is bad. How do we fight *another* Rank 6? He's going to kill Noah and then find out that Noah doesn't stay dead, and then who knows what'll happen. Damn it all. Why can't the world just leave us alone?"

"Sneak in again?" Lee suggested. "We could blow up his house."

"We can't do that! Jalen is ancient," Moxie said. She stopped by her table and stared at the papers on it, as if the solution was just hidden somewhere within them. Unfortunately, it wasn't. "He's not the same as Evergreen. She was trying to make a point and was a family figurehead. The Linwicks didn't do that, and you felt his domain. He's too strong. We can't fight him directly."

"Can we get some of the Linwick family's enemies to somehow cause shit?"

"Not an impossible solution," Moxie muttered. She chewed her lower lip. "Normally, that would be my family. The Torrins are too busy right now, though. They won't get into a bunch of trouble right now. The situation is too precarious already."

"What do we do, then?" Lee asked worriedly. "And where is Noah? Why's it taking so long?"

Moxie shook her head mutely. Scenarios were flashing through her mind, each worse than the last, but she refused to entertain any of them. Panicking would only make everything worse. All they could do for now was wait for Noah to return.

Minutes ticked by. They stretched into an hour, and that stretched into two hours. The worry that Moxie felt only grew the longer that Noah was missing. Death wasn't exactly a big threat for him, but getting captured or imprisoned was.

"I don't get it," Moxie said, her hands clenched at her sides. Her eyes caught on the stuffed Mascot that sat on the corner of her bed and she grabbed it, hugging the plushie to her chest. "He couldn't have been captured, right? He can just blow himself up if he needs to."

"Maybe he's just talking?" Lee offered, but she didn't sound very confident in her own suggestion.

"For this long? There's no way they'd still be talking. Something happened."

"Maybe we could try to find Brayden. He's got Space Magic. We could rescue Noah." Lee paused. "Wait. I have Space Runes too. I don't know exactly how to use them yet, but—"

"By the time you make it to the Linwick estate, who knows what could have happened." Moxie shook her head. "Not to mention you'd never be able to find him. If Noah actually got captured, he'd be held somewhere, probably unconscious. If he wasn't, he'd have blown himself up by now."

"Maybe we should find an Enforcer like Contessa wanted to."

"They clearly didn't care. Nobody showed up." Moxie started to pace again. "We'll have to go to someone else. Maybe Father. He might be able to figure out where Noah is, and then we could try to get over there and break him out with your magic. Brayden might be able to help too."

Lee started to nod, then froze. She sniffed at the air, then scrambled to her feet. "Jalen is coming."

Moxie grabbed for her runes and tossed the plushie onto the bed, dropping into a fighting stance. Lee readied herself beside Moxie. It was futile to go up against someone as powerful as Jalen, but Moxie didn't care. Rank 6 mage or not, she wasn't about to let someone kidnap Noah and then come back to gloat.

It's not like we can run from someone with Space Magic as powerful as Jalen. I'll go down fighting rather than running like a coward.

Whorls of purple magic intertwined in the air before Moxie and Lee. They both tensed for Jalen's return, but Jalen wasn't the one that stepped out of the portal. It was Noah. The purple energy evaporated. Nobody followed him into the room.

Moxie practically threw herself forward, grabbing Noah and pressing her lips to his. He stiffened in surprise, then wrapped his arms around her back and returned it. Moxie held him as tightly as she could, as if letting go would let him disappear again.

"What in the Damned Plains happened?" Moxie asked when she finally, reluctantly, broke the kiss. "What did Jalen do? Where is he? Are you okay?"

"I'm fine," Noah said. "I'm sorry I worried you. I... uh, I think Jalen wine-and-dine'd me."

"He what?"

Noah stepped back, and Moxie realized that he was holding a bottle. He held it out, and Moxie took it numbly, trying to put the pieces of what had happened together.

"I was confused too," Noah said. "I thought he yanked me away from Arbitage to try and kill me safely, but instead he kind of just... complimented us. Then we played darts for two hours and he sent me back."

"That's it?" Moxie asked, not sure if she was meant to be pissed, relieved, or just purely confused. She settled for something in the middle of all three. "He played fucking darts with you?"

"Yeah. The bottle has orange juice in it. He gave it to me to share with the two of you."

Moxie rubbed her forehead and wandered over to her bed, sitting down on it. Her head felt light. "You got kidnapped by the head of the Linwick family. A Rank 6 mage. And he kidnapped you because he wanted to play darts? That's it?"

"Yeah, that kind of sums it up. I didn't really get a chance to ask him what else he wanted or what the point of any of this was. He basically just said he was bored. I think he wanted the Records of the Deceased back, but either he forgot about that or he's biding his time because he didn't press too hard."

"I am glad that you are not dead," Lee declared. "What's in the bottle? I want to drink it."

Moxie felt like she was made out of rocks. She slowly popped the top of the bottle off and took a sniff at it. It really did just smell like orange juice. Too mentally drained to care any further, she took a drink.

It was, admittedly, good.

"I wish it was alcohol," Moxie muttered. "I wouldn't mind getting drunk right about now."

Lee took the bottle from her hands. "Did you want more of this?"

"I think I'll be fine."

"Thanks." Lee stuck the bottle—the entire thing, glass and all—down her mouth and bit down. Glass cracked and shattered and she chewed a few times before swallowing. "Tasty. I like orange juice. It's crunchy. Is Jalen going to give you more the next time he shows up?"

"Next time?" Moxie looked up, glaring. "He's coming back?"

Noah cleared his throat. "I... may have agreed to meet him again next week."

"Make sure he brings more orange juice," Lee said. Her eyes narrowed. "And tell him that if he kidnaps you again, I'm going to kill everyone in his family that isn't strong enough to stop me."

Noah gave Lee a quick hug. "I'm sorry I scared you. I'll be sure to pass the message along. If I had a way to get back and tell you what was happening earlier, I would have. This is definitely better than the alternative, though. Jalen turned out to be a surprisingly decent guy."

"That's fine. He didn't smell too bad when he showed up, but he had you for so long that I thought he was trying to steal you," Lee said. Her tone lightened back up as she shrugged. "You're back now! It's okay."

"Do you think you could do me a favor?" Noah asked.

"Sure," Lee said. "What is it?"

"I think I need to apologize to Moxie more thoroughly. Could you give us a little time?"

"'Kay," Lee said. "I'll go tell Karina and Contessa that they don't have to worry about Jalen anymore. Unless he's still sending assassins?"

"He shouldn't be. Probably," Noah said. He didn't sound too confident about it, but that was enough for Lee. She waved goodbye, then slipped out the door.

Noah walked up to the bed and sat down beside Moxie. He wrapped his arm around her shoulders and pulled her against his chest.

"I'm just glad you're okay. I thought something had happened and you were unconscious or something," Moxie said into his chest, pressing herself against him.

"It definitely could have gone a lot worse," Noah said, his tone turning grim. "I guess we finally got a stroke of luck after all the unlucky ones. Jalen is crazy, but I don't actually think he's an enemy."

"He'd better not be, considering you agreed to meet up with him again," Moxie grumbled. "I'm still pissed at him, even if he's not trying to kill you. Couldn't he have just talked to us like a normal person without all the theatrics?"

"Sorry," Noah said, giving Moxie a squeeze.

"I know it isn't your fault. It's fine."

"Oh?" Noah pulled her chin up gently so that their eyes met. "That means I don't need to apologize, then?"

A tiny grin pulled across Moxie's lips. "It depends what you had in mind."

"I'd have to show you."

"Go on, then," Moxie said. "Show me."

Noah showed her, and Moxie decided that she didn't ever want Noah to apologize to her in any other way.

Chapter Thirty-Six

"Did you really do nothing other than play games with Jalen?" Moxie asked, leaning against Noah's side while he flipped through his grimoire.

"Surprisingly, yes. After the initial shit, which was basically just a dick measuring contest, we just played darts. I won."

"I'm still finding it hard to believe that Jalen didn't want anything else. He didn't fish for information or try to get you to reveal how you progressed so fast?"

"Nope. After we started playing, the only thing he talked about was how much he hated the dart board for trying to avoid his darts. He said it was cursed. I don't think it was, though."

Moxie shifted, turning so she could look directly at Noah. "Wait. I was so caught up with your disappearance that I forgot. You were combining your runes, and Jalen's domain barely affected you. Did you manage to..."

"Oh, shit. Yeah, I did," Noah said, his eyes lighting up. "I honestly didn't even remember why I was looking through my grimoire. I couldn't shake the feeling that I still needed to do something, but I think I forgot that I'd already did the thing I was trying to do."

Moxie grabbed Noah's shoulders, delight in her eyes. "You hit Rank 4? That easily?"

"I don't know if I'd say it was easy, but it wasn't anywhere near as hard as I was worried it would be. I tested everything out again too, and it all seemed just about right. I think I'm finally done reworking it."

Moxie let out a breath and rocked back, shaking her head in disbelief. "That's incredible. Reaching Rank 4 without the backing of a noble family and doing it with completely Perfect Runes... your abilities are completely unfair."

"Hey, don't complain. You'll be using them too."

"Oh, trust me. I'm not complaining. I'm just in awe. You've got a domain, then. Can you feel it? What's it like?"

Noah's brow furrowed as he sought the words to properly share how the domain felt. The sensation wasn't as intense as it had been when he'd first reached Rank 4, but the area in a fairly large sphere around his body still felt like another limb—but, at the same time, it didn't.

He could feel it, but he couldn't actually move anything. It was just a general awareness and the faintest feeling of control.

"It's kind of like having a phantom limb that you can feel but can't move," Noah said thoughtfully, rubbing his chin. "But it's everywhere around you. Kind of a warm and fuzzy feeling."

"Can you feel me? Or just magic?"

"No, I can definitely feel your presence. It might be the magic inside you, though. I can't say for sure."

Moxie dug through one of her pockets and pulled out a seed. She held it between two fingers, and it cracked as she sent a tiny tendril of magic into it. All that emerged was ash, and Noah felt a tickle at the back of his mind.

"It blocked my magic," Moxie said. "Whoa. No effort at all? You just instinctively did it?"

"Yeah. I'm going to have to figure out how to turn that off when I need to." Noah's forehead furrowed in concentration, and he tried to picture his domain pulling back. Something shifted, but he wasn't sure exactly what it was. "Can you try again?"

Moxie shrugged and took out another seed, repeating the process. This time, it sprouted without trouble, and a vine curled around her fingers. It reached out toward Noah, continuing until it reached the end of the area he'd pulled back. A hiss rose up as the vine fizzled and the magic was destroyed.

"Damn," Moxie breathed. "This is a really strong domain. I'm pretty sure Allen's domain was so weak that it barely affected anything that wasn't directly touching his skin. If he knew that some upstart Linwick had a domain this powerful, he'd probably cry."

"That would be a sight to see," Noah said, a grin pulling at his lips. "We'll have to get you to catch up to me soon. Lee too."

"You'd better count on it. There's no way I'm letting you sprint past me when I've been doing this for so much longer than you. Are you trying to leave us behind or something?" Moxie teased.

"Never," Noah said, his features turning serious.

Moxie smiled up at him, then leaned back against his side. "I can't believe you somehow forgot about reaching Rank 4 less than a day after doing it. That should be one of the crowning accomplishments of a mage's life, you know."

"I was playing darts," Noah said defensively. Moxie craned her neck back to send a withering stare at Noah, and he grinned down at her. "Hey, I had more important things on my mind when I got back."

Moxie's cheeks reddened and she moved to give him another quick kiss before sliding off the bed and fixing her crumpled clothes. "Have you tested the new rune out yet? Is it still Natural Disaster?"

"Tested, no. But yes, it's still Natural Disaster. Just... right, this time around." Noah lifted a hand and rubbed two of his fingers together. Electricity crackled between his fingertips as he pulled them apart. "The magic comes so much easier now, and it's controlled as well. I want to find something big to train against the next time we go out to practice with the kids."

"Speaking of them, how do you think they're doing?" Moxie asked. She tried to adjust her long hair, but it had decided to stick out in every which direction and was no longer under her control. She scrunched her nose in annoyance and pulled it back into a ponytail, using a thin vine as a hair tie.

"I'm sure they're fine. Isabel and Todd are much better at bringing other people into their group now, so I don't think there's anything to be worried about," Noah replied. "We'll know for sure next class. Have you thought at all about what you want to teach, or should I get into music and Formations in addition to the normal training?"

"Let's do that for now. I've got some ideas, but you've already gotten started with your stuff, so you might as well run it through. And,

I'll be honest, I'm pretty curious to learn about Formations myself. I imagine this should be enlightening."

"In that case, I'll probably just head to bed. It's been a pretty long day."

"Tell me about it," Moxie said dryly. "Go wash off before you get under my covers. I'm not letting you get them dirty."

Noah gave her a mock salute and strode for the bathroom, grinning at the eye roll she sent in his direction.

* * *

Renewal yawned. Souls stretched out through the cosmos around her, as they always did. It wasn't like it had been that long since something interesting had happened. The past few months had been some of the most eventful ones in recent memory, but somehow that just made things worse.

She'd gotten so used to complete and abstract nothingness that even the slightest taste of anything else had her hooked. To her growing annoyance, the fools that made up her so-called church on the world where the interesting mortal had landed were startlingly incompetent.

"One of my followers literally sat across from the table from him and didn't notice a damn thing," Renewal groaned, pulling at her hair and looking up into the endless sky above with a groan. "If any of them actually had enough power to hear my actual commands instead of just tiny snippets of them, this whole thing would have been done weeks ago. I don't want to wait any more."

The temptation to just go to the world herself was strong—but not nearly strong enough to make her abandon her senses. A transgression of that magnitude would result in her complete and utter annihilation.

And, as boring as waiting was, it was nowhere near as bad as oblivion. At least, Renewal was pretty sure that was the case. She'd never tried oblivion, so it was always possible that it wasn't that bad.

I won't give up my chance to ascend further through the godly realms because of one stupid little mortal. I should just forget all about him. No matter what power he stole or enlightenment he may have stumbled into, it'll all be worthless. It's beneath my attention.

Yeah. I should just focus on the important things. I'll pretend I

*never even saw him. In a few hundred years, he'll be nothing but a blip.
In a thousand, he won't even register in my memory anymore.*

I—

A ripple of energy passed through the air beside Renewal. She looked down as a tiny tuft of white fur trotted into her domain, red horns shimmering with faint energy. Her eyes lit up and she knelt beside the cat. It had been a while since she'd seen it. Making something from her own form also made it surprisingly difficult to track when it didn't want to be seen.

"Hello there, little avatar. You've certainly taken your time." Renewal's body shrank as she drew her energy in, shrinking down to the size of a normal human. She scratched the cat's chin and it purred, arching up against her legs. "Come on, then. What have you been up to? Are you going to bring me that mortal?"

A flicker of judgment passed through the cat's eyes, and Renewal's face heated.

"I know I just decided I didn't care anymore, but that was before you came back," Renewal said defensively. "It's not my fault. Forget that. I changed my mind. Tell me everything."

The cat let out a low purr. That was it. No information arrived in Renewal's mind. Her brow creased in confusion.

"What are you doing?" A note of annoyance entered her words. "That was a command, little avatar. I made you from my power, and I can unmake you just the same. Show me what you found when you located the man who stole my energy."

The cat meowed, its face scrunching up. It hacked a hairball up on the ground, then licked at its paw. Dark eyes watched Renewal slyly.

"You've always been an annoying little shit," Renewal growled. She scratched the cat's back. "Come on. Give me the information. I only kept you around this long because of how useful your shenanigans are with the other gods. You are *not* turning them against me."

Her avatar let out one more meow, then trotted away from her. It turned, looking at Renewal over its shoulder. Her frown deepened and she rose to her feet, extending a tendril of energy toward the cat. It was acting strangely.

The little brat has been mischievous ever since I made it, but it's never disobeyed a direct command from me. What's going on here?

Renewal's energy reached the cat—and brushed across it. Her eyes widened in shock. Her runes didn't match with the cat's anymore. It had changed. The runes that fueled the avatar had shifted enough that they were no longer hers.

"No," Renewal muttered. "Impossible. I *made* you. Nobody could have corrupted your energy!"

The cat let out another meow, and this time, Renewal realized what it was. It hadn't visited to share information with her. No, it had come to say goodbye.

"Who?" Renewal demanded, although she was starting to get the feeling that she already knew the answer. The only person who could have possibly modified any aspect of her avatar would have had to be someone who had access to her runes.

And, throughout all the cosmos, there was only a single person other than her in existence who had a rune that could have done such a thing.

Renewal watched as her avatar turned tail and slipped into one of the streams of energy that connected the universe, vanishing from the astral plane. It was doubtlessly returning to its new partner.

"You little shit," Renewal muttered, staring at the space where her cat had once stood. "If you think I'm letting you get away with this that easily, you're sorely mistaken. We're going to have a chat, even if I have to break a dozen Rules to do it."

Chapter Thirty-Seven

Noah woke the following morning to Moxie lying on top of him, her face on his chest. And, stacked on top of her like the head of a snowman, was Mascot. He yawned, trying not to move too much and wake one of the two up by accident.

That didn't stop him from sending a glare up at Mascot, though.

Little shit. I still can't tell if you're actually on my side or if you just enjoy causing trouble in my general vicinity.

Moxie shifted and blinked, her eyes fluttering open. She started to move, but Noah caught her before she could.

"You've got a cat on top of you," Noah said in a low whisper. "No moving allowed."

Blinking as her consciousness streamed back, Moxie tried to twist to get a better look at Mascot without waking him up. She gave up on the idea and just laid her head back down with a huff. "Why'd he decide to stack on us?"

"Why does Mascot do literally anything?" Noah countered.

"Fair point," Moxie said. "What time is it?"

Noah glanced out the window. "Somewhere around the morning. Maybe an hour or two past sunrise?"

"We need to get ready for class soon."

"Probably," Noah agreed. They were both silent for a few seconds. "So... are you going to move?"

"No. There's a cat on me. Are you going to teach about Formations today?"

They lay there for another ten minutes. Noah was far from bothered by that development, but Mascot was showing absolutely no signs of planning to wake up in the near future. And, as tempting as it was to keep lying right where they were, Noah and Moxie did have responsibilities to get to.

Fortunately for them—and unfortunately for Mascot—they weren't alone in the room. Out of the corner of his eye, Noah just barely saw a flash of Lee as she stood up, reaching for Mascot.

She plucked the cat from Moxie's back, eliciting a surprised yowl as she clutched it to her chest. Mascot hissed and batted at her nose before vanishing in a puff of smoke. Lee stared at her hands in shock.

"I thought that was the plushie."

Moxie pushed herself up and sat back on Noah's legs, brushing the hair out of her face. "That was either very lucky or very unlucky. It depends on how much Mascot takes offense to it."

I'm still not sure if there's anything that should be done about Mascot. Actually, I don't know if there's anything that can be done about that cat. It basically just does whatever it wants. It's the oddest passive for a rune I've ever heard of.

"I'll have some snacks for him," Lee said sheepishly. "I wanted to check if you were still busy. We have to go to class soon."

"So we were just thinking." Moxie slipped out of bed and changed into a new set of clothes. "We aren't late, are we?"

"Not yet."

Noah got up as well, joining Moxie in readying for the day. He brushed his hair back as best as he could, but quickly gave up on taming it. Vermil's hair had always been fairly long, and despite what he'd told Father during their first ever meeting, he hadn't exactly had a haircut since arriving at Arbitage.

After the hasty preparations were done, the three of them set off for the transport cannon. They arrived a short while later to find that the students had all arrived well before them.

All five of them sat in a small circle at the base of the transport cannon, eating breakfast. It looked like they'd been walking around for at least a little while since none of them had the telltale signs of a recent awakening.

"You're cutting it close today," Todd said through a mouthful of biscuit as the professors approached.

"There was a cat on me," Moxie said. "A particularly irate one."

"What will we be training today?" Alexandra asked. "Another hunt trying to catch Lee?"

"Possibly. We'll be opening with something a little different," Noah said. The students all stood up, finishing off the last bits of their breakfast. He couldn't quite tell if they'd all become friends overnight, but a lot of the awkward air from their previous class had evaporated.

"Different? The last time we had a different class, you baited a monster to chase after us," Todd said with a suspicious glare.

"That sounds like something Revin would do." James grimaced. "The trick is to run the monster back toward him so he has to kill it."

"He and Moxie hid," Isabel said. "We couldn't."

"Ah. Smarter than Revin, then."

"I don't think that's a very high bar," Emily said with a snort. "Is the thing we're going to be doing secret or something?"

"No. It'll just be a lecture," Noah replied, starting toward the stairs at the base of the transport cannon. "I doubt it'll get to anything practical today. We'll just see how it goes and if there's interest in continuing it. I imagine we'll have quite a bit of time to do more physical training in the coming days. I want to test something different out."

Everyone followed him up to the top of the tower, where Tim wasted no time in bidding them good luck and sending them off to the Windcorned Plateau. After confirming that there weren't any monsters in the area around them, everyone sat down in front of Noah.

"Is there a reason we aren't just doing this in a classroom?" Emily asked.

"There's nothing wrong with a little sunlight," Noah said with a shrug. "Also, I hate the classroom they gave me. The thing is completely run down. I'd use it if I needed a chalkboard, but I doubt I will today."

"You could have used Moxie's," Emily pointed out.

Noah opened his mouth, then closed it again. He probably could have used Moxie's. Somehow, the thought of teaching in her room instead of his own hadn't struck him. He cleared his throat.

"You'll live. Besides, this'll let us transition to the second half of our lessons easier. But, today, we're having a normal lecture to start with."

"About what?" Todd asked.

"I'm getting there!" Noah exclaimed, giving them a mock glare. "Good god. When did you all become so impatient? We'll be talking about Formations and the basics of what goes into them."

That caught Todd's attention instantly, while simultaneously losing the interest of just about every other student.

"Formations aren't really something we can use, though," Isabel said. "It would take so long to get good at using them that by the time we could actually use a Formation, we'll have outgrown the runes we learned the Formation for."

"That's because you're looking at them wrong. There are several reasons to learn about Formations. To be frank, I think they're being completely misused. Formations are, at their core, a way to give your runes more guidance and power to achieve something you can't normally get."

"You need to be an Imbuement master to use Formations, though," Todd said. "Are you saying you can do that? You barely knew how to do Body Imbuements a month ago, much less the more difficult ones."

"You definitely don't need to master Imbuements to use Formations," Noah said with a shake of his head. "But we'll start from the beginning. Does everyone know what a Formation actually is?"

He waited for a few moments, watching his students' expressions. Isabel and Todd both exchanged a knowing look the moment he finished speaking. They clearly remembered the first class he'd taught them, which filled Noah with pride. Evidently, some lessons had stuck.

Unfortunately for the other three students, they hadn't been subjected to Noah's unique method of learning about runes.

"They're just really complicated Imbuements that are optimized for a set of runes to make them way stronger," Alexandra said, her brow furrowed. "Everyone knows what Formations are. The problem is actually using them."

"That's all?" Noah asked, arching an eyebrow. "They're just rune circles?"

Alexandra paused for a moment, digging through her memory to see if she'd missed something, then nodded. "Yeah. As far as I'm aware, they are."

"What about you, Emily?" Noah asked. "What do you think?"

"Pretty much what Alexandra said."

"Isabel? Todd?"

"Pass," Todd said.

"Same here," Isabel said.

Noah chuckled. "There's nothing wrong with trying to answer a question. Being wrong is fine, so long as you're willing to accept it and continue to learn."

"You're saying Formations *aren't* rune circles?" Emily asked.

"Do the people that use Formations through music work with rune circles?"

"I mean, I don't know. I guess not? But music is just a way to show off how good you are at Formations. It's basically a gimmick." Emily's brow furrowed. "It's just a different way to do a Formation."

"One you didn't consider, which means your understanding of Formations is flawed. If there's one thing you don't know about them, don't you think there's more?"

"I don't know a lot of things about Formations, but I still know they're practically impossible to learn," Alexandra said. "Especially for me."

"Perhaps. That'll be up to you to decide. Here's the thing. I think Formations are much more than what they seem to be. I've been working on them for quite some time now, and I've come to the conclusion that not only are Formations actually considerably easier than we've been led to believe, they're also deeply tied to runes themselves."

"You? You're a Formation Master?" Alexandra asked, blinking in surprise. "Aren't you a Rank 3?"

Rank 4, actually.

"And there's the problem. That's the big fallacy that everyone has arrived at," Noah said, thrusting a finger at Alexandra. "Everyone says that Formations only work for one set of runes, but that's wrong."

He held his hands out, and his violin materialized in them. Isabel and Todd's eyes widened in shock, and Emily's mouth dropped open. Alexandra just watched him, a mixture of confusion and doubt painting her features.

"No damn way," Todd said. "You use music?"

"Music isn't a trick to using Formations. I'm convinced it's actually the best way to do it, and this whole rune circle bit is bullshit." Noah paused for a moment, then corrected himself. "Well, maybe I should correct that. It's not just music. It's pattern."

"Explain." Todd leaned forward, his features unreadable. It did make a degree of sense—his father had been an Imbuer, and Todd had held the man in very high regard. There was a good chance that Noah was insulting practices that Todd's dad had engaged in.

"I want you to think about your runes," Noah said. "And I mean *really* think. This is something that I ruminated over for a long time, but why is it that runes hold power at all? What makes them special? I mean, seriously. Why doesn't a random circle I draw on the ground turn into a rune?"

Nobody responded to that. It was a pretty ludicrous question, of course. Noah could practically read their thoughts.

They're just runes. That's how they work. Who cares?

"Well?" Noah asked. "That wasn't rhetorical. Give it a shot."

"Because you need energy in the first place?" Emily tried, starting to get a little more interested in the lesson. "You can't just take it from nothing."

"Okay. Let's say I've got a filled rune. Why can't I just stuff all that power into a circle I draw? Why do I need to draw the same rune?"

"The rune is a representation of the energy it holds," Alexandra said. "And energy can't change."

"I like the first part of what you said." Noah gave Alexandra an approving nod. "A rune is a representation. Let's hold onto that and touch the second half of your claim before wrapping back."

Noah pressed his hand to the ground and called on Natural Disaster. He'd yet to use the rune, but he was delighted to find that the energy flowed exactly how he wanted it to. A mound of dirt rose up beneath his palm, trembling as it was pressed in on itself by a miniature earthquake.

He then took a small pebble and set it at the top of the mound. "What would this be?"

"A rock," James said.

"Thank you, James. I'm going to call it something else. This is potential," Noah said. He flicked the rock with his finger, and it rolled down the hill, coming to a stop at the bottom. "And I just used that potential."

"What does this have to do with energy changing?" Alexandra

asked, her brow furrowed. The question wasn't meant to be inflamma-tory—she was definitely trying to figure out what he was saying, but it hadn't quite clicked yet.

"I'll admit I'm not an expert on this particular part, but there are basically two kinds of energy in this case," Noah said, picking the rock back up and returning it to the top of his hill. "The first part is the potential. While the rock is at the top of the hill, it has the potential to roll down. That's the energy in your runes before you use it."

"Okay," Alexandra said with a small nod. "That makes sense."

"But what about when the rock is halfway down the hill?" Noah moved the rock, holding it in place on the side of the mound. "Half of that potential energy is gone, right? Did it just vanish?"

Alexandra nodded. Noah could see the gears turning in her head as her brow furrowed. "It's moving now."

"Exactly. The energy changed. Instead of potential, what we now have is kinetic energy," Noah explained. "The potential energy is turning into motion. Thus, energy changes."

Alexandra rocked back and nodded her understanding. "Okay. I'm with you. In that case, what does it have to do with the patterns runes have? Are you saying that they're potential energy before you use them, then kinetic energy while you use them?"

"I don't know if using runes would be kinetic energy, but the analogy is there, yes. Let's pull in the other thing you said. The shape of a rune is a representation of what it is, right?"

Nobody said anything. They all watched him with either curiosity, confusion, or a combination of the two.

"Well, my claim is that a rune's physical form is more than just a representation. It's a pattern that holds the energy. Or, in other words, I think the natural state of runic energy is kinetic energy—the rock in freefall. By drawing a rune out, we're holding the rock at the top of the hill."

He paused for a moment to let his thoughts sink in—not just for the kids but for himself as well. The more Noah had practiced with Formations, the more he'd come to the conclusion he was drawing no. Still, this was the first time he'd put it to actual words.

"That means that runes are basically just patterns," Todd muttered. The blood drained out of his face and his eyes went wide.

"Gods. Are you claiming that Formations can use musical patterns to basically make a new rune?"

"It's a new way to control the magic," Noah said with a smile. "And that's what I want to try to take advantage of. Understanding Formations means understanding your runes better, and the same goes in the other direction. So, shall we get started?"

Chapter Thirty-Eight

"Music is an expression of emotion. It can be pretty much whatever you want it to be," Noah said, placing the bow of his violin against its strings. "And making Formations with it is the exact same principle. We make a pattern—a song—with music, and that holds the magic within it."

"How?" Alexandra asked. "Music isn't a tangible thing. How can you contain music with nothing more than sound?"

"Not sound. Pattern. As we discussed, runes are literally just patterns that hold energy. Sure, they're more visual than music, but a pattern is a pattern. It doesn't matter what kind of pattern it is. That's my theory, at least."

"Wait," Isabel said. She shifted her position, having gone from mildly interested to completely transfixed. "Are you saying that we could make Formations with methods that aren't music? If Formations are just patterns, couldn't we do the same thing with a stick in the sand or body motions?"

Noah's grin expanded and he nodded. "I'll admit that I haven't tested it yet, but if music works, I don't see why dancing wouldn't. What matters is the pattern. Rune circles are functionally the same thing, but they're locked in stone. Frankly, I think they're a crutch."

"They're the main way Formations are done, though," James said. "Are you saying that everyone is fundamentally wrong about the way Formations and runes work?"

"Yes," Noah said. "Just because everyone does something in a certain way doesn't make it the right one. I have reason to believe that there's some very serious misinformation about how runes function. I'm not sure if it's because the noble houses have spread it on purpose or for some other reason, but just take my word for it."

"You can't say that and not tell us what it is," Emily exclaimed. "Why does it sound like you're implying—"

"Yes, I can." Noah cut Emily off and chuckled at the annoyance on her face. "We don't want to get too distracted from the original lesson, and trust me. This one is more important right now."

"Is this even something we can use, though?" Todd asked reluctantly, clearly hoping Noah would calm his worries. "Pattern or not, Formations take years to master. You'd have to teach us all music and then start showing us how to use it for Formations after we learned. It would take forever."

"Good question, Todd. If we were trying to learn rune circles, then yes. It would take forever. And if I were trying to teach all of you music from scratch, it would take me years to accomplish it. That's why I won't just be teaching music. We're going to be focusing on finding the way that *you* see patterns."

"Doesn't everything need to be perfect to use Formations?" Isabel asked. "If we make a mistake, it could blow up in our face. I don't mind some danger, but is there a way we can avoid that? I don't want to shatter my runes or kill myself."

Noah could tell Isabel was thinking back to their early training in the Scorched Acres, and he couldn't blame her. It was probably the farthest thing from safe that he could have done. While it had been effective, the training had also been a pretty big risk.

"You won't be starting by trying to push magic into the patterns. You don't try to sprint before you know how to walk. We'll start by learning the patterns themselves and how we can use them, and then only put magic in once we're comfortable." Noah pulled the bow of his violin across the strings, drawing forth a long, beautiful note. Everyone tensed, waiting for something to happen, but it didn't come. Noah played a few more notes, not ashamed to say he was more than slightly amused by the concern in the kids' expressions.

"Where's the Formation?" Todd asked.

"It's just music," Noah replied. "There is no Formation. That's what I'm saying. I mean, think about it. You've definitely done some form of pattern in your life before, but you didn't randomly blow up by triggering a Formation by accident. Just like everything else in magic, it takes intent."

He paused, waiting for them all to fully process his words. Even Moxie and Lee were paying close attention to his words. It filled Noah with a sense of satisfaction and pride that he hadn't felt in a long time. It felt good to be properly teaching a class again.

"How do we start?" Todd asked.

"By looking inward. Think about what in life speaks to you that you can find pattern within. Something that you'd be comfortable really investing time into. It could be art, motion, nature, anything. Feel free to talk amongst yourselves if you're struggling."

Noah was rewarded by a burst of conversation as everyone started talking at once. Not a trace of the initial apprehension at the start of the lesson remained. Moxie caught the smug grin on Noah's lips and poked him in the side.

"Ouch," Noah yelped. "What?"

"Nothing. I just thought that was a little cool," Moxie replied. She lowered her voice so the others wouldn't be able to hear it over their conversation. "Do you really think they can start doing Formations in a short period of time? I mean you... well, died a lot."

"And in doing so, I figured out the problems. It's just a mixture of pattern and intent. I definitely won't have them trying to make Formations immediately, but I'm confident that they'll be able to handle it as long as we take things one step at a time. Nothing in this world is safe. Giving the kids tools to punch above their weight is worth the risk."

"In that case, what do you think my pattern would be?"

Noah tilted his head to the side in thought. "Your room has a lot of work put into it with all the vines you've used to decorate it. Do you like art in nature?"

"I guess I've never really thought about it," Moxie admitted with a small frown. "I think I do, though? I didn't have much opportunity to really put much thought into it while I worked for the Torrins, but I do rather like my room."

"It's a good start, then."

"What about me?" Lee asked. "What is my—"

"Food, probably," Noah said, only half joking. "Maybe flavor? I'm not actually sure if you prefer the taste of food or the act of eating, but I suspect your path lies along those lines."

"Huh," Lee said. "That might be true. How'd you figure that out?"

"Call it intuition," Noah said, suppressing a laugh and ruffling Lee's hair. He raised his voice so everyone could overhear him again. "And guys, please make sure you don't go about doing anything without my permission. Moxie just reminded me that this is far from safe—don't let my confidence delude you into thinking Formations are easy. You could easily kill yourself by accident, so stay with the pace of the class."

He got a round of nods from the students, who promptly returned to their conversation. Evidently, his warning wasn't that much of a problem for them. The temptation of power and knowledge was too great—but Noah wasn't concerned.

All of them had shown enough maturity that he was confident they'd listen to his instructions. He waited, content to just listen in, for the next few minutes until the chatter started to die down.

"Figure it out?" Noah asked once it seemed like everyone had finished. "Todd, care to share what you decided on?"

"Fire," Todd replied confidently. "It was my dad's favorite Imbuement, and it's the element I understand the most. There are patterns to how it works. I think."

"Definitely true, but you're gonna have to work on the confidence," Noah said with a chuckle. "Isabel?"

"Swordwork," Isabel replied without a second of hesitation. "The movements in a fight have a pattern to them, and figuring them out is the way you win a fight."

"Brilliant. I take it that's yours as well, Alexandra?"

Alexandra blinked, then nodded. "Yeah. It only made sense."

"What about you, Emily?"

"Ice and frost. There are patterns in snowflakes. Really clear ones, when you look closely enough."

Noah nodded. They were pretty solid choices that he couldn't find any fault in. Fire seemed to be the one with the most randomness in it, but nature in general tended to follow patterns of some sort.

"What about you, James?"

"I might go with music," James said. "I rather like humming."

"That's kind of lame," Emily said.

James shrugged. "It's easy."

Somehow, that fits him perfectly. Never thought about trying to hum a Formation, but I can't see why it wouldn't work.

"Okay. Great. For the second half of this class, we're going to be doing one thing. You'll spend it in your mindspace, trying to envision and get closer to the pattern you want to follow. Really think about how it works and just get to know it. Don't worry about actually doing anything, and don't put any magic into it beyond maybe forming something like a small snowstorm or a ball of fire to study."

He didn't need to tell them twice. Everyone sat more comfortably, closing their eyes to slip into their mindspaces. Isabel and Todd leaned against each other, and a small smile drifted across Noah's lips at the sight.

Cute.

He also couldn't help but notice that Emily and James were sitting pretty close together, and their hands weren't too far from touching. It wasn't hard to read their body language—the two had clearly gotten a lot closer over the summer.

Noah called on Natural Disaster and sent a minuscule tremor through the ground, bumping up the dirt beneath Emily's hand to push it closer to James. Both of them stiffened for an instant, but neither moved their hands back.

Moxie caught what he'd done and arched an eyebrow, but he just shrugged in response.

"Keep watch over us?" Moxie asked. "I'm giving this a shot."

"I'm gonna try it too," Lee said, sitting down beside Noah. "Can I have some jerky to test with?"

She didn't wait for a response before reaching up and snagging Noah's rations from his bag.

"I'll keep an eye out," Noah promised. "Good luck, everyone. And remember, you aren't trying to force anything. There's nothing but you and your pattern. It's kind of like meditation, but not boring."

Nobody replied. They were all already sinking into their mindspace. Noah raised his gaze, looking out over the plateau to make sure no monsters would be able to take advantage of their distraction.

This is more than just Formations. It's about improving their funda-

mental understanding of magic as well. Hell, I barely even know what I'm talking about, but the more I try to learn so I can teach, the more I discover myself. I can't wait to see what we can all do in a few weeks.

Chapter Thirty-Nine

A zel was waiting in Lee's mindspace when she arrived in it. That wasn't all that unusual. He'd taken to hanging around in it more in recent days, but that didn't stop her from sending him a suspicious look. Azel was watching her with a pensive look in his eyes, his hands crossed behind his back, and the flames that smoldered along his clothes contained to faint embers.

"What?" Lee asked. "Why are you doing that?"

"Doing what?" Azel asked. "I am just relaxing."

"No, you're leering at me. Are you going to try to convince me not to practice Formations?"

"Absolutely not." Azel shook his head, and something that might have actually been respect passed through his eyes. The emotion vanished so quickly that it might as well never have been there. A demon such as Azel could not have respect for anyone that wasn't himself. "Vines has actually stumbled into something interesting. I think it's worth looking into, and I'll certainly be studying it myself."

"Right," Lee said. She stared at Azel for a second, waiting for him to elaborate. When he didn't, she pressed on. "So why are you standing here like that?"

"Am I not allowed to? It's a free world."

"No. You aren't. This is my soul, not the world."

"Ah, yes. I suppose it is." Azel picked at his fingernails, then curled the corner of his lip down in a grimace. "Alas, you've got some of my runes in you, so there's at least a bit of my soul in here as well."

"For now," Lee said. "It'll fade away as my soul completely envelops your runes."

"It will," Azel agreed. "But until then, there isn't all that much you can do to keep me from spending time with you. Is it really such a horrid concept?"

"Depends on if you're trying to convince me to do things that I'm not going to do. If you weren't such an asshole, then nobody would mind spending time around you." Lee crossed her arms and glared at Azel. "And don't try to pretend otherwise. You know Noah and Moxie wouldn't mind that you were a demon. Their problem with you is *you*."

Azel held his hands up defensively. "Yes, yes. Unfortunately, I cannot change my nature. I am who I am. And so are you."

"What's that meant to mean?"

"It means we both know why you've avoided reaching Rank 4 for so long," Azel said, his brow darkening as he lowered his hands. "It's not because you haven't been able to figure out what runes you want to use. Noah has an offer to get you anything you want, and he already *has* the runes you need."

"I've just been thinking. I don't want to get a bad combination and have to go through another Sundering and healing."

Azel's laughter echoed through the dark recesses of Lee's soul. He shook his head and let out a sigh. "Lee. You do realize I'm a demon, don't you? That was a good lie, but you're literally speaking to a master of twisting the truth. The reason you haven't reached for Rank 4 is because you know that the Rank 4 change for demons isn't the same as it is for humans. We don't get a domain. Are you going to tell me what happens instead, or do I have to remind you?"

It was several seconds before Lee responded.

"Our Demon Rune evolves."

"Exactly," Azel said, walking in a circle around Lee and forcing her to turn to keep her eyes on him. "And you fear that you're going to lose yourself in the process. With how closely our bodies and souls are tied together, it's only natural."

"Are you telling me I won't?"

Azel stopped walking and sent Lee a strange look. She wasn't actually sure what the emotion on his features was meant to be, but it wasn't one that she'd ever seen Azel wearing.

"No, Lee. I'm not. I don't have any reason to lie about that. You will change. Perhaps it will be for the better. Perhaps not. But you will change. There's a reason the gap between weak demons and powerful ones is so great. And I certainly hope you don't plan to remain as a pathetic Rank 3."

"Why do you care?" Lee demanded. "And so what if I do? I'd rather stay the way I am and stay with my friends than lose everything and become like you."

Azel's expression flickered. Strands of Lee's inky mindspace twisted around them, writhing like an angered squid. He watched them for a moment, then straightened his smoldering suit out and pursed his lips.

"Do you really believe you can remain as you are and still keep them? Noah and Moxie are both growing in power. I won't try to convince you that they'll abandon you. Even if I were right, you wouldn't believe me."

"You're right," Lee said. "I wouldn't."

"But you *will* become a liability. Right now, you're strong. But Noah has only been on this world for months, and he's already Rank 4. In a few more months, he may reach Rank 5. His ability to grow is unbelievable. He eclipses even Archdemons in potential. Do you really think he'll want to worry about protecting a Rank 3 when his opponents are Rank 5 or 6?"

Lee opened her mouth, but she found that she didn't have an answer. Azel was far from finished, though.

"And, beyond that, what of the Inquisition?" Azel pressed. "Those pathetic fools and their Holy Runes only worked so effectively on you because your soul and body do not yet match. Demons of Rank 3 and below are easily detected and struck down, but once you begin reaching true union of body and soul in Rank 4, you will not be such a liability. There is no way around it, Lee."

"Well, I'll find one!" Lee yelled, clenching her fists and baring her teeth. "I won't become like you!"

The two demons glared at each other. Even though no magic was flying, tension filled the air like a thick syrup, twisting and winding through Lee's mindspace.

"Why are you doing this?" Lee asked. "Why do you care so much? It's none of your damn business."

"Because I'm bored," Azel growled. "And I'd rather help you than the damn mortal. He doesn't need my help."

Something about his answer felt... lacking. Lee couldn't place what it was, and she didn't really feel like trying to figure it out either.

"Well, I don't want your help."

"I didn't ask if you wanted it," Azel said. "You are receiving it nonetheless. You do realize that you can't have everything you want, right? If you want power, you have to be willing to change. If you don't want to change, then you will remain as you are and will eventually be left behind."

"Well, I want everything. I don't care about logic. It's stupid."

Azel blinked. A snort of laughter escaped his lips and he shook his head. "Spoken like a fool. And spoken like a demon, I suppose. I can't fault you for that. But I will warn you—there will be a time when you need power. And if you continue to refuse it like you have been, the people you care about will die. Noah may survive, but Moxie is not as much of a roach as he is. Isabel, Todd, Emily, and the others—they are all fragile. You must be powerful enough to protect what is yours, or it is not yours. Even if you do not push to Rank 4 now, I suggest you start preparing to reach it as soon as possible. Intentional weakness *will* destroy you."

With that, Azel vanished in a puff of embers and black smoke. Lee stared at the space where he'd been standing, her shoulders slumping forward in defeat. No matter how infuriating the demon was, he actually had a point.

I can't just stay like this. I need to get stronger somehow. I don't want to become like Azel, though. I don't want to be so consumed by the emotion I feed on that I become a terrible person.

But... I suppose getting the rest of the runes I need to reach Rank 4 and filling them up would be a good idea. I don't have to push ahead until it's time, but Noah relies on me. If something shows up that he needs help fighting, I can't let him and the others down.

Lee's face creased with determination and she sat down, crossing her legs and bracing her palms on her knees. There were several forms of power, and the process of pursuing one of them had just been interrupted by Azel.

There would be time to figure out her runes and progression in the future. For now, she was going to focus on the thought of food. She needed to figure out Formations and see if the power she sought could be achieved in a different way.

Chapter Forty

Noah stood as everyone delved into their mind spaces, playing a quiet song on his violin as he waited for them all to finish. There weren't any monsters in the area, and he wasn't sure what else to do with his time.

Besides, it's nice to be able to just play for no purpose. Having music and Formations tied together so closely is nice, but it's not the same as playing just for the sake of playing. I hope the others don't take too long, though. I'm itching to test out Natural Disaster in its new form.

Unfortunately, there wouldn't be any testing until everyone was awake again. Noah wasn't about to just leave them sitting around undefended in an area full of monsters. And so he played.

A little under an hour passed before Moxie opened her eyes. She glanced over at Noah, pausing to appreciate the music for a few seconds before she rose to her feet and brushed the dirt off her backside.

"Any luck?" Noah asked, pausing his song.

"I think so. It's definitely something I'll have to practice a lot of," Moxie said with a frown. "Guess I can see why you blew yourself up so many times doing this, even with your pattern practice."

"It's not like I *like* blowing up. If I'm doing it, it's for a reason."

"Could have fooled me," Moxie said with a snicker.

It wasn't long before the others started to awake as well. Isabel and Emily opened their eyes shortly after Moxie did. Alexandra was next, followed by Todd and James. Lee was the last of the group to stand back up.

They all had pensive expressions on their faces that told Noah his lesson had been at least marginally effective. He waited for another minute after everyone had stood up, just to make sure they were all back in the present.

"Right," Noah said. "Did anything completely not work for anyone? I'm assuming that isn't the case because of how long you spent in your mindspaces."

The students all exchanged glances, then shook their heads one by one.

"I'm not sure I'd say I was anywhere near good at it, but I get what I'm meant to do, and I was making progress," Todd said.

"Same." Isabel flexed her hands as if she were holding a sword. "I still don't really know how I can use magic in conjunction with this, but I can work on it."

Nobody else added anything, so Noah clapped his hands together. "In that case, the first part of class today is over. No point lecturing forever or you'll get so bored with me that your brains will leak out of your ears. We'll be moving on to the next half."

"Getting points for the Master Rune?" Todd asked eagerly. Judging by the looks on the other students' faces, he'd voiced all of their thoughts. Noah chuckled. If everyone had been paying attention before, now they were laser-focused on him.

"No. We won't be doing that today—instead, you'll be doing it on your own time. The next challenge will be to understand the pattern you're focusing on as much as possible by our next class in two days. Whoever can demonstrate or prove their understanding the most extensively will win. The top three of you will get points."

"What are we doing now, then?" Alexandra asked.

Noah turned to Lee. "I was actually hoping Lee could take over the second half of this class again. There's something I need to do on the Windscorned Plateau, and I know she's been hoping to get some physical practice in. It's been a while since we've done anything of the sort, so I think it would be a good idea to stay in the habit."

Isabel, Todd, and Emily all paled as one. James and Alexandra gave the others confused glances, but that was fine. They'd understand soon enough.

"You good with that, Lee?"

"Yep!" Lee said, though it took her a second longer than normal to answer. She seemed slightly distracted, but it wasn't the time to press. Lee rubbed her hands together and grinned. "Stretching is good for your health."

"Not when you're the one leading it," Todd muttered under his breath.

Noah suppressed a laugh. "I'll be back in a few hours; I have a monster to hunt. If any big explosions happen, don't come looking. I'll be fine."

Moxie gave him a small frown as Noah handed her his bag and gourd. She raised an eyebrow slightly in question, and he tapped the side of his head, mouthing the words *Natural Disaster*.

Understanding bloomed in Moxie's eyes and she shrugged. Noah took his flying sword out and laid it on the ground. He sent a tendril of energy into it, lifting himself into the air while Lee had everyone sit down on the ground to get started with her stretches.

Then he was gone, zipping through the air and squinting against the nip of wind against his eyes. Noah made sure to put a decent amount of distance between himself and the others. The last thing he wanted to do was mistakenly summon something strong enough to cause them a real threat anywhere where it could go after one of the students.

And I don't exactly know what the powerful monsters are in the Windscorned Plateaus. Just because there isn't a Great Monster doesn't mean I'll have a cakewalk. Accidents can always happen, so it's better to be safe than sorry.

He flew for just under an hour before landing on the edge of a plateau that looked largely uninhabited. It was, like all the other plateaus, covered with bulbous blue flowers. However, it looked like a herd of Fluffants had gone through at some point, as most of the flowers were withered and drained.

You know, I have to wonder how those things get from one plateau to the other. They didn't seem particularly mobile, and I can't picture them scaling a wall for the life of me. Ah well. It hardly matters.

Noah returned the sword to his waist and drew on Sunder. He needed to put off enough power to draw the attention of a monster, but preferably not one that was so powerful that he couldn't fight against it.

Sure, the likelihood of doing that was probably pretty low, but it wasn't the time to push his luck. Noah let some of Sunder's energy trickle out of his palm and rise into the air. Chances were, any strong monsters in the area would probably be Wind-based and would come from the sky rather than beneath the ground.

Some time passed. Nothing came, and Noah intensified the strength of the magic he was letting pour out. It was an alarming waste of energy that would have drained his reserves dry just a few weeks ago, but the advancements he'd made in reaching Rank 4 had given him much more power to resist Sunder with.

More power swirled into the air above Noah, tiny wisps of black smoke twisting and swirling through the sky beneath the path of the sun. Part of him was starting to suspect that the fishing strategy only worked when the monsters were underground when he heard a screech in the distance.

Out of the corner of his eye, Noah saw a large shape moving through the air in his direction. It was a bird of some sort, but it looked more fluffy than feathered. It strongly resembled a storm cloud the size of a small house, but the two burning red motes in the center of its face and the jagged, black beak gave it away as a monster.

There's my target. Something that big is definitely at least a Rank 2. Maybe even a Rank 3 or higher. I think I'll call it a Stormwing. Seems kind of cool. Let's find out if it deserves the name.

Noah pulled back on Sunder, lowering into a fighting stance as the Stormwing let out another screech. Its red eyes were fixed solely on Noah, having located the source of power that had drawn it out of— well, whatever it had been doing.

Natural Disaster's magic flooded through Noah's veins as he called upon it. A grin stretched across his lips at the tingle of magic, and he rubbed his fingers together, generating the faintest amount of static electricity. That was enough to kickstart his magic.

Power poured into it, arcing between the fingers and coiling into a ball in his palm. Noah thrust his hand forward and a peal of thunder split the sky. Lightning screamed forth in a flash, slamming into the Stormwing with a brilliant crash.

The bird spun through the strike, squeaking in surprise and now thoroughly angered. It didn't look particularly hurt. It dove straight at him, and energy crackled at its own beak. Idly, Noah noted that using lightning against a monster that clearly had some form of Storm or Lightning Runes to call on probably hadn't been the best idea.

Crackles of gray electricity enveloped the Stormwing as it dove for him, aiming to run Noah through with its beak. He spun out of the way, calling on Natural Disaster to gently boost his movements with wind.

A gleeful laugh slipped out of Noah's mouth at the ease at which his rune responded. It was almost as if he were just using a pure Wind Rune, though it was still just a little more work to filter the magic.

The Stormwing shot past him, dragging its feet through the soil and spinning to face Noah. It charged at him like an ostrich, raising its wings above its head to loom over him. The smart move would have likely been to reposition, but Noah wasn't feeling particularly smart at the moment.

A bolt of lightning shot from the Stormwing's beak—and evaporated the instant it reached Noah's domain. He didn't even have to dodge. The monster was Rank 3 at most, and that meant it was doomed.

Wind gathered around his body and shoved him forward in a burst of motion. He let out a roar, bounding straight toward the Stormwing. The monster faltered in surprise, clearly remembering the intensity of the magic he had been putting off, but it was too little and too late.

Noah released the wind and summoned a power he hadn't touched on in quite some time. Tremors vibrated his fist as he filled it with Vibration magic, poised to strike. Noah vaulted into the air, rearing back. The air around his hand thrummed with might an instant before his fist collided with the monster's chest.

There was a loud crack. All the magical pressure that Noah had gathered surged forward at once, rushing out of his fist and into the Stormwing's head. A violent shudder raced through the bird's entire body before a series of muted snapping noises rang out from inside the monster.

The Stormwing didn't get a chance to scream in pain. Its body shattered, bones ripped apart, and internal organs were shredded. It crumpled to the ground, small pieces of bone jutting out of it at odd angles.

Noah stared at the dead bird, then looked over to his hand and flexed his fingers. Natural Disaster waited within his soul, willing and eager to give more energy. He'd used a decent amount of it, but nowhere near as much as he'd thought.

"Oh, yeah. I think I might be able to get used to this." A slow grin crept across his face. "But first, I think I need to do a little more testing."

Chapter Forty-One

Ferdinand froze halfway through taking a bite out of his sandwich. Energy tickled the back of his mind, just barely prickling against his senses. It wasn't the first time he'd felt a use of power large enough to draw his attention, but this was different.

It was so faint that someone less trained may have construed it as irrelevant. But Ferdinand, while not the most fervent member of his church, had not slouched. He knew the sensation of his goddess's power, and he knew the power of the Apostles.

The energy he felt now was, without doubt, reminiscent of Garina's. His eyes shot over to hers, panicked thoughts flashing through his mind.

I thought Garina said that there wouldn't be any more of the Apostles here. What is one doing putting out enough power for me to pick it up? They should be more than capable of hiding their energy usage, so whoever that was had to have used so much that they couldn't conceal it.

But the emotion that Ferdinand found on Garina's features wasn't recognition. It was surprise and confusion. She didn't recognize the power any more than he did—and now, the more that he thought about it, the more the power felt... off.

It only took a brief instant for Ferdinand and Garina to come to the exact same conclusion. The power hadn't been used by anyone they knew. But, without a doubt, it was the power of the Apostles.

The hair on the back of Ferdinand's neck stood on end. He couldn't bring himself to swallow the bite of the sandwich he'd taken. The food tasted like it had turned to ash.

That's it, isn't it? Garina wasn't searching for somebody with Renewal's powers. She was searching for someone with her Demon God's powers—or, perhaps, someone who was strong enough to steal from them both.

But, if that's true...

If it was true, then everything would end. Their partnership, as tenuous as it was, would be over. The chances of two different people just happening to piss off two different gods at the exact same time and location were so unlikely that Ferdinand dismissed it immediately.

They were dealing with someone powerful enough to rob two gods, and they were trampling all over the Rules by existing within the restricted zone. Ferdinand couldn't bring himself to properly care about any of that, though.

The moment he acknowledged the existence of the magic at the edges of his mind, he and Garina would return to being enemies. She'd know what he sought and would be unable to do anything but strike him down.

He could always make an excuse to try to leave, but he doubted it would fly. And, even if it would, Ferdinand found himself reluctant to even consider the idea. Completing his mission—if such a thing was even possible with an opponent such as this—would mean that all would return to how it had been.

Even if Garina didn't kill him, Ferdinand would go back to the Church of Repose. He'd never speak to Garina again. The past few months would be nothing but a surprisingly pleasant memory in an endless sea of nothingness.

Ferdinand swallowed. He lowered his sandwich, staring down at it. He could feel Garina's gaze boring into his forehead. She'd finished her meal already, but he'd made a second sandwich for her. It was sitting in his bag, waiting for when she declared that she was still hungry.

There's always another path. Life is not black and white. But... what is mine?

"Is something wrong?" Garina asked, her voice even. It was a measured question, one without the slight notes of genuine interest that had crept into their conversations in recent times. Ferdinand might have been mistaken, but it almost felt like there was a faint undercurrent of fear within it.

Not fear of Ferdinand, but fear of what his answer would be. He didn't respond for several seconds, not willing to let himself say anything that he would regret. Ferdinand scored his mind, trying to find a solution that didn't result in death or, worse, a return to the days of just a few weeks ago.

And, in the midst of his search, Ferdinand found an answer. A solution so simple that it was laughable. Even the mere thought of it should have been ridiculous. It was the choice of a fool who cared nothing for their future.

"No," Ferdinand said, a small smile drifting across his face. "I don't believe there is."

"Don't lie to me. I felt it as well, Ferdinand. You need to leave, don't you?" Garina asked. Her shoulders were ever so slightly hunched forward, a position of disappointment that Ferdinand suspected no other living being beyond the other Apostles had ever seen. "I—I'll let you have a head start. If you're smart, you'll be out of the empire before the day is over. I can't bend the Rules."

Ferdinand shook his head and reached into his bag, pulling out the second sandwich. "I'm afraid you're mistaken. I do not need to leave."

Garina stared at Ferdinand, confusion playing across her features. "This isn't a trick offer. It's the only one you're going to get. I'm not an idiot. I know you're after the same person I am. I figured it out a long time ago."

Ferdinand's lips pulled up in a grin, and he shook his head once more. "You are incorrect, and you cannot act on assumptions when I have done nothing to make you believe that I plan to move against the Rules. I am not searching for the person whom you just felt."

It wasn't a lie. Ferdinand wasn't searching for the person who dared spit in the faces of two different gods. Not anymore.

"Do you perhaps need to leave?" Ferdinand asked, holding the sandwich out. "Because I did make this for you. It would be a shame to let it go to waste."

"I don't understand. Are you stupid?" Garina demanded. "When you return to the Church empty-handed, they'll know you failed. It will be easy to see through your lie if even I can break it this easily."

"It is not a lie. I no longer search for the person you believe I do."

"No longer? Who are you searching for, then?"

"I believe I have already found them."

It took a second for her to process what he had said. And, in that moment, Ferdinand became the only living man to see Garina of the Apostles blush. She gathered herself quickly, but it wasn't enough to completely wipe the spots of red from her cheeks.

"You're full of shit," Garina said, snagging the sandwich from Ferdinand and taking a huge bite out of it.

"I take it this means you don't need to leave?" Ferdinand asked.

Garina glanced at him out of the corner of her eye. She finished off the rest of the sandwich, and the two sat in silence for several seconds. Finally, a small smile pulled at one corner of her lips.

"No. I don't suppose I do. I'm rather content where I am."

* * *

"You have to be kidding me," Renewal said, staring at the shimmering image of Ferdinand and Garina in the air before her in disbelief and more than a little amusement. "That did not happen. I refuse to believe it."

She didn't expect an answer. The universe rarely gave her them, but for once, something was different. A ripple of energy pressed into the back of her mind, and she spun away from the screen, drawing on her runes.

Cracks of black light splintered through the sky above her, and a bolt of severing energy carved through the air. It crashed down before her, sending souls scattering and screaming in terror. She hardly noticed them.

"Decras," Renewal said, closing the image with a snap of her fingers and narrowing her eyes. "What are you doing here? Do you really dare challenge me twice in a row?"

A throaty laugh echoed from Decras's throat and he held his hands up. "As amusing as that would be, I prefer not to play the same game twice in a row, especially after we both ended up on the losing team to a party that wasn't even meant to be playing."

"Why are you here, then?"

"Boredom. Why else?" Decras snorted, then walked up to stand beside Renewal. He raised a hand and strands of black energy coiled up from the ground, forming a chair. Decras glanced over to the screaming souls and flicked his hand.

Time slammed to a halt around Renewal. Or, more accurately, the time that the souls perceived slammed to a halt. Decras wasn't anywhere near powerful enough to actually stop time, but pulling a few measly souls to a spot where they couldn't feel its passing was well within his might.

"That's it?" Renewal asked. "You came by just a few months ago. I'm going to start thinking you're clingy."

"I am," Decras said, not a single shred of sarcasm in his voice. "And I'm here for the exact same reason. You're watching something interesting, and I've always found it more fun to do such things with others."

Renewal studied Decras for some time. She hadn't truly run into many gods in her solitary role in the universe. He was one of the few that she did know, even if his attention tended to be fairly destructive.

Their last sparring match had been the reason that Renewal was currently missing a tiny chunk of her power, but she took no small amount of satisfaction in knowing that Decras was no better off.

"How are you going to apologize for causing my loss of power?" Renewal demanded. "Do you have any idea—"

Decras held a hand out, and a small golden core materialized within it. Energy crackled within it with enough intensity to catch even her attention. Renewal's words died before they could leave her mouth.

"Will this suffice? I'll have you know that we will be splitting it. I do not give donations."

"You definitely know how to apologize," Renewal muttered. She flicked her hand and flowers twisted into a pink throne beneath her. She sat down beside Decras and snapped her fingers, summoning the image of Ferdinand and Garina back to the air before them.

"Cute," Decras said, squeezing the small marble into two separate halves and giving one to Renewal.

"Where did you even manage to get this?" Renewal asked, staring at the half of the marble in her palm.

"There is great freedom in refusing to be beholden to the universe's will."

"More like danger," Renewal said. "It's a miracle you haven't been killed yet. If you'd chosen a different Goddess of Reincarnation to screw with, your head may have been severed from your shoulders by now."

"But I did not, and it has not," Decras said idly. "Are you asking me to stop?"

Renewal paused for a moment. Then she let out a sigh and shook her head. "No. I'm not. It adds a bit of excitement to my life, and you're more interesting than the other Reincarnation Gods and Goddesses."

Decras grinned and stuck his tongue out, placing the marble on its tip before swallowing it. He drew in a deep breath and let it out with a satisfied grin. "Ah, raw energy never fails to satisfy. If you do not object to my company, you should not be so confrontational when I arrive. Unless it's actually the sparring that you enjoy?"

Renewal reddened, and Decras let out a burst of laughter.

"It is, isn't it?"

"Just because my runes are those of life does not mean I don't enjoy a good match," Renewal said defensively. Her lips pressed together. "Unfortunately, my fellows disagree."

"Then I shall be sure to bother you further in the future, no matter how much you request me to stop," Decras said. He nodded to the screen. "Now, you have much better eyes for the world than I do. What is happening? I am bored."

"Well," Renewal said, drawing the word out before letting out a laugh and shaking her head. "I think your subordinate is flirting with mine."

Chapter Forty-Two

A deep, echoing laugh slipped from Decras's mouth. "Garina? Your subordinate is going to die. I hope you weren't close to them."

"I don't know much more than some of their names, and I've only picked that up in passing," Renewal said. "I just recognize the mimicry of my runes in his soul. You can't be telling me that you're actually interacting with your followers directly, Decras. That's—"

"Against the Rules, yes," Decras yawned, then stretched his arms over his head. A black table rose up from the ground before him, and he kicked his legs up on top of it. "I believe we've been over this particular part already. So long as you don't break the order of the universe too badly, nobody cares. Life is nothing when lived entirely under the thumb of someone else."

Renewal shook her head in a mixture of jealousy and exasperation. The Rules existed for a reason, and both she and Decras were nowhere near the peak of power in the universe. Playing too much with fire was a great way to get burned.

"You're going to get yourself killed, you know?"

"I highly doubt it. The High Gods don't give a shit about what the rest of us do. If they did, don't you think they'd have done something by now? I've had my fingers on that particular little world for hundreds of years."

"Hundreds of—what have you been doing?"

"Training some disciples, mostly. Unfortunately, most of them weren't worth the effort. No potential. But a few have potential—such as Garina. Unfortunately, while she's got great potential, it's completely ruined by her personality. She's basically a dog with anger issues. Shame, really. Can't say she isn't fun to watch, though. It's a good thing you aren't attached to your people, because I don't think that bald one is going to live much longer."

Renewal looked from Decras to the image. They were both silent for a second.

"Is this going to update? Why are they just frozen there?" Decras asked. "You need to upgrade the speed of your magic."

"It's in real time," Renewal said. "They're actually just sitting."

Decras's brow furrowed in confusion and he leaned forward, squinting at the image. Garina was locked in place, still staring at Ferdinand. Then, slowly, she shifted her position to let her shoulder brush against his.

Renewal burst into laughter as Garina leaned against Ferdinand in full. The look on Decras's face was one of such abject shock and disbelief that Renewal suspected it wouldn't leave her mind for thousands of years.

"Impossible," Decras said. "She doesn't even like *me* that much!"

"You've actually met her?" The smile on Renewal's lips faded.

"No, of course not. I'm not so stupid as to manifest myself on a mortal world." Decras scoffed, then shook his head. "But I've occasionally projected some conversation to a few of them. It's a good way to kill some time."

"They're actually strong enough to understand you? My followers barely manage to make out half the words I send them."

"That's because I actually picked mine out. You've just got a gathering of rabble." Decras snorted. "My men and women are those of quality. They have the potential to reach our strength. Well, some of them do. They're superior to yours in every way."

"Except for Garina, who appears to be in love with one of mine," Renewal said dryly. "Unless you've got another explanation for this? Ferdinand is a whole rank below her, and it's a big one."

Decras looked back to the image, then pursed his lips and sank lower into his chair. "Perhaps it is an attempt to manipulate him."

Renewal arched an eyebrow. "You're deluding yourself. Do you not see the way they're looking at each other?"

"At this point, I've decided to look a little less. It seems inappropriate," Decras said. "I'd much prefer if they were trying to kill each other, if it's all the same to you."

"It isn't. This is much better." Renewal leaned forward without even so much as trying to hide her interest. "Love is far more interesting than war. Not to say I don't like fighting, but you get the best of both worlds with the former."

"Has anyone ever told you your beautiful visage hides a terrible demon within?"

"Far too many, but most of them aren't around to complain any longer."

"Can't say I'm surprised. Do you really know nothing about the bald one, though? I have to say that I'm slightly interested. I've never known Garina to care about anything but power. She was a failure of a project, and I've been far too busy to actively keep up with her. I must assume her change has something to do with your subordinate."

"I could probably find out more if I wanted to, but there's a good chance that contacting my church would result in Ferdinand getting ripped apart when they misinterpret my message," Renewal said with a sigh. "The idiots running it have no idea what they're doing."

"Do any of us?" Decras let out a chuckle and straightened back out. The table disappeared and he rose to his feet, letting his chair sink into the ground behind him. "If that's the case, I suppose I'll have to take matters into my own hands."

Renewal's eyes narrowed and she snapped her fingers, banishing the image. She stood as well, squaring her shoulders. "How so? Don't interfere with them. This is some of the best entertainment I've had in ages."

"Unlike you, I don't have that many subordinates. I'm actually invested in mine, and I'll not see one wasted."

"Wasted? She's changing—no thanks to you. Keep your nose out of their business," Renewal warned, taking a step closer and thrusting a finger into Decras's chest. "You hear me? Don't interfere."

"Hm. Are you going to stop me?"

Renewal's eyes narrowed. "Don't try to bait me into a fight, Decras. It's much easier if you just ask me directly."

"But it's much less fun that way."

"You'll find out what fun feels like when I stick my foot up your ass. Don't screw with my entertainment. I already lost my damn cat. I'm not losing this when I just found it. Just the look on your face when you saw them being cutesy was incredible. There's no way I'm letting you break this off."

Decras crossed his arms and tilted his head to the side. "Does that mean you wouldn't mind if I continued dropping by to watch them?"

"I suppose not. It's better than watching alone."

"Fine. In that case, we shall be perverts together."

"What? That's not—"

"Now who's trying to delude themselves?"

Renewal glared at Decras. "It's appreciation of art in life."

"Which is a fancy way to say that you are a pervert that watches others while they don't know. What is this of a cat, though?"

Renewal opened her mouth to refute Decras's first statement, then thought better of it and closed it again. There were some arguments that she wasn't going to win, and something told her that this was one of them.

"It was one of my avatars," Renewal said with a sigh. "I sent it out to look into the mortal that stole my energy—your fault, by the way—and the little shit stole the cat."

Decras threw his head back in laughter. "He stole from you *again?*"

"Yes," Renewal snapped. "You don't have to rub it in, you know. I'm more than aware of how humiliating it is."

"You're cute when you pout," Decras said. He pressed his palms together and stretched them apart. Strands of black matter twisted between his fingertips, gathering into a bubbling mass in the air.

The mass bulged outward, taking shape into a small black cat. It dropped to the ground, a faint yellow glow appearing behind its eyes as it came to life. The cat yowled, then arched up against Decras's leg. He flicked a finger and it trotted over to Renewal before curling up at her feet.

"There," Decras said. "A new cat."

Renewal looked down at the cat, then back up to Decras.

You can't just replace a cat, much less an avatar. It was a part of me.

But... this was surprisingly sweet of Decras. I haven't seen this side of him before. Is he feeling sentimental about Garina?

"I—thank you, I suppose," Renewal said slowly, reaching down to scoop the cat into her arms. It purred and rubbed its head up against her chin. A small grin flickered across Renewal's face. "Feisty."

"Most things about me are. Of course, we can't just let the mortal get away with stealing from you twice."

"I'm more than aware. As soon as my church finds him, he and I will be having a very extensive talk."

Decras let out a snort of derision. "As if those incompetent fools will find anyone. I had my own people looking for him as well, but it appears the two that were the closest have gotten entangled with each other instead of doing their jobs."

"No interfering," Renewal warned.

"I won't." Decras raised his hands and laughed. "But that doesn't mean things can be left as they are. Perhaps a few nudges are in order. If a mortal wishes to play with us, then he should prove he deserves the power he has taken."

"As much as I hate to admit it, I feel like he may have proven that by stealing it in the first place."

"Perhaps." Decras inclined his head. "But that doesn't mean we can't have a little fun in the process, does it? I think we could add a little more excitement to this and watch how it all plays out. It could be enjoyable."

"What are you thinking?" Renewal asked.

Decras's smile grew as he told her. And when he finished, Renewal found a small grin starting to form on her own face.

"That," Renewal said, petting her new cat and already picturing the scene that Decras had described, "sounds like it could be interesting."

Chapter Forty-Three

Noah took down several more monsters over the course of the next few hours, trying to push Natural Disaster to its absolute limits. His efforts rewarded him with a small increase in the rune's overall strength but an incredible increase in his confidence in his abilities.

It was exactly what he'd pictured the rune to be when he'd first made it. Unlike its previous form, Natural Disaster was now completely responsive, as if it were an extension of his body rather than a badly forged tool.

And, even with all the elements to call on, he found himself heavily leaning on Vibration and Lightning. It had been some time since he'd really had a chance to use Vibration offensively, but it was just as devastating as he remembered it being.

By the time it came to return to the others, he couldn't have been more pleased. He landed his flying sword beside the group while they were all sitting in a small circle, likely trying to work on their patterns.

"Welcome back," Moxie said with a small nod. She was the only one that wasn't sitting, keeping watch over the others to make sure a monster didn't get the jump on them while they were distracted. "How'd it go with Natural Disaster?"

"Perfectly," Noah replied with a huge smile. He rubbed his shoulder and let out a wistful sigh. "I wish I'd managed this earlier. It's not exactly that new, but it feels like everything finally clicked. I can use Vibration again as well, which is great. I'm going to need to remake my Imbuements again, but they should be much better now that I can combine vibration with air and earth more effectively."

Moxie let out a slow whistle. "So this completely confirms it then, right? We've genuinely cracked the secret to making a Perfect Rune."

"Certainly seems like it," Noah agreed with a nod. "You're next, by the way. How far away are you from Rank 4?"

"I'll be actively pushing for it when we've got free time. I need to get some new runes to replace the ones I've lost and fill everything up, but Lee and I will just go hunting together. I think we should be able to make it without too much time with the speed we kill monsters at. I'll value it, because this will likely be the last time we can brute force our way through getting enough energy to rank up."

"Yeah, I can imagine. I barely got anything in my Rank 4 rune from the hunting I did today, and I'm pretty sure that it would have given me a hefty chunk if I'd been trying to fill up a Rank 3. I don't even want to think about how much power we'd need to reach Rank 5."

"It'll be more than we can get hunting monsters near Arbitage. Not if we want to make it anywhere anytime soon. There's a reason so few people make it past Rank 3, much less 4 or above. That's a problem for later, though." Moxie brushed a strand of hair behind her ear and looked down at everyone seated near her. "Your class is going well, though."

"Not that I'm even teaching it right now," Noah said with a chuckle. "You and Lee took over. I thought I'd come back to everyone stretching."

"Lee decided to do more pattern practice after she finished up with all the stretching and physical workouts. I don't think anyone was complaining, though. We're all pretty excited about this. I'm just a little concerned about how everyone will practice."

"As long as they don't do anything when I'm not there, it'll be fine. Don't forget that I'm Rank 4 now. As long as they're in my domain, they can basically practice without any trouble at all. The magic won't be able to take form."

Moxie slapped her forehead and let out a burst of laughter. "How did I not remember that? I'm an idiot. Especially with your domain, it shouldn't be too much of a problem at all to keep their magic repressed.

What about when they actually start doing the Formations for real, though?"

"That's a different scenario. I haven't fully figured it out yet, but I think the most important part will be getting used to Formations. Once they've really understood their patterns and everything else down, only then can they add in real magic. It'll be safer for them than it has been for literally anyone else that has learned Formations."

"You've put a lot of thought into this."

"A lot." Noah nodded. "And I still fear it might not be enough, but there's no point staying paralyzed by fear. To advance is to risk. I don't want anyone to get themselves killed for no reason, but danger is part of the process. I'll do everything I can to guide them, but in the end, it'll be in their hands."

"You know, it's hard to believe you're the same person that encouraged fighting without a Shield."

"Look, it was effective. Mages rely too much on Shields. Being able to fight without knowing that you'll be protected from most forms of magical attacks and a good amount of physical ones is important. Shields build bad habits."

"I'm not arguing with you. Your methods definitely have merit. You've just come a long way." Moxie raised her hands in surrender. She glanced at the others to make sure everyone still had their eyes closed, then leaned in and gave Noah a quick kiss on the corner of his lips. "It's cute."

"I try," Noah said with a smile, touching the side of his face. "It helps to have someone to care about. When it was just me... well, never mind. It doesn't matter anymore. It isn't just me, and I don't even want to think about the possibility of something like that ever again."

They stood together, watching over Lee and the students for the next few hours. Eventually, their transport cannon's allotted time ran out, and Isabel vanished in a beam of blue light. The others followed soon after her, disappearing one by one until none remained.

After returning to Arbitage, the students broke off to get food and Lee zipped off in pursuit of some poor small animal that caught her eye. Noah joined Moxie in heading back to Building T. When Moxie opened the door to her room, a slip of paper on the ground caught Noah's eye.

"What's this?" Noah asked, kneeling to pick it up. It was an envelope, trimmed with the faintest lines of gold. There was no sender or addressee listed on its face.

"Oh! I was wondering when that would arrive," Moxie said, holding a hand out. Noah handed it to her, and Moxie ran a fingernail along the top of the letter, ripping it open and pulling out two slips of glossy paper from within. The first was plain white, while the one behind it had golden lettering all across both of its sides. Moxie started by reading the first one. "It's the schedule for the year. I imagine you got one as well, but it was probably delivered to your actual room."

"Eh. I've got yours. What's it say?" Noah asked. "Do we know what the exams will be and when they'll take place?"

Moxie scanned through the letter, then nodded. It took her a moment before she started to speak. "Yeah, it does. The first exam is in about three weeks. It's a 'retrieval exam,' and the purpose will be to hunt down a specific monster and bring it back. I think it's meant to mostly test how far everyone has come and show off to their respective houses."

"Lovely," Noah said. "I don't think any of the kids are going to have trouble with that considering they're Rank 2s. That's well above the expectation, right?"

"Yes. None of the exams should pose even the slightest amount of difficulty now that they're Rank 2. As long as everyone uses their heads, it'll be a shoo-in," Moxie said with a grin. "The second exam should be interesting. It's a tournament between all students in Arbitage. They can choose a bracket to compete in and will be assigned rewards based on their performance from the noble families that sponsor the event."

"What about the third?"

Moxie shook her head. "No information on it, for some reason. They're keeping it secret to build anticipation. It's probably some new noble they hired that cares more about making a spectacle for the nobles with money to throw at the school than they do about any of the things Arbitage is meant to stand for."

"What is Arbitage meant to stand for in the first place? As far as I can tell, the only things it actually cares about are money and rune research."

"Okay, fair point." Moxie rubbed the back of her head sheepishly, then thumbed over to the second piece of paper. She read over it, her brows knitting further with every word.

"What is it?" Noah asked. "That's not a good look you're wearing."

"I'm... not sure what to think, actually. Look. Read it for yourself." Moxie held the paper out and Noah took it, flipping it around to see the front. There, written in flowing gold, was what amounted to an invitation.

Moxie Torrin, we have found the performance of your student(s) during the previous exam to be exemplary and would like to invite you and them to participate in the advanced curriculum this year. Students in the advanced curriculum will be given access to unique opportunities and graded against their peers, with rewards going to the most deserving. Should you wish to accept the invitation, please drop this note off in the office or with the Enforcers before the dawn of the following week.

"The hell is this?" Noah asked. "There's an advanced track?"

"I didn't know it existed either," Moxie said. "Do you think it's real?"

"It certainly seems official, and it's not like they're asking for anything," Noah said, chewing his lower lip. He turned the paper over, but he wasn't even sure what he was searching for. It seemed perfectly legitimate. "And the kids did do pretty damn good."

"What do you think?"

"Maybe I should see if I've got one as well," Noah said. "One second. I'll be right back."

He stepped out of Moxie's room, heading back to his own. No more than a minute later, Noah returned with a pair of papers in his hands. One was the white paper that talked about the exams they had that year, and the second was the gold-trimmed one with the exact same message that had been on Moxie's.

"They actually invited Isabel and Todd? Even though they aren't nobles?" Moxie's eyebrows rose. "That's... surprising, actually. Maybe it doesn't speak well for me that my first thought was that Arbitage would never do something good for people without money."

"Trust me, you weren't the only one to wonder," Noah muttered. He glanced between the papers again, then folded them back up and slipped them both into the envelope they'd come in. "I think this is something we'll need to speak with the kids about. I don't want to make the decision for them one way or the other. I don't know what kind of opportunities the advanced track has, but I'm far from an expert on this stuff. I've just worked a few things out. If we could get any other forms of advantages, we should try to take them."

"I agree. Next class, then," Moxie said with a nod. "Do you have plans for the rest of today?"

"None in particular other than messing with Natural Disaster a bit more and continuing to work on Formations."

"In that case, do you think you could play your violin for me?" Moxie reddened and glanced to the side. "It helps me concentrate, and I want to try to work on figuring out my pattern for Formations."

"For you? Always." Noah's violin materialized in his hands. "It'll be a good opportunity to get some more Formation practice in anyway. I want to work on swapping styles and songs on the fly. Just let me know when you want me to stop or I might just keep at it."

"I can think of worse fates."

Noah laughed, then let the bow flow across the strings of his violin as he started to play. There was something else he wanted to test with Formations now that Natural Disaster had reached Rank 4, but it wasn't quite the time. For now, he was more than content just to play.

The testing could come after everyone else was asleep.

Chapter Forty-Four

Noah played for an hour, until Moxie's eyes had closed and she had retreated deep into her mindspace to completely focus on her pattern. Only after Noah was completely certain that she no longer heard anything he was playing did he allow himself to stop.

He sat down on the floor in front of the bed, leaning back and crossing his arms behind his head. The ground wasn't particularly comfortable, but he didn't want to distract Moxie by lying down beside her while she was working.

There was still some time until night fell, so he focused on repairing some much-needed Body Imbuements. Now that Natural Disaster had far more elements of Vibration within it, remaking his tremorsense Imbuements in his feet and ears wasn't a daunting task.

He worked through the day, slowly putting layer by layer of the Imbuements down and keeping his intent as honed as a razor. Noah was pretty sure he could have worked far faster, and he had done so in the past, but he didn't want to need to go back and re-do anything again.

These Imbuements were going to last all the way until he reached Rank 5, so they were going to have to be the absolute best work he could do. Hours slipped by and the sun dipped below the horizon, casting the room in shadows.

It took Noah a little time to notice that the day had left. When he was focused on something, time just seemed to slip through his fingers like grains of fine sand. He stood, shaking off the stiffness that came with lying on the ground.

Moxie had slumped against the wall, her chest rising and falling in gentle breaths. Noah suppressed a laugh. She'd fallen asleep. He gently scooped her into his arms and laid her down in the bed, taking care to make sure he didn't wake her by accident.

Pulling the covers over her, Noah paused to make sure she was still asleep. It was tempting to get into bed with her, but he wasn't anywhere near done for the night. Noah turned and slipped out of the room, heading for the garden.

A calm night greeted him. Stars twinkled overhead, the faint light of the moon illuminating the ground in grays. Many of the flowers in the garden had closed themselves from the night, and the world felt muted and silent.

Noah made his way through the tall, twisting hedges until he was deep into their protective walls. It wasn't like the garden was a perfect hideaway, but he was pretty sure that barely anyone else visited it—and it was pretty late, so the number that might have visited was even lower.

It's too bad my Imbuements aren't quite finished yet. They'd be pretty useful here, but this is fine. As long as I'm hidden away, I should be able to hear if anyone is coming and react in time.

He sat down in a small nook made by a thorny rosebush with flowers the size of his head, pausing for a moment to smell the faint honey scent emanating off them before he summoned his violin and got back to work.

Patterns make up Formations and runes alike. Right now, there's nothing special about the actual patterns. I don't think that the type of pattern I use is relevant, but that should also mean that if there actually was something special about the pattern, it should hypothetically still work.

So, if I were to make a musical Formation with some form of magical music instead of normal music, that would still work. That would just give me an even more effective Formation, right?

Of course, the alternative was that Noah would blow himself up.

Considering the likelihood of that was considerably larger than zero, he'd elected to save this particular idea until he was away from the others and couldn't kill anyone other than a few bugs.

There were a variety of ways he could have tried to get magic into a song to test his theory. In fact, he wasn't confident that his song didn't *already* have magic. After all, the violin itself was laden with it. There was always a chance that the notes it played had more power than just mere notes.

But hey—a little extra power never hurt anybody.

Noah studied the violin. A small marking near the base of the strings caught his attention and he frowned, leaning in closer to get a better look at it—only to find that there wasn't just one. There were seven small white scratches, each one directly below a string.

Wait. Those aren't scratches.

They were little circles, connected by flowing lines so thin that he could barely make them out. The design was so small that it was easy to miss, but Noah had inspected every single part of the violin.

It definitely hadn't been there before, but there was no way this was some form of accident. There was a very clear design to the lines, which meant they were intentional.

"Seven circles. Seven parts to a rune," Noah mused. "Is this what I think it is? Are you reading my thoughts?"

The violin didn't respond, which Noah was thankful for. He was more than aware that the violin had a will of its own, but having sapience was a little more concerning. But, no matter what it was, the temptation was too strong to resist any longer.

Noah drew on Natural Disaster, taking the faintest sliver of energy from it and letting it travel into the violin. He felt a faint tugging sensation at his fingertip, but nothing changed. There was definitely something there, but he was missing it.

Chewing his lower lip, Noah tried again. This time, instead of taking energy in general, he focused purely on the elements from Thunderstorm. Another trace of energy slipped out of his fingertip.

The violin hummed. Thin lines flickered to life within the circle beneath the first string. Noah had to squint, but he could just barely make out the shape of the Thunderstorm Rune within the circle.

A grin split his lips. Noah summoned the bow of the violin and played a soft note on the string connected to Thunderstorm. Faint energy crackled, tiny arcs of lightning rising up and coiling around the bow as he pulled it.

The shape in the circle faded away, and the power went with it, but Noah's smile only grew bigger.

Oh, yeah. I think I'm going to like this.

Noah drew on more energy and sent it back into the violin. Thunderstorm reappeared in the violin's wood. He increased the power he was drawing, releasing the thunder elements and trying to transition to Cyclone.

A surprising wall of resistance met his efforts. Noah's brow furrowed and he pulled more power, driving a metaphorical shoulder into the force pressing against him. Slowly, he felt his hand tingle as energy slipped out and entered the violin.

The second circle in the row lit, taking on the Cyclone Rune's shape. Noah went to try to fill a third, but this time, the wall had turned into an impenetrable fortress. No matter how he tried to approach or get around it, the violin firmly resisted his attempts.

"Two strings it is," Noah said, not discouraged in the slightest. He pulled the bow across the strings once more, letting just a little music slip out. The violin still repressed its sound, so it couldn't travel far, but he wanted just enough to hear what he was doing.

Energy thrummed in the strings as he played, waiting for direction that Noah was more than willing to give. His bow started to move faster. Wind swirled around his hands and whipped at his hair as sparks of electricity danced from every note he played.

Noah continued to pour energy from Natural Disaster into his violin. While he couldn't fill it past two runes yet, he could replenish the runes that were already there with no difficulty—so long as he still had energy to use, at least.

The violin drank his magic hungrily, going through it far faster than he normally would have himself. But, in turn, the intensity of the power pouring off the instrument was intense. It was amplifying his magic.

How, exactly, Noah wasn't sure. There was only one way to find out. Noah wasn't sure exactly what guided his movements. Perhaps it was instinct, or perhaps it just felt right. As he swept his bow across the violin, he flicked his hand.

Responding to his will, the power swirling around him leapt forth. A bolt of lightning and a blade of wind leapt from the violin in unison, twisting around each other as they arced out and struck the ground with a loud crack. It blackened the dirt where it struck, setting a small pile of leaves on fire.

Noah cursed and ran over to stomp it out, but he couldn't wipe the grin from his face as he realized exactly what the violin was offering him. He could combine his magic, of course. That was nothing new.

What *was* new was the way he had simultaneously cast two different spells. Mages could only cast one kind of magic at a time, and they had to release their energy and re-draw on their runes if they wanted to swap. It wasn't the same thing as casting a bolt of wind empowered with lightning—he was functionally casting two different spells at once, and he could hypothetically put energy from other runes into the circles as well.

You know, I've never actually tried calling upon Natural Disaster as a single concept. I don't even know what would happen if I tried that. I don't think this is the place to practice, though.

Noah was too excited to worry about it. The violin was basically a pseudo-Formation. In addition to his normal abilities, it would eventually let him use up to seven different forms of magic at the same time, so long as he could maintain a pattern that let him control them. Noah couldn't keep himself from laughing.

Patterns really are everything, but this violin is incredible. I'm sure I could replicate this with something else, but it wouldn't compare. Moxie really did get me the greatest gift I've ever gotten. I hope her cloak is half as useful. We still haven't figured out exactly what it does.

Noah made to start playing again but paused before his bow could meet the strings. He wasn't certain, but it almost sounded like the leaves had crunched somewhere near him. Dismissing his violin with a thought, Noah brushed his hands off on his jacket and tilted his head to listen.

A faint crunch broke the still night, followed by two more. Noah lowered his stance, not quite preparing to fight but still making sure he could move quickly if he needed to. People generally didn't wander around at night aimlessly.

I don't count, of course. I'm different and unique.

A silver leg stepped into view, followed by the travel clothes of a soldier. A salt and pepper beard just barely failed to hide the faint grin present on Silvertide's face as he stepped into view.

"Vermil," Silvertide said, coming to a stop and resting his hands on the top of his cane. "It's a nice night, is it not? I was hoping we might run into each other again."

Chapter Forty-Five

"Silvertide! I was under the impression you hadn't returned to Arbitage yet," Noah said, raising a hand in greeting. Silvertide certainly liked his dramatic entrances. It didn't seem like the elderly soldier ever chose a different way to arrive.

"I just got back recently. How are Isabel and Todd doing?"

"Good. You took great care of them." Noah inclined his head in appreciation, thankful he'd dismissed his violin before Silvertide had showed up. As kind as Silvertide seemed to be, Noah had already shared a few too many secrets with him. "And thank you for the help with Todd's neck. I was saving up to buy a potion for him, but it looks like you already did the hard work."

Silvertide chuckled. "I'd heard that you visited Dawnforge, so I imagine you tried your hand at adventuring. And, if you did, you've probably found that money is not hard to come by when you know how to earn it."

How'd he hear that we went to Dawnforge? That's a little concerning.

"It certainly paid better than being a professor," Noah said with a shrug. "How'd you hear about my travels, though? I didn't realize they were well known. There aren't rumors going around, are there?"

"Nothing like that. I've just been keeping an eye on your where-abouts for Isabel and Todd's sake. They wanted to know what you were up to, and when you live to my age, you build up a few connections."

That's a polite way to say you've got an extensive information network.

"I suppose that makes sense. I don't imagine you found much interesting. We just went to Dawnforge for a little while, then got wrapped up in a few unfortunate events. All ended well, though."

"Unfortunate events indeed," Silvertide said, a glitter in his eyes telling Noah that the soldier didn't believe his words for a second. "What brings you out so late at night?"

"Presumably the same thing that brought you out. Solitude. Peace. The gardens are beautiful when there isn't anyone else around."

"So they are," Silvertide agreed, craning his neck back to look up at the moon. Neither of them spoke for several seconds.

A thought struck Noah and he reached into his pocket, pulling out the letter that had arrived at his room. He flipped it open and pulled out the gold-lettered piece of paper, showing it to Silvertide. "I know you're not a professor here, but do you know anything about this?"

Silvertide took the paper and glanced over it. An eyebrow inched upward and he handed it back. "Most impressive, but I can't say I'm surprised. Isabel and Todd have made some incredible advancements, surpassing the average student at Arbitage by wide margins. I'm unsurprised they got an invitation."

"This is real, then? Not a trick?"

"You are a very suspicious man," Silvertide said with a low chuckle. "That will serve you well. But yes, this is not a trick. The advanced track is something present in all four of the Bastions. It's fairly selective, and everyone enrolled in it is... motivated."

"Motivated?" Noah tilted his head to the side. "The way you said that doesn't sound particularly reassuring. Almost like it was a bad thing."

"Not a bad thing, but an intense one. It takes great skill, effort, and talent to become a truly powerful mage. The majority of the students—and teachers—at Arbitage lack that motivation. They are here because it is safe and because it provides an easy path forward in life. The teachers get paid to do babysitting with a little bit of extra effort, and the ones that are competent can research runes without worrying about fighting or killing monsters to get them. But, as with all things, there are outliers."

"So the advanced track is made up of students and teachers that aren't content with how things are and want to get genuinely powerful," Noah concluded. "That sounds like a good thing."

"It is," Silvertide said. "But the competition is intense, and nobles will be displeased to see Isabel and Todd standing at their level. It will be quite an amusing sight to behold, should you and your students enter the advanced track."

"So that means you aren't against it, then?" Noah asked, folding the paper back up and returning it to his pocket. "I just want to make sure I don't put them in excessive danger. I'm more than capable of teaching them everything they need about fighting."

"That confidence is interesting, considering that on all official records, you're still a Rank 2. They're technically not that much weaker than you are. Or, at least, that would be true if you were actually the rank you claimed."

Noah kept his face straight and gave Silvertide a one-shouldered shrug. "I tried telling the office I'd advanced some time ago, but the attendant just ignored me. It's unfortunate, but the amount of money Arbitage pays really wasn't worth the hassle."

"No, it isn't," Silvertide agreed with a chuckle. "But you are not just a Rank 3. I can feel your domain—and it is powerful. When did you reach Rank 4, Vermil?"

Ah, shit. Well, I can't say I'm surprised. I knew this would happen, and I'm about 60 percent sure that Silvertide is on our side.

"Just recently. I'll get around to reporting it soon enough," Noah said. He stretched his arms over his head and yawned as a chilly breeze rustled through the hedges, caressing his skin and sending a small shiver down his spine.

"There are certainly advantages to keeping your power concealed," Silvertide mused. "Though it is not a technique that many utilize properly. Power comes with so many benefits that the only ones who hide it possess more than others can give."

That didn't sound like a question, and Noah had absolutely no desire to answer it. It didn't seem like Silvertide actually wanted a response either. He just scratched at his chin and looked back at the sky.

"Do you happen to know a way for my domain to be... ah, less noticeable?" Noah hedged.

"Practice control and pull it inward. It will become more difficult the more powerful you get, and anyone that gets close enough to you and has sufficient sensitivity will be able to figure it out, but it can work in a pinch," Silvertide replied. "It is very difficult to hide power such as that from anyone if you are within the reach of their own domain. I am aware of everything that passes through my area of influence."

A flit of white caught the corner of Noah's eye, and he nearly choked in surprise. Moxie was walking up behind them, her cloak pulled tight around her shoulders. Silvertide, peering at a flower on one of the bushes, missed Noah's reaction and continued on.

"The stronger your domain, the more aware you will become of everything within it. When you get to my strength, there will be nearly nothing that can slip beneath your notice. And the closer they get to you, the easier it is to feel the disturbance."

Moxie came to a stop a few feet away from Silvertide, a small frown of concern on her features. "I didn't realize we'd all decided to go on midnight walks."

Silvertide leapt nearly a foot into the air, spinning toward Moxie and bringing his staff up defensively as he dropped into a fighting stance. Power coiled around his body, but it evaporated the instant he saw who was there.

"Damned Plains. How did you do that?" Silvertide asked, aghast.

"Do what?" Moxie blinked in confusion. "I didn't do anything."

"Impossible. I can't feel you," Silvertide said. His brow furrowed and he squinted at Moxie. "Vermil, can you see her? Am I hallucinating?"

"No, she's right there," Noah said, equally as confused. Silvertide's speech about awareness felt considerably less impactful when he'd gotten snuck up on by someone who didn't even realize she was sneaking.

Silvertide reached out and poked Moxie's shoulder with the tip of his staff. His befuddlement grew even further. "I can't sense her. At all. What rank are you?"

"Three?" Moxie half said, half asked. "Are you okay? Did something happen?"

The old soldier didn't respond. He squinted at Moxie, then walked in a circle around her. "This shouldn't be possible. You aren't here."

"I'm pretty sure I'm here."

"Yes, as am I. But you shouldn't be."

Noah blinked as a thought struck him. Moxie was wearing the cloak he'd helped Olive make her—the same one that Mascot had fiddled with. And if there was one thing Mascot was good at, it was sneaking up on people.

That and pissing people off, but Noah doubted there was an Imbuement for that.

Silvertide came to the same conclusion that Noah had as his eyes fixed on the furry cloak around Moxie's shoulders. He raised a hand, then paused. "Where did you get this cloak?"

"Vermil gifted it to me," Moxie said, her brow furrowed in confusion. "Why? I'm not following what's going on."

"Fascinating," Silvertide muttered. He pulled his gaze away from Moxie and looked back to Noah, who suppressed a grimace. The interest in Silvertide's eyes had increased. Again. Every time they met, he got a little more of the soldier's attention.

"I worked with an Imbuer to make it," Noah said. "We put a few bits from pretty rare monsters in there."

"I don't suppose you remember what monsters?"

"Afraid not. Some of them were his, and some I didn't even know the name of," Noah said.

"I see," Silvertide said. He let his hand drop and took a step back, leaning on his cane once again. "That is a kingly gift. I have never seen an item that can obscure your magical presence to such an intense degree. Even now, as I am fully aware of it, I can sense nothing but the faint Imbuements on the cloak itself."

Moxie looked down at the cloak in surprise. "I didn't realize it was so powerful."

"There are many things we do not realize," Silvertide murmured. He shook his head and let out a sigh. "The moon is getting a bit high. I did not plan to have any excitement tonight. I hope to see both of you in the advanced track."

"Wait, you're part of it?" Noah asked.

Silvertide gave Noah a small smile. "I am not an Arbitage Enforcer, but I have worked with them before. I was planning on enrolling my foolish apprentice in the program, and this only solidifies my plans. I think we have an interesting year ahead of us, Magus Vermil. I look forward to seeing what you do in the future."

He set off, the leaves crunching beneath his feet as he walked past Moxie and toward a turn in the leafy maze. Silvertide paused at the edge, turning to look back at Noah. "And, Vermil?"

"Yeah?"

"You need a better lie for when you reached Rank 4," Silvertide said. "Your domain is too powerful for only having reached it recently. If I didn't know better, I would have thought you were implying you only had a single Rank 4 rune. And, if that were the case, I would be *very* interested indeed."

With that, Silvertide strode off. A chill ran down Noah's spine, and it wasn't because of the chill.

"What was that about?" Moxie asked in concern, walking to stand beside Noah. "Did he figure out you reached Rank 4?"

"Yeah," Noah said. He let a little more power seep out from the Combustion Rune imbued in his soul, warming his body to combat the deepening cold. "And I think he was giving us a warning. It sounds like the advanced track could be interesting, though."

"Getting more training from Silvertide would be incredible," Moxie said. "If we have a chance to work together with him, we should. I think he's on our side."

"I think so too," Noah said, and he was grateful for it. Silvertide was far too perceptive for his tastes, but he couldn't help but like the man's forthrightness. It was a nice break from all the political scheming that surrounded the noble families.

Moxie nodded, then paused. She put a hand on Noah's arm. "You're warm."

"It's my Imbuement. It was getting chilly, so I made it stronger. Is it that noticeable?"

In response, Moxie leaned up against Noah. "No, but I'm cold. Walk me back to the room. I only came out here because I woke up and couldn't find where you were."

Noah wrapped an arm around Moxie's shoulder and let out a soft laugh. "I'll leave a note next time. Sorry."

"It's fine. I knew where you'd go."

"Maybe I'm getting predictable. We should head back either way. We've got a lot to do in the coming days."

"Yeah," Moxie agreed. She let out a large yawn. "But that's a problem for then. Right now, all I want to do is curl up and sleep. The bed is cold, so you're coming with me."

That was an idea that Noah had absolutely no problems with. There would be time for testing his powers even further tomorrow. He'd gotten enough answers for one day.

Chapter Forty-Six

The next morning, Noah and Moxie awoke to Lee sitting on top of them. Noah blinked the sleep out of his eyes, unentangling his limbs from Moxie as he squinted.

"Lee? What's going on?"

"Nothing. You were warm," Lee replied, sliding off. She raised her eyes to the window. "And it got really cold outside. Cold and white."

Noah followed Lee's gaze and his mouth dropped open. He scrambled out of bed, nearly tripping over his own feet as he ran over to get a better look. A plump layer of fluffy white snow blanketed everything in sight.

Lights poked out from beneath it, their glow muted in the early morning by the small flakes raining down everywhere. Moxie got out of bed and walked up to stand behind Noah.

"What is it?" Moxie asked.

"Snow!" Noah exclaimed, words muffled and nose pressed into the cold glass. If it hadn't been for Combustion heating his body, he probably would have started shivering. "It's beautiful. I've never seen snow in person before."

Moxie sent him a bemused glance. "Really?"

"I've seen pictures of it, but never this much. It looks so comfortable."

"It doesn't taste very good," Lee supplied. "I tried eating some. It's just water. And other things."

Noah scrunched his nose, then laughed. He started pulling on his clothes, still not taking his eyes off the window. "I don't need to know what the other things are. I'm not trying to spoil it for myself."

"Whatever it is, it's cold," Lee said. She scrunched her nose. "And I am still hungry."

"Well, we can go get some food, then. I'm feeling like something across campus. Something kind of far."

Noah was pretty sure Moxie knew his only real goal was to walk through the snow, but she didn't say anything. She just sent him an amused grin and pulled her cloak on, fastening it around her shoulders.

To Noah's surprise, it was Lee that hesitated.

"Actually, there was something else I was hoping we could do first," Lee said. She edged toward Noah's bag, peering inside it. "Could... you help me fix my runes today?"

Noah blinked. He'd been wondering when Lee would get around to it, but he'd started to think that she was going to hold off for much longer. "You're ready to do it?"

"Yeah," Lee said. "I don't want to wait anymore, and I've already figured out all the changes I want to make. I think I know what I need as well. Also, there's that Master Rune... If I can still have that, I'd like to start getting used to it."

"Of course you can." Noah picked his bag up and ruffled through it, pulling out the folder bearing the Catchpaper with Lee's runes on it. He had to admit that he was mildly surprised that his grimoire hadn't found a way to eat it yet, but small blessings were still blessings.

All the runes were still where he'd left them. The Broken Enveloping Dark Master Rune, two Moonlit Shadow Runes, and three Light Runes. All of them were at Rank 4, aside from the Master Rune, which was unranked.

Noah doubted the Light Runes would be of much use to Lee, but the rest of them had function. He held the paper out so Lee could inspect it.

"What are you thinking?"

"My Demon Runes are already good, but I'll need to rebalance them a little bit. I want to modify the Umbral Body Runes I got from that cat monster. My Shift Runes need a little modification as well, but I think it should be pretty minimal. I think one Moonlit Shadow should be enough to fix everything."

"Okay," Noah said with a nod. "This shouldn't be too much of a problem, then. To avoid putting extra stress on your body, I'll take the Moonlit Shadow Rune in myself and chop it up inside my own soul. Then I can just feed you the runes one by one and we won't have to rush."

"That works," Lee said. "Do we still have a Mind Meld Potion?"

"We do. I've been saving it," Moxie said. She headed over to her desk and pulled a drawer open, revealing the small blue potion. Walking back over to them, she handed the potion to Lee.

"Is now a good time? Or should we do it later?" Lee asked.

Noah shrugged. "I'm already awake. The snow got me up fast, so I'm ready whenever you are. As long as you feel ready, we can go now. It's not like I'm going to be doing much work. I'll just be splitting some runes apart for you. You're the one that's going to have to do everything else."

Noah studied the paper, memorizing the Rank 4 rune on it. After he was confident that everything had been firmly committed to memory, he closed his eyes and sank into his own soul, letting power gather at a fingertip.

Just a minute later, he'd succeeded. Drawing runes into his soul had become a relatively simple task, so he'd managed to get it on the second try. Noah could feel his soul shifting at the new Rank 4 within it, but it didn't have nearly as much power as Natural Disaster did, and the change was trivial in comparison to what he'd gained from going from Rank 3 to Rank 4.

The rune didn't get to enjoy its new home for long. No more than a few seconds after Noah ensured it had formed properly, he unleashed the power of Sunder upon it. With a loud crack, the rune shattered and its components spewed out amid a wave of energy.

Glowing Moonlight – Rank 3
Glowing Moonlight – Rank 3
Glowing Moonlight – Rank 3
Shrouded Everlasting Night – Rank 3
Shrouded Everlasting Night – Rank 3
Shrouded Everlasting Night – Rank 3
Shrouded Everlasting Night – Rank 3

All the runes were... average. Not great, not terrible. Either way, they were enough to work with. Noah drank in the excess energy, converting it into Natural Disaster. Unfortunately, the conversion between energy types was brutal.

Of all the power that had come from the rune, Noah barely filled Natural Disaster by five percent.

Huh. Does it get harder to convert energy the more powerful a rune gets? I suppose that makes sense, but it's going to be a huge pain in the ass. I guess I can' t just completely brute-force my way through the ranks.

It was still 5 percent that he hadn't had before, though. Noah returned his attention to the real world and looked to Lee.

"I'm ready, Lee. Whenever you are, go ahead and drink the potion."

Lee's brow set and she nodded. Digging a finger into the seal of the potion, Lee popped it off. She crossed her legs and sat down, leaning against the bed. After one last look at Noah, she tipped it back and poured half the liquid into her mouth.

Noah took the potion from Lee and pulled out the second seal, pouring the rest of it into his own mouth. He sat down beside her as a familiar buzzing sensation enveloped him, setting the piece of Catch-paper down between them. They both put their hands on it. No more than a few seconds later, the world turned black.

Lee's soul was exactly how Noah remembered it. A dark, shadowy expanse reminiscent of his own, but with strands of darkness stretching out in every direction and clinging to her runes like a ball of messy yarn.

As soon as he arrived, Noah did a quick check for Azel. It had been a while since the demon had shown himself, but that only made Noah more suspicious. But, to Noah's surprise, the only people in Lee's soul were the two of them.

"What's wrong?" Lee asked.

"I was checking for Azel. I half expected him to be here."

"Oh. He won't be," Lee said with complete confidence. "He wants me to do this."

"He wants—wait. Have you been speaking with him?"

"Yeah," Lee said. "He's been bugging me a lot recently, but he hasn't done anything bad. He just wants me to get stronger. I'm sure he's got a motive, but I don't know what it is, and I don't think it's an issue yet."

Lovely. That explains where the firey asshole has been these last few weeks. It doesn't seem like Lee is too bothered by him. Maybe he's started to mellow out a bit.

"Well, let me know if he ever starts bothering you too much," Noah said. "We'll find a way to make him stop."

"Okay. For now, I just want to fix my runes."

Her sudden determination to improve made Noah hesitate for a moment. If Azel had been speaking with her a lot, there was a pretty good chance he'd influenced Lee into pushing forward. But, on the other hand, improvement was important.

If he'd just motivated Lee, Azel had technically done her a favor. But, somehow, Noah suspected that there was more to it than that. He studied her for a few seconds, then inclined his head. When it came down to it, he trusted Lee.

"What rune do we start with?" Lee asked. "The Master Rune?"

"Nah. We'll leave that alone for now." Noah shook his head. "I've got the pieces of the Moonlit Shadow Rune waiting for you in my soul, so we'll start by fixing up your normal runes."

"Okay."

Noah told Lee all the runes that had come from Moonlit Shadow, then waited for a minute as she thought about them.

"I'll start with my Demon Runes actually," Lee said. She held a hand out and one of her Demon Runes pulled closer to them, the strands of darkness stretching as they tried to keep it bound in place. It smoldered with faint purplish-red intensity, still completely unreadable to Noah. "I've got some Space Runes left that I can use to patch it, but I'll need you to Sunder this so I can use them."

"Remember I can only use Renewal's power once," Noah warned, "so don't push yourself too hard. I don't want you collapsing on me. We can always come back and fix everything up later if we need to."

Lee nodded, but Noah could tell by the look in her eyes that she had absolutely no plans of holding back. He didn't blame her. If he'd been in her shoes, he would have done the same. Even though it was only a minor delay, Noah understood impatience more than anyone else.

He flexed his fingers and called on Sunder. His veins turned jet black as power pumped through his body, rearing to be used. He didn't relish the pain he was about to cause Lee, but it was the way things were—and he wouldn't hold her back. If there was ever a way that he could find to Sunder Lee's runes without hurting her, he'd figure out how to do it in a heartbeat. But, at the moment, there wasn't.

"Just let me know when you're ready to begin."

"Yeah," Lee said. She swallowed, then set her jaw. "Let's make an order on what we work on to save time. I don't know how much I'm going to be able to say after we get started. After we do all three Smoldering Warps, let's do the Umbral Body Runes and finish with the Shift Runes. I'll just point to the runes I need you to Sunder. Does that work?"

"It does."

Lee pulled her first Demon Rune closer to Noah. He gave it one last look, then extended a hand and laid his palm against its crackling surface. Energy poured out of his hand and into the rune.

A line of black energy streaked across the air, splitting the rune straight in half with a loud, shattering crash. Energy poured out and Lee gritted her teeth, staggering forward and pulling a Space Rune from the reaches of her mind closer.

She got to work, racing against the clock, before the pain or exhaustion took over. Noah had never realized quite how infuriating it was to sit back and hope that his friends would succeed, but there was nothing else he could do.

Nothing but watch. Nothing but wait until the next time she needed Sunder's power.

Chapter Forty-Seven

The stench of a demon infused the ground. It wound into the dying grass and bored deep into the soil. Even though there was no sign of the battle that had taken place here, Rafael knew the smell all too well.

"This is where Inaros and Johan fought," Rafael mused, pressing a hand to the grass. He rubbed the dry soil between his fingers, then rose to his feet. Anger swirled in his chest. This was where his men had died.

Pure incompetence is the only reason that the culprits still walk free. If I had been permitted to pursue them immediately after they went missing, the demon responsible for this would already be flayed at my feet.

By how much energy they let leak out, they have to be a low tier. Rank 3, at the most. I find it hard to believe that Inaros or Johan would fall to something so pathetic. The demon has aid, then. Either another demon or someone else of a higher rank.

The Inquisitor rose to his feet, brushing the soil off on his beautifully decorated shirt. A sword hung at his side, its hilt sculpted into the form of the head of a dog. He barely even noticed the stain that it left behind. Two men were dead because the Inquisitor's Guild was busy playing politics with the Linwick family.

"Power-hungry fools," Rafael growled. He hadn't even been sanctioned to look into the deaths of his men, but they couldn't keep a Rank

5 from taking the leave that he had stored up. It had been years since Rafael could last remember taking a vacation.

There had been no need for one. Ripping the filth of demons from the mortal plane had always been reward enough. Freeing the world from their wretched grip was his purpose for living.

He had less than a month to track down the wretched being that had killed his men before the guild would recall him. And, as much as Rafael hated the idea of leaving his targets alive, there were far greater threats known to them.

This was a personal vendetta. He knew that well. There were many demons to kill, and he was a Rank 5 Inquisitor. There were duties expected of him. Duties that were far greater than his own desires.

But, for the next month, those duties didn't matter.

And I won't even need a month. A demon such as this will be unable to hide itself, and I suspect it will still be together with whatever force or alliance it used to strike down Johan and Inaros.

I will return to the Inquisition with their corpses and have their bones formed into weapons to slay demons a generation from now.

Rafael's hand clenched around his rosary. The bone pearls, each crafted from the corpse of a different Rank 4 demon, trembled at his touch. Some small part of them remained, trapped within the polished bone. Every time he forced his power through it, they screamed in agony. He'd never been able to determine if he despised or loved the tool.

The idea of turning back even a small amount of the suffering that the demons inflicted upon the world brought him delight, but relying on demons in any way disgusted him. Unfortunately, without the bones, it was difficult to force the demons from hiding.

Nothing comes without sacrifice.

Rafael drew in a deep breath and let it out through his clenched teeth. He drew a small dagger from his side and pulled it across his palm. Blood welled up from the cut and Rafael turned his hand to the ground, letting it drip onto the grass.

The blood sizzled as Rafael's energy worked into the ground, drawing out the dried blood beneath the earth. Even though the trail was cold, blood carried knowledge for long after it was spilled.

Scents mixed in Rafael's nostrils. His eyes closed as he filtered them apart, processing each piece and dismissing it before moving onto the next. Blood Magic was complicated, but it was the greatest tool in the arsenal of all the most powerful Inquisitors.

Blood Runes were some of the rarest and hardest to find in the wild, and their sale was heavily regulated. Very few people had managed to get access to them outside the order, and it was for good reason.

Rafael's eyes sharpened as he found what he was looking for. The stench of the demon grew stronger. His hand clenched and the blood flowed up from the ground, pooling into an orb above his cut palm. A cold smile stretched across his lips.

"Found you," Rafael breathed. It was just a general direction, but it would be enough. The blood would react when he grew closer, and then his men would be avenged. Rafael pulled a vial from his pocket and let the blood slither into it before sliding the cork in.

Count your days, demon. I am coming for you.

* * *

It wasn't a pretty sight. Blood dripped from Lee's nose and eyes, streaking down her face and splattering on the dark ground of her mindspace. Noah's arm wrapped around her back, propping Lee up as she pushed through the pain.

Cracks ran throughout her mindspace, faint energy piercing through the darkness in a discomforting manner. It didn't belong, and Lee's soul knew it.

Lee trembled against him, and her body temperature felt lower than it should have been. He wanted to tell her to stop and rest, but it would have been nothing but an insult. The Fragment of Renewal could repair the damage she took, so this was a matter of her willpower versus her nature—and it was not the spot for Noah to butt in.

Sunder did clearly make the process easier than just ripping the runes out, but with the amount of changes they had already made, the damage was adding up—but so was her work. She was nearly finished. Lee had already repaired all of her Demon Runes and turned her Umbral Body Runes into Umbra Runes.

She'd even managed to repair one of her Shift Runes, though its appearance and name didn't change. She'd moved so quickly that

Noah had barely even had time to see what runes made it up, but there were definitely some Monster Runes within it. Grabbing pieces from the Moonlit Shadow Rune Noah had brought in for her, Lee mercilessly ripped her own body apart in the process of remaking it.

Lee nodded her head in the direction of her final Shift Rune, barely even able to muster the energy to move her arms to point. Noah pressed his lips together as the rune drew closer to them. Lee was just inches from collapse.

He clenched his jaw and raised his hand, drawing on Sunder and shattering the final rune. The strands of Lee's soul connected to it snapped. Energy washed past them and Lee spasmed, stumbling. If it hadn't been for his support, she would have collapsed.

She coughed blood onto the shadowy substance beneath their feet, and it bucked beneath them, groaning in pain. Noah prepared to call on the Fragment of Renewal, but Lee's eyes fluttered to stay open.

Mutely, she drew runes from the spiral of energy surrounding them and pulled them together, dragging out pieces left behind from their other combinations and forcing them together.

I could use the Fragment of Renewal now, but that might mess with the creation of the rune because of the way it works. Renewal isn't necessarily proper healing as much as returning to the proper state. If it registers Lee's proper state as the one without the new rune formed, it could cause problems.

"Come on, Lee," Noah heaved. "You can do this. Just one last push."

Blood dripped from her nose and fell onto his sleeve. Noah's clothes were already soaked with it, so he barely even noticed. Her arm struggled to raise at her side.

Noah reached down, taking her wrist and lifting it. Lee drew in a shaky breath. Her eyes, unfocused and blurry, sharpened for an instant. Baring her teeth, Lee clenched her hand. The runes snapped together.

A flash of light lit Lee's mindspace, and Noah was momentarily blinded. He'd been so focused on Lee that he hadn't been ready for the flash. He squinted through the bright light, desperately hoping that they wouldn't need to remake the rune.

He didn't think Lee would be able to survive another modification at the moment, and they'd need a new Mind Meld Potion. And, as simple as that was, it felt like admitting defeat.

The light faded, and a new rune became visible beyond it, the excess energy from the combination pouring back into it. A relieved grin crossed Noah's face. A second remade Shift Rune floated, identical to the first. Strands of black rose up from her soul, winding around the rune and pulling it in.

He went to draw on the Fragment of Renewal, but Lee wasn't done. She bit her lip so hard that blood dripped from it, joining the rivers running down her face. Energy pulsed from the last rune as Lee drew on it, testing her final creation to ensure it was flawless.

The pressure didn't change.

A tiny smile flickered across Lee's lips and her hand dropped. She collapsed into Noah's arms, her body going limp. He instantly ripped power from the Fragment of Renewal, letting the refreshing energy course out from his fingers and into Lee's body.

She let out a small, relieved breath. The jagged cracks running all throughout her soul started to seal over, and a cool, pink mist swirled behind her eyes. Noah lowered her to the ground, sitting beside Lee as he waited for the Fragment of Renewal's magic to do its work.

Lee was definitely awake, but she was so mentally exhausted that she couldn't even muster the energy to speak. Noah didn't mind. He just sat beside her, looking out at her soul as it started to heal.

Minutes passed.

"I did it," Lee said, her words breaking the silence. She wiped some of the blood from her face with the back of her hand, then pushed herself upright. "I fixed all my runes."

"Damn right you did," Noah said, ruffling her hair. "I don't know if anyone else could have had the willpower to push through it like that. But... maybe the next time we need to fix this many runes, we do it one at a time."

A small grin passed over Lee's face and she nodded. "Okay. Hopefully we don't have to do this again, though. They're all flawless now."

"So they are." They fell silent for a few more seconds. Noah nodded in the direction of Lee's new Shift Runes. "Why'd you add Shadow to your Shift Runes? Couldn't you have just tried to make True Shift Runes?"

"I could have, but I've been moving much more toward the stealth aspects than the shape-changing ones," Lee said. "This fits my soul better. It makes it easier to blend in with the shadows, at the cost of not being able to change my form for as long as I used to be able to. It's limited to two or three hours now. That's fine, though. I only needed to shift bodies so much because I was hiding, and I don't need to do that when I'm with you guys."

"I'm glad to hear that," Noah said with a small smile. Many of Lee's runes had lost a good portion of their energy in the conversion, but the power in the Moonlit Shadow Rune that he'd brought her had done a lot to make it up.

Its energy hadn't been too different from the energy that most of Lee's runes needed, so many of her new Rank 3s were still nearly full. It probably wouldn't take too long until she had enough energy to push to Rank 4.

That was a problem for a different time, though. Noah had already seen his fair share of rune modification today—Lee deserved a break.

They sat there in silence, watching the damage to Lee's soul patch over, until the Mind Meld's effects finally wore off and they were whisked back into the real world to see what had passed in their absence.

And, when they got back, there would be a Master Rune waiting for Lee.

Chapter Forty-Eight

Noah's eyes opened to a concerned frown on Moxie's face. She sat in front of them, a bloody cloth in her hand, as she dabbed at Lee's face. Mercifully, Lee's eyes fluttered open a moment after Noah's did.

Moxie had clearly been ready for Lee's rune modifications, because there were several other clothes sitting on the ground beside her, all completely stained through. Lee blinked several times, pulling herself back into awareness.

"Did it work?" Moxie asked, lowering the cloth.

"Yeah," Lee said through a yawn. She shifted and Moxie moved back, watching Lee with her hands out to catch the smaller woman in case she fell. "I did it."

"Perhaps we should have done this in two sessions, but it's all repaired," Noah confirmed. He pulled out the final one of Lee's runes —the Broken Enveloping Dark Master Rune and held it out to Lee. "Will taking this in cause trouble?"

"No," Lee replied, a grin crossing her lips. She wiped at her nose and took the paper from him, running a thumb across its surface. "I've never had a Master Rune before."

"It's broken," Noah pointed out. "I assume that means it's weaker than it should be, and I suppose the multi-word name reinforces that. Then again, it could just be that the Master Rune is the peak of

Enveloping Darkness and got broken. I still don't know all the rules of how they work yet, but there's clearly a degree of hierarchy between them."

"Too many words." Lee put her hand on the paper and closed her eyes. Moxie and Noah both stiffened as Lee's lips pressed thin and her forehead creased in concentration. A minute passed, and the paper fizzled.

The rune on it burned away, taking the Catchpaper with it. Tiny wisps of ash drifted into the air as the last of it vanished, and Lee opened her eyes to watch the remains of the paper float off.

Moxie flicked a hand and a vine reached out, pulling her window open. Catching her thoughts, Noah sent a small breeze out to carry the embers away instead of letting them land on her very flammable room.

"Huh," Lee said, looking down at her hands and flexing her fingers. "That... isn't what I expected."

"Did it work?" Noah asked.

"Yeah. It's in there. Feels really different than the rest of my runes. Kind of like someone stacked an extra rune on top of them. I feel like I could remove it pretty easily if I wanted to."

"Maybe because it's not bonded to your soul as tightly as the other ones?" Noah suggested.

That's odd, though. I didn't notice anything like that with Sunder or the Fragment of Renewal—and I can't really remember much about how I felt after getting Combustion. I was in a bit of a delirium, and now it's imbued into my soul.

"Could be," Lee said with a shrug. She looked out the open window as a chilly breeze blew through it, ruffling her hair. "I want food now."

Noah suppressed a laugh. No matter how much changed or how hard she worked, she was still hungry. And, now that she mentioned it again, food did actually sound pretty good to him.

"I wouldn't object to getting something to eat," Noah said.

"Neither would I." Moxie already had her cloak on, so she was ready for the cold. Noah dialed up the heat from Combustion just a bit to fight off the increasing chill, then looked back to Lee. "Before we head off—you're sure everything is fine, Lee? No adverse effects?"

"I feel normal," Lee confirmed. She rolled her neck, then licked her lips. "Just hungry."

"In that case, you can lead and pick the place. You've done enough work today to earn it."

Lee didn't need to be told twice. She zipped out the door, and the others had to run to catch up with her.

* * *

After a surprisingly fun walk through a foot of snow, they all had a hearty breakfast at one of the local restaurants. They ate near a large window, watching snow fall outside. The large, glistening snowflakes mesmerized Noah to such a point that he could barely take his eyes off them.

When they finished eating, Noah couldn't bring himself to head back inside. It wasn't like the snow was particularly cold because of his Imbuements, so it was basically just a soft blanket covering everything around them.

"I have never been more jealous of your runes," Moxie informed Noah. "If fire wasn't so opposite to the path I'm trying to take with my own runes, I'd have considered imbuing myself with it purely to stay outside longer."

"Is the cloak not enough?"

"It does a lot, but not to the point where I can lie down in a foot of snow and not get cold in the slightest. It's fine, though. I've been thinking about what I'm going to teach, and I think I want to try to get ready for class tomorrow."

Noah scrunched his nose, but he wasn't going to argue. Moxie had been wanting to start teaching again before they'd even returned to Arbitage. It would have been unfair to stand in her way or even offer to help—this was something she wanted to do on her own.

"Sounds good," Noah said. "What about you, Lee?"

"I think I'm going to sleep. I'm tired." Lee rubbed her stomach and licked her lips. "And, when I wake up again, I'm going to be hungry."

Noah snorted and shook his head. "If all you do is eat and sleep, you're going to turn into a slug. Or a sloth. Something that doesn't do much. I don't know. I never really paid much attention to animals. But, in that case, I am going to go frolic through the snow like a newborn deer. I trust there are no objections?"

Lee's response was to yawn and head into Building T. Noah

chuckled and took his gourd off, handing it to Moxie. She arched an eyebrow and took it from him. "Why are you giving me this? Don't tell me you—"

"No plans for it," Noah promised. "I do quite literally plan to just run around in the snow and explore the campus, but it's just a normal gourd. I don't know how great the cold and wet will be for it."

Moxie's eyes widened and she nodded, taking the gourd hurriedly and cradling it in her arms. "Good point. It's clearly treated to last, but there's no point in taking a risk. I'll keep an eye on it."

"Thanks," Noah said.

Moxie raised a hand in farewell and headed into the building while Noah turned, setting out in the opposite direction.

Snow fell around him as he walked to nowhere in particular. Small mounds of it built on his head and shoulders, but Noah couldn't be bothered to brush them off. He intentionally dialed Combustion back, letting a little bit of the chill nip at him.

Arbitage looked oddly beautiful covered in snow. He wandered down the streets and past the markets. A tiny smile pulled at the corners of his lips as he passed by other people. It was really easy to figure out who had Fire Runes and who didn't—while most people were bundled in heavy clothes and waddling around with distaste, there were a few that looked like they'd dressed for a normal summer day.

He continued walking, not paying any particular attention to where he was headed. Noah wasn't even sure how long he walked. There wasn't anywhere in particular he needed to be. At some point, he got back to working on his Imbuements, not bothering to stop moving while he did.

At this point, he knew Natural Disaster's power enough to work with it in the back of his mind. The Imbuements were already almost done, so it wasn't too difficult to continue tracing them on while enjoying the beautiful day.

The sun's light was muted, hidden behind the thick clouds pouring snow down on Arbitage. It felt like it was still early in the morning, even though it was probably approaching midday.

It wasn't just Arbitage's appearance that had changed. The snow seemed to have muted it as well, and the air was still aside from the faint rustle of the wind through trees. Silence hung all around him.

Noah finished the last of the modifications to his Imbuements and finally came to a stop, drawing in a deep breath and enjoying the fresh air. Snow even *smelled* crisp.

To his surprise, he found himself standing at the ruins of the building that Moxie had taken him to before they'd headed to the Linwick Estate. A small grin pulled at his lips. For some reason, it felt oddly fitting.

I must have been walking for quite a while. Time really slipped away from me. I think this would have been nicer if Moxie was here with me, though.

Noah watched the soft light filter through the cracks of the building, enjoying it as it played across the snow-covered stone. He drew on Natural Disaster and hopped into the air, using a soft gust to propel himself up onto the roof.

He landed, sending up a soft puff of snow and trudging over to the spot where they'd watched the sun rise. Noah drew in another deep breath and craned his neck back, looking into the sky.

It was beautiful. It was—

A faint ripple nipped at the back of Noah's mind. The newly finished Imbuements in his ears picked up an abnormal shift in the air behind him. Noah turned, picking up on a humanoid shape moving toward him before he could even see it.

On the roof across from him stood a cloaked man. He wore heavy leathers from head to toe, and a mask concealed the part of his face visible beneath the hood. Not a single part of his skin showed, and two swords were sheathed at his side.

"Can I help you?" Noah asked, squinting. "I'm kind of trying to have a moment here. Maybe come back tomorrow?"

The man didn't respond. He just reached down, drawing the blades and shifting into a fighting stance. Something about his movements felt off, but Noah couldn't quite put his finger on it.

"Oh, come on," Noah said. "Look up, man. I'm busy."

The man didn't say anything, but he aimed the blade of one sword at Noah's heart in a clear refusal of his request. For some reason, he didn't seem to plan to attack until Noah was ready.

If I just ignore him, will he screw off?

Noah considered the thought for a moment, then dismissed it.

"What are you? Another assassin?"

The man didn't respond, but his stance tightened even further. It didn't look like he was going to wait around for Noah to make a move for much longer. Heaving a sigh, Noah drew on Natural Disaster.

"Can't I just have one day of peace? Come on, then. You've got to be the politest assassin I've ever met, though. I appreciate the consideration."

Wind whipped around the man's body, swirling into tight blades that enveloped his sword. He lunged, blurring into a streak of white wind as one of his blades shot for Noah's neck.

He was faster than Noah expected, but not nearly fast enough to surprise him. Noah vaulted back, releasing a blast of wind from his palms. It launched him into the air and sent the assassin skidding back against the roof.

Noah landed on the ground beneath the building, raising his hands. A blur streaked into the air as the assassin leapt off the roof and plummeted down for Noah, swords aimed straight for his heart.

Power roared around Noah as he took advantage of the snow surrounding him. Thick streamers of snow erupted from the ground and shot out like tentacles. They slammed into the assassin, enveloping him in a ball of dense ice and snow with a loud crunch.

The ball crashed to the ground with a thud. Noah looked down at it, then scrunched his nose in annoyance.

"At least I got to test out Blizzard. Thanks, I guess."

A figure appeared in Noah's mental map of the area around him. He groaned, turning to find the assassin standing at his side, completely unharmed. The man hadn't moved fast enough to avoid his attack—which meant he hadn't moved at all.

"You've got Space Magic?" Noah asked, his eyes narrowing. "Has anyone told you that using Space Magic is cheap? The only one that gets a pass is Brayden."

The assassin just pointed his sword at Noah's heart again. Noah lowered into a fighting stance once more, drawing deeply on Natural Disaster and letting a howling snowstorm start to pick up around him.

This guy isn't going for killing blows. Is he testing me? Or is there something else he's looking for? Either way, I might need to start taking this seriously. Letting my guard down against someone with Space Magic is a stupendously bad idea. Maybe this was what today needed. Can't appreciate peace without war, or some poetic shit like that.

"Right then," Noah called over the roar of his magic. "You're clearly a little more competent than I'd hoped. Let's see what you've got."

Chapter Forty-Nine

The assassin blurred toward Noah, who released the violent magic that he'd been gathering. Screaming whorls of snow and ice ripped across the ground, picking up the snow before them and forming into a miniature, horizontal avalanche.

A pop of faint purple light was all the warning Noah needed to know the assassin had avoided the attack. He didn't wait for the man to reappear before dragging magic from Natural Disaster once more.

Against an opponent that could teleport, there were two main methods to fight. The first was to try and get lucky with a fast enough attack and hope they were either too slow to avoid it or they teleported into its path by accident.

The second was a little more interesting, but it wasn't time to use it yet. He'd have to bide his time for just a bit longer.

Noah's neck prickled and his tremorsense picked up the assassin as he appeared in the snowdrift several paces behind him. Noah twisted to the side, leaning his head until his ear touched his shoulder.

The sword flicked over Noah's neck and he spun around, whipping his leg up. The assassin vaulted back, avoiding the attack before disappearing once more and reforming ten paces away from Noah. His leg passed through the air where the assassin had been, just barely missing.

"Is this really how we're going to do this?" Noah asked, his eyes narrowing. "What are you after?"

He didn't get a response. The assassin disappeared in another blink of purple energy. Noah drew in a deep breath, then gripped onto the wind around him with his magic and *yanked.*

Even as the assassin took form, he was pulled off his feet as a powerful gale pulled the snow, dirt, and everything else around them directly toward Noah. The assassin contorted his body, just barely managing to avoid Noah's hand as it passed over his head.

He drove his foot into Noah's stomach, sending him stumbling backward. An instant later, the man blinked and reappeared out of reach, his swords at the ready. He'd already teleported several times, but it didn't look like he was getting tired yet. That seemed odd. Brayden had talked about how difficult it was to constantly use Space Magic, and this man didn't seem stronger than Brayden at all.

On top of that, he's avoiding using magic inside my domain—but he doesn't seem to have one of his own. That doesn't make any sense. He shouldn't be able to sense my domain at all if he's a Rank 3.

Unless...

"You aren't human," Noah said, narrowing his eyes. "You aren't even in control of yourself, are you?"

The assassin didn't respond, and Noah didn't expect them to. He'd gotten a pretty good grasp of the situation now. The assassin hadn't been surprised or reacted to his domain because the person controlling them wasn't actually present.

That means I was right to avoid using any of my strongest moves. Revealing Sunder or my violin to kill this guy would have been a waste. That said, if someone wants to play, I can play.

Noah's fist clenched as power gathered within it. The assassin sprinted at him again, blinking as soon as it drew close. Noah considered using Combustion to suck the air away, but he wasn't even convinced the assassin was breathing.

Instead, he let crackling electricity leap from one of his palms to the other. An orb of lightning started to grow between his hands, steadily growing more powerful. Noah's hair stood on end.

The assassin teleported as he grew close, reappearing at Noah's side. Noah hurled the ball of lightning. Energy leapt off it, melting the snow instantly as it passed by it. As soon as he released the magic, Noah drew more power from Natural Disaster.

With the power contained within the lightning orb, Noah knew for a fact that the assassin would teleport again instead of trying to dodge it. Sure enough, the man blinked out in a flash of purple, reforming on Noah's other side.

The assassin lunged, entering Noah's domain as he swung the swords for Noah's neck. And, in that same moment, Noah's fist whipped up. Normally, trading one punch in exchange for two sword strikes would have been a pretty good trade for the one with the swords, but the assassin had already shown that he was prioritizing avoiding attacks from Noah. Sure enough, the man vaulted back, abandoning his attack—but he was still inside Noah's domain for a brief instant longer.

Noah released a blast of wind, throwing himself toward the assassin and keeping the other man trapped within his domain. It only went a few feet out of his body, but that was all the room that he needed.

The assassin adapted to Noah's strategy quickly, thrusting his swords to try and push him back. Noah ripped the snow up around them, slamming the assassin's swords to the side. It was tempting to tank one of the sword strikes in exchange for landing a blow himself, but he didn't want to give away his regenerative properties either.

As the assassin tried to raise his swords again, Noah used Natural Disaster to rip a stone out of the ground, using the snow to hide it until it was too late for the assassin to use his impressive speed to dodge it.

The rock struck his arm with a loud crunch, sending one of the swords spinning from his grip. As Noah had expected, the man didn't even respond to the pain. He rolled to his feet, swinging his other sword to try and force Noah back.

Unfortunately for the assassin, the tempo of the battle had shifted the moment Noah had figured out the other man's strategy. He flicked a hand and a pillar of stone shot up, slamming the second sword from the assassin's hand.

The blade spun to the side and impaled itself in the ground, just barely poking out over the snow. At the same time, the ground bucked beneath the assassin, tossing him into the air.

Noah grabbed the unarmed man by the neck, then twisted his entire body and pelted the assassin into the ground with all his might. He ripped all the snow away from the impact point and was rewarded with the satisfying crunch of a bone breaking in the assassin's arm.

And then—instead of finishing the man off, Noah kicked him in the face. The assassin rolled back and out of Noah's domain. As soon as he was free, he blinked, reappearing beside one of his fallen swords and grabbing it.

Noah walked over to the other sword and picked it up, studying the blade for a moment before tossing it through the air to the assassin, who caught it using his broken arm without even flinching.

"I'm crushing you the old-fashioned way," Noah said, a grin stretching across his lips. "And I take it back. You clearly aren't an assassin. Whoever is controlling you had best pick up the pace. If you want to see how competent I am, I'd appreciate it if you actually put up a fight."

The hooded man sprinted toward Noah, leveling his swords. Wind whipped around him, boosting the man's speed just before he reached Noah's domain. It was a pretty clever strategy—he wouldn't lose his momentum, even if the magic ran out.

Unfortunately for him, Noah wasn't interested in playing fair and finding out which of them was faster. He set off a blast of wind directly beneath where the assassin would be, sending the man flying into the air.

Noah jumped, colliding with him and grabbing both of the man's wrists before he could spin the swords around to face him. His opponent struggled with surprising strength and managed to free one of his arms—but that also meant that one of Noah's hands was free as well.

Normally, taking a sword cut in exchange for a punch would be a pretty poor idea. Noah wasn't just hitting the man with a normal punch, though. The air around his fist hummed with energy as he whipped it forward, driving deep into the cloaked man's stomach and unleashing a powerful wave of vibration.

A dozen loud cracks split the air, and the assassin rocketed downward, slamming into the ground with one final crash. His swords flew from his hands, disappearing into the snow as Noah dropped to the ground in front of the man, power still humming around his knuckles.

The fallen man twitched, clearly still trying to move, but the vibrations ripping through his entire body made it impossible. Noah put his foot on the man's chest and leaned forward. "How's that for a show?"

He sent one last pulse of energy into the man through his foot, ripping his innards to shreds with violent tremors. Despite the serious damage, no blood leaked into the snow. Noah knelt by the mangled body, digging through his pockets.

His fingers found a letter, and a thin smile crossed over his face. He pulled it out and flipped it open. There, written in familiar golden letters, was a message addressed to him.

Congratulations, Vermil Linwick. Turn around.

"Well, if you aren't a cheesy bastard," Noah said with a dry laugh.

He turned, squinting into the snow falling all around him. A woman stepped out from behind the ruins of the building, an umbrella open over her head stopping the snow from touching her shoulders.

She walked across the top of the snow instead of through it, but her feet were making imprints in the ground. There was no way she was actually that light, nor was she flying, so she had to have some form of Ice or Snow–based runes.

"Vermil Linwick," the woman said, inclining her head. She wore a veil that obscured most of her features, but her lips were a bright ruby-red that were clear even through the obscurement. "You knew?"

"It wasn't hard to figure out someone was screwing with me when an assassin was actually waiting for me to make a move," Noah said with a shrug. "You're with the advanced track teachers."

It wasn't a question. The woman nodded, a smile playing across her lips.

"Yes. We take our applicants and their teachers very seriously. The teachers already in the advanced track met, and we decided that you needed to be tested. There were some that did not believe you deserved to join our number, given your... colorful past."

"I see," Noah said. "Well? Did I pass?"

A pained grimace passed over the woman's lips. "You shattered a puppet that I spent two months building so badly that I no longer have even the slightest shred of control over it. Why did you intentionally avoid doing serious damage to it at the start of the fight? You made it seem like..."

Noah's grin grew as realization set in on the woman.

"You baited me into committing to the fight, thinking you couldn't do severe damage, purely to destroy the puppet before I could ask you to stop?"

"Let's just call it the price of screwing up my day," Noah said. "I told you that I was having a moment, you know."

The woman walked past Noah and knelt beside the shattered remains of her assassin, prodding it. She let out a groan and stood back up. "Has anyone ever told you that you're an asshole?"

"I could say the same to you. Next time, if you want to test me, say it to my face. Don't try this shit."

"Point taken, Vermil." The woman held her hand out. "For what it's worth, you pass. My name is Ulya."

"I haven't decided if I want to join the advanced track yet." Noah took Ulya's hand. "I'm surprised you aren't mad about the puppet."

"Mad? No, Vermil. I am livid. You were supposed to be a Rank 3. That puppet was meant to crush you, and you would have been judged on how long you fought against it. I did not expect... this." She waved her hand around them, then sighed. "You did give me quite the show, though. How many Rank 4 runes do you have? Three? Four?"

"Enough."

Ulya's lips quirked up in a grin. "Secretive. I suppose I should have guessed. I look forward to seeing how your contributions hone the rest of us. It has been too long since we got new talent. Especially talent as... abrasive as yourself."

"I'm not sure that was a compliment, and I haven't said I was joining the advanced track yet."

"You will," Ulya said, not a shred of hesitation in her voice. "You are too powerful not to. Nobody gets to your level of strength while avoiding chances to improve. And you are correct; that was not a compliment. I just respect power enough to know when I have been thoroughly bested. My only request is that you choose to humiliate someone else the next time someone chooses to try you."

"Why would I come after you again if you aren't screwing with me? I already smashed your puppet into little pieces, so there's no grudge."

"I'm the newest teacher in the advanced track, so I was given the privilege of being the one to test you. It may happen again."

Noah let out a snort of laughter. "Well, I suggest you either have a good throwaway puppet or respectfully decline the next time the opportunity comes up. But, now that you're here, I don't suppose you'll tell me how you had a puppet using magic?"

And could you give me any insight into the clone Evergreen had taken over? If this lady is a puppet user, maybe she can actually be of use.

"Join the advanced track, and I'll be willing to exchange information." Ulya knelt beside her puppet again, running a finger over a ring on her thumb. There was a faint pop, and the body vanished in a streamer of purple energy, zipping into the ring. Noah's eyes widened.

The hell was that?

"Until next time," Ulya said, her voice still slightly pained. She turned on her heel and set off, heading back into the snow. Noah watched her leave, a thoughtful frown on his face.

Interesting. I can't say it didn't feel good to kick that puppet's shit in, though. I wonder how she'd react if she knew I'd only hit Rank 4 a bit ago. Either way, it got me a little bit of exercise.

I almost wish it was stronger, though. If you're going to make me fight, you might as well make it worth my time. That was too easy.

Noah stuck his hands into his pockets and set back off toward Building T, whistling to himself.

Maybe the advanced track was a little more interesting than he'd initially thought.

Chapter Fifty

Moxie and Lee were back at the room when Noah got back, and he wasted no time in telling them what had transpired while he'd been trying to enjoy the weather. Lee waited until Noah had finished speaking to promptly fall back asleep in a ball on Moxie's bed, not even remotely interested.

"It sounds like it could have gone worse," Moxie said, pursing her lips and crossing her arms in front of her chest. "And you definitely made an impression on them. It sounds like Ulya isn't going to be forgetting you anytime soon."

"Probably," Noah agreed. Moxie handed him back his gourd, and he returned it to its spot on his waist. "Either way, she seemed reasonable enough. I'm surprised she had her puppet wait until I was ready to fight to do anything."

"Well, they aren't trying to kill you. It makes sense."

Noah copied Moxie's favorite gesture and arched an eyebrow, tilting his head to the side. "Do you have any idea how many people that weren't supposed to try to kill me have done just that? I'm not particularly inclined to believe that the people that are meant to not kill me will actually refrain from attempting to kill me."

"Okay, fair enough," Moxie admitted. "Does this mean you're planning on joining?"

"I'm certainly interested, but I'm not sure yet. I think it'll depend on what the students say," Noah said. "It's their decision in the end.

I'm sure there would be a lot to learn in the advanced track, but if it causes more trouble than good by giving us too much unwanted attention, it might not be the wisest idea."

"Then I guess we'll find out tomorrow."

"Yeah." Noah nodded. "How about you, though? Any luck with your lesson plan?"

"I know I said I didn't want to just teach them so that they could pass exams, but considering both of the upcoming exams are fighting-related, with the first being hunting and the second being a tournament, I think it would be a good idea for me to focus on combat and ways to defeat your opponents with more than just magic. You're definitely better than I am at the moment-to-moment parts of fighting, but I think I could have some interesting things to offer on fighting as a whole."

"Sounds like a good idea to me. I'm focusing on my pattern lessons right now anyway, so having some extra fighting between you and Lee should be more than enough to round everything out."

"Yeah. Lee and I were actually discussing some potential lessons for after you finish up your normal lecture tomorrow," Moxie said, a spark of excitement lighting up in her eyes. "I think this should work really well."

"I'm sure it will." Noah grinned, then glanced out the window at the soft snow still falling outside. There was still a good bit of time left in the day, but he'd had enough excitement already.

That worked out just fine. This was the perfect opportunity to think about his lesson plan for tomorrow to make sure they made the most of their time. He already had a few ideas brewing, and all of them promised to be interesting.

* * *

It was still snowing when the next day dawned. Noah, Moxie, and Lee arrived at the base of the transport cannon early in the morning, only to find the students had beaten them there once again.

There was a nervous energy in the air that Noah hadn't been expecting. Isabel and Todd were exchanging nervous glances with Emily, and even James and Alexandra looked on edge. A small frown flickered across his face as he trudged to a halt in the snowdrift.

"What's going on?" Noah asked, glancing around. "Why do you all look like you threw a ball through my window?"

"Nothing," Isabel and Todd answered hurriedly. Alexandra and Emily both added in empathetic nods, making Noah even more certain that something had indeed gone wrong.

For whatever reason, they didn't seem to want to tell him *what*, though. Noah shrugged to himself. There would be time to quiz them shortly, but there was no point doing it while half of them were still freezing.

"Let's go to the classroom for today's lesson," Noah said.

"Moxie's?" Emily asked hopefully.

"We'll use the normal one this time. It's a little more out of the way and it's also larger," Noah said with a shake of his head. He set off in the direction of Building G and the others trailed behind him, not particularly pleased with that decision.

"Wouldn't it be easier to just use the transport cannon?" Todd asked. "It could get us out of the snow."

"I like the snow," Noah replied over his shoulder. "Besides, you've got a Fire Rune. It shouldn't be bothering you that much."

"It's just... fluffy," Todd grumbled.

Noah didn't grace that comment with a response, and they all arrived at the dimly lit classroom a short while later. Moxie joined the students in sitting down, while Lee discreetly scaled the wall and found a crack in the ceiling to hang off. Noah did his best not to stare at her hiding place.

"So?" Noah held his hands out.

"So what?" Emily asked.

"Are you going to tell me what in the world you're all glancing at each other about? I'm not blind, guys. Something happened. What is it?"

Silence reigned. Noah's eyes narrowed. Whatever they'd done couldn't have been that bad—all of them were still standing around in one piece. He waited for another minute, but it quickly became clear that nobody was going to spill.

Ah well. I'll just shock it out of them, then.

"Fine," Noah said. He reached into his pocket and pulled out the folded letter from the advanced track. He tapped it against his other hand. "I got this in the mail yesterday. It's an invitation to—"

"The advanced track," Todd finished, staring at the paper like a cat watching a bird through a windowpane. "We got one?"

"Way to take the wind out of my sails," Noah muttered, letting his hand drop. "Yes. You were all invited."

"I got a letter for you as well, Emily," Moxie put in.

Noah paused, then cleared his throat. "James, I don't think you officially count as one of my students, so this might not apply to you. I can ask."

"Don't worry about it," James said. He reached into his pocket and pulled out an identical-looking letter, giving Noah a weary sigh. "Revin dropped this off in the morning. He already signed me up for it."

"Figures," Noah said. He looked from the paper in his hand to the one in James's, then narrowed his eyes. "Is that what you were all hiding?"

"Yeah," Isabel said with a sheepish grin. "We were worried we didn't get in, and we didn't want to make you feel bad."

Noah rolled his eyes. "We don't even know if this program is good. That said, it does seem to have some opportunity. Do you know much about it?"

"Silvertide mentioned it while we were training over break," Todd said. "That's it, though. I just know it's a bunch of extra resources and training for students and teachers that are able to qualify."

"Then the question falls to you," Noah said. "Do you want to join?"

"Why wouldn't we?" Emily asked. "More resources mean we can get stronger faster, and we'll have more people to train against. It's just objectively good!"

"Unless the people don't want you there," Alexandra said, her voice soft. "Not everyone here is a noble."

Emily's smile fell away. "You don't think that's going to matter? The advanced track should be for people that care about runes and fighting, not just for nobles."

"How many non-nobles do you see making it very far at Arbitage?" Todd asked. He shook his head before Emily could answer and held a hand up. "It doesn't actually matter. Even if it's a risk, I think I'd like to take it. Any chance I can get to get stronger is one that's worthwhile."

"Even if I could get you the resources myself?" Noah asked.

The students fell silent for a few seconds, but Noah could tell they'd all come to an answer before anyone spoke again.

"Yeah," Isabel said. "Even then. I want to prove that they screwed up by blacklisting us. If we crush all the nobles in the advanced track, there won't be any way to refute it."

"You're correct, but it's also going to put a lot of pressure on you," Noah warned. "Hitting Rank 2 put you at the peak of all the students in the school, but I wouldn't be surprised if that wasn't the case in the advanced track. It could make things a lot harder."

"Don't care. If things are harder, we'll just do better." Todd crossed his arms, and Alexandra nodded.

"I didn't come here because it was easy. I want to get stronger," Alexandra said. "Even if it carries the risk of failure."

"Personally, I'd have loved to do absolutely nothing," James put in. "Unfortunately, Revin registered me already. I don't have a choice."

"Then it sounds like it's settled," Noah said, feeling a pang of sympathy for James. He was sure the boy would be fine, though. Despite how much he claimed to be lazy, Noah was pretty sure James hadn't gotten as competent as he had by doing nothing. It was probably more of a defense mechanism against Revin. "I'll deliver the letter to the office today and confirm that you're all entering the advanced track."

I'm glad they decided to join. There's some risk in this, but it would be really interesting to see how big the difference is between the average researchers and students that don't care about anything related to getting stronger and the ones that are really dedicated to learning and growing.

The students all exchanged excited glances, and Noah gave them a few moments to let everything sink in before he started to speak again.

"Don't let that distract you, though. You've all still got to deal with me, and I believe we were having a competition on who could get the best understanding of their pattern before today," Noah said, tapping the chalkboard leaning against the wall behind him. "Did everyone manage to make progress?"

He got a round of nods, though some were definitely a lot more hopeful than others. In particular, Alexandra and Isabel seemed particularly excited. Noah grinned at their expressions and stretched his arms out at his sides.

"In that case, I think we should get started. Who wants to go first? Walk up to stand beside me and demonstrate what you've learned with your pattern, but don't put any magic into it."

And, if you do accidentally put magic in somehow, my domain will smother it before anything can go wrong. It's like the perfect way to practice.

"Can I start?" Isabel asked.

She was using swords as her pattern. Hm. Both Isabel and Alexandra had the same pattern, and they both looked pretty excited. I wonder if they practiced together. That would have been a good way to really refine their magic.

Noah beckoned Isabel over. "Go ahead, Isabel. Let's see what you've got."

Chapter Fifty-One

Isabel walked up to the front of the classroom. She came to a stop several paces away from him, then pushed a few desks back so that she would have more room to move around. Once she was satisfied, she turned back to him.

"I think my pattern is a little easier if I have something to practice against. It's awkward just swinging a sword at the air," Isabel said.

"I can do it," Alexandra volunteered, rising out of her chair. She and Isabel looked to Noah, who shrugged in response.

"Go for it. Whatever works the best to demonstrate your pattern is fine, but you'll probably need to get to the point where you can practice it alone at some point in the future. You won't always have a sparring partner. And remember—no magic."

"That's fine," Isabel said. Alexandra drew a sword from a second, smaller sheath hanging at her side beside her normal one and held it out to Isabel hilt-first. Giving her an appreciative nod, Isabel took the blade. She held it at her side, shifting into a fighting stance.

Alexandra drew her own sword and raised the weapon. Noah was struck by just how different their stances were. Alexandra stood on the balls of her feet, shifting her bodyweight like a palm tree in a strong breeze.

On the other hand, Isabel stood completely still and unmoving. From what Noah knew, he was pretty sure that being light on your feet was a pretty important part of not getting injured, but the look on Isabel's face told him she wasn't doing it for no reason.

Noah moved closer to them, making sure both were within his domain, then nodded to Isabel.

"Whenever you're ready, you can start. Stop whenever Alexandra calls out or whenever you finish your demonstration. Please do your best to attack her sword and not her. I'm confident in her abilities, but I'd rather avoid an incident."

Both of the girls nodded, then exchanged a glance that told Noah this definitely wasn't the first time they'd done this. A small grin crossed over his face as Isabel drew in a deep breath and squared her stance, wrapping both of her hands around her sword.

She raised the blade, and her whole body twisted as she swung it. A resounding clang rang out as she struck Alexandra's sword. It scraped past Alexandra harmlessly, carving through the air, but Isabel didn't seem bothered.

The sword lifted once more, this time coming from the other side. Noah's eyes narrowed as he watched Isabel start to rain blows on Alexandra's sword. It took him a few moments, but there was something *off* about Isabel's movements.

At first, he'd thought it was merely the fact that she was standing in such an odd stance, but that wasn't it. Isabel's whole body seemed to be committing to every single blow, not even considering the possibility of missing.

The feeling of confusion intensified as Noah realized that Alexandra seemed to be losing ground. She should have been naturally stronger than Isabel because of her Body Runes constantly empowering her, even if she wasn't actively using them.

But, despite that, Isabel's strikes were actually having an impact. Alexandra's features were tight in concentration. She was struggling to keep her sword up. Every strike Isabel sent forth seemed to have even more force than the last.

The pattern started to take form. Noah could see it—a gradually building avalanche of blows, each one stronger than the last. Isabel was purely using swordwork, but by using the momentum of each strike and steadily putting more and more of herself into every attack, she'd effectively created a crescendo.

Isebel finally relented and the lines of concentration faded from her face as she let her hands lower. Alexandra lowered her own sword, discreetly shaking her hands off.

"Well?" Isabel asked. "Did I do it?"

"I'd certainly say so," Noah said with an approving nod. "I could see what you were going for, even if I didn't understand it perfectly. Can you describe the exact goals your pattern had?"

"I was trying to envision a landslide and how all the small rocks falling started to build up into something bigger," Isabel explained, turning the sword around and handing it back to Alexandra. "I tried to do that with my sword. Having every single blow lead up into and intensify the next one. I feel like that fits really well with my Stone Runes."

"Perfect theory. Keep up the practice. You might want to work on doing that while letting yourself continue to move," Noah suggested. "I saw a lot of potential there, but you don't want to be stuck standing in one spot during a fight. Maybe your body could be one of those falling stones? I'm not sure if that's the best suggestion, but try to make sure your pattern isn't something that puts you in an unfavorable position."

Isabel nodded her understanding, and Noah could already see more ideas flashing through her eyes. "Okay. Thanks."

Noah gave her a thumbs-up. "Keep up the good work. Alexandra, since you're already standing, do you want to show your pattern off as well?"

"Sure," Alexandra said. "I don't need a partner."

Noah shrugged. "Whatever lets you show it off the easiest. Whenever you're ready."

Isabel headed back to her chair and sat down as Alexandra turned toward Noah. It struck him how differently she stood now than she had when Gentil had been controlling her. Her movements had become far smoother and more controlled, to the point where it almost seemed like a different person was holding the sword.

Alexandra's blade started to trace through the air, its tip flitting about like a butterfly. It zipped from side to side, seemingly completely opposite to what the directions for their assignment had been.

Instead of having a pattern, Alexandra's movements felt completely random. The blade darted to and fro, flicking and stabbing random points—but never stopping for more than an instant.

Whoa. Her moves are so erratic that the pattern is the complete lack of a pattern. She's wrapped it all the way back around?

Alexandra continued her demonstration. She moved, locked in a dance with an invisible enemy. Noah could practically envision her batting blows out of the air, but instead of ever putting in the energy to deliver a killing blow, her sword just continued to flit around.

Death by a thousand cuts. She's keeping the sword moving quickly and avoiding committing to anything, which lets her react much faster and constantly wear her opponent down. That's an incredible strategy, so long as you've got the stamina to outlast them, and the longer I watch, the more I like the pattern. It fits her perfectly.

As Alexandra's blade slowed to a halt, Noah had no doubt in his mind that Alexandra was further along than Isabel was. Both girls had made great progress, but Alexandra completely understood every move she made. They felt completely natural, while Noah could tell that Isabel was still working to completely come to terms with her pattern.

"Absolutely brilliant," Noah said. "Well done, Alexandra."

A small smile flitted across her lips before her normal expression took over again. "Thanks."

"Feel free to sit back down. Both you and Isabel put on a great showing. Who wants to go next?" Noah asked, turning his gaze to the rest of the class.

Todd, Emily, and James all looked to each other, then back to Noah. None of them made any moves to stand.

"I don't want to go after them," James said sullenly. "I'll look bad."

"You always look bad. You just don't want to go because you didn't study," Emily said with a snicker.

"I don't see you volunteering," James said.

"I volunteer you to go next," Emily countered. Todd just sat back, clearly more than willing to let the two of them duke it out so he could avoid going too close to Alexandra. Noah suppressed a laugh as James gave in and trudged up to the front.

"My pattern is the pattern of not being noticed," James said. "Can I start?"

"I thought you were going to try for humming?"

"I was, but then I got tired."

Noah wasn't sure if he wanted to laugh or sigh. Instead, he just shrugged and gave James an encouraging gesture. "Well, let's see it."

James nodded, then sat down on the ground, crossing his legs and leaning his chin in a palm. And then—he did nothing.

A minute ticked by, and it struck Noah that James wasn't kidding. He was quite literally doing nothing. And, to his complete bafflement, he could actually somewhat see it. James wasn't just sitting there and idly looking around or daydreaming.

He was very intentionally doing absolutely nothing. Noah was pretty sure James wasn't even breathing. The boy was completely and perfectly still.

Well, I'll be damned. Doing nothing is somehow a pattern as well. I wonder how long he can hold his breath, though.

The answer to that was an impressive three minutes. James finally drew in a deep breath and clambered back to his feet, brushing his backside off. "Okay. I did it."

"You didn't do anything!" Emily exclaimed.

"Actually, he did," Noah said, shaking his head in amusement. "There's no way to get that degree of nothingness without intention. James actually has a pattern of doing nothing. Honestly, pretty damn impressive."

"I know." James sat back down in his chair beside Emily, then leaned back and yawned. "You next, Emily."

Emily's cheeks reddened. "I... uh, don't really have anything to show yet. I'm working on it, but I haven't really figured out the patterns in the ice yet. I mean, I know they're there, but I haven't found out how to apply them to myself."

"Nothing wrong with that," Noah said. "We're all going to move at our own pace. Luckily for you, it is currently snowing. Maybe try to spend some time around it and really try to feel how it affects you and how you can incorporate it into a pattern and your fighting style alike. James might be able to give you so
me guidance."

"So I don't have to present?"

"Not if you don't have anything to present yet," Noah said with a laugh. "I'm not going to make you stand up here and do nothing."

Emily let out a relieved sigh. "Thanks."

"That just leaves you then, Todd," Noah said. "Have you made progress?"

"I have, but it's not really in the same way," Todd said. He stood up and approached Noah, pulling a metal bracelet off his wrist and handing it to Noah. "I've been trying to work my patterns into some Imbuements I've been testing."

"Interesting idea," Noah said. He took the bracelet and studied the designs covering its surface. It was covered with flowing lines that ebbed and flowed in a mesmerizing pattern. It took Noah a moment to realize that the runes weren't actually concealed, and Todd had actually just played with their sizes and shapes so much that they were difficult to spot.

He wasn't actually sure if the Imbuement would even work with how much Todd had modified the runes, but he could see the understanding within the bracelet. Todd had tried to capture the feeling of something burning away, and he'd done it quite well.

"This is impressive," Noah said. "Does it work?"

"I don't know," Todd admitted. "I haven't tested it. I don't think the quality of the Imbuement is safe enough to test yet. I know I can do better."

Noah nodded and handed the bracelet back to Todd. "I'll admit I don't know much about Imbuements, but this is impressive. You were smart to avoid testing it, but by all means, keep practicing. Wait until you've got something you're confident in, and then we can test it together."

"Thanks," Todd said with a grin. He headed back to his chair and sat down.

"So who gets the points for today?" Emily asked.

Noah thought for a moment, but the answer was pretty clear in his mind. "You all clearly put in a lot of work, but Alexandra understood her pattern the most. She gets three points, Isabel gets two, and James gets one."

A flash of satisfaction lit in Alexandra's eyes, but she didn't gloat. Noah paused to see if anyone would protest at his rankings, but nobody did. They all just nodded, as if they'd already predicted the answer Noah would give before he spoke it.

"Great," Noah said. "Again, great work, everyone. For today, we'll continue working on those patterns. Everyone will partner up and discuss what they're struggling with, and you can all see how you can help each other. Then, anyone who wants to test their pattern further can come stand next to me to make sure they don't accidentally let any magic seep in. Any questions?"

Everyone shook their heads. None of them questioned why Noah wanted them to stand right next to them, and he was fine with that. It would be a lot more amusing to reveal his domain at a more opportune time, and there wasn't any rush to let anyone know about it yet.

"Great. Then let's get to it."

Chapter Fifty-Two

The rest of the class went without further incident, and everyone set off in their own directions once it ended. Alexandra politely refused an invitation to lunch from the other students, setting a course for her own room.

I've got too much to work on, and I don't want to let my thoughts slip out of my head before I can get them worked out. It's just a change of mindset, but I feel like my swordsmanship improved tremendously in just a few days of practice. If I can keep working on patterns, I could make up for the Body Runes that'll hold me back when everyone else can keep getting stronger.

She couldn't tell if she was impressed or terrified by Vermil's abilities. She'd seen firsthand what he could do back in Dawnforge, and something told her that he'd been holding back in the fight against Gentil.

Something about him and the other professors felt... off. Not necessarily in a bad way, but they didn't fit. At least the differences were obvious with Lee—she was just a bit odd, but it was easy to read her intentions.

Moxie was a bit harder to understand, but even she wasn't too far beyond the realm of comprehension. She cared deeply about Emily and the other students, though she clearly didn't like showing it too much.

But Vermil was something else. He was considerably stronger than he appeared, but instead of flaunting his power or using it to claw his way up the ranks of his family, he was completely content sharing it with his students.

He was content sharing it with her—someone he'd only run into because he was in the process of slaughtering the criminal group that she was part of. And it wasn't like the information he was sharing was common knowledge either.

Vermil was basically giving away secrets that people would kill for and asking for nothing in return but their own secrecy. It made absolutely no sense, but Alexandra definitely wasn't going to complain.

I'll make sure I live up to whatever it is that he wants from us. If this is what Vermil is willing to share now, he definitely has even more hidden away for the future. I don't know what it is, but I'll do whatever he wants me to if it means I'll learn more.

Alexandra was so lost in her thoughts that she almost didn't realize that someone was standing in the path in front of her until she was nearly upon them. She jerked to a halt as she stepped into their shadow, looking up.

A heavyset man with a large mouth and matching nose stood before her, his clothes marking him as a noble. He only had a few wisps of hair left on his head, but Alexandra wouldn't have put him a day over thirty.

"I didn't scare you, did I?" the man asked, holding his hands up and giving Alexandra an easygoing smile. It was made slightly less comforting by the width his mouth stretched to and the unnaturally wide molars behind his lips.

Her guard went up instantly. She'd met more than enough dangerous people in her life to recognize when someone was more interested in her than they should have been—and the way that the man's beady eyes were locked onto hers told Alexandra that he hadn't been just standing around for no reason.

"No," Alexanda said, stepping to the side to walk past him. "You didn't. Excuse me."

She made to move past him but skipped back as she felt the man shift. His smile lengthened as they stared each other down, and it struck Alexandra that there wasn't anyone else in the area. Her eyes narrowed.

"I'd like to have a moment of your time, if you don't mind," the large man said.

"You've already taken a moment. Now you're taking more."

"I can be a bit greedy." The man let out a greasy chuckle, then held his hands out by his shoulders. "You got me. I'll ask for more than a few moments, then. My name is Gero."

There wasn't an obvious change, but the air around him seemed to grow more intense. Alexandra shifted her hand to the pommel of her sword. Even though she couldn't sense domains yet, something told her that the man before her was at a higher rank than she was.

"What do you want?"

"That depends on your answer," Gero said. "Your professor—Magus Vermil—recently received an invitation to enroll himself and his students in the advanced track."

Alexandra kept her features flat, not willing to give any information away until she found out what Gero's goals were. "Is that so?"

"Cautious. Interesting. Yes, that is so. The thing is, we know about Vermil. We know his other students—but we don't know you." Gero tapped a finger on his flabby chin. "Hence the purpose of my visit."

"That hasn't explained anything at all. If you want me to tell you something, you'll have to be more specific about what you want."

Gero chuckled. "Not just cautious. Very cautious. That's perfectly fine with me. To be blunt, I am here to determine if you deserve to be in the advanced track. We only allow students of a certain caliber to enter, and considering you only just joined Arbitage, your abilities are unknown."

Alexandra tilted her head to the side. "So you want to see if I know how to fight or something?"

"Precisely. We have no interest in allowing those without potential into the program. I'm glad you understand. Of course, it's up to you. Feel free to continue past me and go back to your rooms. But if you do, you will not be permitted into the advanced track."

It only took Alexandra a moment to decide. She drew her sword and let energy ripple through her body as her Body Runes pumped magic through her muscles. "What's the test?"

"Eager to prove yourself as well," Gero observed, as if he were narrating notes to the air. He gave Alexandra a small nod. "The test will be the same as any test in the real world. I will try to kill you. You will try to survive."

Alexandra smirked and lowered into a fighting stance. "Do you make it a habit to kill students in the advanced track?"

"No," Gero replied with a wide smile. "But you are not in the advanced track yet. Last chance to continue on. If you remain, then we will begin."

She didn't budge. It was hardly a surprise that the advanced track was going to try to vet everyone that entered, and she hadn't even been at Arbitage for a month. When they'd gotten the news that they were being offered entrance into some fancy program, it had been fairly obvious that it had been meant for the others and not for her.

That's fine. I'll just earn the way in myself.

"If you don't make the first move, I will," Alexandra said.

Gero smiled. Then he blurred. A fist hurtled toward Alexandra's face like a crashing meteor. She swayed out of the side, not letting herself get surprised by the large man's speed. Her sword flicked out, biting for Gero's side.

To Alexandra's surprise, the blade struck him. It passed clean through his body, but there was almost no resistance. Her sword came free and she skipped back, narrowly avoiding a brutal tornado kick. The wind from it whipped her hair and made her squint.

"Good reaction time," Gero said. He drove his foot down, throwing himself forward in an open-armed charge. Alexandra met his dash, vaulting into the air and bringing her sword down for Gero's shoulder.

Once again, the blade passed through his body as if nothing were there. Even though Alexandra was watching for some sort of trick, she found nothing. It truly seemed like her attacks were going right through Gero.

She landed on the ground behind Gero and dodged back as he lunged for her, her mind whirring as she tried to figure out what magic Gero was using.

He's definitely physically here. That kick nearly took my head off, and I could feel the wind from it. Either Gero is some master of illusions, or he's got a way to make his body incorporeal.

Gero intensified his assault, forcing Alexandra to dance and weave around him as she sought a way to fight back. His fists hurtled past her face, each one coming closer and closer to connecting.

The sheer force behind his strikes told Alexandra that even with her reinforced body, she was incredibly unlikely to remain in fighting shape if even a single one landed.

If he's using magic to change himself, then the best way to fight back would be to use magic of my own. My Body Runes hardly lend themselves to a fight like that, though. I could use the Imbuement on my sword to set it on fire, but I feel like that might not do much better. It's not like I've got a choice, though.

Alexandra abruptly shifted from her retreat to an attack. She sent a wave of runic power into her sword, and the blade erupted in flame as she sent it snaking out to bite at Gero's stomach. Or, at least, it should have ignited.

Instead, as soon as the magic left her palm, it sputtered and dissipated as if it had never been there. Alexandra suppressed a curse and ducked under a spinning kick. Gero had a domain, and he was using it.

How is a student supposed to fight against someone at a minimum of Rank 4? Even if he's clearly holding back, I can't use my magic at long ranges! I don't have the power for it.

Alexandra crouched, then threw herself back as hard as she could. Gero's hand shot out, but he just barely missed grabbing her collar. She vaulted back, putting more space between them as she tried to reassess the fight.

"Quick to respond to inconveniences," Gero observed as he strode toward her. "But she has still yet to inflict any lasting damage or determine a functional strategy."

"Surviving is a strategy," Alexandra countered, but she could feel the stress starting to build. Fighting someone at or above her level was one thing, but Gero's domain was an entirely different problem.

If he had a way to prevent her physical attacks from connecting and he had a way to keep her from using magic to empower them, there wasn't any way for her to actually win. Her teeth gritted, she sprinted at Gero, spinning out of his grip and slashing at his shoulder.

As soon as the first attack passed through him, she jabbed again, trying to catch him off guard. Once more, her sword passed harmlessly through Gero. His leg shot back, nearly colliding with her chest, but Alexandra managed to lean back just far enough to avoid it. She spun to the side and hopped back again, dodging out of the way of another punch.

There's no way I can damage him if I keep this up. I'm eventually going to get hit, and if I don't land a single blow, there's no way they'll let me into the advanced track. I need to find a way to get around this.

Her arm tingled as a memory from just a few minutes ago surfaced. The Formations they'd been practicing. If she couldn't actually damage Gero, perhaps she could impress him enough with her swordwork.

It was a long shot, but it was the only thing that Alexandra could come up with. Summoning the state of peace that she'd needed for the demonstration in class wasn't easy, but she'd been in far worse situations before—and, in the time that Gentil had controlled her body, Alexandra had gotten remarkably good at sinking into her own mind and tuning out the outside world.

Alexandra drew in a deep breath. Gero's hand flicked past her head as she tilted it out of the way. She stepped to the side, avoiding a kick, exhaling, and steadying her nerves.

Another punch flew at her stomach. Alexandra stepped to the side. Her sword rose, flitting out like a stinging insect. It brushed across Gero's sleeve to no effect, but came back an instant later to strike at him from a different angle.

Gero lunged forward and Alexandra nimbly hopped back. The world almost felt like it was slowing as her assault continued. Each individual sword strike held little strength behind it, but they passed through Gero's body with increasing speed.

A flicker of confusion passed across Gero's face, and for an instant, Alexandra felt as if the tip of her sword caught on something. She didn't let herself get distracted for long enough to figure out what, though.

Her entire body was in complete concentration. There wasn't room for any distraction. All that mattered was the flow of her blade as it carved through the air. In the complete chaos of the aggressive, rapid attacks, there was order.

There was a pattern—and Alexandra was wholeheartedly focused on it. Her runes burned as she pushed her body to its limits, trying to drag every last drop of energy to push herself further.

And then the concentration snapped. She lost her spot in the intricate weave of movements and stumbled. The world snapped back to its normal speed, and Alexandra drew in a ragged breath, nearly dropping her sword as a wave of exhaustion slammed into her.

Shit! My runes are nearly empty! How did I drain them so quickly?

Alexandra tensed, preparing to dodge another attack, but it never came. She blinked in surprise. Gero stood across from her, his head tilted to the side. If he'd continued his commentary over her last assault, Alexandra couldn't remember any of it.

"What are you doing?" Alexandra rasped, taking the moment to draw in deep, ragged breaths. "I'm not done."

"Yes, you are," Gero replied. "Sheath your sword. This exam is complete."

Chapter Fifty-Three

Disappointment gripped Alexandra's chest at Gero's words. Her hands tightened around the hilt of her sword until her knuckles turned white. "I can still fight."

"You have demonstrated more than enough," Gero said, crossing his arms behind his back. "Leave. I look forward to seeing what you accomplish."

Alexandra opened her mouth to protest, then pause. "What?"

"You passed," Gero said with a low chuckle. "There's nothing more that I'm going to be able to pull from you without causing serious injury. You've more than demonstrated your abilities, and you'll fit right in within the advanced track."

Alexandra squinted at Gero, trying to figure out if the whole thing was some sort of joke. She hadn't actually managed to do anything. It didn't seem like Gero was joking, though. His face was dead serious.

"I—okay. Is that really it?"

Gero snorted. "Not everything in life is a trick. I told you what we were doing. We did it. You passed. End of story, girl. Now on with you. I have better things to be doing than sitting around and chatting with a child."

A flicker of annoyance passed through Alexandra at the dismissal, but she just shrugged and, after carefully stepping around Gero just in case he attacked her again, continued on toward her rooms.

She threw a few glances over her shoulder as she left, but Gero just stood there with his back to her, any interest that he might have had at any point now long gone.

Huh. That was odd. I still have no idea how I passed, but I guess I'll take it. Maybe he was impressed enough with my swordsmanship to decide I was worth keeping around? I'll have to ask Vermil what he thinks the day after tomorrow when we have our next class.

* * *

Gero stared at his palm. Blood welled from a cut that he'd concealed, threatening to drip onto the ground. He glanced around, then pulled a handkerchief from his pocket and wrapped the wound. A droplet of blood rolled off his palm and fell to the street as he worked.

"Fascinating," Gero murmured. "A mere Rank 3, both ascended and crippled by her Body Runes, was able to cut me through my domain. She certainly didn't overpower my magic—that would be ludicrous. And yet, there's no way a mere sword could have cut me. My Matter Runes would never have let such a thing happen. The only possible way she could have hurt me should have been by making space and getting out of my domain to use her magic from afar, but instead of adapting, she managed to brute force it."

The wound stung, but not nearly as much as it piqued his interest. Gero couldn't remember the last time someone had managed to cut him with a mundane weapon. It had to have been years—back when he was still a Year One at Arbitage.

"Who are you, Vermil Linwick?" Gero murmured. "How is it that every single one of your students is so unique?"

Gero's body folded in on itself, transforming into a tiny sliver of energy and flitting away in a flash, leaving no trace of his passing behind but a single drop of blood on the ground.

* * *

"Moxie?" Lee asked.

"Yeah?" Moxie quickly pulled her attention away from the stuffed version of Mascot sitting on her bed, reddening slightly at having been caught staring at it.

"Someone's at the door," Lee said. "And I don't recognize them. I was hoping it was Noah, but he's still out getting dinner for us. This person smells different—and they smell kind of strong. Rank 4, I think."

Moxie's brow creased and the blush vanished from her cheeks. She rose to her feet, glancing out the window to make sure there weren't any assassins waiting. Even though Jalen had supposedly made up with Noah, she wasn't fully sold on it.

The window was empty, though. Of course, that didn't mean nobody was there, but Lee had only pointed out the presence of one person. Moxie drew on her runes, then approached the door and pulled it open.

A man stood before it, a hand raised to knock. He had dirty blonde hair and a black cloth bandage wrapped around his face that covered his eyes. The man let his hand lower and tilted his head to the side.

"Ah. I was just about to knock. Would this be Magus Moxie's room?"

"Depends on who's asking," Moxie replied, resisting the urge to look at the metal nameplate right beside her head. The man had a bandage over his head, so it wasn't like he could see.

"A faculty member," the man said, tapping his jacket. A metal nametag above his right breast pocket identified him as *Will*. "I'm here to speak with Magus Moxie about her and her students' invitation to the advanced track."

"Oh. Well, yes. I'm Moxie. But shouldn't you have confirmed that before you told me what you were doing?"

"I already knew," Will said. He made no move to step past Moxie into her room, and she made no move to allow him in. "Is now a good time?"

"Depends on what you want," Moxie replied. "But we're already talking, so if you've got something to say, you might as well do it now."

"Very well. Emily has proven that she deserves to be in the program, but some of the professors have raised questions as to your own eligibility." Will scratched the back of his head sheepishly, but his expression didn't so much as shift. "Some of us have brought the incident at the Torrin Estate up."

"What of it?" Moxie asked evenly. Something about Will rubbed her the wrong way—perhaps it was the way that he was acting as if nothing that was happening was actually his fault and that he was just a messenger.

Sure, that might be true, but that doesn't make me like him any more. I don't know why, but something makes me feel like this guy isn't even blind.

"There are rumors that your runes were shattered," Will said. "If that is true, we need to determine if your skill level is still high enough to permit you to join the advanced track. Emily's path will not be hindered, but we will not spend resources on a mage that has no future."

"I'm not letting you stroll around in my head," Moxie said. As tempted as she was to be snarky, it would have been a poor idea to get too snippy with the person from the organization she and Noah were trying to join. It would have been nice to have at least one group of people that were actually on their side. "I'd be more than happy to demonstrate that my runes are up to par if need be, though."

As Moxie spoke, she reached into a pocket and found a seed. She rolled it between her fingers, sending a tiny amount of magic into its shell. The magic wormed out and a vine writhed near her palm, brimming with energy.

"A demonstration will not be sufficient," Will said. "We will fight until you are no longer able to continue fighting back."

Cocky little shit. Isn't this basically just threatening to beat the shit out of me?

This guy doesn't even seem that strong, relatively speaking. If he's a Rank 4, then his domain isn't active right now. I'm pretty sure it's fairly difficult to turn your domain off unless you're a complete pushover, which means he's probably Rank 3.

"That's bold of you. Not even giving me a chance to surrender if I need to?" Moxie asked through a yawn. Her vine snaked up her arm and along her body, slithering down one of her pant legs. "Works for me, though."

"Good. In that case—"

The vine snapped out, wrapping around Will's right leg and yanking it out from under him. He let out a startled curse as Moxie surged forward, diving an open palm for his chest. Will yanked himself upward, narrowly avoiding Moxie's attack.

He slashed a hand through the vine and dropped to the ground, spinning toward her as he rose to his feet. If he was blind, he had a fantastic sense of direction. Moxie wasn't particularly interested in finding out just how good of a fighter he was, though.

"Cocky," Will said, clicking his tongue in disapproval. "But there's something to be said about being aggressive. It's certainly a strategy. Just remember—"

Moxie's vine shot out again, widening as she pumped more magic into it. Will ducked, narrowly avoiding the vine as it roared past his head—but he wasn't ready for the floor beneath him to crack. Vines ripped up all along it, writhing like the grasping hands of an undead horde as they rose up to grab at him.

Will scrambled to avoid the plants, but there was a seemingly endless supply. They pushed their way through cracks in the walls and squirmed from the ceiling, filling the entire hallway with grasping, thorned vines in the span of just a few seconds.

Moxie gritted her teeth as she ripped power from her runes, but she didn't have any desire to enter a long fight with Will. The faster it ended, the less time she'd have to waste on him.

Will let out a startled curse as thorned vines wrapped around his limbs, yanking them in every direction. Before he could so much as react, a set of blood-red vines rose up before him, their thorns glistening as they wound around his throat, threatening to squeeze shut at a moment's notice.

"Is that demonstration sufficient?" Moxie asked, not letting on how much the demonstration had exhausted her.

Will swallowed heavily. "How did you do that? There's no way you should have been able to summon that much magic so quickly. Aren't you a Rank 3 that isn't even close to reaching Rank 4?"

"I'm not sure. It sounded like you knew everything about me," Moxie said dryly. The thorny vines tightened around Will's throat. "What do you think? Am I too weak to join the advanced track?"

"You'll fit right in," Will squeaked.

The vines unraveled, dropping Will to the ground as they slithered back through cracks in the stone and receded out of view. Will didn't even bother trying to look dignified—it was far too late for that.

He just beat a hasty retreat down the hallway. Moxie shook her head, glancing around the rubble that now littered the ground. Her brow furrowed as she used Sowed Earth to try and pull the stones back into their proper places.

It was difficult, as the rune was far more targeted at dirt rather than stone, but stone was still a part of the earth. After about five minutes of work, she decided that she'd done more than enough and headed back into her room.

The vines within it still writhed, and Moxie shook her head. Only an idiot would come after a plant mage in their own domain and expect them not to be prepared to fight back. Granted, she'd learned a few lessons from Evergreen's death and had taken a few extra measures in recent days to make sure that she'd be able to fight back quickly against anyone trying to attack her in her own home, but that was Will's fault for not figuring it out.

If they knew so much about me, then they should have been able to catch on. Can't blame me for your incompetence, after all.

Moxie pulled the door shut, then looked down at Lee, whose eyes were wide with delight.

"That was awesome!" Lee exclaimed. "The whole room just came to life and started moving! I didn't even have to do anything. I was going to stab him."

Maybe I should have been a bit slower. That might have been fun, but I really shouldn't encourage Lee. He was arrogant, not deserving of death.

Moxie grinned and ruffled Lee's hair. "Thanks. I just figured there was no reason to not have everything serve an extra purpose. Vines can be comfortable when I want them to be, but it's not hard to hide some thorns beneath the surface."

Lee started to nod, then paused and glanced back at Moxie's bed. Her eyes narrowed. "Is it spiky if I dig deep enough?"

"I don't suggest finding out."

Chapter Fifty-Four

M oxie filled Noah in on what had happened when he got back to the room. There wasn't much he could say—it wasn't like Will had actually managed to pull anything off —so all they could do was sit down and enjoy their dinner together.

But, even though there wasn't anything he planned to do yet, a small frown fixed itself on his lips. The advanced track was testing them. He couldn't say he was surprised, of course, but it rubbed him the wrong way.

If the teachers in the advanced track hadn't been sure about the quality of their abilities, then they should have thought things through more before sending the invites. Still, it wasn't entirely unreasonable to ensure that the people they were inviting were actually competent.

At least, that was Noah's view on it right up until the end of the students' next class two days later. As everyone dispersed and he made to head back to his room with Moxie, Alexandra caught his eye. She was standing by her desk, making no move to leave.

"One moment," Noah said, stepping away from Moxie and Lee to walk over to her. Moxie and Lee both nodded and continued on, leaving Noah and Alexandra alone in the classroom. "Is something bothering you, Alexandra? You've been doing great with your patterns, if that was your question."

"That's one of them, but no." Alexandra shook her head, then glanced around the classroom one more time to make sure nobody else was there. "I just wanted to talk to you about something."

"Well, I'm here. Hit me with it."

"I got approached by a faculty member claiming to be part of the advanced track," Alexandra said. Noah's smile fell away and his eyes narrowed.

"Who? What did they want?"

"His name was Gero, and he said he was there to test me and determine if I was strong enough to enter the advanced track."

"He attacked you?" Noah asked.

"He gave me a choice between leaving the advanced track and fighting him," Alexandra said. She chewed her lip in thought. "I passed, I think, but it didn't make sense. I don't know *why* I passed, but he certainly wasn't going easy on me."

This is going too far. If you want to test me, that's fine. Then they tested Moxie when they thought she was crippled by sending someone who was meant to beat the shit out of her. That's one check against you. But if you want to test my students as well, you need to do it through me, not jump them on the roadside. It seems the advanced track might have overinflated egos if they're just going around throwing their weight like this.

"I see," Noah said, keeping his voice even. "How difficult was the fight? Was he just pressing to see your abilities?"

"It was hard to tell," Alexandra admitted. "He said he was going to try to seriously hurt me and that it would be dangerous, or something like that. I can't remember his exact words."

"I assume you're asking to find out if everyone else has been tested?" Noah asked.

"Yeah. I don't know if the others would have been able to pass," Alexandra said with a worried frown. "I only made it because I'm a Rank 3 and had Body Runes that let me keep up with him. I mean, Gero was obviously holding back because he's a Rank 4, but he wasn't holding back completely."

"Understood," Noah said. "I don't think any of the other students have gotten tested, but rest assured that it won't happen again. Not in any unofficial manner, at least."

"It won't?" Alexandra blinked. "I was going to ask if you'd be willing to give us more combat training that incorporates patterns so we could get ready for it. I figured this was how things were going to be now."

Noah snorted and shook his head. "We can definitely do that, but this is not how things are going to be. Class is time for learning and practice. You need rest, and that time is when you're off class. If those idiots are going around attacking you after you've already been to class, you'll be worried about saving your strength for them. Trust me, I'll handle things."

"Okay. Thanks," Alexandra said with a small nod of appreciation. "I'll be off, then. I need to practice my pattern more today. I think I'm really starting to get a hold of it."

"So I can tell. You're still the farthest along out of the entire class," Noah said. He flashed her a grin and raised a hand in farewell. Alexandra returned the gesture, then headed out of the class.

As soon as she was gone, Noah's smile fell away and anger crossed his features in its place. He stormed out of the Building G and set a course straight for Moxie's room. His mind spun in thought—if the advanced track wanted to play games with him, then he was more than willing to play back. He just needed a few things. Fortunately, Moxie and Lee were already there when he got back.

Moxie took one look at his face and her own eyes narrowed. "What's wrong? What happened?"

"Those advanced track pricks attacked Alexandra," Noah said. "Their egos are the size of clouds if they think they can just go around terrorizing my students. I was already on the edge with what they were planning to do to you, but this is two times now. I'm not giving them a third."

"Should we withdraw?" Moxie asked.

"Hell no," Noah replied. "From what I can tell, the advanced track is a bunch of professors that argue over shit. Ulya—the lady that tested me—didn't even seem like she wanted to be doing it. Out of all of them, she seemed decent enough. But now I'm pissed off."

"That sounds like it's going to be fun," Lee said, a small grin slipping across her face. "Do I get to help? It can be just like the Dayton thing again. And if you have anyone you need to get rid of, I'm hungry."

"Yeah, I think I just might need your help," Noah said, more pieces of a plan sliding into place.

"I hope you aren't planning on killing anyone too important," Moxie said. "We don't want to go overboard."

"No plans of killing anyone," Noah said with a shake of his head. "Not yet, at least. Moxie, could you watch over my gourd? You never know what will happen."

Moxie nodded and Noah took his belongings off his waist, pulling a change of clothes out of the bag before handing it and the gourd over to Moxie. He then leaned his grimoire against the wall and turned to Lee.

"Here. You're going to need these."

"I'm going to be you?" Lee's eyes lit up and she pulled her clothes off, her body shifting even as she moved. Her skin bulged and changed shades, hair shifting to match Noah's as she grew larger.

By the time she'd finished changing, she'd already started to pull Noah's clothes on. She stuck her hands through the jacket, then turned to Moxie. "How do I look?"

Moxie reached out and ruffled her hair, messing it up so that some strands hung in front of her face. "There. But what are you planning, Noah?"

"Just a little demonstration," Noah replied. He sent Moxie a quick smile to show her that he wasn't going to do anything *too* stupid. "Lee, do you think you can sniff out the idiot that came after Moxie?"

"Easily."

"Good. We need to make another stop first, but I'll need something different to wear. Moxie, can I borrow a cloak from your closet? I kind of only have one outfit."

Moxie snorted and turned to ruffle through her closet. She found a green traveling robe after a few minutes of searching and threw it around Noah's shoulders, tightening the clasp at his neck.

She pulled the hood up over Noah's head, then took a step back and tilted her head to the side.

"It hides your face, but not perfectly. Aside from that, it fits."

"That's fine," Noah said. He pulled his badge off and handed it to Lee, who fixed it on her chest. "I won't be long. No more than a few hours."

Moxie nodded. "Just make sure that, if you die, you don't leave anything behind."

"Will do," Noah promised. He pulled the door open, keeping the hood low over his face. "Let's go, Lee."

They left Moxie's room and swept out of Building T, moving at a brisk pace. It was already well into the evening, and there weren't too many other people walking around to bother them. It didn't take them long to reach the dormitories, and Noah led Lee up to Todd and Isabel's room, rapping on the door when they drew up to it.

It opened a few moments later to reveal Todd, a confused look on his face. He looked over Noah's shoulder at the fake Noah.

"Professor! What's going on? Are we doing an exercise?"

"Nothing like that," Noah said. Todd jumped at his voice, and Noah took the opportunity to step inside, pulling the hood back. The boy stared at him, then turned his eyes to Lee.

"What the—wait. You're doing something."

"Very apt," Noah said dryly. "And I'd like your help. By the way, where's Isabel?"

"Out for dinner with Alexandra." Todd broke into a grin. "You should have started with needing help. What can I do for you?"

"Hopefully nothing too difficult. I need something imbued, and I couldn't think of anyone better to go to."

"Imbued?" Todd blinked. "Yeah, I could probably help with that. What do you need?"

Noah smiled.

* * *

A little over an hour later, Noah and Lee left the room. A stone mask rested on Noah's face, obscuring it. He hadn't needed anything particularly fancy, but Natural Disaster wasn't suited to creation—only destruction.

Todd had only needed a short while to form a mask out of the stone of his room's walls and shape it into a snarling visage, carving out holes for Noah's eyes and imbuing it so that it would hold its shape. The mask had stone loops to hold it in place that probably should have been incredibly uncomfortable, but Todd somehow imbued them to be just soft enough to not be a nuisance.

Todd had warned him that the mask wasn't a permanent Imbuement and would only hold for about three hours before it fell apart and he ran out of energy, but three hours was more than enough time for Noah to work with.

Lee took the lead as they left the dormitories, and Noah kept his hood pulled low over his face to conceal the mask that was now covering it. They stuck to the side streets, staying out of sight in case anyone happened to see them passing by.

Some time later, the two of them arrived at the edge of a dark alleyway. Across from them was a fairly nice house in a quiet neighborhood. It was stone and marble, with just enough quality to make it apparent that its owner was wealthy. Lee nodded to the house.

"He's in there."

"Perfect," Noah said, his smile concealed by the cool stone against his face. "Thank you, Lee. That's all for this part. Can you go back to Building T and make sure to take a long trip through the market?"

Lee beamed at him with his own face, which was admittedly a strange experience that he still had yet to get used to. "Okay! Have fun! He's in the room with the big window above head height."

She slipped back into the darkness, vanishing just a step away from Noah. A small shiver ran down his back. Lee was getting *really* good at slipping through the shadows. He didn't even know if she was there anymore.

Noah wiped those thoughts away. Lee was on his side, and now wasn't the time to be thinking about her. He pulled his cloak lower and strode up to the side of the house, flexing his fingers as he considered the best way to do this.

If I were Lee, I'd stealth in. That would be pretty scary—but I'm not Lee. Oh well. We'll be doing this the fun way, then.

Noah drew up to the house, letting Natural Disaster's power pulse through his veins as he lifted a hand and pressed it against the wall. A violent tremor ripped through the stone. There was a deafening crack followed by an explosion as the wall shattered.

A scream rang out from within the room, and Noah stepped through the cloud of dust and falling rubble. On the other side of the room stood a blonde man, his eyes wide with terror and shock.

"What in the Damned Plains? Who are you?" Will demanded as Noah strode toward him. Noah's lips creased in a smile as he saw the man try to reach for his magic to no avail. He'd already closed the distance between them, and Will was within Noah's domain with no way to resist it.

"You tell me," Noah said, letting his voice drop into a lower octave. He drew on his meeting with Jalen, channeling the man's dangerous aura as best he could into his words. "You've been the one fucking with the people I've been teaching, Will. You and the advanced track—did you really think I'd just sit around while you interfered with my work?"

Will took a step back, his eyes darting around the room. Moxie had certainly been right about one thing—the little prick wasn't actually blind.

"You're Vermil?" Will asked, aghast.

Noah let out a raspy laugh. "No, Will. Did you really think he'd just figured everything out on his own? Even the most talented students need some guidance. No. I'm not Vermil. I'm the one who taught him everything he knows. Congratulations. You got my attention. I hope you're going to do something worthwhile with it, because the only thing I hate more than having my time wasted is being disappointed."

Chapter Fifty-Five

Will backed up against the wall, his eyes bulging and flicking around the room, searching for escape. The door was several steps to his left, and Noah had no plans of letting him run out and lead him on a chase.

Snapping his fingers, Noah sent another ripple through the earth. A jagged crack raced out across the ground, cutting Will off from the room's exit, ripping the stone open, and sending debris plummeting into the darkness.

"Eyes on me," Noah said softly. He stepped past the rubble behind him, using a small gust of wind to keep the dust swirling around his body. The chances of Will identifying him were low, but the more distracted the other man was, the easier everything would be.

"What do you want?" Will stammered. "I was just—"

"Testing them," Noah finished. "Yes. I am aware of what you were doing. But what gives you the right to interfere? They weren't in the program yet, Will. But that's in the past now, isn't it?"

Will nodded hurriedly. "Yes, exactly. We—"

"We don't need to hold grudges," Noah interjected. A crackle of electricity trailed across his fingertips, then vanished into the air with a hiss. "There's nothing wrong with a little testing. It's only natural."

"That's how we see it as well. We meant no harm, but ensuring the quality of every student in the advanced track is vital for its success.

That's how we can make sure we only put out the most competent students."

"A logical solution," Noah said. He tilted his head to the side as if in thought, then tapped a finger on his mask. "But if you test those that enter—who tests *you?*"

Will blinked in confusion. "Me? I'm a member of the track already. They tested me when I was first invited, and I—"

"I don't believe I was present for that," Noah said, not letting Will finish his sentence. He wanted to keep the other man on the backfoot and avoid giving him a chance to start mustering any form of properly coherent thought, and it was working pretty effectively. To a normal Rank 3, a powerful Rank 4 mage wasn't all that different from a Rank 6. They were both effectively insurmountable—which meant Will would have trouble placing his strength when he recounted it to anyone.

"You? No, I don't think—"

"No," Noah agreed. "I wasn't. You're right. So how can I know how competent you are? As far as I can tell, you're nothing but a sniveling Rank 3, barely able to stand in my presence. Is there more to you than that?"

Will's face flickered, likely recalling Noah's first threat about how little he liked being disappointed, and gave him a firm nod. His hands clutched at the wall, trying to claw through it to no avail.

"Ah. You are. Fantastic," Noah said. "In that case, I'm sure you wouldn't be opposed to letting me test you. After all, tests aren't any harm. They're just to ensure the quality of every student and faculty member participating in the advanced track."

This is pretty much the same offer you gave Moxie, right? Fight me until you can't fight any longer, or something like that? Turnabout is fair play.

Will winced. Noah had completely wrapped his own words around him, and he knew it. There was no way for him to refuse without angering him. A second of silence passed as Will desperately dug for a solution, but there wasn't one. The only thing he could do was swallow heavily.

"You should feel free to refuse, of course," Noah added. He waited just long enough to see the hope flicker on Will's face before he continued on. "But if you do, I expect you to withdraw from the advanced track. I can't have the unworthy dealing with my students or their students."

The hope died. Will gritted his teeth and lowered into a fighting stance. "I'd be more than willing to prove myself, but I am one of the younger members in the advanced track. I'm close to Rank 4, but I haven't achieved it yet."

"I'll be sure to keep that in mind," Noah said. He would have pulled his domain back if he was actually good at controlling it yet, but he was still working a bit on the finer aspects. That was an unfortunate outcome for Will, but Noah also wasn't very interested in playing fair at the moment.

He'd given Will more than enough time to get ready. He shifted forward, using the wind to accelerate his movements as he whipped a leg up for Will's head. The other man dipped back, dodging to the side and narrowly avoiding the strike.

Noah spun, a hand snapping out to strike Will in the chest. A bright flash lit the air as shimmering gold armor snapped to life over Will's body. Noah's fist struck it with a loud crack and Will skidded back, uninjured.

There was a Shield bracelet on his wrist, humming with energy. They were close enough that Will didn't have any way to use his magic, but that evidently didn't translate over to imbued objects.

Now that's good to know. Since a Shield is drawing magic from within him rather than sending it out of his body, it can still activate. So domains, at least at my rank, don't protect from imbued weapons. That probably changes at higher ranks.

Noah didn't give Will much time to recover. As much as Noah disliked him, Will was clearly competent and knew what he was doing. If this was an actual test, he might have been somewhat impressed.

Unfortunately for Will—it wasn't a real test, and Noah wasn't interested in being impressed. He was interested in sending a message.

Water gathered in the air around Noah as he ripped it out of the surroundings, sending bullets at Will from every direction. Will lifted his hands in front of his face as the magic pattered against his armor, sending ripples of energy running across it.

The Shield was clearly of fairly good make—at least a Rank 4, by Noah's estimate. Will's hands started to lower, but Noah wasn't done.

The temperature in the room dropped sharply as he drew in the heat, freezing the water now covering the ground.

Will's foot hit a patch of ice as he shifted to try and get out of the range of Noah's domain. He stumbled and fell, catching Noah's vibration-empowered foot on the way up. A deep thrum ripped through Will's armor as he was launched into the air, tremors racing through the Shield.

The Shield shattered with a tinkling crash, fragments of light spiraling away from Will. He hit the wall and let out a pained grunt as all the air was knocked from his lungs. Wind gathered in Noah's palm, wisps of white spilling over his fingertips. Noah nearly sent it out in a spike to pierce straight through Will's heart before he stopped himself at the last moment.

Shit. Don't want to kill the idiot. I need him alive.

Will crumpled to the ground, coughing and gasping for air. The ball of magic faded away, and Noah clenched his hand, letting it return to his side.

"Is that all? I wasn't even trying."

"You broke my Shield in just one spell," Will wheezed. "How am I supposed to fight against that?"

"If you rely on a Shield to fight, then you are a pathetic warrior," Noah growled. He extended a hand and a powerful blast of wind shoved Will off the ground, sending him stumbling right into Noah's grip.

He gripped the man's shirt and lifted him into the air, the power from his runes coursing through his body like a raging river. It had been a long time, but Noah could feel the tickle of Azel's influence in the back of his mind.

Strangely, the demon felt weaker than he had been before—or perhaps Noah had gotten stronger. Either way, the power Azel had over him had drastically weakened, and Noah was able to crush Azel's desires out without too much effort.

Will struggled in Noah's grip. His feet kicked pointlessly and his arms pried at Noah's arm, but it was completely ineffective. It felt like he was holding a runaway toddler, not a mage. Noah was lucky he was wearing a mask, because the scorn and disbelief on his face likely would have driven a blade straight through Will's heart on the spot.

"Is this all you can do?" Noah demanded. "This pathetic excuse can boast about being in the advanced track?"

"I'm a researcher and an Imbuer." Will wheezed. "I don't ever need to fight without my magic."

"Then don't go throwing your weight around like you're anyone of interest. You're pathetic," Noah said, trying to picture exactly what Jalen would have said if he were in his position. He was annoyed enough that it wasn't hard, and perhaps that should have been concerning.

"There are a lot of ways to be strong. I'm not a warrior." A glint passed through Will's eyes as his gaze flicked past Noah's shoulder. There was relief in his expression—relief that shouldn't have been present. "But she is."

Noah didn't bother turning. He threw Will back and dropped to the ground. A sword ripped through the air where his neck had been, letting out a keening wail in its wake. He set off a powerful blast of wind in the air above him and was rewarded with a loud crash a moment later.

Noah rose, spinning toward the new threat. A man rose from the rubble of a new hole in Will's wall, the cloak hanging ragged around his body and a long sword in his hand. His face was blank and expressionless—not the features of a human, but a well-carved mask. Noah nearly laughed as he spotted Ulya on the street, her brow creased in concentration.

"Decent attempt at a surprise attack," Noah said with a low chuckle. "It's too bad your friend is a brainless idiot—but it's not like that would have hurt me in the first place."

Will scrambled to his feet across from Noah, running back until he was out of the range of his domain. As soon as he was safe, glittering cubes of light sprung to life all around him.

"You're outnumbered," Ulya said. "I don't know who you are, but I suggest you surrender now if you want to live."

"Outnumbered?" Noah burst into laughter. "No. You're just saving me time, Ulya. I didn't realize you and Will knew each other so well."

"Will?" Ulya's expression flickered when she heard his name, her gaze moving to Will. "What's going on?"

"Forget it!" Will yelled. A beam of light ripped from one of the cubes, slicing through the air toward Noah. Noah didn't bother waiting to see if the magic would make it through his domain—considering it had originated outside it, there was a decent chance it would. He hadn't had enough time to test out the domain's full abilities, and now wasn't the time to do it.

He dodged to the side, then slammed Will into the wall with a powerful blast of wind. Will slid down with a cough as dust rained around him.

"Sit," Noah growled, turning back to Ulya and her puppet. "Come on, then. I hope you prove more interesting than your friend."

Chapter Fifty-Six

Despite Noah's words, he didn't actually have anything against Ulya. Sure, she'd technically tried to jump him, but nothing she'd done particularly stuck out as rude. He had no desire to break yet another one of her puppets and had been planning to track Gero down after dealing with Will.

Hell, I would have gone after Gero first if I could have, but I had no idea where he was. The only one I could track was Will because Lee knew what he smelled like. Unfortunate for Ulya—I'm not backing down now.

The puppet lurched toward Noah, its blade driving for his chest. He set off a blast of wind between them, throwing the puppet back across the ground. She clearly valued her puppets a lot, so unless he had no choice, Noah preferred not to damage them too badly.

Will shifted, and Noah turned to send him a look. He didn't even have to say anything. Will hadn't been seriously injured yet, only slightly roughed up. In comparison to what he'd threatened to do to Moxie, it was nothing—but Noah was more than willing to rectify that if Will tried to rejoin the fight.

Ulya's puppet dashed at Noah, grabbing its sword with both hands and pulling it apart at an invisible seam to split it into two blades. It swung one at his head and the other at his midriff, trying to force him to choose one to dodge and get struck by the other.

Noah sent a wave of power into the ground, making it buck

violently beneath the puppet and launching it into the air. The puppet shimmered and vanished as soon as it left the range of Noah's domain.

With the way Ulya fights, she's going to try to send it at me from a different angle. There's no point getting wrapped up fighting her puppet, though. Especially not if I'm going to try to avoid smashing the stupid thing to bits.

Noah launched himself forward—and straight through the crumbling ruins. Ulya's eyes widened in surprise when she realized that Noah was headed right for her. Her hands came up and a swirling mass of purple magic formed between her palms.

It streaked over his head as he read her motions, predicting where the spell would go and dipping out of the way before it could strike him. It was pretty apparent that Ulya wasn't used to fighting people herself, and she hadn't been expecting to fight someone tonight.

Noah slammed to a halt directly in front of her, using a small gust of wind to make sure he didn't accidentally plow her down. A tiny spark of magic had already started to reform in her hands, but it sputtered as she stared into Noah's mask.

"I wouldn't do that," Noah said, a note of warning in his voice. "I know I told you to be entertaining, but it doesn't seem like you're prepared for a fight."

Ulya swallowed and eyed Noah warily, but she didn't step back. "Who are you?"

"Someone your group annoyed," Noah replied. "Going around and threatening my students is an effective way to get on my bad side. As Will and I discussed, some tests are entirely understandable. What I take offense to is the way you've executed them."

"Tests?" Ulya's brow furrowed in confusion. "Are you—"

"Shit," Will said, staggering upright and clutching the back of his head. "You gave Moxie runes, didn't you? That's why she was so strong."

Took him long enough to make the connection. He's technically not even wrong. About time, though.

"A fact she likely would have been more than willing to warn you of had you actually just *asked* what she was capable of instead of threatening to assault her to prove her incompetence," Noah drawled. "You're fortunate she decided that you weren't worth the effort."

"Your students—Moxie?" Ulya blinked, then paled. Her puppet

stepped out of the house, but she made no move to have it attack again. "Vermil too? They called you?"

"Called? No. I typically don't enjoy getting involved in their problems, and to be frank, they're more than capable of handling any issues themselves. I just have a vested interest in seeing them and wanted to see the mettle of the advanced track for myself."

"And you did that by... attacking Will?" Ulya asked in disbelief. "What would you get out of that?"

"Get? Nothing. I've always been a believer of treating others the way they treat you. If you threaten to assault those you believe to be weaker than yourself, shouldn't you be prepared to receive the same treatment?"

"That isn't what happened, though. All of us were to approach our respective targets and test them politely but efficiently. Acceptance into the advanced track relied on their performance in the fight. That's it. There should have been no threats."

Ulya seemed to completely believe what she was saying—which meant she probably had absolutely no idea about the wording Will had used with Moxie.

"Which sounds entirely reasonable, except I don't believe that was what happened. I believe Will's offer to Moxie was that he'd be fighting her until she was no longer able to continue, while fully aware that she should have been functionally crippled."

Ulya looked to Will in surprise, confirming Noah's thoughts. Will had gone off-script. That alleviated some of Noah's anger almost instantly—she hadn't been lying. Testing wasn't unreasonable if they were going about it the proper way, though he still had objections to hounding his students while they should have been focused on work.

"Will?" Ulya asked. "What's he talking about? That wasn't the assignment."

Will looked like he wanted to respond, but one look at Noah made him settle for just clenching his jaw and looking away. A few pieces of stone fell from the hole Noah had left in the wall and clattered to the ground.

"I think I may have to apologize," Ulya said. "It seems Will may have gone considerably further than he was meant to. I can swear that the advanced track doesn't value itself on bullying members. We just want to ensure the quality of everyone within it. Was there any significant damage from Will's actions? We would be—"

Noah raised a hand, cutting her off. "I'm not here because I'm babying my students, Ulya. I can see how you'd view it as such, but as I've already said, they can handle their own problems. I'm here because I wanted to see the extent of your arrogance and to entertain myself. I have much better things to be doing than going around, crushing the weak beneath my heel."

He sent a very pointed glance at Will that Ulya didn't miss. She grimaced, nodding her understanding.

"We'll deal with that, and we'll make sure to avoid your lot in the future."

"Avoid? On the contrary. Feel free to treat them like anyone else," Noah said with a laugh. "Challenge is good. And, as fun as it is to turn someone's words in their face, you and Will don't have much to fear from me. I can't go around crushing people weaker than me in the neutral zone, but Vermil and Moxie are both perfectly capable of challenging you themselves through the normal channels—and they don't have to hold back."

Ulya winced, sending a glance at the puppet standing by the hole in the wall. "I'm more than aware. Vermil destroyed one of my puppets."

"Then perhaps you should have told him you didn't want it broken before you started fighting. Words are effective, but it seems like you all have some difficulty using them," Noah said. "No matter. You'll learn—and I'd suggest you pass the warning along to Gero."

"You're going to go after him?" Will asked nervously.

"Did you hear anything I just said? No, I'm not. Why would I waste my time? I've already passed the message along. I don't need to do anything. If he tries something as stupid as threatening to kill one of Vermil's students in a training exercise, then Vermil will kill him himself."

"He cares that much about his students?" Ulya asked. "You're referring to Alexandra, right? Gero is a pretty brutal teacher, but he's very effective."

"Perhaps, but Vermil doesn't enjoy when other people threaten to kill his own. As far as he's concerned, the only person allowed to try to kill his students is him. He's rather territorial."

Ulya looked like she couldn't tell if Noah was joking or not. With his expression covered as it was by the mask, it was impossible to tell. Either way, it got the point across. Hunting Gero down as well would have been a pain in the ass, and Ulya had definitely gotten the message even if Will hadn't.

All in all, that's pretty much everything I wanted. Cocky little shit got his own words tossed back to him without making me step too far over the line; people have a good explanation as to why Moxie is strong again; the advanced track isn't going to try their stupid shit again unless they do it through me instead of trying to just go after my students; and the mysterious benefactor can disappear without a trace. The only thing I still need to do is establish a few hooks that I can pull on later.

"I'll keep your words in mind," Ulya said. "And I'll ensure Will and Gero do as well. There are other tests throughout the advanced track, though. I assume from your comments that you want them involved, just in the proper way?"

"See? Look at that. Words work," Noah said. "They're just considerably less fun than punching people. That's precisely what I want. If you want them in the advanced track, then treat them like everyone else. If you don't, then don't. I really don't care. There's nothing you have that I don't. I just don't want to deal with the fallout of Vermil killing off another group of idiots. It gets tedious."

Ulya started to nod, then paused when she registered what Noah had just said. He'd seeded more than enough questions in her mind to make sure that she'd have a vested interest in learning more about him —which meant that, when they next spoke, Noah would have the upper hand in getting information.

Now I'm satisfied. Moxie would be proud. I didn't even have to kill myself.

"Then I believe we're done," Noah said. "Keep this in mind for the next time you decide to twist your orders, Will. You never know how strong someone is until the fight is over. A little respect goes a long way, but at least you gave me something to do tonight. I wouldn't suggest you draw my attention again."

With that, Noah turned and strode down the street. It would have been better if he had a way to theatrically disappear or teleport away, but his only fast-departure move was blowing himself up. And, while that definitely would have left an impression, he wanted bragging rights that he'd solved a problem and lived through it.

Ulya and Will's stares bored into his back until he turned the corner and vanished into the darkness. Noah was pretty certain that Ulya would hold true to her word. He was less sure if she'd tell the other advanced track teachers about the fake master cleaning up after Vermil's messes, but something told him that she'd likely give as little information away as possible.

Everything he'd learned about this world told him that information was one of the most valuable resources, and the advanced track teachers were unlikely to treat it any differently. She and Will would likely warn Gero off while giving away as little as possible and trying to figure out what they'd learned to their advantage.

He suspected he'd find out soon enough. With all the seeds he'd just planted, it wouldn't be long before Ulya showed up at his room, trying to fish for information about him—and in turn, she'd tell him everything he needed to know about the advanced track.

Noah grinned as his steps faded into the night.

Not bad. Not bad at all.

Chapter Fifty-Seven

Ulya didn't let out the breath lodged in her throat until the man's footsteps faded into the darkness. It wasn't like he'd actually *done* anything that dangerous. His magic hadn't been that out of ordinary. Sure, it had been fairly strong, but not by any degree greater than Vermil's.

There was something else about the man that screamed danger, and it wasn't any of his techniques or abilities. It was the way he carried himself, as if success were inevitable and there was absolutely nothing either she or Will could have done against him.

It was almost like he put so little importance on our abilities that we might as well have not even been fighting back. The only people that don't give even the slightest amount of respect to an opponent's abilities are the ones too stupid to realize they can die or the ones that know without a shadow of a doubt that they can't lose.

"Damn that asshole," Will muttered, rubbing his arm and brushing the dust and rubble from his clothes. "Arrogant prick."

"Was he telling the truth?" Ulya asked. "Did you really go after Magus Moxie like that? We're not meant to be making enemies here, Will. What were you thinking?"

"You can't tell me you believed that guy. He clearly just had it out for me!" Will exclaimed as he let his hand drop and sent an affronted glare at Ulya. "Aren't you supposed to be on my side? We're working together!"

"And Vermil will be soon as well. They all passed the tests," Ulya pointed out. "I don't think that man was lying about Vermil either. I fought him, and he's not the kind of person to hold punches. We don't need to be making enemies for no reason."

Will scoffed and shook his head, turning back to his house. "Coward. If you want to bend over and kiss his shoes, that's your prerogative. I didn't do anything that odd. I was just testing them. That's all."

What in the Damned Plains is up with Will? I swear he's never been this argumentative before. He's always been a bit arrogant, but this is ridiculous. He never would have gotten into the advanced track if he always acted like this.

"Is everything all right?" Ulya asked. "Nothing odd happened, did it?"

"Someone just broke into my house and tried to murder me," Will snapped. "Of course something happened!"

He ducked to step through the hole in the wall, and a small frown crossed Ulya's lips. There was a small green nub at the base of Will's neck, just above his spine. She only saw it for an instant before he stepped out of sight.

"Hold on," Ulya said, following after Will. "You've got something on your back still. Let me get it for you."

Will, midway through shifting some stones off his desk, glanced over to Ulya. "Yeah, I know. Dust. And rock. A lot of it. Did you miss the part where my wall got smashed in? Or was it the part where I got thrown into the wall?"

"Oh, stop whining and turn around," Ulya said irritably. She stepped around Will, pulling the collar of his shirt down with one hand.

The green nub she'd seen still stuck out of the back of Will's neck —not a piece of plant debris like she'd originally thought, but thoroughly worked into the back of his neck. It wasn't stuck to him. It was inside him. The flesh around it had been twisted and sewn shut, but several small stitches had torn apart in the fight, allowing the green substance to push its way out.

"What in the Damned Plains?" Ulya asked, staring in disbelief.

"What is it?" Will asked, twisting to look back at Ulya. "Is something wrong?"

"Turn back around. You've got—"

A bladed vine erupted from the side of Will's chest, ripping through his clothes and snapping out for Ulya. She threw herself back to the ground, hitting it with a pained grunt and sending a mental command to her puppet.

It snapped to life, disappearing in a sparkle of Space Magic and reforming before Ulya as she scrambled to her feet and backed up.

"What's wrong with you?" Ulya demanded, retreating another step. "Are you insane?"

Will's body bucked. His muscles writhed beneath his clothes, bulging and shifting unnaturally. Thin seams formed all along his skin, growing taut and ripping apart with loud snaps as plants writhed out from within him.

"It seems I must apologize," a scratchy, warped voice that definitely wasn't Will's said as his body distorted even more. His skin ripped apart and fell to the ground as lurching plant matter pushed out of him. "I got sloppy. Didn't realize the puppet was damaged. I hope you'll forgive me, but I can't have you telling anyone."

Magic roiled out of the disgusting, squirming mass, and Ulya didn't bother saying another word. The creature in front of her wasn't Will. She threw her hands up and her puppet launched itself—not toward Will but toward her.

It grabbed Ulya, but there was a loud crunch before they could teleport. A series of loud pops within her mind announced all the Imbuements within it shattering at once. Ulya staggered as her puppet was ripped away from her by a swathe of sharp-thorned vines. Half a dozen of them had driven into the back of the puppet in a split instant, completely destroying it.

Ulya coughed, blood trickling from her lips as the backlash of the damage to her runes echoed through her body. She staggered against the wall, wiping her mouth with the back of her wrist.

"Who are you? What did you do to Will?"

"What was your name again?" the monster that had once been Will asked. "Ulya, was it? Do you have a convenient diary I could read? I'm going to need to polish up on what you should know for when I replace you."

Ulya turned and sprinted, mentally cursing her decision to work with puppets and put all her power into Imbuements, leaving none for herself to work with. Her nearest puppet was nowhere in the area. She risked a glance over her shoulder and immediately regretted it.

Vines were racing down the alley, digging through the stone and rising up behind her like the maw of a malevolent dragon. Ulya threw herself into an alley, hitting the wall in her haste and knocking the breath from her lungs.

She choked on her own blood as she ran but didn't dare let up. Whatever magic was chasing her was more than what her meager domain could ever hope to resist, which meant the only hope was finding someone else to help her fight.

A spike of pain raced up her leg, and Ulya felt it get yanked out from beneath her. She cried out, throwing her hands in front of her a moment before she hit the ground. A vine had wound around her ankle.

She grabbed it, ignoring the jagged thorns as they ripped into her palms as she tried to rip it free, but it felt like she was trying to cut iron. Rocks scraped against Ulya's legs and back as she was dragged back toward the teeming mass.

"Help!" Ulya screamed, kicking desperately at the vines. She tried to reach her runes, but every single one of them was still reeling from the damage, and she could barely muster even the slightest amount of magic.

The vines rose up above Ulya, blocking out the moonlight and casting her into pitch darkness. She let out one last scream, drawing on the last of her magic in an attempt to do anything.

There was a faint flicker of purple energy.

The vines crashed down, and then there was only silence.

* * *

Wizen lowered his hand, the last of the magic fading from his construct. Hidden within the whorls of swirling wood that made up a mask covering his face, his lips pursed.

"How displeasing."

He stood in the center of a dark cave, his hand resting on a massive dirt orb. Five more of them surrounded him. Each was easily seven feet tall and half as wide, sticking halfway out of the ground like the bulb of a flower waiting to sprout.

One of them had shattered, its top completely destroyed. Fragments of its shell lay on the ground around it.

"Perhaps more than displeasing. What a waste of a perfectly good construct," Wizen said as he took his hand off the bulb. The flow of power that had been running out of it and into his body faded, and the Plant Runes contained within it faded back into dormancy. "I took so much care to avoid blowing my cover, but I did promise you that I'd show just how badly you'd played your hand, didn't I? Never let it be said that I don't keep my promises."

He crossed his arms behind his back and sighed. It wasn't like he'd lost his only construct. There were more, and he'd learned a fair amount from this one. It had done its job.

"To think I lost it purely because that bumbling idiot smashed the fool's head into a wall and damaged the housing," Wizen said, a flicker of anger passing through his posture as his hands tightened at his sides. The anger faded as quickly as it had arrived, and he shook his head, patting the dirt bulb with one hand.

He could feel power roiling within it, desperately trying to find its way out of the cage he'd built. A small smile stretched across his lips and he chuckled.

"Is something wrong?" Wizen asked the orb. "This was our deal, was it not? A way to escape the games you were trapped in so you could focus on growing more powerful. A way in which you could truly comprehend the magic that you've sought to master for all these years. Do you not feel more in contact with the earth than you ever had before? Soon, you will bloom into a beautiful flower. Your runes will be consumed and made part of something far greater than you ever could have been, Evergreen."

More emotion roiled within the orb, causing the smile on Wizen's lips to grow even wider. "Perhaps you are displeased that the woman you thought to have outplayed was actually the one that outplayed you. That seems to be happening a fair amount as of late. Losing to a mere Rank 3 as a Rank 6. Pathetic, really. I suppose it only makes sense. You were so determined to reach power that you have not earned that you lost your diligence. You fell at the hands of your own family, trying to avoid drawing too much magic and risk severing our connection. I suppose you succeeded—you clung onto life, and I brought you here, just as I said I would. And just like I assured you, you were reborn. And now, just as you begged me, your new form will have power. It will *be* power. You just won't be the one to wield it."

Chapter Fifty-Eight

Ulya's fist pounded against the door, her fist matching up with the throbbing headache gripping her skull. Her breath came out in short gasps, and her runes were completely drained to the point where her stomach had clenched itself into knots that felt like they never might unscrew.

She raised her hand to knock again, but it swiped through the air as the door swung open.

"What in the Damned Plains do you want?" Gero demanded. "It's the middle of the—"

The rest of his sentence faded into the darkness as he got a look at Ulya's harried expression and damaged clothes. Blood has soaked her leg where the thorns had grabbed her, and blood still dripped onto the ground at her feet.

"D-Did anyone show up tonight?" Ulya asked, bracing her hands against her knees and doubling over in an attempt to catch her breath. She could barely even believe she was alive. By all means, she shouldn't have been.

"What happened to you? No, nobody showed up."

"Turn around," Ulya ordered.

"What? You're talking nonsense. What's going—"

"Turn around, damn it!"

Gero blinked, then slowly turned to follow her directions. Ulya grabbed a small dagger from her waist and poked at the back of his neck. The blade passed through it harmlessly, and Gero glanced over his shoulder at her.

"That's not going to do anything."

"Turn it off," Ulya snapped. "Now."

"Why?"

"Just fucking do it," Ulya snarled, clutching the dagger before her. "I'll explain after. I need to cut you. Just a little."

"If this request was coming from anyone else, I'd think them insane." Gero turned away again. "Go ahead."

Ulya's breath caught in her chest as she pressed the dagger to the back of Gero's neck, drawing a thin line of blood. The lack of anything green nearly made her weep in relief. Her hands dropped.

"Satisfied? Now tell me what in the Damned Plains is going on," Gero demanded. "Were you attacked?"

"Will is dead," Ulya said bluntly, pushing past Gero and stumbling into his house. He closed the door behind her, a frown deepening on his features.

"At your hand? What did he do? That's an over-reaction, Ulya. Are you insane?"

"Not my hand," Ulya snapped. "He was killed. Some form of powerful plant mage had turned his body into a puppet. Completely replaced his innards with some disgusting plant magic. Will got slammed into a wall and I noticed the plants inside him. Barely made it out with my life."

"You were fighting Will?" Gero crossed his arms in front of his chest. "If you've come here to avoid the law, you made the wrong choice."

"That's not it," Ulya's exasperation built and she dropped into Gero's expensive chair, staining it with blood. Gero walked to stand in front of her, not looking particularly pleased—it was hard to tell if the anger was about what she was doing to his furniture or what had happened with Will. "Someone else attacked Will. A powerful mage related to Vermil's group."

"Another one?" Gero asked in disbelief. "How many are there?"

"Two, as far as I've found." Ulya pulled her wounded leg up, rolling her ravaged pant leg back to examine it for any remaining pieces of plant matter. She didn't know what the plant mage could do, but she had absolutely no plans of sitting around to find out. "I was visiting Will to discuss the results of the tests, but there was someone already there toying with him."

"He was strong enough to beat both of you?" Gero asked, tilting his head to the side.

"Hard to say," Ulya replied. She pulled her shirt up, biting into it as she dug into the wound on her leg and ripped out a thorn. Letting out a muffled hiss of pain, Ulya dropped the thorn to the floor. "He was willing to talk when I got there, but his demeanor felt like a powerful mage, and he had a domain. Claimed to be Vermil's teacher. Didn't get a chance to see how large his domain was, but it doesn't matter. After he left, I saw a green nub sticking out of Will's neck."

"And he attacked when you pointed it out?"

"Yes. I think he was going to try to steal my body," Ulya replied with a shudder. She spotted another thorn and ripped it free, repressing a curse at the daggers of pain that tore through her. "Barely managed to muster enough magic to teleport out. The plant bastard destroyed my puppet in an instant."

That isn't true, though. I know for a fact that I didn't have enough magic to teleport. I should have died—but I somehow teleported anyway. Damn it. Why is my memory so blurry?

"Shit," Gero said, his expression darkening. "Will's definitely dead, then?"

"Absolutely dead. I saw his corpse pop like a full waterskin in front of me. The plant mage would have killed me too if I hadn't been on guard already. I was worried he came after you already."

"The plant mage?"

"Or the other one," Ulya said. She twisted her leg to try to get a better look at it, then looked up to Gero. "Do you see any more thorns in me?"

Gero reached down to the back of her calf, yanking a thorn that Ulya had missed free without warning. She let out a pained yelp.

"You could say something," Ulya hissed.

"Faster to get it over with," Gero replied, dropping the thorn and letting it join the pile. He held a hand toward them, and a translucent pink box of energy materialized around the thorns with a subtle pop. The box floated up to Gero's hand, then sank in on itself and vanished. "I'll contain these."

"Thanks," Ulya said through a grimace. "You'll need to keep an eye on me as well. I—I don't know how his magic works. I could be infected."

"Your domain appears natural. If there was another mage's influence on you, it should have been apparent," Gero said with a shake of his head. "Did you find out what the mage wanted?"

"The first one was mad because Will threatened Moxie and because you messed with Alexandra's training. The second one—I have no idea."

"Meaning the plant mage was likely the one that antagonized the first one," Gero concluded, completely ignoring the part that he'd been involved in.

Ulya glanced around Gero's living room for something to use as a bandage. She spotted a shirt lying discarded on the ground and limped over to it, ripping it into strips before Gero could protest.

"Probably," Ulya said as she started to wrap her leg. "I just don't know why. Do you have a healing potion, by the way?"

"No."

"Figures," Ulya muttered, grimacing as she tightened the makeshift bandages. "What do we do? Tell the others? Confront Vermil?"

"How do we know the plant mage and Vermil's benefactor aren't working together?" Gero asked. "If someone was strong enough to catch you this badly off guard, we have to assume that they're probably controlling more puppets somewhere. Vermil might *be* one."

That was a harrowing thought. Ulya swallowed heavily, then finished tying her bandages off. She sank back into the seat with a groan. "We should get Enforcers on this."

"We will," Gero said. "Silvertide is in the area, and he recently joined the advanced track as well. He'd be a perfect resource."

"Shit, I nearly forgot," Ulya said. The tension in her shoulders didn't completely vanish, but it receded. "What about Vermil? If he isn't involved in this, he probably will be. The plant mage was pretty pissed that he got revealed because Vermil's teacher went around beating Will up."

"Did you get the feeling that this first mage—the one that claimed to teach Vermil—was powerful? Would he be able to help us, assuming he wasn't working with our opponent?"

"Probably," Ulya said after a moment of hesitation. "He seemed reasonable. A little insane, but reasonable. He didn't ask for preferential treatment for Vermil's group—just that we not single them out."

"Then you should establish contact with Vermil. Test his group. Find out if they're with the plant mage and see if you can convince the strong one to stick around. If someone's powering puppets with enough strength to give you this much trouble, their true form is going to be uncomfortably strong. Rank 6 at the minimum, possibly with multiple runes. I hate puppet and construct users. Annoying little bugs are impossible to root out." Gero paused, then glanced down at Ulya. "Present company excluded."

"Thanks," Ulya muttered. She tested her weight on her leg again, then slowly rose to her feet. "Why do I have to be the one to interact with Vermil?"

"You already met his mentor. We don't want it to seem like we're leaking information. Also, you're down two of your puppets. You can't fight properly until they're fixed, so it makes no sense to have you hunting this plant bastard. I'd direct your searches toward Moxie—she's a Torrin, and plants are their domain."

Ulya let out a sigh. Her stomach was still clenched, and her headache was only just starting to pull back, but the adrenaline was fading. "Okay. Fine. You need to go check on Will's corpse, though. I don't know what those vines are doing, but we need to make sure they don't spread."

"I will. I'll get an Enforcer while I'm at it," Gero said. "Good job on surviving and delivering the message. First thing tomorrow morning—find Vermil and figure out what in the Damned Plains is going on. Avoid bringing any other members of the advanced track into this. They may be similarly infected, and we can't give away our plans."

Ulya grimaced. She didn't want to do anything other than sleep for the next week, but she settled for giving Gero a nod. Then she slumped back in his chair—it was already bloodied, so there wasn't going to be any saving it—and let an exhausted sleep take her.

It was hard to tell how long Ulya slept, but when she woke, she determined that it hadn't been enough. She let out a groan, squinting through the sunlight filtering down on her through a window.

There was a loaf of bread out on the countertop that hadn't been there the previous night, but no sign of Gero. Ulya stood, wincing at the flicker of pain that ran down her injured leg, and walked over to the counter.

"Who eats a bloody loaf of bread for breakfast?" Ulya muttered, taking a bite out of it. Gero's diet was about as much of a mystery as how his Matter Runes actually worked. Ulya's leg throbbed again and she cursed under her breath, limping out the door to go buy a potion—and possibly something a little stronger.

If she was going to have to talk to Vermil after the shitshow that was last night, Ulya got the feeling that she might need it.

Chapter Fifty-Nine

Someone knocked on Moxie's door, and Noah sent Moxie a smug look.

"Told you they'd show up," Noah said.

"I never doubted it," Moxie said through a yawn. "But they really didn't waste a second. I thought they'd at least wait a day. This seems a little more sudden than I would have expected."

"Maybe they work fast," Noah said. He pulled his jacket on and adjusted the badge that Lee had returned to him after he'd gotten back the previous night. Once he was certain he looked as presentable as possible, he walked over to the door and pulled it open.

Ulya stood on the other side, and it looked like she hadn't slept a wink. There were dark bags under her eyes, and she looked like a strong breeze would probably push her over. Noah blinked. He definitely hadn't gone *that* hard on her.

"Ulya. I wasn't expecting to see you again so soon," Noah lied. "Or were you looking for Moxie?"

"I was looking for you." Ulya's eyes flicked past Noah, taking in the room. Something flickered over her expression—it was hard to tell exactly what the emotion was, but it could have been either discomfort or disgust. Either way, it definitely wasn't the reaction that Noah had been expecting.

"Why's that? Are there more tests or something?" Noah asked innocently. "Also, are you okay? It looks like you had a rough night."

"You have absolutely no idea," Ulya said. "I was going to ask why there are two random women in your room, but I've realized that I no longer actually care. They said I could find you here. We need to talk."

"We're doing that right now."

"Alone," Ulya said.

"I trust Moxie completely," Noah said, shaking his head. "Unless you've got a really good reason as to why you can't say something in her presence, I don't see a reason to exclude her. Anything in relation to the advanced track is going to affect her as well."

Ulya's lips pressed thin and her fingers twitched at her sides. The emotion passed across her features again, and this time Noah realized that it wasn't discomfort or disgust—it was fear. And, not of him, but of Moxie.

The hell?

"It won't take long. I need to speak with you first," Ulya insisted. She shifted her weight and glanced over her shoulders, then shook her head. "I need to confirm something."

Is she assuming that the fake mage that supposedly taught me didn't teach Moxie? That can't be it. I specified he taught both of us, and she definitely heard it. What's going on here?

"It's fine. I'll go to the bathroom," Moxie said, stepping through the bathroom door and poking her head out. "Just knock on the door when you're done."

She closed it behind her, and Noah stepped to the side so Ulya could enter the room. Ulya hesitated for a second, then stepped inside. She tensed as Noah closed the door behind her, only increasing his confusion even further.

"What's going on?" Noah asked. "Something feels off."

Ulya drew a dagger from her side, but in a slow motion that made it clear she wasn't about to try to run him through. Even still, Noah nearly blasted her with a wave of power from Natural Disaster.

"You know, if you're going to pull a dagger on someone, they'll assume you're going to use it," Noah said dryly.

"I need to test something," Ulya said. She swallowed, then waved the tip of the dagger. "I need to cut you."

"That is an incredibly concerning statement, and not one that I'm inclined to let happen."

Did she somehow lose it last night? This barely feels like the woman I spoke with yesterday or the one that tested me a little bit ago.

"It's just a small incision. There's... something going around campus," Ulya said lamely, but Noah didn't miss the fact that she'd yet to remove her eyes from him. She was watching him warily—ready to burst into motion if he made a move.

What move she was waiting for, Noah wasn't quite sure of. After all, she'd come to him, not the other way around.

She didn't hear of my old shitty reputation and think I'm going to be a creep, did she? But if that was the case, why would she just be asking to stab me? Just to prove she can? That doesn't make sense.

"I'll do it to myself if you let me cut you first?" Ulya offered.

"Now it just sounds like you're trying to get me to join some creepy pact," Noah said. "Why don't you tell me the reason you need to cut me in the first place? Saying something is going around isn't really that explanatory."

"I suppose I've already said enough, so it's not like it would matter one way or another," Ulya said, more to herself than to Noah. Her gaze refocused on him. "There's a puppet user going around and stealing bodies. That's all I'm saying until you let me test you."

A what now? Oh, screw it. The worst she can do is stab me.

"Fine," Noah said. "Go ahead."

"Turn around," Ulya said.

"The hell are you doing with the dagger? Sticking it up my ass?"

"I didn't say bend over," Ulya snapped. "Just pull your hair away from the back of your neck and don't make any sudden moves."

Can't say this is how I saw I'd be starting the morning. I know Moxie is probably listening in. I wonder what she's thinking. At least my gourd is hidden. It would be awkward if she ran me through and I popped out right in front of her, naked as the day I was born.

Noah turned around and, in slow motion, pulled his hair out of the way. He felt Ulya press the steel of her dagger against the back of his neck with just enough pressure to draw a thin line across it.

She let out a relieved sigh and Noah heard her step back. "Okay. You're fine. You can turn around."

Noah moved to face her as Ulya returned the dagger to her side. She edged toward the desk chair and sent Noah a questioning look. When he nodded in response, she flopped into it.

"Are you going to tell me what's going on now?" Noah asked.

"Your teacher showed up yesterday," Ulya said through a grimace. She pinched the bridge of her nose between her fingers. "He kicked Will around a bit before telling us to watch what we were doing before dipping again. I need to know if he's still around."

"He did?" Noah blinked, but the surprise wasn't even entirely false. This wasn't at all how he'd pictured this conversation to go, but for the time being, he stuck to his original plan. "Is Will okay? I didn't realize he was doing anything like that. He can be a bit impulsive, so I hope he didn't go over the line. I don't have a lot of contact with him, so he kind of does as he pleases. What did he share? Not too much, I hope."

The best play is to really lean into the semi-crazed person that half these powerful mages seem to be. It gives more credibility to any bullshit I need to spin in the future.

"About you? Not much. Just that he taught you, and that he would be displeased if we treated you unfairly." Ulya's eyes tracked Noah's expression carefully as she spoke. "But Will is not okay."

"Shit, I'm sorry to hear that," Noah said, hiding his bafflement. He'd barely roughed Will up—he'd gotten hit harder in sparring matches with Lee than what he'd done to him.

A ploy to make me feel bad, maybe?

"Me too," Ulya said. "Will is dead."

Noah nearly choked. "What? How? Are you saying my teacher killed him?"

Seeing the genuine surprise in his expression, Ulya relaxed further. "No. Will was apparently replaced by a plant mage's puppet. After your teacher left, I noticed plants coming out of Will's neck. He tried to kill me—nearly did."

This is not at all how I thought this was going to go. Will was a construct? Does that mean he was a construct when he came after Moxie? The guy I attacked clearly knew what had happened, so it had to be the same one.

"You're shitting me," Noah said. "Have you told Arbitage yet? This sounds like something pretty serious and way over my pay grade. Why have you come to me? You can't suspect my teacher is somehow related to this plant guy, do you?"

"Hardly," Ulya said with a snort. "If anything, your teacher is the only reason I lived. If I hadn't noticed the plants, I never would have been on guard. Then again, maybe he wouldn't have attacked me at all. It's a moot point now. And the Enforcers have been alerted already, but your teacher is clearly a fairly powerful mage. We wanted to see if he'd be willing to help us."

Noah didn't respond immediately. He was too busy processing all the information Ulya had just given him. She looked far too sincere to be lying—and that meant that there probably really was a plant mage that had been puppeting Will's body.

And if that was true, they'd sent Will after Moxie. They were related somehow—he couldn't afford to sit this one out, even if he wanted to. Anyone that came after them once was liable to try it again, especially since Noah had absolutely no idea what their goals were.

"It's not easy to get in contact with him, but if it's interesting enough, it's possible," Noah allowed. "I can try. Is the way to test everyone just cutting the back of their necks?"

"I don't know," Ulya admitted. "Will wasn't bleeding—he just had the plants, and the back of his neck is where I saw them first. It's a bet more than anything, but it's all I've got to go off."

"Well, if the entirety of Arbitage is looking for him, I'm sure we'll root the guy out soon enough, even without my teacher's help."

Ulya shook her head. "Unlikely. Do you have any idea how many serious threats arise in Arbitage and are snuffed out without being revealed to the general public? This is one of the Four Bastions, Vermil. Arbitage doesn't want people to think things go wrong, and they'll cover everything up all the way until it's too big to be concealed."

"You're saying we're on our own?" Noah asked in disbelief.

"Not on our own. The Enforcers will be on it," Ulya said. "That includes a few members from the advanced track. My job was to test you to confirm that you hadn't somehow been replaced, and then try to see if your teacher would be willing to lend us aid. A mage that can make a puppet as strong as Will is going to be a menace. Gero thinks he might be midway through Rank 6."

"Shit," Noah said, and he genuinely meant it. This wasn't the first time they'd dealt with clones, and this wasn't the first person that had been interested in Moxie in particular. The pieces were pulling together in a way he didn't like in the slightest.

During the survival exam, Evergreen's clone had been controlled by someone that they'd never determined the identity of—but Revin had warned them off pursuing him any further. And then there had been Gentil's master. He'd been interested in connecting with Moxie, but he'd never said why, and they'd never found out.

I could just be pulling together unrelated assholes, but somehow I doubt it. I think the shit we've stirred is finally coming up to the surface.

Wizen is making a move.

Chapter Sixty

"Can I come out now?" Moxie asked through the door of the bathroom, nearly startling Ulya out of her chair. "Despite how it may appear, I don't actually enjoy sitting in here."

"Yeah," Noah said without waiting for a response from Ulya. When she shot him a look, he just raised an eyebrow in response. "What? You can't think Moxie is the one doing these attacks. If you did, it would have been pretty dumb coming here on your own."

"I didn't say that, but she's a Torrin. The chances of the culprit being from her family are abnormally high."

The door opened and Moxie stepped out of the bathroom. "I was functionally exiled from the Torrins. If they had some murderer strolling around Arbitage messing with shit, I can assure you that they wouldn't be very well disposed toward me."

Ulya's features paled. "You could overhear our conversation?"

"It's a bathroom door, not a soundproof wall," Moxie said dryly. "Though sometimes I certainly wish it was."

"Relax, Ulya," Noah said. "Moxie is who she claims to be, and we haven't been apart for anywhere near long enough for her to go around killing people and replacing them with puppets. I know all of her runes as well—none of them would allow them to do what you were describing to Will. On top of that, she's still just Rank 3. There's no way she has the ability to do what you're claiming, even if she wanted to."

That didn't seem to completely sate Ulya, but her shoulders relaxed slightly. "I still want to test her."

"No," Noah said. "I don't trust you enough to let you near Moxie's neck with a dagger. If she's willing, I can do it myself."

Moxie tilted her head to the side. "Can't say I'm a huge fan of it, but I'll try everything once. Well, most things. Don't use that against me."

"I'm definitely using it against you."

Moxie glared at Noah and pulled a dagger from her side. Noah took it and turned to Ulya. "Is this going to be enough? Because if you're going to complain about it later, then I'm not even going to bother. We're only doing this for your sake."

"Just make sure I can see the blood," Ulya said flatly. She rose to her feet, her fingers twitching at her sides. Noah wasn't sure if she could actually do anything without a puppet present, but there was no point pressing the issue.

Moxie pulled her hair out of the way, and Noah carefully pressed the dagger against the back of her neck, drawing a thin line across it with just enough pressure to draw a droplet of blood. He lowered the blade.

"Happy?"

"No," Ulya said. "But I suppose that will work for now. At least for the duration of our current conversation, I'll believe that neither of you has been taken over."

Damn, she's suspicious. I can hardly doubt her given the circumstances, though. This is a pretty serious issue, and even knowing that it's Wizen doesn't help me all that much. We never found out what he wanted, who he really was, or what he could do.

"You next," Noah said. "Not that I actually think you're a puppet, but at this point it's just a matter of pride."

Ulya huffed and pulled her hair back, turning around and running a dagger along the back of her neck—where there were already several other small cuts. It drew a line of blood. She turned back to them as she sheathed the dagger, expression flat.

"What's the plan, then?" Moxie asked, taking her own dagger back from Noah and sliding it into a sheath at her waist. "Did you just come here to tell us that you need our... teacher's help?"

"And yours," Ulya said. "It seems like the person who killed Will has some degree of interest in you, Moxie. I don't know why, but it's basically the only lead we have to go off. When the Enforcers get involved, we'll all need to work together."

"I've never been opposed to killing assholes, so you can count on us," Noah said with a shrug. He paused, then tilted his head to the side. "Well, at least as long as we don't have to detract from our practice. I've got students to teach, and the show must go on."

"Aren't you a little unconcerned about this?" Ulya asked. "We don't know what this man is capable of. There could be a Rank 6 mage after you—is there really nothing you can think of that drew his attention?"

"I don't think I'd use *unconcerned*. It's more that I'm used to it," Noah said with a shake of his head. "And there's no point panicking. We don't know what this guy wants, and I'm not a detective. The best thing I can do is be prepared and ensure all my students are prepared as well. Nothing else would change the situation."

Ulya's features scrunched. "Yeah, sure. He could be *anyone*, though. I can't just go around cutting people to test them every time we speak. I mean, I could, but it wouldn't work. And if I did try to cut someone who happened to be under his control, I could get killed before I reacted. The only people we know are safe are the ones in this room—and I don't even know you!"

"So why lose sleep worrying over it?" Noah asked. "It's just putting you in a worse position. If there's nothing you can do to improve a situation, the least you can do is try to avoid making it worse. And there are definitely things you can do to prepare. Where are your puppets?"

Ulya blinked, then shook her head. "Oh, right. I left it out."

Her hand flicked, and a shadow passed over the window. Noah and Moxie both turned to see churning mandibles chittering against it, and just beyond them, a maze of jagged teeth. It had black, sleek flesh the color of the night, and wore ratty gray clothes, but Noah couldn't make out what its form was actually meant to be with how close it was.

"God, what is that?" Noah grimaced.

"Could you let it in?" Ulya asked. "It's not very good at opening things without breaking them."

Moxie sent Ulya a doubtful look, then extended a vine tendril to pull the door open. The creature on the other side of the window chittered and shifted, several limbs working their way into the room with a series of clicks and pops.

The puppet vaguely resembled a preying mantis that had been clothed in the robes of a human. It stood a foot taller than Noah, and he could feel the magic radiating off it from where he stood.

As they watched, the puppet seemed to fold in on itself. Pieces shrank in and limbs snapped together until it was only a little over five feet tall. What appeared to be a child in an oversized cloak sat on Moxie's bed, the hood pulled far over its face to obscure its features.

The puppet hopped to its feet and walked over to stand beside Ulya. If Noah hadn't been watching its motions, he likely wouldn't have even realized that it was anything other than a small child.

"That might be the creepiest thing I've seen in a while, and that's saying a lot," Noah said. "Is that your main puppet?"

"Yes," Ulya replied, putting a hand on the puppet's shoulder. "And before you ask, I didn't murder a child to make it. It's just that a smaller form is easier to move around and hide."

"Do you get that question a lot?" Moxie asked.

Ulya pursed her lips. "Yes."

"Well, I hope I don't have to see it in action," Noah said, but he did have to admit that he was more curious than he would have admitted as to what Ulya was capable of when she went all out.

She had to have been accepted to the advanced track for some reason, and nothing she'd shown thus far had seemed like she was any stronger than the other people he'd come up against. It was possible that their standards weren't nearly as good as what they wanted people to think, but from how Alexandra had described Gero's abilities, he suspected that it would be unwise to underestimate the advanced track professors.

But if that's the case...

"Why was Will in the advanced track in the first place?" Noah asked. "Was it because he had really competent students?"

"No. He wasn't actually a professor," Ulya said, looking slightly surprised at the change of topic. "He was a researcher. A good one. We invited him because of how much he'd deduced about rune theory on his own."

"Do you think it was possible he was targeted?" Moxie asked. "Was he working on anything special?"

"I'm not sure. I think he was studying artifacts recently, but nothing that should have made him a target," Ulya admitted. "We were friendly, but Will was pretty secretive with his work. I can speak with Gero and the other advanced track professors, but I'm not sure how much information we'll get from any of them. Oh, speaking of which—you're all in, if that wasn't already obvious. None of you failed the tests, and you pretty much all outperformed them."

"Thrilling," Noah said. "Do we get anything upon entry?"

"There's a meeting tomorrow," Ulya replied. "You can ask then. Normally, it would be a little more exciting than this. I don't suppose you'd be able to get your teacher to show up?"

"I was under the impression we were trying to keep things on the down low," Noah said, stretching his arms over his head. He'd been standing around for too long. He wanted to *do* something. This wasn't at all how he'd pictured the morning going.

"The advanced track is not a cohesive unit," Ulya admitted reluctantly. "A lot of us are—how would you put it?—at odds."

"Reassuring," Noah said.

"It's just how things are when you put a bunch of competent people in one room," Ulya said as she raised her hands in a defensive wave. "Half of them think you're worthless and cheated your way up somehow, and I don't even want to get into what the others think. I was one of them, if I'm being honest—but you can't cheat your way through crushing one of my puppets like that. Right now, the only ones I can properly trust to not be the murderer are you two and Gero."

Moxie's eyes narrowed. "Wait. Are you saying you think the person that killed Will might be another part of the advanced track?"

"I don't know, but it's possible," Ulya said. "That's why any support we could get is vital. If your teacher could show up and just attend, I'll cover for it. The sooner we can all meet, the better," Ulya said.

"I'll see what I can do, but no promises," Noah said. "As I've said, it can be difficult to get in contact with him."

Ulya nodded, then let out a sigh. "This is not how I pictured any of this going. For what it's worth, I'm sorry you've all gotten wrapped up in this. Getting into the advanced track should be something to celebrate."

"We've dealt with worse," Moxie said with a dry laugh. "Vermil can be a bit heartless, but he does have a point. There's no need to get distracted by what you can't change. Just focus on what you can."

"Thanks," Ulya said, but she didn't seem too convinced. "Sorry again about how rough the introduction to the program has been. With any luck, we'll be able to handle this easily and things can continue as normal. I'm going to go get back to fixing my other puppets. They took quite the beating."

She didn't wait for a response before slipping out the door. Her small puppet pulled it shut behind her with a gentle click, and Noah listened her footsteps fade down the hall before he spoke again.

"Well, that was something."

"I don't suppose you planned it?" Moxie asked.

"Unfortunately not. I think our friend from the survival exam might be back," Noah said, starting to dig through his bag. "I don't like it, but I think I know what the next steps are."

"Jalen?" Moxie guessed.

"Probably worth trying, but I can't speak with Jalen until he shows up, and that's not for a bit longer. There's another source of information that could be useful for this," Noah said. He pulled a folded slip of paper over, uncreasing it to reveal a rune on its surface. "I'm going to speak with Father."

Chapter Sixty-One

Noah waited for Moxie to leave her room before he tried to contact Father—though he made sure to remove his gourd and other belongings, stashing them out of sight. He did feel a little bad about forcing her out of her own room, but he couldn't exactly do it in his, and Moxie claimed to have some work she needed to handle anyway.

Lee, who had been waiting at the door and likely listening in to the entirety of their conversation with Ulya while making sure nobody got too close and overheard anything that they shouldn't have, went with her.

Once they'd left, Noah let his finger touch the faint rune on the paper. He could feel distant power shimmering within it. Not enough to do much, which was likely intentional. Any form of Imbuement was a connection, and connections could always go in two ways.

Either that or Father was cheap. As far as Noah was concerned, either was equally possible. No matter what it was, faint energy tingled in response to his fingertips. It receded quickly, but before Noah could even start to wonder if it was working, the energy returned.

At first, it was nothing more than a growing hum. Then energy started to gather, burning at the edges of the paper. The power rapidly increased and Noah dropped it just as the entire slip ignited, going up in a puff of flame.

A purple tinge flashed within the fire as it faded, ballooning out into a crackling portal of matching color. Arcs of energy popped along its edges, and shapes took form within it until Noah found himself looking into Father's room.

As usual, Father sat at his desk. A strange black creature that vaguely resembled a cat was curled beside Father's interlaced fingers. It had been a while since Noah had last seen the small monster, but it looked about the same as it had before—rotund and largely indescribable.

"Vermil," Father said, a faint trace of what might have been annoyance tinging his words as he unlocked his fingers and leaned back in the chair. It was difficult to tell how much of his action was genuine and how much was just another layer of acting that he was putting on. "I'm surprised. I didn't think you'd actually use the contact form."

"If you didn't think I'd use it, why'd you give it to me?"

"I can hope," Father said dryly. "That portal isn't going to remain open for long, and I'm not giving you another contact unless you make this worth my time and energy."

"Have I ever reached out to you when it wasn't?" Noah stepped through the portal and into Father's office. The biggest thing he'd learned from all his dealings with just about anyone of worth in any noble family was the importance of never backing down or showing any weakness.

A part of me wonders if Father could somehow be under Wizen's control. The Records of the Deceased said that this isn't Father at all, so he could easily be a clone of some form. But that wouldn't make sense, as Father had a chance to get something from Moxie and didn't take it. Wizen seems more interested in the Torrin family than Father is.

The portal snapped shut behind Noah. Not looking back, he pulled the chair in front of Father's desk out and sat down.

"What is it this time?" Father asked, tilting his head to the side. "Killing another Rank 6 mage?"

"I have no idea what you're talking about," Noah said without missing a beat. "Evergreen's death was a convenient tragedy."

"One that I regret not participating in. I'm one of the few that is well aware that you are responsible for her death, Vermil. I'd use the name we agreed upon, but I'm wondering if giving you respect may be a poor move for my prolonged health."

Father's words didn't fool Noah in the slightest. The flattery was a thin veil for Father to let him know he was more than aware of what Noah had been involved in, which wasn't really all that much of a surprise.

He'd hardly tried to hide it when he'd come to Father for aid before. Moxie's life had been on the line. Fortunately for Noah, there would be absolutely no benefit for Father to reveal that he'd done anything, because that would just end up lumping the blame on his own head. They were part of the same family branch, after all.

"I suspect your health will be just fine," Noah said. "Did you finally get into the main branch like you wanted to?"

The corner of Father's lip twitched—a practiced, controlled movement that lasted for exactly a second before returning back to its normal position. "Yes. You were invaluable, Spider."

"I think I much prefer Vermil," Noah said. He matched Father's posture. "I think there's something going on at Arbitage that I believe you'd be interested in knowing, considering you've got a vested interest in it."

"What makes you think you know anything I don't?" Father asked. "And, for that matter, why would you presume I care about Arbitage any more than anyone else?"

"Call it a hunch," Noah said, pausing to glance around Father's room. He didn't see any bottles of the mango-flavored wine, which was a slight disappointment. "You sent Vermil there for a reason, and you were also directly involved with the Hellreaver being replaced. It's hard to claim that you don't care at all."

"I never did. I just said you were presuming," Father pointed out. "What are you looking for?"

"The wine. You don't have any more of it, do you?"

For an instant, a flicker of what might have been genuine annoyance danced over Father's features. It was so fast that Noah would have missed it if he hadn't gotten used to how placid and controlled the man's expressions normally were.

"No. I do not."

"Bummer," Noah said. "Well then. We were talking about what you were going to give me for the information that you want."

"The information that I likely already have."

"You don't know that, though," Noah pointed out.

"Nor do you know that I don't have it."

They stared at each other, and Noah was struck that they likely strongly resembled two children arguing over a hypothetical toy in a playground. That thought completely broke his mask and he snorted.

"Fine. I'll tell you, but if it's genuinely a surprise, you've got to help for free without trying to attach a bunch of your damn strings to everything. How's that sound?"

"You're letting me determine if the information is valuable?" Noah could feel the disapproval in Father's voice, as if he'd expected more from him.

Noah just grinned. "Yeah. All you. After all, I don't particularly care about Arbitage. It can burn down around me for all I care. The pieces of my own plans are not immobile."

After considering Noah for a second, Father gave him a slight wave with one of his hands. "Go on, then. Speak."

"Do you know of someone called Wizen?" Noah asked, watching Father's expression carefully to see if he could pick up on anything. "I was involved in the destruction of one of his clones, and he seems to have some plans with regard to Arbitage."

For several seconds, Father didn't speak. Then, slowly, he pushed himself up from his chair. Noah tensed, preparing for an attack—or to blow himself up if Father did anything in an attempt to capture him.

Instead, Father just walked over to the shelf and took down two crystal glasses with one hand, reaching behind a book and drawing forth a bottle of wine. He turned back to the table and set the glasses down.

"I thought you didn't have any left."

"I lied." Father removed the cork from the top of the bottle and poured each of them half a glass. "And you have my interest. How is it that you were able to determine the identity of Wizen's clone?"

Aha. I actually have something Father doesn't. At least, I would have had something if I'd done anything in particular. I just got lucky throwing the guy into a wall and Ulya happened to be at the wrong place at the wrong time. Or perhaps it was the right place at the right time. That remains to be seen.

"Does this count as admitting that I have information you want?"

"Yes," Father said, much to Noah's surprise. That wasn't the angle he'd been expecting Father to take—and, if anything, it concerned him. He'd been confident that Father would have danced around the topic, trying to pry information from Noah without revealing his own hand.

Instead, he'd laid his cards out on the table face-up. And, as far as Father was concerned, Noah was pretty sure that wasn't even a viable move.

If it seems like Father is being open, then I get the feeling we aren't even playing the same game. Either that, or Wizen is such a massive threat that Father isn't willing to screw around with him. I'm not sure which option would be worse.

"You have yet to say how you located the clone."

"It attacked someone that was part of my plans, and I went after it," Noah replied with a shrug. "A—"

"Torrin," Father finished.

"Yes. Your information network told you already?"

"No," Father said. "But I am aware of his interest in the Torrin family."

"Care to share what it is?"

"I have yet to figure out *why* he cares about them." Father shook his head and took a sip of his wine. "It does not logically make sense. Wizen is a powerful mind mage. One strong enough that even I hesitate to directly challenge him. He has an obsession with the Torrin family and something they possess, but I do not know what it is."

Noah couldn't tell what it was, but something poked at his mind. It wasn't like he knew Father anywhere near well enough to actually read the man, but something about his words felt off. For an instant, he felt a twinge of Azel's presence flit through his mind. Then it was gone, and Noah had no time to linger on it without giving away more than he was willing to.

"Hold on. I've heard Wizen was a Mind Rune user," Noah said, raising a finger as his brow furrowed. He paused to take a sip of the wine—it wasn't mango-flavored, much to his disappointment—and then continued. "But he was using plants to puppet the clone around. That seems pretty damn split up. What's he going for with his Rank 7 rune?"

"Wizen is a difficult opponent to read," Father said noncommittally. "He is not rational, and it makes him a very difficult opponent."

So he's like literally every other powerful mage I've met.

"I see the thoughts on your face," Father said dryly. "He is not an idiot or a buffoon. Wizen is very much in control of himself, and he works toward a singular goal without hesitation. And yet, the actions he takes to get there are entirely irrational. It is like the flight of a bee, flitting from flower to flower without purpose and arriving at the hive all the same."

Bees have purpose in their flights, though. I think I read back on earth that they can follow the same routes or something like that—but I get what Father is saying.

"So you think some part of his plan involves making a move on Arbitage?" Noah asked.

Father drained the rest of his wine, then set the glass down on his table with a clink. "I think he already has."

Chapter Sixty-Two

"You're going to have to give me more than that to work with."
Noah drained the last of his wine and set the empty glass to the
side, interlacing his fingers and leaning forward. "You know
things about everyone. What's the gap in his armor? I could find it
myself, but it would save a lot of effort if you just told me."

"If he had a gap wide enough for me to take advantage of, I would
have already done it." Father shook his head. "There are mannerisms—
repeated mistakes—that Wizen is prone to making, but none of them
are significant enough to properly turn against him. He is arrogant, as
all of us in power are. He is irrational, which works both for and
against him. His people are loyal."

"Voluntarily?" Noah asked. "Or are they puppets?"

"Wizen, despite the appearance he has put on thus far, is not a
puppet master," Father warned Noah. "Not in the literal sense of the
word. Only recently have I seen him working with anything construct
or puppet-related, and just now am I hearing about plant-related abilities. He is—or at least, I believed him to be—a mind mage."

Did he get his hands on a bunch of runes? That seems a little odd.
Something isn't adding up here.

"When you say mind mage, what do you believe are the full extent
of his powers that you do know of?" Noah asked carefully. He didn't
want to give away that he had basically no idea what a mind mage was
actually capable of beyond possibly telling if someone was telling the

truth or not and doing whatever it was that Wizen had done to Alexandra.

"His main ability has always been his ability to read his opponents' plans. It is not proper mind reading, but it is very close to it. He can pick up on your intentions and react before you can adjust as long as you're within his domain," Father said. He poured himself another glass of wine and looked to Noah, who shrugged and nodded.

"What else?" Noah asked while Father poured him a glass. "That can't be all."

"He can forcibly take control of someone's body if he has sufficient time by imbuing them with a portion of the Mind Rune," Father said, his features narrowing in distaste. "It is not an effective strategy against an opponent who can fight back, and it's very easy to tell who has been affected by it. The binding is very literal, and those under his control can ignore commands not directly given. He uses it more to show his power than as a real weapon, though he can reinforce the bodies of people he imbues."

So exactly what he did to Alexandra.

"How long would it take to do that?"

"Days, at the minimum. Possibly weeks."

It sounds like that particular power isn't going to be a direct issue, then. Not as far as protecting others, at least. The most pressing matter is to figure out how to deal with his puppets, and then I can work on the other crap later.

"Wizen can only mind-read you when you're near him?" Noah asked.

Father nodded. "Yes. And last I was aware, the range of his domain was one hundred feet around him."

I wonder what the chances are that Wizen is in Arbitage. Something tells me he isn't. If he was actually able to do all this Mind Magic crap, I don't see why he'd resort to having plant clones strolling around. This is probably the same situation that Evergreen's construct was in, so he's off somewhere else, probably nice and safe.

Works for me, though. It means I should be able to focus. It doesn't matter how Wizen started getting puppets. What matters is finding a way to recognize them.

Noah leaned back in his chair, idly going to take a sip from his glass before realizing that it was empty. He didn't know if Ulya's strategy of cutting the back of everyone's necks was the best one to use. They'd have to do it every single time anyone left their sight for more a few seconds, which sounded like a huge pain if nothing else.

Wizen is using plants to make his puppets and can steal control of other people's constructs. I don't think anyone other than Evergreen has a construct just strolling around casually, so I can focus on the plant shit.

Seconds ticked by. He'd narrowed down the scope of the immediate problem, but it didn't change the fact that he had absolutely no idea how he could figure out if someone was made out of plants without just cutting them open.

Noah could feel Father's gaze boring into his skull, reminding him that this fight was far from just him and Father versus Wizen. It was a three-way battle, and Father was only a temporary ally—if that. There was still a chance Father was going to double-cross him somehow.

"Do you have anyone that uses puppets that you could bring in?" Noah asked, deciding that sitting silent any longer would show more concern than he was willing to reveal.

"Perhaps," Father allowed. "Why?"

"I want to test something."

"Will you kill them?"

"Do you care?"

"Yes," Father said. "They are an important part of my family."

Ah. Someone you still need alive. Not like I was planning on killing anybody for no reason in the first place. Good to keep up some degree of appearances, though.

"I won't harm them," Noah promised. "I can't say the same for their puppets, though. I'd like to test a few theories."

Father considered him for a moment, then inclined his head. A moment later, the door rumbled open to allow Janice entrance. If she was surprised to see Noah, it didn't show on her face. She just gave him a small nod of greeting before turning her attention to Father.

"What can I do for you, Father?"

"Get Ian and tell him to bring one of his puppets with him. One that isn't important."

Janice stepped out of the room without another word. The next few minutes passed in silence, with Noah and Father sitting on either side of the table wordlessly. Fortunately, Janice worked fast and they didn't have to wait long.

Three pairs of footsteps walked back into the room, and Noah resisted the urge to turn and look over his shoulder. Janice re-entered the room, accompanied by an average-looking man. He had curled brown hair and matching eyes. A beard covered the lower half of his face, and his hands were stained with grease.

Standing beside him was a scraggly-looking animal. Noah wasn't sure what animal it was meant to be. It walked on four legs and was vaguely reminiscent of the monkeys he'd seen in the Scorched Acres, but it didn't have any hair—nor was it alive.

Instead of skin, it had exposed gray muscle. It had indents for eyes and an open hole for a mouth. Once the creature was close enough to Noah to enter his domain, he picked up a faint amount of energy curling off its form.

"You called for my services, Father?" the man asked, wringing his hands together. His eyes darted around the room, barely lingering on Noah for more than an instant.

"Thank you for coming, Ian. Magus Vermil has requested to inspect your puppet," Father said. "You may leave. Remain outside the room."

Ian let out a breath, not even trying to hide his relief. He hurriedly shuffled back out of the room and stood just outside the open door. Janice sent one last glance at Father, but when he gave no further command, she followed after Ian.

The door ground shut behind them, leaving Noah and Father in the room with the gray, hairless monkey.

"Do what you will with it," Father said with a vague gesture, but Noah didn't miss the subtle interest in his posture.

Noah examined the puppet. He walked in a small circle around it, trying to figure out what similarities it would share with something under Wizen's control. The monkey obviously wasn't made out of plants, but they both functioned with Imbuements.

That didn't narrow things down much. A lot of things had Imbuements, and many mages had Body Imbuements. Besides, even if the Imbuements had stood out, it wasn't like he could check everyone for them. He needed something more obvious.

There had to be something that set the puppets aside from

everyone else and made it possible to immediately identify who had been replaced and who was safe.

Minutes passed. Noah studied the puppet, keeping his thoughts to himself. Father seemed content to do nothing but watch, which was just fine with Noah. He preferred to work in silence, but the silence didn't change the fact that he was finding precious few similarities he could actually rely on.

Wizen's plants had been supposedly able to infiltrate Will's body and completely control it, so shape and appearance were out the window. The faint amount of magic coming off the monkey wasn't particularly noteworthy in comparison to other mages either.

There were a lot of things that would have caused similar effects, including just about any imbued item with more than a little power stored inside it. That didn't stop Noah, though. He continued to dig through his mind, searching for a solution as he walked circles around Ian's puppet. The most obvious signs were the ones where he'd have to look so closely that it would be obvious. He needed something he could pick up on in just a few instants.

I wonder if my domain would be able to do anything. I haven't fully tested its abilities yet, but I can feel the area covered by it a lot better than anywhere else. Maybe there's something internal I could pick up?

Noah focused his senses on the area of his domain and the puppet within it. He could feel it sitting there, empty eye sockets staring into the wall. Streamers of magic tickled his senses, but they still didn't stand out any more than they should have.

The puppet was just... that. A puppet. It had absolutely nothing remarkable about it. Noah's fingers twitched in annoyance. He was so focused on his domain and the information filtering in from it that he realized he was amplifying just about everything in the room.

He could feel the blood rushing through his own body and hear the gentle thump of Father's heartbeat across the table—a slow, steady rhythm that Noah suspected rarely ever changed.

And then it struck him. The solution was so simple that Noah nearly scoffed at himself for even daring to think of it, but the more he thought, the more he realized that simple was exactly what they needed.

The puppet was just a puppet. It was a mass of magic, flesh, and whatever else Ian had thrown into it—but it wasn't a human. It wasn't alive, and it certainly didn't have a heart.

It's not that easy to pick up on unless I'm really amping my senses to the max and feeling for everything, but now that I know what I'm looking for, it's obvious.

There was no noise from the puppet, and plants would be no different. If Wizen replaced someone's body with a bunch of magic, then their heart would no longer be beating. All they had to do was look for people without a heartbeat and blood flow and they'd root Wizen's clones out without any difficulty.

"Ah," Noah said. "That helps."

"What does?" Father asked, tilting his head to the side. "Did you find what you were looking for?"

"I did. And I didn't even have to break anything. Proud?"

This answer is so simple that it makes me wonder why Father didn't think of it himself. Or did he already figure it out and just didn't tell me? Damn it. I can never tell with Father.

"That would depend on whether your solution works. Do not say it aloud," Father warned, raising a hand before Noah could say anything else. "The fewer people know about what you have determined, the better—myself included. Fewer people means there are fewer targets he can steal information from."

Just how strong is Wizen if Father thinks he can breach his sanctum? Then again, Father is a paranoid bastard.

"Noted," Noah said. "In that case, you've given me what I needed. Now that I know you won't be interfering, I'll return to Arbitage and deal with the remainder of this issue."

Father nodded idly. "I'm sure you will. I will give aid. Any opportunity to inconvenience Wizen is too tempting to pass up on."

"You will?" Noah tried not to sound too surprised. "Who?"

Father lifted a hand, pressing his other palm to a rune circle on his desk. A hum filled the room and a purple swirl hummed to life behind Noah, twisting out into a portal as energy crackled at its edges.

"Someone talented in dealing with scurrying little rats," Father replied, the corners of his lips twitching. "I will send Brayden."

Chapter Sixty-Three

If Father had been looking for the exact set of words that would have made Noah happy, he found them. Noah nearly let a grin slip across his face before he caught it mid-formation, settling for a mildly uninteresting nod in its place.

"He should prove beneficial. I have one more question before I leave, then. Do you mind?"

"You'd ask it whether I said yes or not," Father said wryly. "Ask. I do not guarantee a response."

"What will Wizen do if I go around killing his clones? Unless he's obscenely powerful, he can't have all that many of them. So when they all get squished, I'd imagine he'll be mad. Is he going to lose it entirely?"

"You're asking if he'll be baited into a stupid decision or revealing himself, yes?" Father tilted his head to the side, considering the question. "It's hard to say. Wizen is a man who often has many layers to his work. I respect him for it, but it makes him a rather difficult opponent. It would be ill-advised to believe he will fold after you inconvenience him."

"I figured that was too much to ask, but it was worth a shot," Noah said. "That's actually everything, then. I don't suppose you've got anything else for me?"

Father's response was to reach under the desk and pull out another slip of paper with a rune on it, sliding it across the desk to Noah.

"Just to contact me should you find more information of any degree of interest. I am quite curious to see how you will end up doing against Wizen. Curious enough that I may be willing to lend more aid than normal, should the situation prove appropriate."

Which is another way for you to say you'll do more if it gets me into your debt and really screws either me or Wizen in the long term. I was wondering why Father was being so open with the information, but I think the answer is staring me right in the face.

Father is pitting two people he wants taken out against each other. Even if he isn't working with Wizen directly, I can't assume he isn't feeding him any information. That's why he stopped me from telling him what I'm going to do. Son of a bitch.

"Is something amiss?" Father asked.

"Nothing at all. There wasn't anything else, was there?"

"There was not."

Noah nodded and stepped through the portal. He didn't bother bidding Father farewell, and Father returned the favor. With a fizzling hiss and a pop, Noah found himself standing back in his room.

I wonder if I should have asked to stick around in the Linwick Estate so I could try to find Jalen, but that might have been a bad idea. I don't think Father knows about my ties to Jalen yet, so I shouldn't over-play my hand.

As the room took form around Noah, he spotted Moxie and Lee standing behind the shrinking portal, watching it warily. Neither of them relaxed until the portal had completely faded away.

"Well?" Moxie asked. "How'd it go?"

"About as well as I expected. And, if I'm willing to risk divine retribution for getting too cocky, I might even say it went better than I had been hoping for."

"So you have a way to deal with Wizen?" Moxie asked.

"Kind of," Noah replied. He filled them in on the entire conversation that he and Father had gone through, not leaving anything out. When he finished, Lee and Moxie both sat quietly for a few seconds.

"So all we have to do is run around and kill all his puppets, right?" Lee asked, miming a punch. "That shouldn't be too bad—but you didn't actually say what the strategy you figured out was. Do you think Wizen might be listening in?"

"I don't know. Probably not, if I'm being honest," Noah admitted.

"I doubt Wizen is so strong that he can just constantly sit around and listen to what we're talking about. If he is, we're already screwed—but if he were that strong, he wouldn't be playing games with us, and Arbitage would already be under attack or destroyed."

"And yet I note you didn't say how you can detect the puppets," Moxie observed. "I take it that was intentional."

"Yeah. Who knows how extensive his Mind Runes are. I'm not going to sit here shivering in terror, but I don't think we should go around spilling our secrets either. Wizen has a lot of cards, so the more we keep close to chest the better."

Lee let out a huff of disappointment but nodded her understanding. "Fine. You'll just have to tell me who to punch. What are we going to do in the meantime? We aren't just sitting around until Wizen's clones show up, are we?"

"Depends on your definition of sitting around. We definitely aren't pausing any of our lessons. The kids just got introduced to Formations —and both you and Moxie have gotten started on them as well, not to mention the advanced track. No reason to give up on that now. We'll just keep plugging along as we have been, but with a little extra in mind."

"Oh, awesome. That means we get to stretch next class, right?" Lee asked. "I've been feeling a little stiff."

How is making the students stretch going to make you less stiff? Actually—I don't want to know. Some things are better off just watched and enjoyed, lest Lee try to bring me in as well.

"What about Jalen?" Moxie asked, changing subjects back to their original topic. "I don't suppose you had any luck contacting him while you were in the Linwick Estate?"

"I considered it, but decided against revealing too much to Father," Noah said, shaking his head and letting out a huff. "It certainly would have been convenient to meet them both at once, but it was just too risky. I'm not so sure Father has our best interests in mind."

"I don't even know if there should be a question. Father is using us to damage Wizen, and the same goes in the other direction. He's only helping because the only one that wins from a conflict like this is the one that wasn't in it," Moxie pointed out. She crossed her arms, but a smirk played across her features. "At least, that would be true if we couldn't take all the power Wizen has when we kill him."

"That definitely does skew things in our favor, assuming we take Wizen out," Noah agreed with a nod. "But for now, let's focus on what we can handle. I've got a way to detect the puppets that I'm... fairly sure should work."

"Fairly?" Moxie raised an eyebrow.

"About as sure as I can get without testing it on a real Wizen clone." Noah rubbed the back of his head and gave them a weak grin. "It should work. The logic is sound. The important part is just to make sure we all keep getting stronger so that when Wizen does pull out his next card, we'll be able to handle it."

"In that case, do you think you could give me some pointers on Formations?" Moxie asked. "I want to brush up as much as possible before the lesson tomorrow."

"Me too!" Lee exclaimed, flopping down cross-legged on the floor. Noah and Moxie both sat down as well.

"Right then. Where exactly are you getting stuck?" Noah asked.

"Mostly in keeping the pattern around after I start to picture it," Moxie said. "Getting started isn't too difficult, but the moment I start trying to hold the pattern in place, I find that it slips away."

"Can you demonstrate?" Noah asked. "If I see what you're doing, I should be able to hopefully point you in the right direction."

Moxie nodded, closing her eyes to concentrate, and they got to work.

* * *

Rafael stood before the towering walls of the enormous Bastion, their shade blocking out the sun overhead. The Inquisitor's hand tightened around his rosary as he drew in a deep breath, letting the myriad of scents in the air filter through his mind.

He could feel it. The demon that had killed his men—the one that bore the answers that he sought—it was close. It was so close that he could almost feel it, but the musk of the city obscured his power.

There were so many people, so many forms of magic, churning and twisting, all striving to block his sight. To block him. They would not. Rafael had the scent, as muddled and faded as it was.

He'd never had a demon scent this elusive before, and he didn't know what it meant—but if anything, that only drove him even harder.

Rafael let his free hand brush against the dog head carved into the hilt of his sword.

Clear energy rang through him, pushing away the feelings of fear and confusion. It shoved back the concern of failure and the magnitude of the task before him. All that remained was completing his duty. There was something of value here. Not just to him, but to the Inquisition.

Whoever this demon was had done a great job of hiding themselves, and that meant figuring out how they'd done it would then unveil countless ways to discover other demons that lurked amongst humans.

I cannot fail. The lives of countless people all rely on this singular hunt. The trail is faint, but it is there nonetheless.

Running a thumb along the beads of his rosary, Rafael stepped into Arbitage. A tingle ran down his spine as he strode down the busy streets. There were powerful beings in Arbitage. Some of them might have been allies should he seek them out, but others most certainly would not have been.

It didn't matter one way or the other. Rafael didn't dare risk the missions for something as paltry as fear. The demon couldn't have advanced much since its fight against Inaros and Johan, so it was unlikely it would be able to properly challenge him.

The demon's ally may be difficult, but demons are fickle creatures. The chances of the ally sticking around the demon this long after the initial fight are relatively low. I can't discount it, of course. I will strike quickly and end the fight before it can properly begin.

His runes churned within his chest, emanating pressure as they worked to track the demon. Blood Magic was difficult to control and using it when there were so many competing sources of information all vying for his attention was even harder.

The blood in the vial and all the years of skill under his belt were the only things that gave him a lifeline to hang onto. And, in the vortex of competing energy that sought to confuse his powers, a thin strand held firm. It was so faint that most Inquisitors would likely have lost it by now, but Rafael was not most inquisitors.

He was the Hound, and the Hound followed until its duty was done.

Chapter Sixty-Four

After an hour of practice on their patterns, Lee and Moxie both broke off to hunt monsters and work on filling their runes so they could reach Rank 4 as soon as possible. Lee was probably considerably closer to it than Moxie was, since all of her runes had already been completed and all she had to do was get the last of the energy to prepare herself for advancement.

Moxie had a bit more work, as she only had three Flawless Runes made and would need to either duplicate them or gather more runes to push the rest of the way through Rank 3. If not for the events at the Torrin Estate, she'd have been equally matched to Lee if not already at Rank 4. Neither of them could complain about that, though—those events had been the way that Moxie had finally broken free of Evergreen's grasp.

As far as both Noah and Moxie were concerned, it was a worthwhile trade. But unfortunately, that meant while Lee and Moxie were out hunting monsters, Noah didn't have a good excuse to join them.

Sure, getting more power would have been a good idea, but there were more pressing matters he could still deal with. He needed more practice with using his violin to simulcast magic, and figuring out the lesson plan for tomorrow was important as well.

So, while Lee and Moxie headed out to fight, Noah spent his time preparing. He didn't particularly mind it—Moxie had been working hard for so long that she deserved some form of break from proper teaching, and he'd missed being able to teach a class of students that were actually interested.

There would always be more things to fight and kill, after all.

Hours slipped by, and the day sank into night. Noah worked through the darkness, preparing both for the upcoming class and for the meeting with the other members of the advanced track that would be happening the following night.

The muted song of his violin, its voice muffled so that nobody would hear it, just barely tickled at his ears. Power coursed through the instrument as he inserted and removed runes from within its strings, growing more and more used to operating it properly.

Noah didn't stop working until it was well into the night. Just around the time he was slipping into bed, the door to the room cracked open with a soft click. Noah, who had been midway through getting into bed, glanced over as Moxie crept in, likely trying to avoid waking him.

They locked eyes and she snorted, stepping the rest of the way into the room and closing the door behind her.

"Why are you awake? It's the middle of the night."

"I was practicing," Noah replied with a grin. He covered a yawn as Moxie pulled her jacket off and hung it over the back of her chair. "How did hunting go? Make good progress?"

"Really good," Moxie confirmed, shaking her head and laughing quietly. "Lee is an absolute monster. It's ridiculous that she's a Rank 3. I'm pretty sure her runes are already full with the way she fights. We must have killed nearly a hundred monsters."

"A hundred? This quickly?" Noah let out a whistle. "That's pretty scary. Strong ones?"

"Rank 2 and 3. We were in an area called the Ardent Desert. It wasn't really that much of a desert, if I'm being honest, but it still had a lot of monsters to fight. Definitely a little too advanced for most of the students."

"Was there a Great Monster in the area?"

"Probably. They did have some patterns in how they fought, but I'm not quite as good at picking them up as you are," Moxie replied, stepping through the bathroom door and poking her head back out. "Give me a second. I need to freshen up before getting ready to sleep."

Noah got the rest of the way into bed and propped the pillow up against the wall so he could sit at an angle. A few minutes later, Moxie returned to the main room, her hair wet. Noah pulled the covers to the side and she got into bed, scooting up to lean against his chest and pressing her wet hair to his chest, drawing out a curse.

"Damn, that's cold," Noah complained, dialing up the heat from Combustion internally.

"You'll live," Moxie said. The bedsheets pulled themselves up of their own volition and Moxie snuggled in, ensuring that her hair was scattered over Noah as much as possible before settling down. "Did you need help figuring out what we're doing in class tomorrow?"

Noah tried to move some of Moxie's hair away from his face before realizing it was a hopeless task and settling for wrapping his arms around her waist. "I think I should be fine. You've earned yourself a break from worrying about that stuff. I'll just be doing some combat training with patterns, seeing if the kids can use patterns while they spar. Alexandra sounds like she already pulled it off against Gero, so I'd rather get that started before they do it on their own."

Moxie let out a murmur of approval and rolled over so that her cheek was pressed against Noah's chest. She wrapped her arms around his back and let out a content sigh, speaking in a drowsy, satisfied tone. "Thanks. I'll be caught up to Rank 4 soon enough, I promise."

"I know you will," Noah said. "That's a problem for tomorrow, though."

Moxie made another noise of agreement and gave him a small squeeze, not even bothering to form words. Noah slipped down so they were lying back and let his eyes close, letting himself drift off to sleep.

* * *

The next morning, Lee met Noah and Moxie at their door when they set off to go to class. She stretched her arms over her head, arching her back and letting out a loud yawn before smacking her lips.

"Good morning, Lee," Noah said. "What did you end up doing last night?"

"Just wandered around mostly," Lee replied. "I didn't really feel like sleeping, and we killed so many monsters that I didn't need to. I already had breakfast. Do you want some?"

Noah nearly said yes, but narrowly managed to stop himself in time. Lee's idea of breakfast was definitely a squirrel.

"I'll probably grab something later," Noah said diplomatically. "Or I'll just kill a few monsters when we all go out to train in a bit. No need to keep the kids waiting."

"Oh, yeah. Are we gonna stretch today?"

"Sure," Noah said as the three set off down the hall and toward the transport cannon. "Why not? It'll be a good way to warm up before we get to sparring."

The students were all sitting at the base of the tower when they arrived, discussing something with each other in hushed tones. James, who was keeping watch to make sure nobody wandered too close to their group, nodded in greeting as they drew up, and the other students all looked over.

"Morning, Teacherman, Moxie. You too, Lee," Todd said, raising a hand. "What are we doing today, and how do I win?"

"You win by settling for second place," Isabel quipped with an easygoing smile. "Are we doing more patterns today?"

Noah took a moment to let his domain sweep over all of them. He highly doubted any had been replaced, but it was important to check just in case. Fortunately, they were all as normal as could be.

"How'd you guess?" Noah gave them a wry grin. "We'll be putting everything we've covered so far together and doing some sparring where you try to work your patterns in. As usual, no trying to use any magic in your patterns."

Isabel, Emily, and Alexandra both exchanged an excited look, while James and Todd both frowned. Noah hid a laugh. It was pretty easy to tell who had patterns that were going to be directly beneficial to fighting and who didn't.

I'm not worried about Todd or James though. They're both far more capable than they let on. I'm looking forward to seeing what they can do.

"But first we're stretching!" Lee proclaimed. "You can't spar without being properly warmed up."

Everyone other than James and Alexandra shuddered. Noah just chuckled and led them all up the tower and into the elevator. Tim was waiting at the top in his normal chair when they arrived, a merry grin on his face.

"Good morning, Vermil. Windscorned Plateau again?" Tim asked.

Noah paused a moment to let his domain sweep over Tim. To his relief, the man's heartbeat was present. He didn't know what he would have done if the kindly old man had been turned into a puppet, as unlikely as it might have been.

I want to find a way to fix his runes, but how do I get around to it without revealing my powers? Maybe I have to knock him out in the middle of the night or something? It would be like a reverse robbery. I take all the crappy runes, replace them with equivalent ones from my book, and use the Fragment of Renewal to fix the damage. I don't know where he sleeps, though. There's no way he just stays in the tower, is there?

"You know, I've only ever seen you here," Noah said. "Not that I object, but don't you ever take breaks to sleep or take a day off?"

Tim chuckled and stroked his long beard. "A day off? Oh no. Who would run the transport cannon if not for me? I prefer not to take long pauses. The service is just too important."

"Can't disagree there, but nobody can run like that forever, right?" Noah pressed.

"When you've got nothing better to do with your life, it doesn't hurt. I just get enough sleep to get by. Meeting old friends and new people is just too exciting." Tim let out a cackle and let his hands fly across the controls of the transport cannon.

The tube shuddered as it shifted, changing directions and locking into place. Tim gave Noah an encouraging wave.

"It's ready for you lot."

Noah considered pressing the matter, but he decided to let it drop with a laugh. Pushing too hard would make it obvious. He had to find a way to help Tim without implicating himself, which was the very same problem he'd had ever since first deciding he wanted to help Tim. Unfortunately, Noah still had no idea what the best way to go about doing it was—but he made a mental commitment to find one before the first exam this year. "Sounds good. Thanks, Tim. Be seeing you."

Moxie lay down in the cannon and vanished in a blur of blue energy a few moments later. The rest of the students and Lee followed after her until only Noah and Tim remained in the room.

After pausing for one more second, Noah lay back onto the cold metal as well.

"Have a good trip!" Tim called from behind his desk. A moment later, energy slammed into Noah and his body was turned into a flash of blue light that went streaking across the sky in pursuit of the others.

* * *

Tim watched the last traces of Vermil's energy fade, then smiled and shook his head. The man was hardly fit to be a Linwick, but he and his group were a pleasant change of pace from the usual people that frequented the cannon.

He leaned back in his chair, looking out one of the windows onto the campus below. Watching all the tiny people mill about it below was one of his favorite ways to let the days pass. It was a bittersweet feeling.

Tim could remember the days when he'd been one of the students below, hopes of becoming something great still fresh in his mind. Fate had other plans, though. All the money he'd gathered was only just enough to pay his way into Arbitage, and nowhere near enough to buy him the runes he needed to advance.

If he'd been a bit better of a fighter, he could have become an adventurer. Unfortunately, the mere idea of hurting something made him grimace in distaste. Tim went to take a sip of his tea, but his hand missed the handle, and he knocked the cup off the table.

Tim cursed and lunged, grabbing the cup from the air before it could hit the ground. It lost the majority of its contents, but at least it didn't shatter. Tim leaned back with a small chuckle and set the cup back on the desk.

"Another reason why I couldn't be an adventurer," Tim muttered to himself. "Clumsy as sin."

He stood, moving to find a towel so he could clean up the floor, and froze in place. A man stood on the other side of the room, a cloak pulled low over his head. Tim hadn't heard the elevator activate, nor had he heard anyone arrive.

"Whoa there," Tim said, smiling in greeting. "I didn't see you there. What can I do for you?"

"Keep the cannon in its current location," the man replied. "Send me after the people that just left."

Tim's smile slipped away. "I'm afraid that kind of thing is confidential. I can't be sending you after others unless you're a staff member. Do you have a badge?"

"No," the man said. "I don't need one. Is the cannon still pointed in the right direction?"

Tim's eyes narrowed. "I won't be answering that question. Is there somewhere in particular that you'd like to go? If not, I'm going to have to ask you to leave."

For a second, the man didn't respond. Then he reached up to his hood, pulling it back. "I'm going to ask one last time. Send me after them."

Tim's eyes went wide.

A minute later, another streak of blue flashed through the morning air, and the transport cannon was silent once more.

Chapter Sixty-Five

As soon as everyone arrived at the Windscorned Plateau, they set off to find a more secluded location to train. Between Noah and James's Wind Magic and Alexandra and Lee's speed, they were all able to make good speed and came to a stop on a platform a few minutes away.

Noah didn't waste any time once they got there. He wanted to see how far everyone had come, and he could tell by their expressions that they were just as eager to show it off. To nobody's surprise, Isabel and Alexandra both volunteered to go first.

"It only makes sense, so go ahead," Noah said with an encouraging nod. "Both of you are still using patterns related to your swords, right?"

They nodded.

"Go for it, then. I know we've got a few healing potions—unless they got used up—but do your best not to actually cut each other. This is a demonstration, not a real match."

"I can blunt my weapon," Isababel said. "And if I use my armor, Alexandra's sword shouldn't be able to break through it unless she's really swinging with all her might."

"I won't," Alexandra promised, drawing her blade and holding it at her side. "I'm ready once you get your armor up."

"No magic, unfortunately," Noah said with a shake of his head, stopping Isabel before she could make her armor. He still didn't have enough control of his domain to actively keep it from suppressing her, and he needed them both within range in case they mistakenly put power into their patterns and risked blowing themselves up. "Todd, can you lend Isabel the Shield? It's far from perfect, but as long as Alexandra keeps her speed under control and focuses on technique, it should be enough."

Todd nodded, pulling the bracelet off his wrist. He handed it to Isabel and took a step back, giving the girls room to spar. The other students backed up as well. Alexandra drew her secondary sword and gave it to Isabel.

"Ready when you are," Alexandra said as she lowered into a fighting stance, her blade flitting to and fro in the air before her. Noah could already see her erratic pattern starting to take form. Alexandra had definitely been practicing—her movements were sudden and jumpy, and yet there was still a sameness to them that kept them from being truly random.

Isabel set her stance and wrapped both of her hands around the hilt of the blade. She drew in a deep breath. As she let it out, her posture changed. Noah's domain tingled—there were faint amounts of magic trying to manifest in both of their patterns, but his domain was suppressing them.

"Ready," Isabel confirmed. "Let's go."

She took a step forward, bringing her borrowed sword down in a powerful, direct swing that had no signs of subtlety or subterfuge within it. Alexandra's sword snapped out, slapping the blow to the side lightly as she ducked out of the way.

Isabel spun, bringing her sword around in a loop and down for Alexandra's shoulders. The other girl was forced to hop back to avoid the strike. She retaliated in a flash, her blade snaking out to nip at Isabel's side.

Instead of trying to dodge it, Isabel activated her shield. A dull glow enveloped her and the blade rang off the magic, not having been thrust with enough power to damage it. She continued her assault, every blow raining down with even more intensity as she advanced toward Alexandra.

Fascinating. If this was a real fight, there would be no match. Alexandra would destroy Isabel completely purely because of her speed and resilience, but because they're only matching their patterns rather than their full abilities, they actually seem to be close to evenly matched.

Alexandra definitely wasn't the only person practicing. Isabel has moved her pattern into her entire body rather than just her sword. It feels like she's literally become the avalanche—but Alexandra is withstanding it without relying on her Body Runes.

She's dodging and poking at Isabel's shield with what would likely be some pretty nasty cuts had she been putting more force behind them. I'd say Alexandra is still a bit ahead of Isabel in patterns, but the gap is closing. Either way, they're both doing incredible. Good shit, kids.

Noah let the match continue for another minute before stepping in, using a small burst of wind to separate the two. They both turned to him, sweating and breathing heavily.

"What? What happened?" Isabel asked, looking around to get her bearings. She'd clearly fallen into a flow state during the fight.

"You both did incredible, but I don't want you completely exhausted. Patterns are too dangerous to push that hard, so taking it one step at a time is safer," Noah said with a smile. "I honestly don't have anything to criticize. Both of you have made huge steps in your respective patterns, and you understand them better than I do."

"What does that mean?" Alexandra asked, blinking in surprise. "You can't teach us more?"

Noah snorted. "Far from it. I just can't find any more flaws in your actual patterns because I don't understand them like you do. The patterns aren't the end goal, though. They're just the first step."

"Oh. That makes sense," Isabel allowed, flipping her sword around and handing it back to Alexandra. "Thanks for the sword, by the way."

"No problem," Alexandra replied idly. She sheathed both blades and wiped her brow with the back of her hand.

"Who wants to go next?" Noah asked. "Any volunteers?"

"I'd like to give it a shot, if that's possible," Emily hedged. She hadn't been able to show a pattern in their previous class, so Noah had been slightly concerned that nothing had changed since then. But, considering she was volunteering, his fears were slightly eased.

"Me too," James said.

"Great. The two of you can come up," Noah said. "Remember, no magic."

"Is there a reason we aren't allowed to use unrelated magic?" Emily asked. "It can't cross over, can it?"

Because my domain would squish it, and I can't stop that from happening yet. Also, there's a chance of someone mistakenly letting something leak. At least, that's what I'll be telling myself.

"Yes, but for now, that reason is just going to be safety," Noah said. There would be a better time to reveal his domain, and he didn't want them distracted from the lesson at the moment. "I know your patterns will eventually be much more tied to using magic, but I want to make sure they're perfect before then."

Emily nodded her understanding. "I can live with that. I don't think my pattern is really great yet, but at least I've got something."

"The only way to find out is to show me what you've got. You can get started whenever you're ready."

"I'm ready," James said through a yawn. He rubbed his eyes with the back of a hand, then sat down and crossed his legs. "Just attack whenever you want to."

I'm curious to see how James is going to use that pattern of doing nothing to fight. Is he just going to sit there and let Emily wail on him? That would be kind of interesting, but somehow I suspect that even he isn't that lazy.

"I'm not really the best at hand-to-hand combat, but I'll do my best," Emily said hesitantly. She shifted her stance, raising her hands before her.

Noah wasn't exactly an expert on fighting stances, but he could tell that Emily wasn't lying. She wasn't exactly off balance, but she was nowhere near as comfortable as Isabel and Alexandra had been.

Emily stood still for a few moments, then flowed forward. Even though James was sitting, she didn't look like she was going to take things easy on him. She spun, trying to hit him with a hook kick.

James blurred, shifting just enough to the side to avoid the attack before returning to his previous location. Emily kept her momentum and drove a palm for his shoulder, already readying another attack even as the first one flew out.

Once again, James weaved out of the way and let the blow just barely pass him by. Emily's next strike missed in the same manner. She didn't give in, though. A flurry of strikes flew out as Emily used her hands, elbows, feet, and just about every part of herself to attack.

James was forced to vault to his feet as her efforts intensified, but he continued to move with the least amount of energy possible. A small grin flickered across Noah's face as he started to see their patterns fully take form.

Emily was a snowstorm. A constant flurry of blows raining down from every direction with blinding intensity. Similar to Alexandra, none of them were particularly strong attacks, but there was a distinct difference in their fighting styles.

Alexandra's attacks were sudden and fast, but they were targeted. Every movement was intentional—Emily had gone in the exact opposite direction and had done her best to perfectly embody the storm.

Her assault came from every direction and every style. No single attack was of any real threat on its own, but when they piled together, he could see the potential within them. As for James—if Noah had to find a word for his pattern, it wasn't just nothingness. It was laziness, and not even in a bad way.

He'd found a way to put the absolute least amount of energy into every movement, optimizing his motion as much as possible. It wasn't actually all that different from the methods that Noah used to fight enemies he was familiar with.

James is further along than Emily is, but that's probably because he's been practicing being lazy his entire life. Emily is doing great for not having had a pattern during our last class.

Noah let them fight for another minute. James didn't attack once, and Emily refused to let up her flurry of blows. When it became clear that neither had anything left to demonstrate, Noah split them up with another small blast of wind.

"Great job, both of you," Noah said. "James, you're going to need to work some offense into your pattern. Purely using it for dodging is great, but you can't just leave it at that. Battles are won through fighting back, not backpedaling. And Emily—opposite advice. You've made some huge steps since last class, but you're focusing entirely on attack. You need to survive your fights, not just win them."

Both of them nodded, and Noah looked to Lee and Moxie.

"Any thoughts from you two?"

"You should stretch more," Lee advised Emily. "If you want to really throw attacks that fast, flexibility will be helpful. I'll give you private lessons."

Emily's face went white, but she gave Lee a nod. "Thanks. I think."

"I don't know much about patterns, but I can see how much work you've been putting in," Moxie said to Emily, giving her a wide smile. "Keep it up. At this rate, you're going to surpass me. James also has one of the more interesting styles of fighting I've seen. I have to admit, I'm pretty interested to see where you both take things."

Emily beamed, but before either she or James could say anything else, another voice spoke up from behind them.

"I'd have to agree. That was fascinating."

Everyone spun as the air wavered and shifted. A robed man appeared from within the distortion, his hood pulled back and a wry grin on his lips. Jalen raised a hand in greeting.

"What have you been teaching these little gremlins, Vermil? And why is it that their motions feel eerily similar to a Formation?"

Chapter Sixty-Six

"Jalen!" Noah exclaimed. "What are you doing here? I didn't think we were going to meet for a few more days."

"We weren't. I got bored," Jalen said. "And that didn't answer my question. Where'd a kid like you learn Formations well enough to start teaching them to other people? I know for a fact that there wasn't anything of the sort in the catacombs."

Letting on just how much I know about Formations is a pretty bad idea. I don't dislike Jalen, but if he gets too suspicious about what I can do, he may start looking a little closer than I'd prefer. But if I don't give him a satisfying answer, I end up in the same spot.

"We aren't working on Formations," Noah said, opting to go for the safest answer he could—the truth. Part of it, at least. "We're working on patterns. They aren't exactly the same thing."

Moxie and Lee nodded, but none of the students made any moves. They all watched Jalen warily, ready to burst into motion at an instant's notice. Noah didn't blame them—even though Jalen wasn't doing anything and his domain was suppressed, he could feel the danger practically enveloping the man.

Jalen didn't miss the way they'd reacted. His gaze swept over everyone, lingering on each of the students.

"Are they not? I was unaware," Jalen said. "Never had much interest in Formations myself. Lots of work and you usually get squished midway through trying to cast them. Why are you teaching kids about them?"

"They're useful," Noah replied with a shrug. "Knowledge never hurts. And, as I said, we aren't exactly doing Formations. This is more about their coordination and understanding of their fighting styles."

"Curious," Jalen said slowly, his eyes twinkling faintly. "I don't think I've met other professors that employ similar methods. This wouldn't happen to be from the Torrin family, would it, Moxie?"

"Is that any of your concern?" Emily asked, her eyes narrowing as she took a step forward. "How is it any of your concern what they teach us?"

Jalen let out a chuckle. "Feisty. I was only asking a question, lass. You should learn that anger can often be just as much of a declaration of guilt as any other emotion. If you can't control it, you're going to give away more than you want to."

"Maybe we should talk somewhere more private," Noah suggested, intervening before any of the students could draw any more of Jalen's attention. He highly doubted Jalen would actually hurt any of them, but Jalen's interest was possibly just as dangerous as his ire.

Jalen shrugged. "Perhaps."

"Moxie, can you take over for a bit?" Noah asked. "Just have them keep at it. I'll catch up with all of you shortly."

She nodded, and Noah beckoned to Jalen before tossing his flying sword to the ground and taking off. He didn't have any concerns about the other man keeping up with him, so he flew several plateaus away before touching down once more.

No sooner had Noah stepped off his sword than Jalen materialized in the air beside him, a thoughtful expression on his face.

"What?" Noah asked. "And was there an actual reason you came to visit early? I can't have my students getting traumatized by the head of the Linwick family staring them down."

"I was bored, I told you. I wanted to see how things were playing out in Arbitage," Jalen replied with a chuckle. "And don't worry. I'm not going to screw with the kids. You've certainly got an interesting lot, though. Not a single one of them was scared of me. Why would that be?"

"Maybe they just didn't know who you were. It's not like you broadcast your identity," Noah pointed out.

"That is true," Jalen allowed, tapping a finger on the side of his chin before shaking his head. "But I don't think that was why. They weren't scared because they seemed convinced they were safe."

"They certainly shouldn't be. I've nearly gotten them killed more times than I can count."

"And yet, convinced they were. You continue to fascinate me. Why is it that they believed a mere Rank 4 strong enough to contend with someone clearly of a higher power?"

"Stupidity?"

Jalen let out a bark of laughter and slapped Noah on the shoulder. "Your attempts to deflect my attention are amusing and entirely pointless. No bullshit can overcome the sheer agony of boredom."

Trust me. You've got absolutely no idea how true that statement is.

"Well, just don't go screwing with their education. They've gotten shafted enough by the noble families as it is," Noah said with a sigh and a shake of his head. "I've just been trying to do right by them in the ways that I can. But—now that you're here, I've actually got a question for you."

"Oh?" Jalen tilted his head to the side.

Noah was pretty sure it was pointless, but he still took a moment to confirm that Jalen had a heartbeat with his domain. If Jalen had somehow been taken out by Wizen, he was pretty sure literally all of them were dead. It was difficult to get a good read on the man because of how much power was packed within his body, even with his domain suppressed, but Noah was able to just barely pick up on the muted thumps within Jalen's chest.

"Do you know of somebody by the name of Wizen?" Noah asked.

"Wizen?" Jalen tilted his head to the side in thought, not speaking for several seconds. "No. I don't believe I do."

"He's some kind of mind mage that had a plant puppet of another Arbitage professor wandering around campus. He nearly killed another professor and seemed to be interested in the Torrin family," Noah said. "I think he also replaced Evergreen's construct at one point. None of that sounds familiar?"

Jalen, to his credit, didn't say no immediately. He paused again, clearly digging through stacks of memories that he hadn't accessed in years. Eventually, he shook his head once more.

"Afraid not. Never heard of him. I'm not particularly up to date with anyone of the newer generations," Jalen said with a shrug. "If you're asking about him, I take it you're concerned."

"I am," Noah said. "He's probably a Rank 6, and a pretty strong one at that. It looks like he might attack Arbitage as a whole. I don't suppose you're interested?"

"Depends on the context." Jalen sent Noah a wry smile and adjusted his shirt. "I don't care about Arbitage, but I'm looking forward to seeing how you handle this. You've already killed one Rank 6, so I don't imagine this is beyond your capabilities. If I stepped in, I'd completely ruin the show."

Somehow, I saw that coming. Honestly, that isn't the worst-case scenario. Jalen isn't going to act against us, but he won't act to help us either. He's just going to sit on the sidelines and watch, possibly tossing in a little bit of aid if he thinks it'll make things more interesting. It's too bad he didn't know anything about Wizen, but that does tell me one thing—Wizen isn't some super powerful old bastard.

Jalen doesn't know who he is, so Wizen is probably somewhere around Evergreen's level of power, likely a little stronger.

"Yeah, I didn't expect you'd be particularly motivated to kill off your entertainment," Noah said with a chuckle. "Although I should remind you that if Wizen manages to get the upper hand over me, you're still losing your entertainment."

"I would be, but it would be a worthwhile sacrifice. The nobles fiddle with their children's affairs far too much and stunt their growth. Better to break a few bones learning a lesson than to baby someone until they turn into a pathetic wretch like Dayton."

Noah blinked in surprise. "Wait. You know about Dayton?"

"I'm not *entirely* removed from my family's affairs, despite how much I would like to be," Jalen said dryly. "Even I occasionally hear things. And, speaking of which, it's my turn for a question. What is your relationship with Father?"

"Enemies," Noah said without a second of hesitation. "Enemies who have recognized we both have bigger problems than each other and occasionally work together. I don't trust him in the slightest, and he offers me the same respect. Why do you ask?"

Should I tell him that Father isn't even who we think he is? The real Father is dead. What would I get out of sharing that information, though? I suspect the only Father I ever knew has been the fake, and I've been benefiting from working with him. If Jalen decides to kill him, all I've done is weaken myself.

"He was unusually interesting," Jalen replied. "More intelligent than most of the other idiots vying to get into the main branch. I'm pretty sure he's after something, but I've yet to figure out what it is. I've been having some fun watching him tug people around like toys, but he's no different than anyone else. Only concerned with control and power."

At least it doesn't sound like Jalen has any plans of helping Father out. Good. The last thing I need is these two teaming up.

"Most people seem to be. Control and power tend to mean you can live comfortably," Noah pointed out. He glanced over his shoulder in the direction of where they'd come from. "I'd be more than willing to entertain you, but I've got a pretty busy day today. I need to finish my lesson for my students and then let them know we'll be attending a meeting with the advanced track professors tonight—that will probably be pretty interesting, actually."

"Oh?" Jalen tilted his head to the side, a sparkle of interest flashing through his eyes. "Why do you say that?"

"There's going to be a bit of a game afoot. I won't be showing up as myself," Noah said with a grin. "If I boil it down, the whole thing is basically going to be a big dick measuring contest. Everyone will be trying to show off how strong they are. I imagine it's going to go awry pretty quickly."

"That does sound interesting." A grin pulled across Jalen's features. "Perhaps I'll attend."

"Just don't blow my cover," Noah said. "Entertainment is great, but this is about the kids, not me."

"I'll do nothing of the sort, I assure you. It's much more interesting to watch the dominoes fall on their own volition—and fall they will. I'll tail you for a bit longer. I'm rather interested to see what else you're going to be teaching those students of yours. Just don't expect me to interfere if things go south."

"I don't," Noah said, stepping back onto his flying sword. "By the way, where'd you even come from? Did you just teleport right to us?"

"I followed you through the transport cannon," Jalen replied. "Interesting little place. Haven't used transportation like that in some time."

"Tim sent you after us?"

"Tim?" Jalen laughed. "Ah. Yes, I suppose so. He needed a little persuading."

"You didn't hurt him, did you?" Noah's tone darkened, and Jalen didn't miss the shift in his stance.

"I don't go around assaulting people for fun," Jalen said through a derisive snort. "The old man is fine. I'm *far* more interested in these students of yours, Vermil. I'm very curious to see what they're capable of."

"Just don't go breaking anything," Noah warned. "I like them in one piece, but I've got some more I need to cover before the training for today is done."

"Me? Break something?" Jalen flashed Noah a sharklike grin. "I'd never do anything of the sort."

Chapter Sixty-Seven

Noah and Jalen returned to find that Lee had taken over the class and had everyone stretching in positions that looked like they definitely shouldn't have been possible for any human to achieve without snapping a few tendons.

"Well, this is horrifying," Jalen observed. "What are you doing to your students, Vermil?"

"Don't look at me. This is all Lee."

"We're stretching," Lee filled in, turning her head a full one hundred and eighty degrees to look straight back at them like an owl. "Thanks for the orange juice, by the way. Do you have more?"

Jalen nearly choked on his own saliva as he tried to suppress his laughter. "No. I do not carry around bottles of orange juice."

"Oh." Lee frowned, then turned her head back—but she rotated it the wrong way, finishing the full circle instead of following the path she'd taken to look at them. "You should."

Jalen looked from Lee to Noah, then shook his head. "Your criticism has been duly noted and ignored."

"Orange juice or not, some proper introductions are in order," Noah said.

"If that's an excuse to stop stretching, I'm taking it," Todd said, unwrapping himself and clambering to his feet. He brushed the grass off his pants and shook himself off, as if trying to throw the memory of what he'd just had to do to the side. "I'm Todd."

"This is—"

"Jalen. Just Jalen," Jalen said, cutting Noah off before he could even properly start his introduction. Noah caught himself as a small frown passed over his face.

Jalen wants to hide the fact that he's the Linwick Family Head? I mean, I won't blow his cover, but I didn't think he'd be concerned with keeping students from finding out who he is. Maybe he doesn't want to get stuck signing autographs or something. He's got the wrong idea of who these kids are if he thinks they'll give a shit about the Linwick family, though.

"Pleasure," Isabel said, standing up along with everyone other than James. Her tone was considerably less friendly than Todd's was, though not so far as to be rude. She'd raised her guard. "I'm Isabel, and the one who's pretending to sleep is James."

Alexandra gave Jalen a small nod but made no move to introduce herself.

"And I'm Emily," the Torrin girl finished, nudging James not-so-gently with the tip of her foot. He mumbled something under his breath and made absolutely no move to stand up. Emily let out an exasperated sigh. "Sorry. He's unbelievably lazy."

"I can respect that," Jalen said with a smirk. "Don't mind me. Vermil and I are just old friends. Very close. Practically attached at the hip. Please, continue with your lessons and pretend that I'm not here."

You're laying it on way too thick. We've played darts once.

"Right," Noah said, clearing his throat to get everyone's attention back on him. He couldn't help but notice that Moxie hadn't said much to Jalen. She was probably still pretty pissed about how Jalen had functionally kidnapped him, and Noah didn't blame her. If he'd been in her shoes, he'd have been furious. "Let's get back on with the lesson, shall we? There's more to cover today, and I've got an announcement for the end of class."

"Why'd you have to tell us now?" Todd asked. "Now I want to know the announcement. Are we getting a pizza party?"

"You'll find out at the end of class."

"I think it's a pizza party," Lee said.

"It's not a pizza party," Noah said. "Now pair up with someone you haven't sparred with yet. We're sparring again."

* * *

Jalen's face was externally flat, but his heart was beating harder in his chest than it had been the last time he'd tried to ask a woman out to dinner—and that had been just about three hundred years ago.

The woman in question had promptly rejected him and had evidently been so motivated to escape his presence that she promptly vanished into secluded meditation to try and advance to Rank 7.

Then she'd vanished.

For that matter, he hadn't really been all that excited at the time. But this—this was excitement. It took every single fiber of self-control Jalen had to keep his expression under control. Vermil was teaching children Formations—and somehow, he was actually succeeding.

Jalen had lost count of the number of times noble families had tried to make themselves Formation Masters. He'd lost count on the trail of corpses their attempts had left in their wake. Every single attempt had failed miserably.

All the kids that had managed to show any aptitude for Formations never managed to progress their runes far enough to actually make use of it, and the noble houses had always pushed them too hard.

The results had been one of the reasons he'd stepped back from his spot as the proper head of the Linwick family. Jalen hadn't lived to his age without doing a few things he regretted, and allowing any of those programs to continue within the walls of his family was paramount among them.

And yet—somehow—a mere Rank 4 had done what he hadn't been able to. Before him were five burgeoning Formation Masters. There wasn't any magic in the patterns they were drawing, but even the motions held power.

The urge to grab Vermil by the shoulders and shake the secrets out of him hung tantalizingly in Jalen's mind, but he repressed it. This was more than mere Formations. The students weren't using music. They weren't using runes at all.

This should be impossible. How does he understand Formations this well? Was Vermil a survivor of one of the noble family programs? I know for a fact that the Linwicks gave up on artificially manufacturing Formation Masters a long time ago.

Jalen watched Vermil teach his class silently. They were sparring again, but the more he watched, the more convinced he became that there was no noble family backing Vermil. He knew too much.

Every single one of his students was doing their own unique pattern, and Vermil was still able to give them advice. He understood Formations with a degree that a Rank 4 never should have.

I'll be damned. He's the closest thing to a Formation Master I've seen at his rank. That makes absolutely no sense. Anyone who spends that much time studying Formations should have a horrible basis of runes. Nobody has the time to perfectly refine and combine their runes as well as understand the intricacies of Formations.

But if he didn't, there would be no way for him to teach these kids to this degree. He's going from understanding, not by reciting textbooks—and by the Damned Plains, he doesn't even realize how ridiculous this is.

We aren't anywhere near close enough for him to be willing to comfortably share this information with me. He should be restraining himself, limiting the information I can get so that...

Jalen's face paled. Vermil wasn't stupid. He'd gathered that much from the conversation they'd had. Vermil *was* restraining himself. There was no way he'd be revealing the full extent of his knowledge to someone that was a potential threat watching them, even if they'd come to a truce.

I'll be damned. Who is he?

Jalen was shaken from his thoughts by a finger prodding his side. The motion was so surprising that he nearly doubled over in surprise. Vermil aside, he couldn't remember the last time someone had dared to speak to him without a waver in their voice, much less prod him.

He turned to see the short girl that had been leading the stretches standing before him, her wide eyes boring up into his without an ounce of fear or concern.

Lee, her name was? Interesting. Why is it that absolutely none of Vermil's party have even the slightest amount of fear? This is... refreshing. She's staring at me like I'm a slice of meat, though. Can't say I enjoy it.

"Yes?"

"Are you sure you don't have any orange juice?" Lee asked. "I smell it on you."

Jalen's eye twitched. He did, in fact, have a small bottle of it in his pouch, but that was for lunch. He sniffed the air, but there was absolutely no trace of it anywhere. The damn bottle was sealed. It should have been impossible for—

Lee had somehow already unhooked the latch on Jalen's bag and was ruffling through it without a care in the world. Jalen stared at her in abject disbelief. She hadn't hesitated for a second.

A second later, Lee found the bottle and pulled it out. "Here it is. You must have forgotten you had it."

"I—"

"Were you going to drink this?" Lee asked, already pulling the cork off with two fingers. She held the cork up, studying it for a moment before sniffing at the bottom.

"At some point, yes. That's generally why someone carries something around."

Lee put the cork into her mouth and chewed once before swallowing. Her nose scrunched in distaste. "That wasn't very good. A bit spongy."

What in the Damned Plains is happening?

Jalen started to laugh. He couldn't help himself. It felt like he'd stepped into a different dimension. A girl half his height and a thousandth of his power had just robbed him while looking him straight in the face.

By the time he'd mustered himself again, Lee had eaten—not drunk—the entire bottle. She licked her lips and grinned at him. "Thanks. I like the way it crunches."

She headed back to the rest of the group and poked Todd in the back as she passed him, causing him to trip over his own feet and fall face first on the ground. Todd lunged forward and grabbed Lee's ankle, pulling her down with him as the others all burst into laughter.

Jalen was confident Lee could have avoided the attack if she'd wanted to. He'd seen her glance down and notice Todd's lunge. Her reaction speed was ridiculous for a Rank 3. She'd *chosen* to let Todd grab her, likely to motivate his studies.

It wasn't just Lee—something about Vermil's entire group felt... different. He couldn't quite place what it was, but it was more than just the Formations. They had power, yes, but there was more to it.

"What do you think?" Jalen was pulled from his thoughts as Moxie walked up beside him, her arms crossed. He could feel the muted hostility from the woman, even though she was doing a fairly good job at concealing it.

She's mad that I took Vermil away to speak with him? I'm still not sure why a Torrin cares so deeply for a Linwick. It makes absolutely no sense. If it had been someone from my generation, sure. I've had my share of fun with the Torrins—they can do some great stuff with those vines. But now? The families hate each other so much that I can't see how they even would have met.

"It... interesting," Jalen said, choosing his words carefully. Everything he told Moxie would doubtlessly go straight to Vermil, and he didn't want to sour the relationship. Vermil was more than just interesting. He was fascinating. "I haven't seen anything like this taught before."

"No," Moxie agreed. "It's unique to Vermil. We'd like it to stay that way."

Is a Rank 3 warning me off? When she knows who I am? Marvelous.

"Not a word will leave my mouth," Jalen promised, and he genuinely meant it. Something as rare as this could not be permitted to fall into the hands of the moronic noble families—his own included. It would only be wasted. "I am only here to observe, as I told Vermil."

"You aren't helping with our little... problem, then?" Moxie asked, tilting her head to the side.

"A flower that cannot grow on its own will wither and die when abandoned."

"And all the hot air you're blowing up your own ass might come out your mouth," Moxie countered. "People are going to get killed because some psychopath is obsessed with my family. You can do something about it."

"I could, but that would rob you of the experience of doing it yourself."

"And it could end in someone here dying."

That... would actually be quite a shame. I won't handle Vermil's problems for him, though. It will stunt his growth.

"It may," Jalen allowed. "Many people die. And you do realize that, if I directly interfere, the others of my generation will be liable to do the same? It could make the situation worse."

"I'm not asking you to kill the asshole for us," Moxie said. "But finding a little information shouldn't be impossible for you. Vermil might not care about letting you watch this class, but I'm well aware just how valuable what you're seeing here is. You're in his debt."

Well, damn. She's right.

A smile flitted across Jalen's lips. "You might be one of the boldest Torrins I've ever seen. How'd you meet Vermil?"

"What does that have to do with anything?"

"Answer the question if you want my help."

Moxie pressed her lips together, then sighed. "I insulted him in the library."

Jalen cackled. "Somehow, that doesn't surprise me in the slightest. Very well. I will look into this—but nothing more. Satisfied?"

Moxie tilted her head to the side, then gave him a short nod. "No, but it'll do. Don't kidnap Vermil again. I don't care who you are. If you're going to pretend to be our ally, then act like it."

And, in that moment, Jalen finally realized what feeling the group had been giving him. The amount of care they all showed for each other, and the ferocity that had no power to back it up other than will— they weren't just a random assortment of mages. They saw each other as a family.

This is what we started the noble houses for.

"You know what?" Jalen asked. "I'll keep that in mind."

Chapter Sixty-Eight

The rest of the class passed quickly, and the time for them to wrap things up soon came. Noah was pretty happy with how things had gone. Even with the wrench that Jalen's appearance had thrown into his plans, it didn't seem like anything had gone awry.

Jalen seemed generally interested in his students and didn't look like he'd be messing with any of them, and he didn't even appear to suspect too much about his teaching methods or contents.

It's definitely a good thing I toned things down. If I started going on about giving a Master Rune away or any of the slightly more detailed things I had planned, he might have picked something up.

But, as things are now, it looks like he's pretty much just watching what's happening and isn't all that more interested than he would be in anything else.

Noah gathered everyone up when there were just a few minutes left before the transport cannon was due to kick back on and draw them back to Arbitage.

"Are you finally going to tell us the announcement?" Todd asked. "Because I've barely been able to concentrate. You can't just dangle something like that over a man's head. It's not right."

"Your complaints have been duly noted and ignored," Noah said without missing a beat. "But yes, it's time for the announcement. It's about the advanced track."

"Did our acceptances get rescinded?" Alexandra asked. "That wouldn't surprise me in the slightest."

"What? No."

"Did they decide to give us a bunch of runes because of how cool we are?" Todd asked.

"Also no."

"They're throwing us a pizza party?" Moxie asked.

"No! Why—" Noah cut himself off and spun to look at Moxie, who wasn't even bothering to hide the grin on her face. "Don't join them! You already know the bloody announcement!"

"Well, get on with it then."

Noah rolled his eyes. "I was getting there, if you'd stop throwing guesses out and give me a second to speak. We've all been invited to meet the rest of the advanced track tonight. Something like a welcoming party."

"So they are throwing us a pizza party!" Isabel pointed out.

"It's not a pizza—oh, whatever," Noah grumbled, throwing his hands up in defeat. "Either way, it's exciting. You should all look forward to it. But, at the same time, don't forget where it is we'll be or who is there with us."

"You're saying you think it'll be another test of some sort?" Alexandra asked, her brow furrowing.

"I don't know if it'll expressly be a test, but you can assume that they'll be paying very close attention to all of us. We're all going to need to put on the appropriate behavior and ensure we make the right impression."

"Isn't the saying putting on our best behavior?" Isabel asked, tilting her head to the side.

Noah grinned. "Yes."

"I take it you didn't misspeak, then."

"No," Noah replied. "I did not."

* * *

Several hours later, after everyone had returned to Arbitage and spent some time decompressing and getting ready, they all met back up in front of Moxie's room in Building T.

They were all greeted by Vermil in his best pair of clothes, which happened to be identical to nearly every other pair of clothes he wore. He chewed on a strip of jerky as he watched all the students pile in, nodding to them as they showed up.

Moxie had donned her fur cloak and wore her normal uniform beneath it. Beside her were two hooded figures. The first wore a gnarled wooden mask, and the second simply had his hood pulled low over his head to hide his features.

"Is everyone ready?" Vermil asked, stretching his arms above his head and yawning. He sniffed at his clothes, then scrunched his nose. "When was the last time these were washed?"

Moxie flicked him in the back of the head. "Yesterday. At least try to act presentable, won't you?"

"Right. Sorry."

"So... what do we do?" Todd asked. "Just sit around here and wait?"

"Yeah. I'm assuming that someone should pop up soon enough to take us," Moxie said with a shrug. "Don't get impatient. If they're anything like the other nobles I know, then we might end up waiting around a bit."

"I'd like to see them try," Jalen growled from the darkness of his hood. "I don't like being kept waiting."

"Please don't destroy the advanced track," Moxie said politely. "We need it in one piece."

"Ah, right. I'm not going to interfere. I did say that," Jalen said, but it sounded more like he was trying to convince himself than anyone else.

Mercifully, they didn't have to wait long to find out if he would be true to his word. After just a few more minutes, hurried footsteps echoed down the hall, and everyone turned as Ulya appeared down the bend, her back pressed to the stone.

The bags under her eyes hadn't abided in the slightest. If anything, they'd grown deeper. Her skin was a shade paler than it should have been, and her nails had been picked raw. She looked horrible.

As soon as she spotted the masked man at the back of the group, some of the tension eased out of her shoulders. Her fingers ran over the hilt of a dagger at her side, and she swallowed.

"Vermil. Everyone. Pleasure to see you. I'm here with the advanced track."

"You look like shit," Vermil said.

"Thank you," Ulya said, her lips pressed so flat that they were nearly white. "I need to check you all, if you don't mind."

"I already checked them," Vermil said, taking a step forward. "No need. You can check me if you absolutely have to, but have you really been living like this?"

"Yes," Ulya said curtly. Vermil turned and pulled his hair back so Ulya could make a small incision at the back of his neck. She let out a small breath and stepped back. "You're absolutely sure they're safe?"

"Yes. They're fine. Have you even met anyone since we last spoke? Or have you been hiding away?"

"Does it matter?"

"I suppose it doesn't, but you should be careful. You might end up getting yourself killed if you're so tired that you can't react properly."

"Your concern is appreciated," Ulya said, not sounding like she appreciated it in the slightest. She sheathed her dagger and jerked her chin over her shoulder. "Let's go."

They all followed her out of the building and along Arbitage's streets.

As they walked, Ulya fell in closer to Vermil and sent a glance over her shoulder at the hooded figures taking up the back of the party. "I recognize your teacher. Who's the other one?"

"His friend," Vermil replied.

Ulya's eyebrows lifted ever so slightly. "Equally as powerful?"

"Yes, but he's not going to be doing anything to help. My teacher might not as well, but the other one is purely here just to observe."

"He's trustworthy?"

"I dare you to tell him he can't come. He's a Rank 6, and a strong one."

Ulya grimaced, then inclined her head. "I was prepared for as much. I'll handle things, then. Stick close to me once we're there. I haven't been able to check anyone other than you lot and Gero, and I won't have seen Gero in the time it took me to come get you."

Vermil just inclined his head, and the rest of the trip went quietly. After about thirty minutes of walking, they'd left the main grounds of the school behind and made their way deep into the city. Ulya brought them several alleyways, then up to an inconspicuous door in a plain stone wall.

She pulled it open, revealing a well-lit stairwell leading underground, then started down without a second of hesitation. Everyone piled in behind her, the masked figures keeping their spots at the rear of the party and closing the door behind them after they entered.

It only took a few more minutes to reach the bottom of the stairs, but the sound of muted chatter and clinking silverware heralded their trip down. About a dozen people sat in a large, circular room with along a table that split the room nearly in half.

The majority of the chairs at the table were empty, and everyone sitting at it sat in very distinct groups. Even within the advanced track, it was pretty evident that not everyone was on the exact same page.

As soon as people spotted the group enter, much of the conversation fell silent. Everyone turned toward them, and a tall man sitting at the end of the table rose. He had a neatly trimmed gray beard and toned muscles covered by red velvet clothes emblazed with a golden heron.

The man spread his hands out, a smile crossing over his lips in greeting. "Ah. Ulya has returned with the newly accepted members of our program. Welcome, all. Please, sit and enjoy some food. We'll get to business shortly, but there's no need to cloud our enjoyment of the night too early."

He seemed perfectly friendly, and the wide grin on his lips was earnest. Even though he was dressed in gaudy, expensive clothes, the wrinkles at the corners of his eyes showed that he was often locked in a perpetual smile.

There was just one slight problem.

The man didn't have a heartbeat.

Chapter Sixty-Nine

U lya felt like her eyes were about to pop out of her head. They ached something furious from constantly looking around, staring at anyone that seemed like they were getting too close for comfort.

Every single shadow felt like it was just inches from jumping out to grab her, and she was pretty sure half of the feast on the table was moving. She could barely remember the last time she'd gotten a proper night's sleep even though it had probably only been a day or two ago.

The only person she knew was safe was Vermil. If she trusted his word, then the rest of his group was probably fine as well, but there was no way to know if he'd actually tested all of them. The smug bastard barely even looked concerned about the whole situation.

As soon as Godrick had told everyone to eat, he'd promptly darted right over to the table, shoved Gero out of the way, and started shoveling food into his mouth.

His students had done much of the same, though at least a few of them had been polite enough to spend a little time greeting Gero. Nobody else from the advanced track made any moves to introduce themselves yet—a fact that Ulya was thankful for.

The tension hanging in the room meant nobody was getting too close to her. She couldn't just go around cutting the backs of everyone's necks to test them. The others would have assumed she was insane at best.

Ulya bit her lower lip, moving to put her back against the wall so she could observe the entire room. Before she could get far, Vermil's mentor stepped into her path. Ulya paused as she felt his gaze fix on hers from behind the whorls of his wooden mask.

"Who's the big guy?" the man asked, nodding over Ulya's shoulder to Godrick.

"That's the second-strongest member of the advanced track. His name is Godrick, and he's a Rank 5," Ulya replied, sending a glance toward the burly man. He'd sat back down at the head of the table and was happily eating away, chatting with Verrud, another one of the professors in the program. "Why do you ask?"

"Curiosity," the man said. The hooded man that had accompanied them walked up to join Ulya, glancing around the room and yawning in clear boredom.

"I hope you're going to make this more exciting soon."

Exciting? I certainly hope not. I'd kill for a nice, peaceful night of rest where I'm not worried about a puppet ripping me apart from within.

"We'll see," Vermil's mentor said with a one-shouldered shrug. "I'd request that you avoid taking steps to remedy that yourself, though."

"Me? I would never," the hooded figure said, pressing a hand to his chest and letting out a chuckle. Ulya sent a faint tendril of magic out to feel how strong the man was, but it evaporated the literal instant she tried to manifest it.

Why is Vermil's mentor letting his domain seep out like this? Is he trying to piss everyone off?

Sure enough, there were more than a few peeved looks being sent their way. Generally, it was polite to keep your domain under control unless one was in a combat situation. Letting it roll across the room without any attempt to even control it was a blatant challenge to every single member of the advanced track.

"I'm not sure we were ever properly introduced," Ulya said, pushing down her apprehension. Puppets didn't have domains, which meant that even if he was rude, the man was probably safe. "You know my name, but I never found out yours. Is there something I can call you by?"

It was a moment before Vermil's mentor responded, "Spider."

"Spider?" the hooded man asked through an amused snort. "That's cute."

"I didn't come up with it."

"I'd certainly hope not. I'd much rather be something more interesting. A butterfly, maybe. Oh! A hummingbird. Ever seen one of those? Fascinating creatures, really. It's unfortunate they're so rare. I'd imagine it's because the stupid things hum so much that they probably accidentally set off Formations and blow themselves up."

Spider turned to his friend, tilting his head in what was either confusion or shock. Ulya couldn't figure out which one it was past his mask.

"Truly?"

"Oh, yes. They've got runes, most of them. Unfortunately, not every song is suited to be a Formation. Leads to quite the spectacular show when one of them lets a little too much magical energy into their singing. One moment, it's beauty incarnate. The next, you're cleaning pint-sized guts off your face."

"Fate is cruel," Spider said. "By the way—this is Ulya. I don't believe I properly introduced her."

"Splendid. You can call me Jay," the hooded man said.

Ulya held her hand out. Jay looked down at it, then back up at her. "No thanks. I'll be honest; I've forgotten your name already. I'll remember it if you do something to keep my attention."

This guy is definitely an old bastard. I've seen that attitude before. Who in the Damned Plains is Vermil? How does he have the backing of not just his teacher but also another Rank 6?

"You don't have to look so stressed," Spider said, scratching the side of his neck and looking around the room. "There's only one person here that's a clone."

Ulya nearly choked on her saliva. "What? I—how—"

"There are ways to tell," Spider said with a low chuckle. He paused as Vermil grabbed an entire roast chicken and—to the utter bafflement of the entire room, shoved the entire thing down his gullet in a single move.

There were several seconds of silence, broken by a round of applause that started with Gero and wrapped its way around the room. Spider heaved a sigh. "Idiot."

"That was a little impressive," Ulya hedged, forgetting what they'd been talking about a moment before—but only for a mere instant. "Wait. You said you could detect the clones?"

"Yes. It's rather simple, actually. I can't tell you how, though." Spider gave her an apologetic shrug.

"What? Why not?" Ulya demanded. "If you've got a way—"

"I've learned more information about our opponent, and I have reason to believe that any information spoken aloud has a good chance of reaching his ears. For that reason, you'll just have to trust me."

Ulya bit back a snarky response. The one person she couldn't afford to offend in the room was Spider. She was pretty sure he'd kill her at the drop of a hat, and he'd only shown up as a favor to her in the first place. Talking back to him now was a foolish of an idea.

"I see," Ulya said, crushing the disappointment in her voice. "Who's the clone? We need to..."

Actually, what would we even do? Accuse them? I have no idea how many clones are around. Accusing him could turn this into a slaughter. Nobody's ready for a fight, and if I go around secretly alerting people, half of them won't believe me or think it's some form of ploy. Damn it.

"We need to what?" Spider asked. "I'd say acting is directly against our best interests."

"It is?" Ulya frowned. "Why?"

"Because as long as we don't make a move, we have the upper hand. We know who to suspect and they have no idea we suspect them. That means we should be able to trace the clone back to the source or otherwise get rid of any other clones."

"You mean through some form of sympathetic magic?" Ulya considered Spider's words, then nodded slowly. "That makes a lot of sense. That's genius, actually. I wish we had an Inquisitor with us. Their Blood Magic excels at sympathetic purposes. I've heard they can take out portions of bloodlines if they're strong enough."

"Do our targets even have blood?" Spider asked.

Ulya opened her mouth, then closed it again. "Oh. Yeah. Good point. I didn't think that through—but there should still be some form of Sympathetic Magic that could work. I think you're onto something."

"Perhaps you should look into that," Spider suggested. "Until then, just stay by Jay's side. He's an asshole, but he'll probably keep you alive."

That was possibly the least convincing thing that Spider could have said. Ulya caught a flash of a cold grin beneath Jay's hood that didn't make her feel even slightly reassured. It looked more like Jay was hoping she'd trip and faceplant on the table.

A few cheers rose into the air as Vermil devoured another roast chicken—along with the plate that it was on. Ulya stared in disbelief, then risked a glance at Spider. She still couldn't tell what the man was thinking, but she suspected he was one step from blowing steam out of his ears.

Vermil is certainly making an impression. I didn't think he'd be this much of a party animal, but I suppose some of the rumors going around campus about him were right. At least he hasn't made any moves toward the other female professors or their students. Maybe Moxie straightened him out?

The commotion died down as footsteps echoed down the stairwell behind them. Everyone other than Vermil, who was occupied dragging another professor's plate over to himself with two fingers, turned toward the stairwell.

Metallic clicks accompanied every step, and it wasn't long before two people made their way down the stairs. A large, uncomfortable-looking boy took the lead, his hands shoved deep into his pockets and his shoulders hunched.

Behind him strode Silvertide, his leg glistening in the faint light with every step he took. Ulya shot a glance at Spider to see if he'd reacted negatively to the new arrivals, but his stance hadn't shifted.

That means he's probably not a clone, right? Who am I kidding—if someone took out Silvertide, we'd all be doomed. Thank whatever gods are listening. Having Silvertide here changes everything in our favor.

"Silvertide!" Godrick exclaimed, raising a hand and beaming. "We were all thrilled to hear you accepted the invitation to join us. That must be your apprentice with you—Tyler, was it?"

Silvertide clapped Tyler on the shoulder. The boy's back was as stiff as a rod, and his face was ghostly pale. "We appreciate the invite. I'm looking forward to seeing what you all have to offer."

Ulya's brow furrowed as she watched Silvertide speak. Something about the demeanor of his apprentice was off. Everything she'd heard about Silvertide said that he was a great teacher and a kind man.

Sure, there was a chance it had been a rumor, but Tyler looked terrified.

"Is Peter with you?" Godrick asked when Silvertide and Tyler stepped off the stairs and into the room. "He was meant to escort you here."

"Peter?" Silvertide tilted his head to the side. His eyes lit up with understanding and he nodded. "Ah, Peter. That was the man that came to bring us to the advanced track meeting, was it?"

"Yes, that was him."

"I'm afraid not," Silvertide said with a frown. "It would have been rather difficult for Peter to make it."

"Why's that?" Godrick asked. "He said he'd be open. Did he give you a message? Everyone that wasn't currently out on a trip or otherwise tied up was meant to come to meet the new members today. He should have known that."

"He didn't give me a message," Silvertide said, tapping his staff on the ground. There was something brownish on its tip. Ulya squinted closer at it, then paled. It wasn't brown. It was dark green plant matter.

"I would have been quite impressed if Peter had said anything at all," Silvertide continued, his gaze cold. "After all, I've found that the dead typically don't speak—and the person using magic to puppet his body certainly wasn't Peter. Would someone care to explain to me why your group sent a corpse to my apprentice's door?"

Chapter Seventy

Noah wasn't sure if he wanted to burst into laughter or slap his forehead. He'd been so proud of his on-the-fly plan. He had a lead, and, at least as far as he was aware, Godrick had absolutely no idea that Noah knew about his lack of a heartbeat.

All he'd have had to do was get closer to Godrick during the party and then find a way to trace him back to the other clones. Ulya's mention of something called Sympathetic Magic sounded like it would have been promising as well.

None of that was going to work out if Silvertide kicked down the door, frothing at the lips. Granted, that would have been the exact strategy Noah would have used himself in nine out of ten other situations, but now that he was the one trying to do a little maneuvering, he felt self-righteous enough to ignore that particular fact.

The entire room stared at Silvertide in a mixture of confusion, shock, and fear. Conversation had dropped to complete silence—at least from everyone aside from Vermil, who was quietly sliding food into his mouth and swallowing without chewing.

"You killed Peter?" Godrick asked, his expression turning dark as his hands clenched at his sides.

"Me? No. He was dead before he ever showed up. The only thing I saw of Peter today was his corpse," Silvertide said. His eyes swept over the room, pausing for an instant as they passed over Vermil. They flicked over to Noah, then to Jalen.

"Was it an undead?" another professor that Noah didn't know the name of asked. "Or a Skinwalker?"

"It shouldn't have been a Skinwalker. That problem vanished quite some time ago," Godrick said, his brow furrowing. He drew in a deep breath and let it out in a sigh. "This is ill news. He was a good man."

It only took a brief glance at Ulya's face to tell Noah that she didn't particularly agree. She didn't seem too distraught about Peter's death, but the stress had clearly taken a massive toll on her. Noah was pretty sure she was a strong breeze away from collapsing.

Godrick doesn't seem to be taking the news of this too poorly. Wizen is obviously a good liar, though. Maybe he's planning to play the impartial card or the like to avoid getting suspicion on himself?

"I'm sure he was, but we've got a bigger problem than the dead," Silvertide said, tapping his cane on the ground at his feet. "Namely, the living. I've always been liable to assume that trouble comes with more than one incident. I don't suppose anyone is aware of what may have happened? Unless this was an intentional test of some sort?"

Glances were passed around the room, but nobody spoke. It was pretty evident that Peter hadn't been meant to show up dead. And, even if he had, Noah suspected the advanced track professors weren't about to say anything otherwise.

"Did you recall what kind of runes were being used to puppet Peter?" Godrick asked with a frown. "That could help us narrow down who we're dealing with."

Several people turned toward Ulya. She held them, not giving any ground.

"Plant Runes of some sort. High-rank ones, likely around five or six."

The people that had turned to Ulya all looked away. Her abilities were evidently pretty well known, and she didn't have anything in the form of plant magic.

"I don't believe we have any Plant Magic users in the advanced track," Godrick said with a concerned frown. "Perhaps that's a good thing. I would prefer to be against an external opponent rather than an internal one."

No shit. That's because you're the bloody opponent.

"Unless they're working with one of us," Gero observed idly from where he sat at the table. "We have no way to know. Who would send someone after Silvertide, though? Nobody here should be that stupid."

Of that, everyone seemed to agree. Nods went around the room, but it didn't do anything to ease the tension surrounding them.

"What happened to Peter's body?" another professor asked. "Is there anything left that we can study? Was the puppet convincing?"

"Very convincing," Silvertide said with a nod. "And there is, unfortunately, nothing left of his body. You'll have to take my word for it."

"If it was convincing, how did you survive?" Gero asked. "Even as strong as you are, a Rank 6 mage getting the drop on you should be enough to do some serious damage."

Silvertide nodded thoughtfully. "Yes, I suppose it should have been."

There were several seconds of silence. Gero cleared his throat. "You didn't answer the question."

"Oh, did I not? I believed the answer was implicit. He did not injure me because I was simply better than my assailant."

Noah nearly choked on laughter, but Jalen was far less subtle. His cackle rang out through the room, drawing everyone's eyes straight to them. Godrick tilted his head to the side.

"I don't believe we were introduced. Remind me who you are?"

"Just a traveler," Jalen replied with a wave of his hand. "I'm with the brat's group and I don't have any Plant Runes, so no need to try to strip me with your eyes."

"I think we can judge that ourselves," Godrick said as he started to rise from his chair. His tone wasn't aggressive, but there was a line of steel in his words.

"It wasn't him," Silvertide said, raising a hand before Godrick could make any moves. "I can assure you of that."

Godrick paused, then lowered himself back down and inclined his head. "Very well. Do you happen to have a suggestion for what we should do, then? I can't imagine you'd just barge in here without a plan."

"Of course not," Silvertide said with a chuckle. "Puppets are still puppets, and I don't believe the controller is in the room with us. It should be a fairly straightforward—though perhaps not easy—task to root them out."

Root them out—was that a pun?

"Please say more," Godrick said with a distressed frown. "This was meant to be a day of celebration, and yet I've found that not one but two of our members have been killed already."

"Wait, two?" The man beside Godrick spun to look at him in surprise. "Who was the second?"

"I was going to properly address it at a later time, but Will was also killed. Gero reported his death earlier today," Godrick said, working his jaw in anger. "We're all aware of the risks that come with pushing ourselves to be more than others, but it has been some time since two of our members were killed in such quick succession."

"Some time? I'd say," another professor said as she crossed her arms. "Granted, Will wasn't a combatant. I assume he was killed in the same manner?"

"He was," Gero confirmed. "But, as tragic as the loss was, it doesn't get us any closer to solving the issue at hand. If Silvertide has a method to locate the attacker, we should use it. I've been completely at my wits end."

"I'm not so sure I'm willing to skip past the fact that nobody mentioned anything until now," the professor beside Godrick said, glaring at Gero. "Why didn't you say anything? Maybe you're the one that killed him."

"Because it would have devolved into a slew of accusations just like that one, Verrud," Gero said, his tone dry. "I'm aware how difficult subtlety can be for you, but not everything needs to be handled with the grace of a stampeding monster horde."

The entire room erupted into conversation as people started to take sides. It only managed to go on for a few seconds before a loud bang echoed out, silencing everyone. Godrick lifted his clenched fist from the table, his expression flat.

"Which is why we should shut up and hear what Silvertide has to say. He may be a new member of the advanced track, but I think everyone here is more than aware of just how capable he is. We will not devolve into an argument like a group of unruly children."

Nobody said another word, but Noah's confusion grew. Godrick had done exactly what a proper leader would have, but that didn't line up. He *was* the puppet. His goal should have been to take away from

Silvertide's legitimacy by trying to poke holes in his claims or otherwise distracting the other professors.

Noah could have seen an argument for the whole thing being a huge ruse to lower their guard—but that would have been unbelievably stupid. Silvertide had basically revealed he knew how to identify the puppets, so he'd probably be able to find out that Godrick was fake.

And, since Godrick had just said to listen to Silvertide, he'd have no way to refuse or try to back out if Silvertide accused him of anything.

Is Wizen dumber than we thought? Or am I just missing the angle he's playing at?

"Thank you, Godrick," Silvertide said. "Fortunately for all of us, I am relatively adept at dealing with plant mages. This isn't the first time I've dealt with one that used puppets, and I am capable of identifying their puppets without too much difficulty."

"The first thing we should do is clear the room, then," Verrud said, his beady eyes lighting up. "Brilliant. Check us. Nobody make any sudden moves."

"Exactly my plan," Silvertide said. "Remain where you are. Tyler, stay at the stairwell. If anyone tries to run past you—well, let them. They won't make it far."

Everyone remained locked in place while Silvertide started walking through the room, pausing as he passed by each individual person.

I have to be missing something. Not knowing what it is that Wizen wants is completely throwing me for a loop here. I can't tell what his goals are with the advanced track or with Godrick—and I don't know what the hell Silvertide is doing either.

Silvertide is far from stupid. He wouldn't play his cards like this unless he had a really good reason to. Why blow our cover? I just don't get it.

Silvertide's expression held no answers in it. He made his way across the room, continuing on until he stood before Godrick. Noah reached for his runes. One way or another, things were about to go south.

"Well?" Verrud asked. "What did you find?"

"There's a puppet in this room," Silvertide said, raising a finger.

"But it isn't a plant puppet. It's a metal one, and it appears to be unrelated to any plant magic."

"That would be mine," Ulya said, her voice strained. "Are you sure there aren't any other puppets?"

"No," Silvertide said, stepping away from Godrick and shaking his head. "There are not."

Wait, what?

Chapter Seventy-One

"That's a relief," Godrick said, leaning back in his chair. He drummed his fingers on the table and tapped his foot on the ground. "It means everyone in the room right now is safe—but it doesn't give us a good solution to the problem."

"Which is for the best," Silvertide said.

"What? How is that good?" Verrud asked, rising from his chair and crossing his arms behind his back. "Even if you have a way to detect the puppets, the rest of us don't. We're also clearly getting targeted for some reason."

"Are you getting targeted, or is our opponent simply after stronger mages and you fit the bill?" Silvertide queried, raising a finger into the air to forestall any further questions. "Either way, it doesn't matter. As I'm sure you all know, letting news about this out would cause panic and do nothing but make it harder to trace the roots of our target."

"We can't exactly sit around and do nothing," Gero said. He picked up a piece of chicken and took a large bite out of it—bone and all—before Vermil could mow through all the food around them. He continued to speak with a full mouth. "Something has to be done."

"Something will be done," Silvertide said. "But this is a job for a surgeon, not a swarm of blundering fools."

"Are you volunteering?" Godrick asked.

"I am. I have extensive experience dealing with threats such as this. I should be able to deal with this threat with the aid of a small team."

"What do the rest of us do, then?" a female professor with pure white hair asked. "You can't expect us to sit around and do nothing while there's a murderer running loose on campus."

"Do you really do anything that different normally?" Silvertide asked with a chuckle. "Just continue as you were and keep your guard up. These are puppets, not mages at your rank. They don't have any information about the person beyond what they can study. If you're aware of your surroundings and put a little thought into your actions, nobody should be caught by surprise."

A few murmurs passed through the room, but nobody spoke up immediately. Silvertide was acting as if the situation was little more than an inconvenience that had drawn his annoyance.

I'm pretty sure he's underplaying this a bit too much, and I still don't understand why he doesn't suspect Godrick. I'd almost wonder if Silvertide himself was a clone, but he still had a heartbeat, and he definitely recognized me. For now, I suppose I should just play along and see what he's aiming for.

"How long do you believe it would take you to handle this threat? If you're asking us all to stand down, there's only so long we can wait before it becomes unsustainable. Unless we're up against an entire group of mages, I refuse to be terrorized by a single opponent," Godrick said. "I'm willing to let you try things your way, but only if it solves the problem quickly."

"I can have this handled in a week," Silvertide said with a dismissive shrug. "And, so long as all of you actually use those heads you're so proud of, there shouldn't be any more deaths."

"A week? You can root out the mage in just a week?" Godrick asked, raising an eyebrow. He shrugged, then gave Silvertide a sharp nod. "Very well. I speak for all of us when I say you've got your week. I assume you wish us to maintain our normal activities?"

"Yes. The less our opponent knows about what we're doing, the better it will be," Silvertide confirmed. "I can assure you that this threat will be completely dealt with within seven days."

The other advanced track professors exchanged glances, but nobody spoke up. It looked like they were satisfied with going with whatever Godrick suggested—for the time being, at least. Even though nobody was speaking, the tension in the room was evident.

"In that case, for the time being, we will resume as we were," Godrick said. He paused for a few moments to gather himself. "I can honestly say that this is not how I saw today going. It is tragic to hear of Peter's passing, but we will continue on as we always have."

"At least he didn't have any students," Gero said through a mouthful of food.

Godrick shot Gero a glance out of the corner of his eye. "That did not make him any less of a valuable member of our group."

Gero shrugged in response, clearly unbothered by the loss of the other professor. Something told Noah that Gero wasn't particularly well liked. The man's abrasive personality was already grinding on his gears, and he hadn't even had a proper interaction with him yet.

I don't care much for the advanced track professors one way or another, but if you've been a part of the group for a while, shouldn't you at least pretend to care that one of your compatriots is dead?

I wonder who Peter was. Did he just end up in the wrong place at the wrong time like Ulya? Or was he targeted by Wizen intentionally?

It didn't seem like the answers to that were going to come tonight. The rest of the people in the room slowly resumed their activities, though an air of unease surrounded them. The only people in the advanced track that seemed completely unbothered were Godrick, Silvertide, and Gero.

But, even though there was definitely a good amount of concern, there was less than Noah had thought there would be. It seemed more like the room had been informed that they had a particularly troublesome exam coming up that they'd have to find out how to study for, not that there was a powerful mage lurking in the darkness to kill them and steal their bodies.

The students looked a little more worried than their respective professors, but that made sense. From what Noah had learned, the advanced track had dealt with some fairly significant issues before. This probably wasn't the most troublesome thing that happened to them—at least, not yet.

Silvertide made his way over to Noah, Tyler trailing his steps like a lost puppy. He looked so different from the last time that Noah had seen him that it felt like years had passed.

At least I didn't punch him this time around.

Noah kept his posture relaxed, but he made sure to keep his runes at the ready. He didn't know what was going on with Silvertide, but on the very small offchance that he'd somehow been corrupted or controlled, he wasn't about to be caught off guard.

"Quite the day, isn't it?" Silvertide asked casually, throwing a glance over his shoulder at Vermil as he continued to stuff his face full of food. "Though it seems like some of us are largely unaffected."

"That's just because he's crazy," Tyler muttered under his breath, though not quietly enough to avoid Noah's detection.

Moxie snickered beside Noah, and Tyler paled as he realized that he hadn't been nearly as quiet as he thought he had been. He looked back to Vermil to make sure that he hadn't been overheard, then shrank even deeper into Silvertide's shadow.

It wasn't particularly effective, considering he was nearly three heads taller than Silvertide was, but the attempt was there.

"Do you know anything about what we're up against?" Noah asked, choosing his words carefully to avoid giving too much away.

"I've fought my share of puppet users in my time," Silvertide said with a shrug. "I'd reckon I know as much as most. Enough to get by, and more than enough to take out someone wantonly attacking other people. I typically did this with more than one person, though. When you're fighting someone with a massive information network, having a few reliable backups is vital."

"I take it I'm being offered that position?"

"Indeed." The corner of Silvertide's mouth quirked up. "You, or whoever it is that you're pretending to be right now."

"Your disguise sucks," Jalen informed Noah. "Mine is much better."

"You don't even have one. The only reason that hood does anything is because nobody knows what you look like in the first place."

"Anonymity is the greatest disguise—and I'll have you know that at least a few people do know what I look like. I used to get around."

Noah suppressed the urge to roll his eyes. It wasn't like anybody was going to be able to easily tell what he was doing with them while the mask was on. "I'm not opposed to helping, but why me?"

"Because you're already wrapped up in it," Silvertide replied. "It's a powerful plant mage. Do you know the last time a powerful plant mage showed up that *wasn't* part of the Torrin family? I've got no better place to start working, and I imagine you'd be wherever Moxie ends up."

"Fair enough," Noah allowed. This was definitely Silvertide—which made it even more confusing as to what his goals were. He glanced around to make sure nobody was too close, then lowered his voice. "Why did you lie?"

"Lie?" Silvertide blinked. "What are you talking about?"

"About Godrick. You said there weren't any other puppets in the room, but he doesn't have a heartbeat. I'm pretty certain he's a puppet."

Silvertide let out a bark of suppressed laughter. "I can see how you'd come to that conclusion. You aren't technically wrong—Godrick doesn't have a heartbeat. That isn't because he's a puppet, though. It's because he doesn't have a heart."

"Something tells me you're not being metaphorical."

"Godrick and I go back quite some time. His heart was destroyed years ago in a really nasty fight, but he was fortunate enough to have a very talented Imbuer on his team. They managed to make an imbued heart that keeps him kicking, and his body is so adapted to it that trying to heal the damage with a potion is pointless at this point."

A flush of embarrassment reddened the back of Noah's neck. Of course he'd run into the one person who somehow didn't have a heart and wasn't a puppet the moment he'd come up with his new puppet-sensing technique.

"Well, that's awkward," Noah muttered. "At least I didn't do anything yet."

"I would have come to the same conclusion if I was using heart-beats to sense puppets," Silvertide said with a grin. He clapped Noah on the shoulder. "Don't beat yourself up about it. The fact of the matter is that you weren't *entirely* wrong. Have you had a chance to scan the whole room yet?"

"No. I've been pretty focused on Godrick."

"Ah. Then you'll be thrilled to know that there is, in fact, a puppet that I didn't mention. No point letting our opponent know that I'm onto him, is there?" Silvertide's lips split apart into a cold grin.

Noah was grateful for his mask, as it stopped anybody from

noticing his eyes widen. He still nearly turned to scan the room before he caught himself. It would be ironic if he gave himself and Silvertide away by acting like an idiot.

"Who?"

"The woman with the white hair," Silvertide replied, not breaking eye contact with Noah. "How do you feel about going on a little hunt tonight, after the party has worn down?"

Chapter Seventy-Two

The party—if it could still be called that—ground on. It was clear that the mood had been completely ruined, and most people stuck to their own areas, glancing furtively around the room as if Wizen's clones could have been lurking anywhere in their midst. And, in their defense, they weren't wrong.

Moxie joined the fake Vermil and the rest of the students at the table, keeping an eye on them while giving Noah, Jalen, and Silvertide more room to speak in private without having such a big crowd that they drew attention.

Godrick did his best to perform proper introductions for everyone, but with the evening's earlier revelations, it was clear that nobody was particularly interested. They already knew who Silvertide was, and Vermil had already plowed through nearly half of the available food on the table with no signs of stopping.

As for the new students, it was pretty clear that nobody was going to be going around doing any proper introductions until the Wizen issue had been dealt with. After all, knowing more people just meant more opportunities for a clone to get closer.

Noah sat with Silvertide and Jalen through the majority of the party, keeping an eye on the white-haired clone while they waited for her to take her leave. Ulya sat a few feet to their side, nervously fidgeting in her chair.

"So, are you going to properly introduce me to your hooded

friend?" Silvertide asked, sending a glance in Jalen's direction. "I don't believe I recognize him."

"Just a traveler," Jalen said with a dismissive shrug. "Nobody of any interest, I can assure you."

"Would you find me odd if I didn't believe that for a fraction of a second?" Silvertide let a wry smile cross his face and shrugged. "No matter. I will not push, even if it causes my curiosity pain."

"Wise," Jalen said. "Though I'm starting to wish someone would. I was expecting a considerably more exciting night. Everything was laid out for a play, but it seems you've gone and shifted the pieces around."

"I prefer to work when the playing field is already stacked to my advantage," Silvertide said. "I would be happy to accommodate you if I knew more of what your desires were."

Jalen chuckled and tapped a finger to his head in a gesture of respect. "A good attempt, but one that will yield no fruit. I believe I promised to avoid causing too much of a commotion today, so I will not be sharing anything about myself."

Silvertide shrugged. "Very well. Does anyone happen to know the name of tonight's target? I must admit that I haven't had time to properly research the backgrounds of everybody in the advanced track yet. I had planned to do it tonight, but that plan changed when a corpse showed up at my door."

"Mayreena," Ulya put in. They all turned to look at her and she shrank in her seat. "Sorry."

"No need to apologize. If we wanted privacy, then it would have been rather stupid to speak in your presence. As far as I can tell, you're in with Vermil, yes?"

Ulya averted her gaze to peer at Vermil, who was currently crushing a large fruit up in his hands to shove it, skin and all, into his mouth. She swallowed, then nodded. "I... suppose so. We have been working together."

"Then nothing here should be much of a surprise to you," Silvertide said. "I'm sorry for your loss, though."

"My loss?"

"Mayreena. She is dead," Silvertide said.

"Oh. I wasn't particularly close to her. She was one of the professors that worked closely with Verrud, another researcher. Mayreena always kept to herself and was pretty standoffish, so while I'm sad to hear she died, I'm not personally affected."

"Or perhaps you're just too tired to register things properly," Silvertide observed. "You could carry a corpse in those bags under your eyes."

Ulya raised a hand to her face, then grimaced. "I haven't had much chance to get proper rest recently. I've been too focused on the plant mage and figuring out how to deal with them."

"Well, feel free to rest well tonight," Silvertide said. "Our opponent will be very occupied tonight, so he won't be doing anything fancy. Puppet users all have a very glaring weakness, especially the ones that use a lot of them at once."

"Really?" Noah asked. "What is it?"

"Attention split," Ulya answered before Silvertide could speak. "The more puppets you try to move at once, the harder it gets. That goes doubly so when they're precise moves like fights or the like. That's why I almost never use more than one or two puppets at a time."

"Precisely," Silvertide said with a nod. "Puppets are a technique that mages adept in Imbuements can use to devastating effect, but they are far from a way to take over the world. A single powerful puppet is often considerably more dangerous than a horde. Is that fast friend of yours around? We may have need of her services."

Noah did his best to avoid looking over to the table, where Lee was still using his body to stuff her face. He'd asked her to draw *just a little bit* of attention during the meeting, so nobody investigated him too heavily, but he was pretty sure this was more than a little.

"She may be," Noah said. "But I wouldn't count on it, especially if we have to leave early."

Silvertide pursed his lips. "That's problematic. Remind me of your name, lass?"

"Ulya."

"Ulya. Are you busy tonight?"

From anyone else, that might have sounded like a proposition. But, from Silvertide, it was practically impossible to take it the wrong way. He spoke like a kindly grandfather finding out if his grandchildren would be willing to spend some time with him—even though he only looked to be in his late forties.

"I—no. I'm not sure if there's anything I can actually do against this person, though. The last time we fought, I barely survived."

"But you did survive."

"Not through any fault of my own. Something or someone saved me," Ulya said, biting her lower lip and frowning. "I still haven't figured out who or why. Part of me fears that it was an intentional move and I was somehow infected, but my domain should have revealed anything like that."

Jalen coughed into his fist, and Noah shot a glance at him. It was hard to see under the shadow of his cloak, but he was pretty sure that the powerful mage was grinning to himself.

"Well, so long as you aren't corrupted yet, I'd imagine you'll be of some help to us," Silvertide said. "How many puppets do you control? Not powerful ones—just in general."

"Right now? I have eight," Ulya replied after taking a moment to think. "But most of them aren't great at combat. Only three can fight properly. All my other combat puppets have met... unfortunate circumstances as of late."

"Eight should be more than enough," Silvertide mused, rubbing his chin. "I don't imagine there will be more than that. Every active puppet is a loss in overall power, and I doubt our plant mage friend is stupid enough to waste an entire rune purely on puppets."

Noah wasn't sure he quite followed with what Silvertide was saying, but if he understood it right, Wizen likely only had a set amount of puppets to work with, and it was hard to use all of them at once.

Like any Imbuement, puppets took energy to make and maintain, so he'd probably only have a limited number of them wandering around. It almost sounded as if Silvertide wanted to find a way to take out every puppet in a single fell swoop, but Noah had absolutely no idea how he meant to do that.

Could it be that Sympathetic Magic that Ulya mentioned? I'm assuming it works by some form of correlation, kind of like Voodoo back on Earth. Do something to a representative and the magic carries on to the other pieces. I don't really know much more than that, but if I'm right, that seems like a pretty reasonable strategy.

"Just defeating the puppet may be more difficult than you suspect,"

Ulya said. "And the plant mage didn't seem like he valued the one that he attacked me with very much."

"Gero did inform me of some of your circumstances," Silvertide said, causing a small frown to pass over Noah's face. If Gero had spoken with Silvertide, then why had Silvertide pretended to not know who Ulya was?

He could have been testing her, I suppose. Testing for what, though? Maybe I'm reading too far into it, and he literally just forgot. It's hard to remember that he's a powerful soldier sometimes. He might really just not remember.

"Do you know what happened?" Ulya asked, leaning forward slightly, but disappointment passed over her features as Silvertide shook his head.

"I'm afraid not. Nothing about our opponent has indicated he has any form of Space Magic, though. If you're a plant, then he is playing an entirely different game than I believe. Regardless, your help will be useful, even if your puppets can't properly fight yet."

"Then I'll do what I can," Ulya said, swallowing in a clear attempt to keep her nerves under control.

Before anyone else could speak, Mayreena rose from her spot at the table. The party had been slowing down for a while, and a few of the other professors and their students had already left.

She started to make her way for the exit, and nobody other than the trio around Noah was watching her. Silvertide inclined his head slightly once Mayreena passed them. He stood up with a yawn.

"I'd say it's about time we get moving. Would be a shame to let her get away."

Noah sent a glance back at Moxie and the others, his brow furrowing. As much as he wanted to follow Silvertide blindly, he wasn't keen on leaving his friends alone with the advanced track.

He wasn't confident something wouldn't go wrong, and if he was nowhere near, he'd have no way to know.

"You didn't have any plans to fight anything tonight, right?" Noah asked Jalen.

Jalen shrugged. "Not at the moment."

"Mind sticking around here and keeping an eye on them? I'm not asking you to go to war for them, but I don't want some random Rank 5 or 6 just showing up and randomly killing everyone the moment I leave."

"Is that something that happens frequently enough that you're accounting for it?" Jalen asked, tilting his head to the side just enough to let the light touch on the amused grin on his face.

"Now that you mention it—yes."

Jalen snorted. "Fine. Don't expect much, but I'll make sure the fight is fair if nothing else."

That was about as much as he could ever imagine getting the strange man to agree to, so Noah nodded in appreciation. He rose to his feet to stand beside Silvertide, and Ulya got up as well.

"We'll be off, then," Silvertide said, his cane clicking at his side as Noah and Ulya followed him up the stairs, leaving the advanced track party behind in pursuit of Wizen's puppet.

Chapter Seventy-Three

As soon as the trio emerged from the doorway leading out into the streets, Silvertide was off. In the few seconds that had passed, Mayreena had already vanished from view, but that didn't seem to hinder Silvertide in the slightest.

He set a brisk pace that forced Noah and Ulya to hover at something between a fast walk and a jog to keep up. They turned down several alleyways, keeping their movements relatively quiet in their pursuit.

After just a few minutes, Noah caught a flash of white hair down the turn of an alley. It was only for an instant, but Silvertide clearly knew exactly where Mayreena was. Noah wasn't sure why they hadn't just sped up to catch her by now, but he suspected Silvertide probably knew what he was doing.

Maybe he's hoping she'll lead us back to the hive of puppets, or something like that. It feels like it would be monumentally stupid to just have every single puppet hanging out in the same spot after hours, though. It's not like there's an evil plant puppet nightclub that they all just kick back at.

Fortunately for Noah's dwindling patience, they didn't have to wait much longer. After a few more turns and about a minute of pursuit, Silvertide's pace finally slowed. They turned a corner, stepping out into an old town square that looked largely abandoned.

They were well into the city at this point, and not the good part of it. The houses were old and unkept, their walls showing signs of age in the cracks that had started to build up along them. A faint, moldy smell just barely drifted into Noah's nostrils, even though he couldn't see any mold in the area.

Mayreena stood at the other end of the square, beside an old fountain that didn't look like it had been used in a dozen years. Her arms hung straight at her sides as she stared at them, face as expressionless as the night sky above them.

"Well, isn't that an interesting coincidence?" Silvertide asked, coming to a stop with a final click of his cane against the stone. "I didn't think we'd run into anyone on our nighttime stroll."

"You say that as if you haven't been following me the whole way out of the party tonight," Mayreena said. "What do you want?"

Ulya stiffened at Noah's side, her eyes darting left and right to peer into the shadows surrounding them.

"Us? We're just walking around," Silvertide said with a small shrug. "And I would never do something as detestable as trail somebody out of a party. Damned Plains, lass. What kind of person do you think I am?"

Noah tried to feel if Mayreena had a heartbeat, but she was still too far for him to check. If they got a bit closer, she'd be within the range of his tremorsense, though he would have preferred to have her within his domain to really get a perfect read.

Then again, if she's a clone, something tells me I won't be getting anywhere near close enough to get her inside my domain.

"Is that so?" Mayreena asked. "You'll have to forgive me if I don't believe you. Perhaps you and your *friends* should direct your stroll in a different direction."

There was a clear threat in her tone—a threat that Silvertide chose to completely and utterly ignore.

"I'm afraid I've never been a fan of changing my plans because someone else decided to be in the area," Silvertide said. He genuinely sounded apologetic about the inconvenience, which nearly made Noah burst out laughing. "Perhaps you should have chosen a different path if you're uncomfortable with my presence. See, we're not just strolling around for fun."

"Is that so?" Mayreena asked. "I couldn't have guessed."

"We were patrolling the streets for some rats," Silvertide continued. He tapped his cane against the cobblestone. "And, as a matter of fact, we've been on the tail of one."

"I think we can cut the games now," Mayreena said with an annoyed sigh. She rolled her neck and massaged the bridge of her nose. "You're a real pain in the ass, Silvertide."

"Many dead men have told me such, but I tend not to listen."

"Cocky old bugger, aren't you? I've always enjoyed a good opponent, but don't go strutting around just because you destroyed one of my bodies. I've got more than enough to work with—but I'll be happy to repay the damage you did."

"Not particularly clever of you to admit to anything," Silvertide observed. "What if there had been other people lying in wait to see if you were what I claimed?"

"There aren't," Mayreena replied. "The only people here are you, the stupid girl that managed to slip out of my grasp the last time, and the masked buffoon. Really, it's quite convenient. The three idiots responsible for destroying two perfectly good bodies, all gathered up in one place. Perhaps I should thank you."

"In my defense, you were the one that got caught," Noah pointed out with a snort. "All I did was toss Will around a bit. You can't blame me for that."

"And, if I'm not mistaken, you're hardly giving me credit," Silvertide said. "You said we've destroyed two—I think that number should be three. We outnumber you."

Mayreena gave them a crooked smile. "No, you don't. I don't make the same mistake twice."

Two people stepped out of the darkness behind Mayreena. Noah didn't recognize either of them—they were both about as plain as plain could go. Both were men, roughly five feet tall, with entirely unremarkable faces.

"Three puppets?" Silvertide asked. "That's all? I'm disappointed."

He's trying to bait Wizen into bringing more puppets out. I guess that makes sense, considering what I learned about puppets earlier tonight. The more of them have to fight at once, the harder it is to control all of them. So, more puppets would actually make the fight easier for us... but there's no way Wizen wouldn't know that.

"Three will be more than enough to handle an old man and a

masked clown," Mayreena said with a laugh. "And I'll be taking your bodies as recompense for the damage you've already done."

The two men at Mayreena's side doubled over in unison. Loud snaps echoed through the square as the bodies bulged and twisted. Their clothes ripped apart and wooden growths erupted from the puppets' bodies, writhing across the ground.

Rotten wood and vines twisted together, rising up and forming into the kneeling forms of ragged, humanoid creatures. Each one must have been over ten feet tall and was covered with ragged thorns.

The monsters rose to their feet to stand at Mayreena's sides. Neither of them spoke a word, but just their movements were enough to shake the ground beneath Noah's feet. They were heavy—and, if he had to guess—quite strong.

"Oh, shit," Ulya breathed, her face paling. "If he can actually control all three of those, we're in a lot of trouble. We need to get out of here. Will's body didn't have anything like that in it. Those are a lot stronger than what attacked me, and he might have more puppets lying in wait if he knew we were coming. He could just keep throwing them at us every time one of the old ones dies."

"Nonsense," Silvertide said. "I suspect we'd be in far more danger if we tried to run. I doubt turning our backs to our friends here would be beneficial for our health."

"Is there even a reason you're doing all this shit?" Noah asked, hoping to wring some information from Wizen's puppets before the fight started. "Isn't this normally the part where you tell us all your plans since you're so convinced we're going to die?"

Mayreena laughed. "You're a mouthy one. That's convenient. Those are always easier to mimic."

Whelp. I guess that would have been asking for too much.

"Shall we?" Noah asked, taking a step forward. "If we aren't getting anything useful out of this, then I've got better things to do with my time than try to banter with a tree."

Silvertide held his cane out, stopping Noah from moving any further. "No need. I brought you two along for a different reason. I'd be ashamed if I had to ask for help dealing with something as simple as this."

"Simple?" Mayreena asked with a laugh of disbelief. "I know who you are, Silvertide. Do you really think I'd come to challenge you without the strength to bring you down? Rejecting help now is a damn foolish move to make."

"If that was true, why would you say anything?" Silvertide countered. "Never stop your opponent from making a mistake. Perhaps you aren't as smart as you think you are."

"And you aren't nearly as strong as you think you are."

"I suppose we'll have to find out," Silvertide said with a wry smile. "Care to tell me your name before we fight? I have my suspicions, but it would be nice to have something to think of you as."

"You already know my name, Silvertide," Mayreena replied. The monsters at either side of her creaked, the wood on their faces snapping open to form jagged maws. Vines twisted down their arms, forming into menacing axes. "Not that it'll matter for long. You're nothing but a Rank 5 soldier that had a few lucky breaks. The only thing I regret is that I won't be able to let anyone know that you fell at my hands. No matter. Your body will suit me well."

The huge puppets surged forward. Noah prepared to draw on his magic, but Silvertide rapped him on the wrist with his cane, shooting him a sharp glare.

"I believe I told you that I'd handle this," Silvertide said, apparently unconcerned about the monsters stampeding toward them. Every step they took made the cobblestone at their feet jump in terror.

"I'm calling my puppets," Ulya said hurriedly, pressing her back to the wall. "They'll be here soon, and we can use them to buy time to run. I—"

Ulya's sentence ended in a scream as one of the puppets leapt into the air, bringing its axe down toward the three of them, likely planning to kill all three with a single blow. Noah wasn't sure how Wizen planned to harvest any bodies if he squashed them all into paste, but he never got the chance to find out.

Silvertide's cane tapped against the stone. A gray blur flicked out, slamming into the massive axe and sending it careening to the side. Before the puppet could even land, a second blur slammed into its chest and threw it across the square.

Wood cracked and shattered as the puppet rolled across the ground and slammed into a wall with a loud crash. The second puppet closed in on Silvertide, but it had no more chance to attack than the first did.

Noah didn't even see what happened. One second, the puppet was bearing down on Silvertide. The second, it was tumbling back, its arm severed right above the elbow. Silvertide's cane tapped against the stone as he advanced toward Mayreena at a leisurely pace.

Holy shit. Is this guy seriously Rank 5?

The puppets staggered back upright, and wood twisted out of their bodies to repair the damage they'd just taken. They launched themselves toward Silvertide in unison—only to be cut down midair by a blur so fast that Noah's mind didn't even properly register the move until it had already finished.

Silvertide continued forward, stepping right past the puppets. They struggled to rise and reach out for him, but every single time they moved, more blurs carved the monsters apart. Within seconds, they'd been reduced to a pile of wooden scrap.

"Is that all?" Silvertide asked, sending a glance back at the puppets with a frown. He turned back to Mayreena. "I was expecting more."

The puppets exploded. Ulya called out a warning as twisting vines erupted from their bodies, wrapping around Silvertide in a split instant. They constricted... and splattered to the ground, leaving Silvertide standing where he had been before, completely untouched.

"What rune are you using?" Mayreena asked, taking a step back. "This is impossible. You're a Rank 5."

"I sincerely hope you've got more than this," Silvertide said, a small smile creasing his face. "I brought an audience, you know. It would be a shame if I made them leave the party for no reason."

"I'm going to kill you," Mayreena growled, her body rippling. Vines erupted from her arm, wrapping around it and forming into a thin blade. "And then I'll rip the runes from your body and take them for myself."

"Do you have any idea how many times I've heard that?" Silvertide asked with a laugh, beckoning Mayreena onward. "And do you know how many people who made that threat are still around? You'd best make your next attack count. You won't get a chance to make another one."

Chapter Seventy-Four

Mayreena burst into laughter, the vines pushing out from beneath her skin and undulating with her amusement. "You can't be serious. That might be the cockiest thing I've ever heard. Do you really think that cutting up two of my puppets is anywhere near enough to justify such arrogance?"

The ground shuddered, and Noah's neck prickled. Two looming forms stepped out of the darkness, vines writhing along their bodies. Wizen had brought out more puppets, and there was no way of knowing how many more he had in the area.

"I told you," Ulya said, her face so pale that it was a miracle she hadn't fainted yet. "If you fight a puppet user on territory they're ready for you on, everything is skewed in their favor. We have no idea how many puppets he's set up and had inactive, just waiting to swap in. We can't win this fight."

Noah was starting to wonder if she was right. He didn't know how powerful Wizen was, but he knew he was strong. If he had dozens of puppets just sitting around, they weren't going to be able to win.

Even if I can die and come back, Ulya and Silvertide can't. Retreating and finding someone that actually has a way to properly deal with Wizen's puppets seems like it might be the smartest option here.

Silvertide didn't seem like he agreed. He'd stopped in the center of the square, leaning on his cane with a slight expression of amusement on his face. The new puppets lumbered to stand beside Mayreena, casting long shadows in the moonlight.

"Well?" Mayreena asked. "You were talking big game, Silvertide. I believe you said that I'd only have one more move. I'd love to see how a mere Rank 5 is going to take out every single one of my puppets in a single blow."

"If we're going to get stuck on technicalities, then I don't believe that's what I said at all," Silvertide said. He drummed his fingers on the top of his cane. "I said you'd only have time for one more move, not that I'd kill all your puppets in one blow."

"Are those going to be your last words?" Mayrenna brought her hand down and the puppets lurched into motion, advancing toward Silvertide. "Snarky—and utterly pointless. Disappointing."

"I do hate to hear that I've failed to live up to expectations," Silvertide said, taking his hands off his cane and brushing them off on his coat. The cane remained in place where he'd left it as he stepped to the side, rolling his neck.

His leg shimmered. Ghostly threads rose from it, swirling in the air around him like the rings of Saturn, and a faint hum started up, quickly turning into a high-pitched keening. Noah's ears stung and he raised a hand to his head, grimacing.

What the hell is the magic Silvertide uses? He doesn't seem concerned, but I'm starting to wonder if it's because he's just putting on a front. I should get ready to grab Ulya and make a run for it. He's just so confident that I can't help but feel like he's going to win... even if I have absolutely no idea how he's going to handle all these puppets before we run out of energy. Maybe he thinks Wizen is bluffing?

Pieces of Silvertide's leg pulled away, and the humming grew even louder. Both puppets bore down on him, roaring as the vines covering them shot out, drilling toward the old soldier. Noah went to run forward and help, but something stopped him.

There wasn't even the slightest amount of concern in Silvertide's stance—he was just standing there. It was only a moment later that Noah found out why.

The ribbons of gray that had been swirling around him erupted forth, carving out through the air in a myriad of slashes so fast that Noah was pretty sure he only picked up a tenth of them. The puppets were ripped to shreds in a split instant. They collapsed to the ground, diced into minuscule chunks.

Mayreena's eyes narrowed. "Cute, Silvertide. But I believe I'm still standing."

She shifted, then froze. Something about her movements felt off—and Noah spotted what it was a moment later. Threads of silver had covered the entirety of the square, so thin that they were almost invisible.

Hundreds of them had wound around Mayreena. She pulled at them with a bemused frown. The threads hardly seemed like they were properly restricting her, and it only took her a second to pull her hand free.

"What is this?" Mayreena asked, pinching a thread between her fingers. "This doesn't even have any runic energy in it. Even I was expecting more than that."

Silvertide smiled in response. He reached over to his cane and plucked it from the ground, spinning it upside down and bringing its head down.

And, in that moment, Noah finally learned where Silvertide had gotten his name. A wave of gray erupted from the soldier's body, racing down every single strand, filling the town square and bringing it to life.

A churning mass of silver flashed out, carving through the ground and ripping apart the square—but Silvertide's attack didn't stop there. Strands flashed through the air and cut clean through buildings.

Loud rumbles shook their surroundings as stones rained down, crashing to the ground and sending up huge plumes of dust. Thin flashes of silver danced through the wreckage, twisting inward toward Silvertide's position—but they didn't come alone.

Strung up on the silver threads like clothes were bodies. There must have been fifteen or twenty of them—all run through in so many different spots that they looked like they'd picked a fight with a dozen hedgehogs and lost miserably.

The threads pulled the limp corpses to hang before Silvertide, and the rest of the silver thread swirled up behind him, forming into the shimmering body of a massive snake nearly three times his height. Thin strands of energy ran from Silvertide's hand to the creature behind him, and every other strand of thread originated from it.

Mayreena's body hung at the front of the row of bodies, as limp as a tablecloth. There was no life left in her—or any of the other puppets that Silvertide had just killed in the span of a second.

Holy shit.

"Well then," Silvertide said, sounding considerably wearier than he had a few moments ago. He righted his staff and leaned heavily on it, letting the corpses drop to the ground as he turned back toward Noah and Ulya. "Good riddance."

"What in the Damned Plains?" Ulya whispered. "I—what? How? You're—"

"A puppet user," Silvertide finished with a wry smile. The snake coiled at his feet, then collapsed into a pile of thread that wound back into his leg. "Yes. Few people expect it. Most puppet users hide behind their puppets instead of using them as another tool. It is a misuse of a powerful tool."

Ulya's cheeks reddened and she looked to the side in shame.

"How did you know who all the puppets were?" Noah asked, swallowing back his disbelief. Silvertide—a supposed Rank 5—had just done the most devastating attack Noah had ever seen and barely even looked more than winded for his troubles. "Did you have some way to sense them at that range?"

"In a way, yes. I can only sense puppets that are within my domain," Silvertide said.

"You can't be claiming that your domain reached that far," Ulya said in disbelief. "If it did, you'd have to be one of the most powerful Rank 5 mages in history."

Silvertide laughed at Ulya's expression and tapped a finger against his leg. "That's because I cheat. My puppet is more than just a puppet. It's part of myself—and anything it takes control of joins that connection."

"Take control of?" Ulya's brow furrowed in confusion. Then she blinked. "Wait. What happened to my puppets? They're all—"

"Destroyed." It was Silvertide's turn to look sheepish. "My apologies. I needed more base points, and I needed them quickly. Taking over other puppets is fairly simple, but if I did it to our opponent, he would have figured out I was trying to check who was in the area. I stole your puppets to make sure there weren't any innocents in the area and used them to locate where all of the other puppets were by expanding the locations my domain could sense."

"But how?" Ulya demanded. "You never even saw most of my puppets! You just asked if I had them!"

"You called them to you when I asked about it. Any smart puppet user would only use a small amount of energy for a summoning like that, so it was easy enough to follow that energy back and overrule your commands in a subtle manner. Unfortunately, when I released my own puppet, the magic ripped all of yours to shreds. It was a necessary sacrifice to make sure I killed every one of our opponent's tools at the same time."

"Why'd you even bother inviting me?" Noah asked. "You didn't need any help."

"No, but I certainly seemed less intimidating when I needed to drag along backup, didn't I?" Silvertide cackled at the expression on Ulya's face, then slapped Noah on the shoulder. "Come on. Ulya, I'll make sure you get reimbursed for the damage I did to your puppets."

How many steps ahead was Silvertide this whole time? I can't tell if I should be offended that I was literally brought in as the peanut gallery or impressed that he took out Wizen's entire battalion of puppets with one attack. Moxie is going to be so jealous she wasn't here.

"What happens next, then?" Ulya asked as they fell in behind Silvertide. "That mage could come back, couldn't he?"

"The hard part is getting the puppets here in the first place. Now that our plant mage friend has lost his army, he's going to have to go through a lot more work and recovery if he wants to try that plan again. I suspect he's smart enough to know that won't work considering how easily we crushed it this time. And, beyond that, I left him a little gift."

"You did?" Noah asked, blinking. "How?"

"Sympathetic Magic..." Ulya murmured, realization setting in on her expression. "You used his puppets to attack him? I thought you didn't know Sympathetic Magic!"

"Did I say that?" Silvertide said, tilting his head to the side. "I must have lied."

* * *

Wizen ground his teeth together, staring at the cracked bulb of dirt at his feet. Evergreen's essence leaked out of it, infused with rancid silver magic. The soldier had sent his power back down the line connecting Evergreen to the clones, and the results weren't pretty.

Several of her runes had been shattered. If it hadn't been for Wizen's own powers, her body and magic would have been destroyed completely. Wizen shook his head, then let out a laugh.

"Well played, Silvertide. I got cocky, and you made me pay for it. That's one nasty Master Rune—and using the corpse of the monster you're so famous for defeating as a mere puppet... I can't even complain."

Wizen set his hand on Evergreen's bulb, sealing it over. There wasn't much left of her, but there was no reason to waste even a little power. If he could wring anything else from the old woman, he would.

"You can take this round," Wizen said, turning to the other bulbs in his room as a smile pulled across his lips. "It was only the first game, after all. Puppets might not be the right angle, but I'm fortunate enough to have options. Perhaps it's time I got more... intimately involved. I can hardly stand back after such a firm blow to my face."

Chapter Seventy-Five

"I am unspeakably jealous of you," Moxie informed Noah, crossing her arms and leaning back in her chair.

He'd returned to her room just a few minutes ago and had been relieved to find that everyone had returned safely—although that relief had faded slightly when he'd realized that he had to tell Moxie that he'd watched her hero show off his coolest move.

"I didn't know he was going to go and do something like that," Noah said defensively.

"I know, I know. That doesn't make me any less jealous, though. It's incredible that he's managed to keep that under wraps this whole time. I never would have thought he used puppets, but it makes so much sense. That's why he's been punching above his weight class so much. He's using the body of a powerful monster, and he's probably been reinforcing it with extra Imbuements and magic this whole time."

"He was certainly something," Noah admitted. "He brought me and Ulya along specifically so we could make him look weaker—and I was supposed to be pretending to be a Rank 6 powerhouse. What a badass."

"Stop talking him up," Moxie groaned, running her hands through her hair. "It's just making things worse. I wish I was there."

"Sorry," Noah said with a cheeky grin. "Maybe you can pretend to be the insanely strong mage next time so that he drags you along instead."

Moxie snorted. "Yeah, right. That'll be the time we get attacked by everyone and their grandmothers. I'll let you stick to that. But what happened after Silvertide killed the puppets? That can't be it, can it?"

"Almost certainly not," Noah agreed. "I'm certain this is Wizen we're up against. I don't think he could read any thoughts through his puppets, or he would have figured out what Silvertide was doing. There's no way he's done, though. And, unfortunately, he didn't give us a scrap of information about what he actually wants."

"Lovely. I was kind of hoping he'd just spout his plans to look cool before he tried to kill you."

"Me too," Noah admitted with a sigh. "I tried, but he didn't bite. He's not an idiot, unfortunately. Silvertide seemed to think it would be pretty hard for him to get his puppets back to Arbitage, though. He might have to come here himself."

Moxie chewed her lip and leaned back on the rear legs of her chair, rocking back and forth in place as she thought. "Then he's almost certainly going to go after Silvertide. After getting stomped that hard, he's got to be pissed."

"Given how arrogant he came off? Almost certainly." Noah nodded. "I think it might be a bit before he pops up again. We should use that time to get stronger and focus on the kids' training. Right now, they're the weak link and I don't want Wizen thinking they're easy targets."

"That's assuming he cares about them at all, but I agree," Moxie said. She let her chair return to its normal position before she could fall. "Some of the other advanced track professors were discussing having training matches. It could be worthwhile to match up some of our students against theirs to see where they stand. The first one is next week."

"Seems like a good goal. More than enough time to try to push them to the next step with Formations," Noah said.

They were silent for a few moments, and Lee took that moment to speak up for the first time since Noah had gotten back, having been in a food coma.

"What did you end up doing with the bodies the puppets had taken?" Lee asked from her spot on the edge of the bed. She'd—mercifully—returned back to her normal form, so Noah didn't have to look at himself when she spoke.

"Left them to Silvertide," Noah replied. "I don't know what he did with them after that. Maybe he took them as proof? Either way, you've eaten more than enough for one night."

"I'm still hungry, though."

"You're always hungry."

"Oh, yeah." Lee blinked, as if she'd completely forgotten that particular fact. "I guess I am."

Noah and Moxie both laughed at the completely innocent expression on Lee's face. Sometimes, it was hard to tell if she was being serious or not. If anything, she was even better of a liar than Noah was.

"What ended up happening at the advanced track party after I left?" Noah asked. "Anything important?"

"I don't know if I'd say it's important, but they covered some of what they'd be providing and doing through the year," Moxie said. "The most important part is that, for the students to stay in the advanced track, they need to score similarly to or above the other advanced track members. So our exams are the ones everyone takes, but if we aren't at the top of the class and also at the level of the other advanced students, they get booted."

"They're expected to be that good right off the bat?" Noah raised an eyebrow, but Moxie shook her head.

"No, there's a warm-up period. They don't have to perform as good as everyone else immediately, but the top performers get access to information on some rune combinations as well as special training areas and sometimes just straight up runes. They treat the students at the top really well."

"Noted. More reason to make sure everyone is ready to crush, but we'll have to approach this in the right way. We don't want too much attention. Not yet, at least. It's something we can deal with tomorrow. I'm hearing the bed calling my name, but I want to know one more thing before I can rest."

"What is it?" Moxie asked.

"What did Jalen do after I left?"

"Oh, he kind of just hung around. I was surprised. I thought he'd start trouble, but he stayed out of our way and barely said anything. He escorted us back to the room and left shortly afterward."

"Seriously?" Noah tilted his head to the side. That really *was* odd. He hadn't expected Jalen to lie, but doing absolutely nothing felt even weirder. It wasn't like Jalen was around to ask what had happened, so all Noah could do was shrug. "Well, that's good. Maybe he's not as insane as we thought."

"Right," Moxie said dryly. "More like we didn't figure out what he was doing."

"Probably. Either way, I'm exhausted from a day of doing absolutely nothing but thinking that I am going to be doing something."

"Me too," Lee declared, about half a second before dropping her head and starting to snore.

It wasn't long before Noah and Moxie got into bed and followed her lead.

* * *

Rafael was deeply concerned. He'd known that this task wasn't going to be simple. Killing demons rarely was—but he'd never expected his target to be this deeply entrenched. The demon wasn't just defended. Everything around them was a veritable fortress.

It had been strange enough when the blood he'd gathered had been more finnicky than it should have been. Instead of leading him right to the demon, it faded and swirled throughout Arbitage, as if it couldn't make up its mind as to where the demon had gone.

If it had gone up a rank, Rafael could have understood a degree of confusion. Demons changed considerably with every rank they advanced—but this was different. It was as if the demon couldn't determine if it existed or not.

And, even in spite of that, he'd tracked his foe. He'd followed its many trails through Arbitage. His efforts had finally led him to a group —a group that was in with one of the most famous soldiers in the kingdom, Silvertide.

It wasn't just Silvertide, either. The group, including several people that appeared to be mere students, also had the support of a man and a woman who had completely suppressed their power. And, if there was one thing that Rafael had learned in his time hunting demons, it was that anything without even the slightest amount of power had *far* more power than anyone else in the room.

Rank 5 minimum, probably Rank 6. I've never felt such a perfectly suppressed... well, everything. I would have thought the hooded man wasn't even there if I'd been looking less closely. The woman... the same. I couldn't get a read of her.

But... which one was the actual demon? Was it the one shoveling food into his mouth like there was no tomorrow? Was it the woman—or the masked man? Damn it.

He'd chosen to remain hidden in the shadows of the meeting he'd followed the group to, staying behind when Silvertide and the masked man had left. The chances of Silvertide being corrupted were low, so the others were far more likely to be his targets.

But, to his annoyance, the night had ended without anything even slightly out of the ordinary aside from the man—Vermil, if Rafael had caught his name correctly—having a seemingly bottomless stomach.

It could be him. Eating that much could be indicative of a demon's unrestrained personality... but he also seems to care a little too much about the people around him. He keeps glancing at the students to make sure they're next to him, and with the discussion that was happening in here earlier, it makes sense.

Demons don't care for others. Shit. Who is it?

They couldn't have *all* been demons, and there was a very good chance that at least a few of them had no idea who they were traveling with. Rafael couldn't warn them either—if they did know and were simply hiding it, then he'd be giving himself away.

Damn it. I could try approaching Vermil, but what if he made a deal with a demon to protect his students? That would make him an enemy, even if it was for a good cause.

No matter how hard Rafael thought, he couldn't think of anything that would answer his questions. Nobody had given themselves away tonight, which meant it was ever more likely that his target was the masked man or, gods forbid, Silvertide himself.

I don't have much time left. I'll have to observe them over the coming days. And, if nothing reveals itself, then I will be forced to try to isolate them as much as possible and confront them one by one.

Rafael took his rosary in his hands and ran his thumb along the beads, forcing himself to take control over his fraying nerves. He was no stranger to great threats, and this demon was no different. No matter how extensive its support network may have been, it was a demon.

And, once it was revealed, he would destroy it. There was no alternative. There were no other paths. Demons were a plague on this world, and they could not be allowed to exist.

Before this week ends, the demon must die.

Chapter Seventy-Six

The next morning, Noah woke up to Lee slipping in through the window. He blinked, locking eyes with her as she froze with one foot in the room, as if not moving would keep anyone from noticing her.

"Lee?" Noah asked, rubbing the sleep from his eyes and sitting up. Moxie had somehow slipped out of bed without waking him up, and it didn't look like she was in the room.

"I was trying to be sneaky," Lee said, pulling the window open the rest of the way and dropping into the room. She shut it behind her and frowned back at it.

"You're normally pretty good at that," Noah said. "What happened?"

"I was distracted," Lee said. "Something about the party yesterday felt a bit weird, so I went back to investigate. I haven't seen anything out of place, though."

"Weird?" Noah asked. "What part of it? I'd say there were half a dozen different weird things all happening at once."

"Most of that was the normal weird." Lee shook her head, clearly searching for the right words. "It was a smell. One that really didn't fit, and it wasn't the puppets—I don't know why, but those didn't smell different. They just smelled like people."

"Concerning, but what was the other smell, then?" Noah asked, fully waking up. He slid out of bed and got dressed, snagging his belongings. "Something we should be worried about?"

"That's what I was trying to find out. It seemed a little familiar... but at the same time, I couldn't place it at all. And, when I went back today to try and see if I could smell what it was, there was nothing there."

"I'm not even going to waste time asking if you're sure it was there, then. Do you think it had anything to do with the puppets, even if it wasn't them? Maybe Wizen?"

"I don't know. I don't think I've interacted enough with Wizen or the puppets to place the smell," Lee admitted with a frown. She fell silent for a second, then shook her head. "Never mind. For now, just be careful, I guess. I don't know what it was."

"Noted," Noah said. "Do you know where Moxie went?"

"Emily and Alexandra stopped by asking to do some extra training today, so she went to practice with them. I saw them leaving while I was headed out to see if I could smell the thing from yesterday."

Noah nodded, adjusting his hair. He went for the door, then paused. Now that the meeting with the advanced track had passed, he wasn't actually sure what he wanted to do today. Originally, dealing with Wizen's puppets would have taken that spot up—but those were, courtesy of Silvertide, handled as well.

Well, shit. Normally, this would be a great time to bother Moxie, but she's doing teacher things. That's honestly for the best, considering she's been trying to find a way to help more in recent classes. Does leave me in a bit of a pickle, though.

Whelp, Formations it is, then. There's still a lot more I know I can get out of the violin, and I need to make sure I'm as strong as possible in the near future. Getting better with Formations and the violin will be a lot more beneficial in the short term than getting some new Rank 4 runes, but I should keep that in mind as well.

That particular thought gave Noah pause. His first Rank 4 rune had been pretty easy to figure out. It had just been an extension of his Rank 3—but he didn't have that privilege anymore. Even if he used a few Rank 4 Natural Disasters for his Rank 5 rune, he still needed something else in the mix.

"What kind of magic would pair well with Natural Disaster?" Noah mused to himself, letting his hand rest on the doorknob.

"Unnatural Disaster?" Lee offered from behind him, snickering to herself.

Noah went to roll his eyes, then caught himself as the idea fully registered. Natural Disaster was all nature-based magic. If he continued down the disaster route, adding magic that originated from areas beyond just environmental ones seemed pretty logical.

That would be a great spot to work in some Space Runes or the like. I'm not sure what rank I'd have to be to create a black hole, but I'm pretty sure that would count as a disaster at some point, especially if it was right on top of some poor bastard's head.

"That's not a bad idea," Noah said with a grin. "Thanks, Lee."

"It wasn't?" Lee blinked, then cleared her throat. "I mean, of course it wasn't. I'm a genius."

"Got plans for today?" Noah asked as he headed into the hall. "I'll probably focus on some practice. I don't know how long we'll have before Wizen is back, but we should have at least a few days of being left alone, if not more. That'll be welcome—it's been far too long since I've gotten any proper free time. Are you close to hitting Rank 4 yet? It might be a good idea to try to push through the last bit and advance."

Lee's features clouded and she remained in the room, not following after him. "I'm almost there. Maybe I'll get there this week. Today, I'll probably just wander around. Maybe I'll follow after Moxie and the others."

"Whenever you're ready," Noah said. "Let me know if there's anything I can do to help."

Lee nodded absently, and Noah headed down the hall while Lee pulled the door shut behind her, likely planning to head out the window rather than take the stairs.

Once I can really get Formations under control, I can look more into my next Rank 4 rune. With any luck, I'll be strong enough to give Wizen a nasty surprise the next time he comes after Moxie.

I still wonder what it is from the Torrin family he wants, though.

* * *

Lee found Moxie, Emily, and Alexandra without much difficulty. It only took her a few minutes of slipping through the shadows and following her nose before she caught up with their scent at the transport cannon.

Tim was sitting behind the counter, fiddling with his thumbs, when he spotted Lee arrive and grinned in greeting.

"Hello! You just missed Moxie and the others," Tim said.

"Yeah. Could you send me after them? I went to say hi to Vermil, then realized I didn't have anything to do today other than bother them."

"I don't normally do that, but I've seen you lot spending lots of time together, so I suppose it should be fine," Tim said. He tapped the console of the cannon and grinned at her. "Besides, it's still set for the same spot. Just hop in and you'll be on your way."

"Thanks!" Lee said, hopping into the cannon. A moment later, she was a beam of blue energy streaking across the sky.

The transport cannon deposited Lee on the Windscorned Plateau, and her nose led her straight over to Moxie and the students. It wasn't hard to find them, as none of them had any Wind Magic.

All three had gathered at the edge of the plateau they'd arrived on, just beneath the sheer wall of a plateau above them. Lee ran over, arriving in just moments and nearly scaring the life out of Emily. The girl, who had been focused on a swirling ball of ice hovering in her palms, lost control of her magic and doubled over coughing.

"Lee! Where'd you come from?" Moxie asked with a laugh. "And are you okay, Emily?"

"I'm fine," Emily muttered. "I just didn't expect someone to come at us so fast."

Alexandra seemed to be the only one that hadn't been caught even slightly by surprise, and that was probably because she'd been looking in the direction of where Lee had arrived, meaning she'd likely seen Lee coming for an instant.

"I just used the transport cannon to come over because I was bored," Lee said with a shrug. "What's everyone doing?"

"Emily is practicing with her magic and trying to get a better feel for it that she can translate into Formations," Alexandra said. "I'm just warming up so I can spar with Moxie."

"I thought Vermil said not to use magic with our practice," Lee said, narrowing her eyes.

"I'm not doing Formations or patterns right now," Emily explained, forming another swirling ball of ice above her palm. "I'm studying how ice looks and feels. How it interacts with things, you know? So I can get better at my pattern. You can't embody something if you don't understand it perfectly, right?"

"Oh, yeah," Lee said with a sage nod. "That makes sense. It means I should probably eat more. To understand it."

Moxie rolled her eyes. "I'd say that you understand food better than possibly anyone else in the entire world, but I do have some jerky you can have if you promise not to eat all of it."

"Why would I promise that when I can just slowly take pieces of it away until it's all gone?"

Emily snickered, but Lee didn't miss her attempt to carefully shift her small travel pack to her other hip. It was pointless, of course. Lee could smell the jerky in it no matter where Emily moved the bag.

"Just make sure not to distract anyone too much," Moxie said. "You're welcome to join us, though. Having someone else to spar with will be a lot of use."

Lee nodded and sat down cross-legged beside Emily, content to bide her time and wait for the opportune moment to claim some of the girl's jerky for herself. Figuring out how to defend food was a core element of training.

Part of her was still concerned with the smell from yesterday, but it had been so faint and unreadable that it was almost certainly something to do with Wizen's puppets. Silvertide had handled that, so there was nothing else to worry about for now. There would be time to worry about getting stronger later. Right now, she was content to sit with her friends.

* * *

A footstep echoed through the room, pulling Tim's gaze away from his favorite window. He hadn't even heard the elevator activate, but a man stood on the lift, his features concealed by a hood.

For a moment, Tim wondered if Jalen had returned, but he quickly dismissed the thought. This man didn't have the same build—his shoulders were broader and he was almost a foot shorter.

"I didn't hear you coming," Tim said with a smile, pushing back from the table and rising to his feet. "Are you new to the transport cannon?"

"Yes," the man replied in a gravelly tone. "This is my first time. I don't often make use of Space Magic Imbuements. They're finnicky."

"They are," Tim agreed, his smile growing even larger. "That's why the transport cannon is so impressive. It's state-of-the-art and has some of the biggest improvements in travel efficiency that the world has seen. Care for a demonstration?"

"No," the man barked as Tim reached for the controls. Tim froze, blinking in surprise.

"You don't?"

"Not at the moment. Please step back," the man said. Something in his tone sent a frown crawling across Tim's face.

"I'm sorry? Why? Is something wrong?"

"Nothing is wrong," the man said, his cloak flowing across the floor as he approached Tim. "Just step away from the controls."

Tim's eyes narrowed. He considered himself a pretty good judge of character, and nine times out of ten, when people showed up with their hoods on and murmured vague threats, they didn't tend to be anyone good.

"I don't think I'll be doing that," Tim said. "If you have any complaints, feel free to take them to the office."

He reached for the reset lever—and froze.

Tim's eyes couldn't even widen. His body wouldn't budge. It was as if every single part of it had completely rebelled against him. He couldn't so much as blink. The man stepped forward, studying the levers beside Tim.

"This one activates the cannon, yes?"

Tim didn't respond. It wasn't like he had a choice. He struggled as furiously as he could, trying to so much as wiggle a pinky toe, but his entire body was locked down.

"There's no point trying to resist," the man said. "It's Blood Magic, and you're in my domain. Without one of your own, it's fruitless."

He held a hand up, running his thumb over a bone rosary. A moment later, the man lowered it. "You have nothing to fear from me. All you're going to do is pull that lever once I'm on the transport cannon. It's still set to the same location, isn't it?"

Tim could do nothing but stare as the man walked across the room and lay back on the cannon. He felt his hand rise up of its own volition and wrap around the lever. It wasn't mind control—Tim could literally feel the blood shifting in his body, forcing him to move his arm.

That did nothing to change what happened. His hand pulled down. There was a flash, and the man disappeared, leaving Tim standing in an empty office. Control snapped back into his body and his face went pale as his blood started flowing properly again.

The cannon isn't set up for any custom controls right now. I can't pull anyone back early. I need to find someone.

Tim sprinted out from behind the counter, nearly tripping over his own feet as he ran into the lift and it started to lower, the rattle of the chains rising up all around him in a mocking cacophony.

All he could do was pray that he'd be able to get help before it was too late.

Chapter Seventy-Seven

L ee was still trying to find the best way to relocate the jerky in Emily's bag to her mouth when the air shifted. A shimmer of energy passed through the sky, and it carried with it a familiar scent.

"Did anyone else see that?" Alexandra asked. "I think it was the transport cannon. Was Vermil also going to join us?"

"I saw it," Lee said, uncrossing her legs and standing up, a frown slipping over her features. "And that wasn't Vermil. He wasn't planning on coming. He's doing his own practice today."

Moxie stood beside Lee, brushing the grass off her back. They both squinted at the edge of the plateau, where a dark form had appeared against the grassy ground. The person's features were obscured by a black cloak, but they were heading toward them.

"It's not Jalen, is it?" Moxie asked, the frown deepening on her face. "That isn't any of the other students, that's for certain. The build is wrong."

"No," Lee said, sniffing at the air. "It's someone else. I think they were at the advanced track party with us yesterday."

"Is it a puppet?" Emily asked nervously. Cold energy swirled around her hands, starting to gather into the shape of a bow. "Do you think they're coming for revenge?"

"Silvertide said he handled the puppets, and I'm inclined to believe him," Moxie said. "It's more likely that it's someone else from the advanced track. I swear, if those idiots are trying to test us again, I'm going to lose my cool. They don't know when to stop."

They all watched the figure approach them warily. He didn't seem to be doing anything other than walking in their direction. There was no indication of hostility in his posture or scent—but, at the same time, something about him set the hair on the back of Lee's neck stand on end.

"I don't like him," Lee muttered to Moxie. "We should leave."

"The transport cannon doesn't reactivate for a few hours," Moxie replied in the same tone. A vine rose up from the ground beside her, forming into an armrest for her to lean on. "And I don't know who we're up against. If they're an opponent, attacking first without letting them know we're aware of a threat might be the smartest way to handle things."

Lee swallowed and nodded. "Okay. On your go?"

"Yeah. We'll be polite first—it's probably just an advanced track member. But if I attack, follow up immediately. Girls, your job is to run for the hills. I know Alexandra should be able to climb the plateau if need be, so bring Emily with you."

"What? I can fight," Alexandra protested. "I—"

"Don't care," Moxie said flatly. "If this is someone strong enough to handle Lee and I, then they're going to be able to kill you two as well. Your job is to stay alive. I'm sure I'm overreacting, though. It just doesn't hurt to be ready."

Alexandra looked like she wanted to protest, but she gave Moxie a small nod and pressed her lips together, turning her gaze back toward the person approaching them.

It wasn't long before he had crossed the rest of the distance separating them and drew up, coming to a stop a dozen feet away. The man raised a hand in greeting, revealing a flash of pale flesh beneath his dark cloak, before he let his hand fall and be swallowed by his long sleeves.

"I hope I haven't startled you," the man said, pulling his hood back to reveal a rather average-looking face. He was middle aged, between forty and fifty by looks, with a deep scar to the side of his lip and above his eye. He wasn't quite bald, but Lee was pretty sure that would be rectified if a strong breeze kicked up anywhere near him. The only reliable hair the man had on his face was in the form of his beard.

"Generally, it's not polite to follow after someone using the transport cannon," Moxie said in a curt tone. "Especially when we aren't friends. You were at the advanced track meeting, right?"

The man paused, the smile on his face locking in place for a second, before he got control of himself again. For some reason, Moxie's words had caught him off guard.

I don't think I actually saw him anywhere. Was he not part of the advanced track? Someone from a competing program or something like that?

"My apologies. I hadn't realized you spotted me," the man said. "My name is Rafael. I was simply hoping that I could speak with you."

"You're doing that right now," Moxie said. "If there's something you need to say, you're welcome to say it."

Rafael's lips thinned. "I would prefer to keep it private."

"And I'll have to refuse. I have no interest in speaking with you privately," Moxie said, letting a hand lift to touch the cloak on her shoulders. "Spit it out or leave."

"I have reason to believe there are... infiltrators in the area," Rafael said, choosing his words carefully.

"We all heard about the puppets," Moxie said dryly. "And if anyone is suspicious, it's you. Get to the point, or leave. I've got students to keep an eye on, and you're looking an awful lot like a threat."

"I can understand how you feel. I promise you, I hold no ill will toward any innocents," Rafael said, raising his hands. His sleeves fell back once more, this time revealing a string of bone beads hanging around his right wrist.

The world slammed to a crawl as Lee's eyes locked onto the beads. A cold hand gripped her stomach and squeezed as she realized what the scent that had been throwing her off was.

Rafael was an Inquisitor.

"I am looking out for the world's best interests," Rafael continued, completely unaware of Lee's realization. "And I do not wish to alarm you, but it is possible that one of your group has been overwhelmed and their body stolen. I simply need to run a simple test that will do absolutely no harm to you, and then I'll be on my way."

As he spoke, his hand went for the rosary at his wrist. Lee went to move, but Moxie was faster. A deep red vine covered in jagged thorns erupted from the ground at Rafael's feet, winding up for his neck.

A deep hum filled the air and the vine was shredded apart before it even grew close to him. Lee's heart plummeted into the pit of her stomach—Rafael was at least a Rank 4, probably higher based on how powerful his domain had to be if it had destroyed Moxie's magic so quickly.

"Run!" Moxie yelled, jerking her hands into the air. Vines erupted from the ground around her, writhing up like the heads of a hydra. Alexandra grabbed Emily and blurred, sprinting for the rock wall behind them.

Lee went to move, but Rafael was faster. His thumb ran over the beads, and a wave of golden energy erupted from the rosary with a melodic chime. A wall of sheer agony slammed into Lee, ripping a scream from her throat as she crumpled to the ground.

Stand up, you little idiot! Move!

Energy slammed into Lee and she drew in a ragged breath, scrambling upright as Rafael's eyes flicked, locking onto hers.

"Demon," Rafael snarled. "Not the one I was tracking, but a demon nonetheless. Stand down, woman. I'm an Inquisitor. It should be apparent—"

The ground beneath Rafael vanished. His eyes only had an instant to widen before he plummeted down, vanishing beneath the earth. Lee spun to Moxie, whose face was pale from exertion.

"I can't do anything through his domain, but that doesn't stop me from digging the ground out from beneath him and then just pulling it open from below. You need to run, Lee."

"I can't leave you to fight him alone!"

"He only wants you," Moxie snapped. "Just go. You're faster than he is, so wait until the transport cannon reactivates and then go find Noah or Silvertide."

Moxie's words made sense. As much as she hated the idea of it, Lee turned to run—and another wave of agony slammed into her, worming its way into her mind. She crumpled to the ground, gasping in pain.

Rafael clawed his way out of the hole behind them, baring his teeth as he stood. "I will only give you one more chance to get out of my way, professor. I do not wish to kill innocents."

"And I'll give you one last chance to leave," Moxie said, but Lee could barely hear her words through the pain. Azel was yelling something in her mind, but it was a swirling mess. Her fingers dug into the grass, trying to find purchase.

Before Lee could even stand, another blast of pain ripped through her. She doubled over, blood splattering from her lips and onto the grass. The resonance from Rafael's rosary was a dozen times stronger than the one that the previous Inquisitor had held, and her innards felt like they were turning to liquid.

A brief instant of reprieve walled off the pain as Azel's power sank even deeper into Lee's body, flooding her muscles and pushing Rafael's magic back. She threw herself forward into the cliff face, her fingers digging into the rock as she desperately started to climb.

"No!" Rafael roared. "She will not escape!"

Lee glanced back over her shoulder as Rafael sprinted after her—only for Moxie to jump forward, thrusting her foot in front of the Inquisitor's feet. The man stumbled, cursing, and Moxie brought her elbow down on the back of his head.

A loud crack rang out, and Rafael hit the ground with a grunt. Lee took the mere seconds that Moxie had bought her to force her screaming body to finish the climb up the plateau, joining Alexandra and Emily at the top. She ignored the terrified look on Emily's face and coughed again, blood splattering against her fist.

"Fool. You chose this. I will not let you interfere!" Rafael roared from behind Lee. A deep thrum burned Lee's ears as Rafael's domain activated. Despite everything Moxie had said, Lee glanced back one more time.

Moxie's vines had all been ripped to shreds, and she was locked in place like a startled deer. Even in the brief look that Lee took, she could tell Moxie's posture was unnatural. She'd literally been frozen solid, and Rafael was drawing a sword.

He's going to kill Moxie!

Forget the woman, you stupid girl! The Inquisitor isn't as fast as you are. Use Moxie's sacrifice and get out of here before you die with her!

"Those in league with the demons will fall with them," Rafael snarled, his eyes burning with fanaticism. The sword fell.

"Moxie!" Emily screamed, beating at Alexandra's arm. "Let me go! I need to help her!"

I'm faster.

Stop!

Lee blurred, diving off the cliff. The sword shot for Moxie's neck, but Lee was far faster than a mere blade. Even as it made contact with Moxie's neck, her fist crashed into Rafael's face, shattering his cheek-bone and sending him rolling across the grass. Rafael managed to keep his hold on the sword, but his blow never finished reaching its mark.

Rafael rolled a dozen feet before skidding to a stop, a snarl twisting his face. Moxie drew in a hissing breath as control returned to her body. Her hand shot up to the cut on her neck.

"We need to run," she hissed. "He's got a Blood-element domain! If he gets close, you can't move at all!"

"Too late," Rafael growled, pressing his thumb to the line of blood on his sword as he staggered upright. Moxie's eyes went wide as her body locked in place mid-step. Rafael stalked toward them, baring his teeth. "Your arrogance will not save you. All who consort with demons will die."

Panic pulsed in Lee's mind. Moxie couldn't move. Alexandra and Emily were nowhere near strong enough to challenge someone this strong, and she was completely useless against him.

Another wave of agony ripped through Lee's body as she turned to run for the cliff, hoping to put enough distance between herself and Rafael to dive-bomb him again. She stumbled, tripping over her own feet and landing face-first in the grass with a scream.

"Your time will come, demon," Rafael hissed. "But first will be the one hiding her power."

Lee forced her gaze up, but she was in the range of the rosary once more. Even with the magic Azel was shoving her way, her body wouldn't respond. Moxie was going to die in front of her, and there was nothing she could do about it.

Chapter Seventy-Eight

L ee's throat clenched. Blood pumped in her ears. Rafael's advance toward Moxie spun in her eyes, every step seeming to come slower than the last. Color shifted as the world turned a faint rose, then slipped into black.

Control snapped back to her body, but it wasn't in the real world. She stumbled forward, finding herself within the darkness of her mind-space. A bloom of flame swirled before her, revealing Azel's form.

"Idiot," Azel snarled. "I told you to run."

"Let me out!" Lee grabbed Azel by his collar. "I need to—"

"What?" Azel shoved Lee to the ground. "What are you going to do, you stupid girl? Your body is locked in place. You can't move. You can't even beg. All I've done is buy you a few meager moments. You can feel it, can't you?"

Lee didn't have to ask Azel what he was talking about. A burning heat swirled at the back of her neck, working its way slowly up toward her brain.

"What did you do?"

"I'm forcing your brain to run faster than it should be capable of, but there's only so long you're going to be able to handle this," Azel said, thrusting a finger into Lee's forehead. "That's your brain stem heating. And, in a minute, you're going to go up like a candle."

"Then help me!" Lee begged. "Kill the Inquisitor!"

Azel let out a bark of laughter. "Do you think me an attack dog, Lee? I don't have a body thanks to Vermil. All I am is energy, and Evergreen did a lot of damage to me. It's taken everything I have to shift the majority of my power to you, and you've been wasting it at every blasted opportunity."

"I—"

"No," Azel snapped. "No more talking, Lee. It's my turn. I've helped you at every turn. If you want to live, you're going to do what I say. Enough of this cowardice. You've got enough energy in your runes to advance to Rank 4, and that's what you're going to do. That's the only way you survive this."

"If I advance, can I save Moxie?"

"Save? You should focus on keeping yourself from dying. Reaching Rank 4 will let you keep Rafael from freezing you in place with his domain, but that won't let you fight him for more than a second or two. He's a Rank 5, and a strong one. Ranking up will give you a chance to run."

"What about Moxie?" Lee demanded. "I can't—"

"You will!" Azel roared, flame coiling off his shoulders and lighting the darkness before it was swallowed by the shadows once more. "You are a demon. Beyond all else, we persevere. I do not know where you got this damn fool notion of sacrifice in your head, but the Damned Plains have no room for sentimental idiots. Rank up. Now. Otherwise, sit around, watch Moxie's throat get slit, and then die afterward yourself."

If I reach Rank 4, I have a fighting chance. It might be enough to catch Rafael off guard for even a second, and that could give me time to grab Moxie and make a run for it. It's my only choice. I don't have another one.

Azel was saying she'd save herself, but Lee wasn't so sure there would be anything of herself left to save after she reached Rank 4. Advancing and forming the Rank 4 rune would very likely be the last time she was ever truly herself—but if she could hold on for just long enough to get Moxie and the others away from Rafael...

"Fine," Lee said, swallowing heavily. "Let's do it. Will you help me?"

Azel's smile was cold. "What do you think I've been waiting this whole time for? I will aid you. You know your emotion, I trust? This isn't going to work if you don't."

Lee's hands clenched at her sides. "I do."

"Then gather your runes and become what you were always meant to be," Azel said, his lips peeling apart in a hungry smile. "And have no fear, Lee. We will take our toll on this fool. Once we get out of here, I assure you we'll return and rip this Inquisitor apart one nerve at a time. We will do it together, you and I."

Azel lifted a hand into the air, curling his fingers into a fist. Lee's mindspace trembled as power arced through it and her runes rose up, the shadows constraining them stretching as they tried to keep their grasp on the power.

"You only have seconds," Azel warned. "But time is meaningless to us, Lee. Demons are instinct. We know what we are. There is nothing that can *ever* change that. All you need is an instant to open the floodgates. Your emotion will guide you. Accept it."

Lee closed her eyes, letting the energy from her runes pulse through her mind. Then she brought her hands together, pulling the runes closer. They were all full—they had been for a while.

Like Azel said, the power was there. It lay in wait, prepared to give her what she sought and take everything she cared about in return. There was only one thing left to do.

She reached out and took it.

* * *

Moxie's magic was failing. All the vines in the world couldn't have helped her when she simply didn't have the power to penetrate Rafael's domain. Her entire body was locked hopelessly in place, and her magic couldn't so much as twitch.

Damn it all. If I hadn't gotten my runes shattered at the Torrin Estate, I'd be Rank 4 by now. I can't die like this. I've come too damn far.

Moxie's thoughts did nothing to slow Rafael's advance. He didn't look like he was in a talkative mood. He raised his sword, striding toward her with murder in his eyes. Moxie desperately fought against the bonds of his domain, but it was absolute.

There was nothing a Rank 3 could do within it. She couldn't so much as grit her teeth. Helpless disappointment and anger swirled within her chest, closing around her heart like the hand of the reaper.

I keep hoping that someone is going to pop out in time to save me, but I think I'm all out of that. Fuck. I'm sorry, Noah. I hope you don't kill too many people because of this.

Rafael reached Moxie and reared back, his muscles tightening as he prepared to swing.

I'm going to enjoy watching you get your shit beat in from the afterlife. If your domain lets up for even a second as I die, I swear I'm going to take you with me.

Out of the corner of her eye, Moxie saw a massive ice arrow streak through the air—and completely evaporate the instant it entered Rafael's domain. Evidently, Emily hadn't followed her orders.

The blade blurred toward Moxie's neck, and she was denied even the option to squeeze her eyes shut and avoid the end. In a way, she was just fine with that. Moxie met Rafael's gaze, hoping he could see the derision within her eyes.

And then Rafael vanished. His sword spun through the air and embedded itself in the ground behind Moxie. An instant later, a crash echoed through the Windscorned Plateau. Moxie's body slipped back under her control, and she spun to see Rafael drop down from a small crater he'd made in the cliff face.

"She's mine," Lee hissed, but there was something off about her voice. It came out overlaid, as if two people were speaking at once. "They're all mine. You can't have them. They're *mine!*"

Rafael rose to his feet, wiping the blood from his lips and pulling his lips back in a snarl. The blood on the ground around him rose up, forming into a pair of twin blades in his hands. "Advancing at the last second to use the burst of power to temporarily match up with me? Not enough, demon. Not nearly enough."

Rafael blurred, and Moxie's body slammed to a halt once again before she could take so much as a step. He reformed beside Moxie, his sword swinging—and a red blur slammed into him. A loud crack echoed out as his chin shot up, blood spraying from his mouth. A second blow drove into his stomach and sent him tumbling across the ground.

For the briefest instant, Moxie saw Lee—but the woman that stood before her didn't look like Lee at all. Two jagged horns had ripped out of her forehead, curling up around her skull. Smoldering flame raced across them and throughout her hair, traveling down her arms and dancing across her knuckles.

Her fingers had sharpened to black claws, and her teeth had grown from pointed to full-on fangs. But, beyond all of it, there was a deep, desperate hunger burning behind her eyes. It was a hunger that Moxie recognized—and it was more than just Lee.

Azel.

"What is this?" Rafael wheezed, staggering to his feet. The blood swirled around his body, forming into armor. He wasn't playing around anymore. "It's impossible. A demon at Rank 4 can't have this much power. Not even with a rank-up. What are you?"

Lee vanished in a puff of soot and flame, reappearing before Rafael and driving her claws toward his throat. This time, Rafael wasn't caught off guard. He spun one of his swords, knocking Lee's arm to the side but failing to cut her.

He drove the other for Lee's chest, but she vanished before the blow could connect. Reforming behind Rafael, Lee sent a brutal spinning kick to the side of his head. He spun out of the way, then let out a roar.

The blood surrounding him erupted, driving out toward her in jagged points. Several of them carved into Lee's flesh before she could disappear once more. Moxie tried to move, but Rafael had her within his domain once again.

All she could do was watch through gritted teeth as Lee flashed and spun around Rafael, desperately trying to kill him. But, with every movement, Moxie could see Lee's strength reducing. She'd used up the huge burst of power that had come with her rank advancement. Even though she still had far more strength than she should have, Rafael was taking back control of the fight.

"I will study you," Rafael hissed, driving a fist into Lee's stomach and sending her flying back. She spun, landing on her feet and skidding across the dirt. Her fangs parted in a snarl, and she flashed toward Rafael again—only to be met with a blast of concentrated blood. Even as it sent her flying, one of Lee's claws shot out. It caught on Rafael's jaw, ripping a deep furrow down across his neck.

Lee hit the ground on her back, hissing in pain. She tumbled, bouncing once before managing to catch herself with her claws. Blood streaked her face, and her chest rose and fell with desperate breaths.

The blood pouring from Rafael's wound slowed. It should have been a borderline mortal wound, but the bastard was cheating—he was literally keeping the blood in his body. Rafael reached up to his neck, then cursed.

"I made the right choice in coming," Rafael snarled, thrusting a hand into his pocket and pulling out a glass vial. "A creature such as yourself must not be allowed to grow any further. I can't believe a newly made Rank 4 pushed me this far, but the fight ends here."

Rafael clapped his hands together, shattering the vial. As he pulled his palms apart, his blood swirled together with whatever had been in the vial. Energy crackled at his palms and Moxie's skin prickled, even from as far as she was.

The energy between Rafael's palms seemed far too powerful for even a Rank 5. Lee recognized it as well, but she couldn't get close to the Inquisitor. Blood swirled around him, carving through the ground in a tornado of sanguine blades.

"You should feel honored," Rafael said, gritting his teeth as blood started to trickle from his eyes. "I've never had to use a bloodline curse on a demon before, but I refuse to let a creature such as yourself roam this plane. The damage could be irreparable if you continue to draw breath."

"I'm going to consume you." Lee's horns burned with dark flame. "You won't take them from me. Nobody will."

"There won't be anything left of you to take from," Rafael replied. His teeth gritted in concentration as he tried to contain the power swirling between his palms, but it was too much to handle. The ground shook beneath his feet, and it looked like it was drawing every ounce of power he had just to keep from falling. "I'm not stupid enough to take any more chances."

"As if I'll let you hit me with that," Lee said with a bark of cold laughter that sounded completely uncharacteristic for her. "You can barely aim. The moment you release that magic, you die."

"I know your emotion, Glutton. And I know how you feel about those who belong to you. You're fast enough that I'd never be able to land this on you anyway. But I don't need to land anything when you'll do it for me." Rafael turned—not toward Lee, but toward Moxie.

He released the magic that had been gathering around him, sending an arrow of screaming blood carving through the air toward her with a howl of magical energy. And, for the second time that day, Moxie could do absolutely nothing but watch as death screamed her name.

Chapter Seventy-Nine

Rafael's magic was fast. Still, if it had been headed straight for Lee, she was confident that she could have dodged out of the way. But it wasn't headed toward her, and with the fuzzy swirl of her newly formed Rank 4 rune pounding in her head, Lee's thoughts were a muddled mess.

There was only one thing that she still knew as a fact—and that was that Moxie wouldn't survive the powerful blood arrow screaming toward her. Lee's skin prickled just from her proximity to it, and every single one of her senses screamed at her to turn tail and flee.

She could feel Azel pulling at her body, desperately yelling something in the back of her mind, but Lee barely even registered him. His words were a droning hum, drowned out by the immense rush of incomprehensible thought and hunger.

Out of the muddled mess, only a single thought managed to take form. And, amusingly enough, it was driven entirely by the sole emotion that Azel had been pushing her to embrace ever since they'd met.

She's mine. Nobody can have her.

Lee blurred, slamming into Moxie and shoving her out of the way. She'd had plans to continue on, diving out of the way of the Blood Magic and letting it hurtle past both of them harmlessly, but she wasn't *that* much faster than Rafael.

The bolt drove into Lee's shoulder. She braced herself for a blast of pain or agony, but nothing happened. Instead, the magic vanished within her, disappearing as if it had never been there. Lee took several stumbling steps, catching herself as Moxie rolled across the ground before her, unable to stop herself while within Rafael's domain.

"Game's over," Rafael said, letting his hands drop and bracing them against his knees with a pained laugh. "I win."

Lee tilted her head to the side. She looked down at her body, then back up at Rafael. The relief in the Inquisitor's eyes flickered, then faded as his eyes widened. "How are you still standing? I poured every ounce of power I have into that. You can't—"

Heat blossomed in Lee's chest. She doubled over as magic erupted from her body, roaring through the air in a current of crimson fire. The rest of Rafael's sentence was lost to the crackling flame as Azel snapped into existence beside Lee, embers rising off his black suit.

"No," Rafael heaved, taking a step back. His back hit the stone cliff, but his eyes never left Azel's form. "Two demons. But how—"

Azel blurred. Fire streaked across the ground as he shot toward Rafael. Blood swirled up around the Inquisitor, starting to form into a shimmering barrier, but Azel crashed straight through it. His fist shattered Rafael's magic, and he grabbed the Inquisitor by the hair, lifting the man into the air.

A loud crack, followed by a wet squelch, ripped through the air. Rafael's arm spun to the side, splattering to the ground behind Azel. The rosary slipped from useless fingers and slid across the grass beside it.

"Well done, Inquisitor," Azel spat, hatred and fury bubbling from his words. "You found me."

Rafael opened his lips to say something, but Azel denied him the opportunity. The demon's hand slammed into the Inquisitor's face with a loud crunch. Fire erupted around the two of them, swirling up into the air before abruptly snapping out of existence.

The Inquisitor's body dropped to its knees, then pitched forward, a large hole running through his head. The body hit the ground with a wet squish and didn't move again. Not even a Blood Rune could save someone when their entire brain had been pulverized.

Moxie scrambled to her feet, raising her hands defensively as Azel turned. His suit smoldered, the ends of his lapels starting to burn away. Lee squinted at him, the world fluctuating around her.

The Rank 4 rune was still shifting her body. She couldn't tell what was changing, but there was an undeniable sense of... loss. Something that had once been there was gone, and more was fading with every passing second.

Moxie was alive, though. The kids would be fine. The Inquisitor was dead. That was what she'd wanted. It had been the trade she made. It had been inevitable. There was no way for a demon to advance beyond embodying their emotion.

Lee's face felt wet. She lifted a hand, wiping away a tear streaking down the side of her cheek. A frown crossed her lips as she stared at the water on her finger.

Why am I crying?

Azel stepped up to Lee, the ashes swirling off his body enveloping them like the setting night. Moxie yelled something, but Lee barely even noticed it. Moxie wasn't the only thing she needed.

There was so much in the world. She'd never thought about it properly before—but the world was beautiful. The plants were lush. The sky was vibrant and blue, and everything between it called her name.

They were hers to take. They belonged to her. Everything belonged to her. All of it but Azel. He was a pillar of sickly fire, a power that was beyond her grasp. She couldn't take his power—but that only made her want it more.

Lee's tongue ran along her lips as her eyes darted around, trying to find a way she could rip the energy from the demon. There had to be a way to claim it. A way to—

Azel's hand moved before Lee could react. His fingers dug into her shoulders, and the ashes pouring off his body grew thicker, plunging the two of them into a deep, murky fog. Lee could only barely see Azel by the smoldering flame that curled off his body.

Before she could rip herself free from the other demon and try to drive a hand through his throat, a dull pang rang through her soul. Her Rank 4 rune bucked, then shuddered. The power pouring out of it and into Lee's body ground to a halt.

"Stupid, gullible girl," Azel said, but it lacked the usual molten heat that his words carried. It sounded—off. Garbled, as if he were speaking through a layer of water. "You used *my* Demon Runes to form this, and you dare think about trying to use it against me? This is my rune as much as it is yours."

Lee's mouth worked, but the enormous hunger that had brought her into its grasp seemed to have abated. Or, more accurately, it seemed to have been stolen. She could still feel it, burning at the corners of her mind and frothing at the mouth to be released, but Azel was holding it back.

At least for a few more seconds, Lee was herself once more.

"Is this it?" Lee asked, her voice wavering. "I don't want to die."

"You aren't going to die," Azel growled. "You are becoming greater. You have so much potential. With Vermil's help, your rune is flawless. A Flawless Demon Rune, Lee. Do you understand what you represent? You can become the most powerful demon in history. Do you not realize what I've been doing for you? I have paved the path. I gave you the seeds and watered them until they sprouted. All you have to do is continue."

"I don't want to be the most powerful demon in history," Lee said. "I just want to be Lee."

Azel's fingers dug deeper into Lee's shoulders as his eyes bored into hers. The fire within his eyes flickered for a second, and he doubled over, releasing one of her shoulders and coughing into his fist.

"You are an idiot," Azel spat, wiping his mouth with the back of a hand. Lee's stomach clenched as the hunger in her mind tried to push forward again, but Azel's presence walled it off. He was suppressing the rune. "I gave you everything, and you reject it?"

"Why don't you just take it yourself?" Lee demanded. "Noah probably would have given you a Flawless Rune if you'd just left us alone!"

"I was going to!" Azel roared, his eyes flaring with flame. He drew in a ragged breath, containing himself before speaking again. "I set everything up perfectly. You took my runes like a trusting little fool, and I wormed my way further and further into your soul with every day. The moment you reached Rank 4, I should have had a Rank 4 Flawless Rune. All the potential that Noah had put into you would have been *mine*."

"And?" Lee demanded. "Why don't you do it, then?"

Azel let out a bark of laughter. "You can't bait me into doing anything, Lee. I'm hundreds of years your superior in everything, and that includes manipulation. Do you really think that losing the Rank 4 rune will let you have a chance of remaining as you are? You wouldn't survive."

"It's a chance. You want the rune. I want to stay the same. Take it!"

"No," Azel said, grinding his teeth. "I will not."

"Why not? I thought you wanted—"

"I did." Azel cut Lee off with another bitter laugh. "Until you went and ruined everything."

"What? What are you talking about?"

"Your gods-damned delusions," Azel spat. Another spasm racked his body and he coughed, but he ignored it and pressed on. "You are, without a doubt, the worst demon to have ever lived. You took everything that we should be and twisted it."

"I think you got hit on the head. Just take my rune—"

"What is Gluttony to you?" Azel shook Lee by the shoulders. "Tell me!"

"It's protecting what I love!"

"Wrong!" Azel hissed. "It is loving the feeling of getting more. It is the endless hunger for more. That is what you should have—but your stupid delusions were so strong that you twisted the damn emotion into some perverse... human feeling. Something that we should not be corrupted by."

"I don't care about any of this," Lee said. "The Rank 4 rune was turning me into what you're talking about. If you take it, you'll have what you want."

Azel's snarl slipped away, turning into a defeated laugh. "I don't want it anymore, Lee. Your delusion ruined more than just your potential. It ruined my own."

He reached down to his burning suit, pulling it to the side. Thick lines of red wound through his body, pulsing with sickly energy. They wound around his chest and up toward his neck, turning the skin around them a dull gray.

"What is that?" Lee asked.

"You are such a little shit. It's the bloodline curse that you jumped in front of. The one that would have killed you instantly if it had connected."

Lee stared in shock. "You took the hit for me? Why?"

"I don't know," Azel said, looking down at the magic carving through his body one inch at a time. "I suppose I may not have been the demon I thought I was. My emotions are Lust and Hatred. I betrayed them. Perhaps this is an apt punishment."

"I still don't understand. What are you talking about?" Lee said, squinting at Azel.

"Why do you think I let you live when you followed me through the portal in the Scorched Acres?" Azel asked abruptly. "Did you really think you snuck through without my knowledge?"

"I thought you just didn't care."

"If only. No. I knew you were there because I held the portal open for you," Azel said. His face twisted in a grimace as the Blood Magic winding around him reached his neck and started to crawl toward his chin. "You were always a poor demon. I had hoped that entering the mortal plane would be the boost you needed."

Lee stared at Azel in disbelief. "What?"

"When I realized just how worthless you were, I decided to harvest your energy once I escaped Noah's body," Azel continued with a wry smile. "At least, that's what I told myself. That's how I justified giving you my own runes. That's why I transferred myself into your soul, even though Noah could have been convinced to perfect my own runes in exchange for leaving you alone. I suppose that excuse doesn't work anymore, does it? I can't take anything when I'm dead."

"Why didn't you ever say anything?" Lee demanded.

"Does it matter?" Azel asked. He coughed, then ground his teeth. "Not anymore. You are not the demon I wanted you to be—and you never will be."

Azel raised his hand, grabbing one of Lee's horns. Then, with a sharp jerk, he snapped it. Lee let out a pained scream as agony raced through her body, but Azel held her in place with his other hand.

Molten lines of pain ripped through her body, winding through her head. They wrapped around the Rank 4 rune in her soul, digging into it like jagged knives.

"There. That won't last forever, Lee. Become more than just a mere demon," Azel said, a smile flickering across his lips despite the pain in his features. "I want the legends of my daughter to travel so far that I still hear them. It'll give me something to think about in that line of Noah's."

"Wait. You can't just—"

"Odd," Azel breathed. The Blood Magic wound up his cheeks and he tilted his head to the side, his eyes staring straight past Lee. "This isn't an emotion I recognize. It feels... warm."

Cracks raced through Azel's face. His body collapsed, crumbling in on itself. The ash that had been swirling around them twisted into a pillar and dissipated with a gentle pop, leaving only Lee to greet the light as day returned.

Chapter Eighty

"Lee!" Moxie rushed over to the demon's side. "Are you okay? What happened? Where's Azel?"

Lee stared at the spot where Azel had stood. The only thing that remained of him was a slightly scorched patch on the grass. She wasn't so sure she actually knew the answer to Moxie's question.

The power of her new rune hummed in the back of her mind, restrained by the other demon's last act. With every passing second, the rune relinquished more of its grip on her. It had still changed her body, but it had been stopped before it could progress any further.

I don't even know what its name is, and I don't know if I want to. It feels like the more I learn about it, the stronger it'll get.

"Lee?" Moxie asked again, taking her gently by the shoulders. "Are you with me? Did you get hurt?"

"I—I'm fine," Lee managed. Her lips felt dry and parched, and speaking hurt her throat. The vestiges of pain from Rafael's rosary still wound through her body, reminding her of just how close they'd all come to death. Numbness gripped her as her mind tried to piece together everything that had just happened. Everything that she'd learned. "Rafael is dead, right?"

"Most certainly," Moxie said with a concerned expression. "What happened to you, Lee? Did this all come from ranking up?"

Lee reached up to her head, running a finger along the horn that Azel had broken. It was rough to the touch and warmer than she'd expected. They were a bad idea to keep out in public. It was basically an advertisement as to what she was.

It should only take a moment to remove them.

Her brow furrowed—and nothing happened. Lee blinked, touching the horns again to make sure that she hadn't imagined it, but they were right where they'd been a second ago. Her brow creased even further in concentration as she focused on her skull.

Almost reluctantly, the horns sank into her skull and vanished from sight. They were far from gone, though. Instead of sinking into her body and turning into mass that she could manipulate, Lee could still feel them waiting to burst free once more.

"How did you manage to defeat Rafael?" Moxie asked. "And what was with Azel? I thought he should be with Noah."

"He's been with me recently," Lee replied. "Azel helped me kill Rafael."

"I suppose that makes sense. I don't imagine he likes Inquisitors much. We got lucky. Again." Moxie let out a relieved sigh. Her skin was paler than usual, and Lee saw some of the stress she felt reflected in the other woman's eyes. "I get the feeling Azel is going to lord that over us for a long time."

"He isn't," Lee said. Her words caught in her throat, but she wasn't entirely sure why. She hadn't known Azel that well. She'd barely known him at all. They'd spoken a few times, but he'd always just encouraged her to do the exact opposite of the right thing.

Why did he die for me?

"Are you sure?" Moxie asked doubtfully. "He doesn't seem like the type to—"

"He's dead," Lee said. "He died blocking the last attack from Rafael. It was really strong."

Moxie did a double take. "Azel... is dead? He died for you? Why?"

Lee couldn't bring herself to voice what Azel had told her. Her head felt like a twisted mess of spaghetti, but even in the confusion and exhaustion, it felt like Azel's final words had been for her ears alone.

"I don't know," Lee said. It wasn't a complete lie, but it definitely wasn't the truth. A small, distant part of her mind felt a flicker of amusement. Azel probably would have approved of her answer.

If Moxie suspected anything, she didn't let it on. She just nodded, then put a hand on Lee's shoulder and pulled her into a gentle hug before releasing her once more. "You're okay?"

"For now," Lee said. "My new rune is dangerous. I don't know if I'll be able to stay myself. You saw what happened in the fight, right?"

"We'll figure something out," Moxie promised. She looked over her shoulder to Alexandra and Emily, who both stood at the bottom of the cliff but far enough away from Lee and Moxie to give them some privacy.

They headed over the moment Moxie turned her attention toward them, giving Rafael's body a wide berth.

"You're a demon," Alexandra said, her features unreadable. "That was an Inquisitor you just killed, wasn't it?"

Lee considered trying to lie, but she was too tired to come up with something that would have been even remotely believable. She half hoped that Moxie would cover for her, but coming up with a lie that could somehow completely deny everything Alexandra and Emily had just seen with their own eyes felt impossible.

But, before Moxie could say anything, Emily shrugged. "Does it matter?"

Alexandra's eyes flicked to Emily before shooting right back to Lee. "Why wouldn't it? Demons are—"

"That's Lee, though," Emily said. "Isabel and Todd told me Inquisitors came for Noah before, and they tried to kill everyone, not just him. This is the second time they've come looking for trouble. They can only blame themselves for finding it."

"But—"

"I mean, even an idiot could have told there was something weird with Lee," Emily said, crossing her arms. "I've been around her for a lot longer than you have, and she never once did anything that made me feel like I was in real danger—aside from a few of the stretching lessons. I don't care what she is."

A flash of warmth swirled in Lee's chest. Emily hadn't doubted her for a second. The warmth was quickly quashed as a thought slipped unbidden into Lee's mind.

Maybe she should doubt me. If Azel hadn't restricted my rune, I would have become the exact thing that everyone thinks I should be. If I can't find a way to fix this, I'm going to be a danger to everyone. The Inquisitors would be right in trying to kill me.

"Wow," Moxie muttered under her breath. "I didn't expect she'd get over it *that* quickly. Now I feel like an asshole for causing such a scene with Noah about you."

"You knew?" Alexandra asked, her mouth agape, overhearing Moxie. "I don't understand. Aren't demons all evil? I thought they only came to this world to kill and feast on human emotion. Why is Lee just... teaching a class?"

"Lee isn't an average demon," Moxie said. She walked over to Rafael's corpse, and a vine twisted out of her pant leg, winding around the rosary laying by his severed hand. It picked the bone beads up and tucked them into Moxie's bag. "Emily is right, Alexandra. Lee wouldn't hurt any of us. She's just trying to live. No different than a certain former criminal."

Alexandra's mouth clicked closed and she winced. She sent one last concerned look in Lee's direction, then bit her lower lip and sighed. "I find that hard to believe, but I suppose that's also a little hypocritical of me. Does this have anything to do with all the people that were dying?"

"No," Lee said, finding her voice again. "It's separate. Inquisitors have been after me for a long time. I thought they'd stopped, but I guess I thought wrong. The other issue is... separate."

"And likely solved for the time being," Moxie added. "Though we should keep that to ourselves until we figure out what the future holds. This could have gone really, really poorly. We're all lucky to be alive— and that reminds me. I ordered both of you to run."

"I'm not leaving you to die," Emily said, setting her jaw and matching Moxie's gaze.

"I think Vermil would have killed me himself if I just ran off while you got killed," Alexandra added.

"He would not have," Moxie said. "I don't want my students throwing their lives away for me. That's not how this works."

"Then you should have been stronger," Alexandra said.

Moxie blinked, then let out a burst of surprised laughter. It was a mixture of genuine amusement and relief from still being alive, all boiling up now that the threat was gone. Moxie quickly got a hold of herself and shook her head.

"You might have a point, but I don't want to hear it from you. I'm working on it. I've been... delayed."

Moxie held her hand out and vines twisted out from beneath the ground, binding Rafael's body and dragging him beneath the earth. They tilled the ground around him, making sure every single piece of land around where he'd fallen had been drawn deep beneath the earth.

"I'm not sure I'm in the right state of mind to practice anything else right now," Emily said as she watched the last traces of Rafael vanish. She swallowed heavily, then stuck her hands into her pockets, hunching her shoulders. "I want to go back to bed."

"Me too," Lee said. "I'm exhausted. We're stuck here until the transport cannon reactivates, though. I—"

A flash of blue carved through the air. Lee's eyes widened and she dropped into a fighting stance, all the exhaustion vanishing in an instant. "Get out of here. Someone just used the transport cannon."

"Damned Plains," Moxie cursed, summoning vines from the ground to rise up around her as her eyes scanned the Windscorned Plateau for any sight of the new arrival. "Another blasted Inquisitor?"

"I don't know," Lee said, sniffing the air. The wind was against them, but she could still pick up the faintest traces of something familiar. Her eyes widened. "Wait. It's—"

A flash of purple split through the air, and an enormous man stepped out, a sword of matching size resting on his shoulder. The sword was new, but Lee recognized the one bearing it immediately.

"I was told there was someone flinging around Blood Magic over here," Brayden said, turning in a circle. His gaze lingered on Alexandra for an instant longer than the others, but it was clear that she wasn't trying to fight back, so he dismissed her quickly and turned to Moxie. "What in the Damned Plains happened?"

Chapter Eighty-One

Lee's shoulders slumped in relief, and she flopped back to the grass, too tired to stay standing any longer. Brayden wasn't going to try to kill them. At least, she was pretty sure he wouldn't. He'd been pretty mad the last time they'd spoken, but he'd also given her some Space Runes.

"You're late," Moxie said, letting out an explosive sigh and letting the vines sink back into the ground around her. "And I don't think my heart is going to be able to take another surprise today. Why are you here? And I swear, if you tell me someone important is dead, I'm going to lose my shit."

"Why would someone important be dead?" Brayden asked, baffled and still glancing around in search of the blood mage. "The transport cannon operator ran me down while I was knocking on the door of Vermil's room, yelling about some blood mage attacking you."

Tim's alive. That's good. He smells nice. Did he really run all the way over to Noah's room to find Brayden, though? That's a bit much, isn't it? There had to be someone strong closer. I'm glad he got Brayden, though. He also smells good.

Moxie studied Brayden for a few seconds, likely trying to figure out how much she could safely share with him. Lee wasn't so sure of the answer to that herself. Brayden liked them, and he'd clearly rushed over to help, but telling him everything could be risky.

He should already either know or very strongly suspect I'm a demon, though. Noah called me in to the room with Father when we first met him, so it's not a big reach to make that the Inquisition would be after me.

"It was the Inquisition," Lee said finally. There was no point trying to hide it from Brayden, considering he'd probably piece everything together pretty soon.

"Was?" Brayden asked, blinking. "You managed to kill an Inquisitor with a domain? I was told they were probably a high Rank 4 or Rank 5. I don't feel a domain from either you or Moxie."

"We caught him off guard," Lee said. She didn't have a domain because she was a demon, not because she wasn't a Rank 4. And talking about Azel... she couldn't quite bring herself to do it.

Not yet.

It wasn't like Azel's existence would change anything for Brayden. All that mattered now was that Rafael had come for them and that they'd managed to defeat him. Everything else was just extra detail.

"This gives me a sense of familiarity that I really don't want to be feeling," Brayden said, drumming his fingers on his thigh. "Where's the Inquisitor?"

"Buried about sixty feet beneath the dirt," Moxie replied. "Along with everything that was around him. I don't know how they managed to track us all the way over here, but I didn't want to take any risks."

"Smart," Brayden said, lowering his sword and driving it into the ground. He crossed his arms over the hilt and leaned on it, letting out a sigh. "They likely tracked you with Blood Magic. From what I heard, there was only one of them. That's a bit odd, as Inquisitors usually travel in pairs."

"You think another one of those guys is going to show up?" Emily asked, her eyes widening in terror.

"Unlikely. They would have shown up by now," Brayden replied, not even looking back at her. His brow furrowed in deep thought, but he gave up after a few seconds and shook his head. "Must have been an Inquisitor acting of their own volition. Maybe a friend of the ones that showed up the last time. Either way, if you really got rid of the blood, it's unlikely they'll be able to track you this easily again. I didn't think they'd be tracking you at all. Father said he'd handled it."

"Evidently not," Moxie said, her voice going cold. "And we all nearly got killed because of it."

"I'd offer to pass your complaints along to him, but I think we both know how that would go—especially coming from a Torrin."

"Do you have a problem with Moxie?" Emily asked, her eyes narrowing.

Brayden let out a bark of laughter. He straightened up and pulled his sword from the ground. A ripple of purple passed over the blade, and the weapon vanished from his grip. "Surprisingly, no. My broth—ah, Vermil likes her. That's enough to vouch for her character, even if she is a Torrin."

"Relax, Emily," Moxie said, walking over to the girl and putting a hand on her shoulder. "Brayden did literally just come running to help us."

"He was late."

"The thought was there."

"Did you say that Vermil was your brother?" Alexandra asked, squinting at Brayden. Lee didn't see what the confusion was. Noah and Brayden smelled pretty similar at first take. It was easy to tell them apart, of course, but the matching blood was there.

"Yes," Brayden said after a moment of hesitation. "We share the same father."

"Capital or lowercase *F*?" Alexandra asked.

Brayden chuckled. "Both. And who would be asking? I don't believe I properly recognize you."

"I'm Alexandra. One of Vermil's students."

"A new one?" Brayden asked.

Alexandra nodded. "Yes. As of this year."

"I see," Brayden said. He glanced at the tilled earth, then back to Alexandra. "And you aren't perturbed by the Inquisitor?"

Alexandra didn't respond immediately. She was silent for a few seconds, her features unreadable. Then she inclined her head. "I don't suppose I am. I had a pretty bad reaction at first, but I think he had it coming, even if his original intentions might have been good. To be honest, I just want to get stronger. I don't care what I have to do to achieve that."

"Interesting," Brayden said. "I can see why you chose Vermil as your teacher."

"What's that mean?" Alexandra asked, but Brayden had already turned away from her. He walked over to Moxie, pulling out a healing potion from a pouch at his waist and handing it to her.

"Here. Drink."

"I'm not that wounded," Moxie said.

"Vermil is going to lose his shit if he sees you hurt," Brayden said, turning away before Moxie could respond. "Drink the potion."

Moxie scrunched her nose, then did as Brayden asked. By the time she'd drained it, Brayden had handed a matching potion to Lee. She threw it into her mouth without a word of complaint—healing potions tasted like cherries, and the glass added a nice, spicy texture.

"What are you—" Brayden raised a hand, then let it lower and shook his head. "Why do I even bother?"

"With what?" Lee asked, swallowing the mouthful of glass and potion. "Oh. Did you want to eat the vial? Sorry. I didn't realize. I could probably throw some of it up for you. It might be a bit digested by now, but—"

"I'm quite all right, thank you," Brayden said hurriedly. "I'm here for twelve hours because I had no idea how long it would take me to find you guys and fight off the Inquisitor. Evidently, you've already handled that. How much longer until you're pulled back?"

"Probably a few hours," Moxie replied.

Brayden nodded. "Then sit down and relax. I'll watch over you, and we can all speak once we return to Arbitage and can get in contact with Vermil. I doubt I even have to say this, but if you want to remain alive, I strongly recommend nobody share a single breath of what happened here. If the Inquisitors find out you've gone and killed one of their own—again—you'll never live in peace again."

* * *

"That," Renewal said, leaning forward in her chair to stare at the shimmering image in the air before her, "was not at all what I was expecting."

"It took me by some surprise as well," Decras admitted from the chair beside her. He reached over to the box of chocolates on the table between them, and Renewal smacked his hand away. She took one of them for herself, throwing it into her mouth without letting her eyes leave the scene playing out before her. "Have you ever seen a demon kill itself for someone else?"

"No, I don't believe I have. I didn't think they had the capacity to feel like that," Renewal admitted. "Not with the damage their runes do to their psyche. Honestly, I feel bad for the poor creatures. Failed experiments."

"Nothing great can come without failure," Decras said. He snagged a chocolate before Renewal could stop him and threw it into his mouth to keep her from reclaiming it. "The girl... Interesting. I didn't think there would be two people in the same group that caught my attention."

"Hands off," Renewal warned. "I refuse to let your stupid acolytes destroy my only good source of entertainment in years."

"I thought you were only keeping the thief around to study his runes once you caught him," Decras said with a wry smile.

"Oh, stuff it," Renewal muttered. "I do what I want. I'm a goddess."

"A very humble one," Decras said with a snort of laughter. "You think the little demon will actually manage to repair her flawed Demon Rune? I don't know if her body would even be able to handle such a change."

Renewal shrugged. "Noah has both of our runes. He has the power to do it, if the demon can live for long enough to survive the change. Why do you ask? Feeling threatened?"

Decras let out a low laugh. "They've got a long way to go before they could come anywhere near threatening me. And I can't believe you bothered to actually remember any of their names. They're a bunch of mortals, Renewal."

"We've been watching them for some time," Renewal said defensively. "And that *mortal* stole more of your rune than he stole of mine. I'd think you'd be smart enough to remember his name before he steals even more of your power from right under your nose."

Decras narrowed his eyes. "We'll see about that. My little surprise should still be on the way. The Inquisitor was interesting, but I want to see what the thief can do, not just the demon girl."

"Your surprise isn't going to make it until they're all two hundred at this rate," Renewal said, eating another chocolate. "Can't you move faster?"

"You've gotten impatient," Decras said. "Better work on that if you don't want to go insane."

"Bah. It's not impatience. Have you seen how fast they're growing? By the time you actually get around to doing anything, they'll be ten times stronger than what you guessed they would be, and the threat won't even bother them."

"Do you really think I didn't account for that?" Decras rolled his eyes. "They've got their hands full already. If my surprise showed up anytime soon, it would be too much for them to handle. I've already accounted for their growth and the time it'll take them to deal with that rune hoarder."

"You're sure they'll beat him?" Renewal raised an eyebrow. "For his rank, he's quite the menace. He might win, and then we're going to lose everything. I'm not going to watch *him* for fun. He's just a scurrying rat dragging around something he stole."

"Is our own target really any different?"

"Yes." Renewal looked away from the screen to glare at Decras. "He's actually comprehended what he took and improved upon it. Wizen is just a power-hungry man with a rune too dangerous for him to handle properly."

"And now you're remembering the names of the unimportant roadblocks." Decras crossed his arms. "Did you get hit on the head, Renewal? How much attention are you spending on these mortals?"

"Oh, get over it. You're doing the same thing, just making up your own names for everyone. If you ask me, that's even more effort just to pretend to be more mysterious than I am."

Decras cleared his throat, immediately telling Renewal that she'd been right on the money. "Either way, I suspect we'll have quite the show. And, if not, I'm sure we'll get our entertainment soon enough. The pieces are already moving, Renewal. Maybe you should focus on getting your Church closer to the scene. Right now, they couldn't be further from actually finding the thief."

"And whose fault is that?" Renewal asked. "Your little temptress got in Ferdinand's way."

"I'd argue the opposite. Garina would have captured the little shit by now if the stupid baldy hadn't gotten in her way and started waving those damn sandwiches around. I swear, when I next talk to her—"

"Interfere and I'll rip your throat out," Renewal growled. "I want to see this play out."

"You'll try," Decras said with a wry smile. "Relax, would you? Garina might not listen to me now, even if I asked her to do something. She's always been rebellious. We'll just let things play out and see what happens. Either way, I think we'll have more than enough entertainment for quite some time."

Renewal couldn't help but agree.

She hoped Noah would find a way to get out of the situation closing in around him in a way that would keep his companions alive. She'd never admit it to Decras, but she was actually starting to get somewhat invested.

It would be a shame if Wizen killed them all.

Afterword

Thanks so much for reading book 4 of Return of the Runebound Professor! I've got a whole lot more content, around 600,000 words as of the time of writing this, over on my patreon page at https://www.patreon.com/Actus

You can also find me by searching up 'Actus Patreon' on google! In addition to Runebound, I've got several other novels you can check out. Make sure to keep an eye out for Runebound Book 4, as it'll likely be out pretty soon after Book 3! I've also got some merch and a clothing brand you can check out at https://www.actuswrites.com

Thank you for reading Return of the Runebound Professor 4

We hope you enjoyed it as much as we enjoyed bringing it to you. We just wanted to take a moment to encourage you to review the book. Follow this link: Return of the Runebound Professor 4 to be directed to the book's Amazon product page to leave your review.

Every review helps further the author's reach and, ultimately, helps them continue writing fantastic books for us all to enjoy.

* * *

Also in series:

Check out the entire series here! (Tap or scan)

* * *

Want to discuss our books with other readers and even the authors? Join our Discord server today and be a part of the Aethon community.

Facebook | Instagram | Twitter | Website

You can also join our non-spam mailing list by visiting www. subscribepage.com/AethonReadersGroup and never miss out on future releases. You'll also receive three full books completely Free as our thanks to you.

* * *

Looking for more great LitRPG?

Check out our new releases!

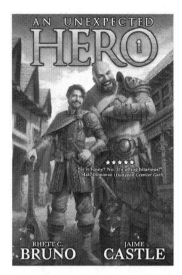

Order Now!

(Tap or Scan)

A magical new world. An ancient power. A chance to be a Hero.
Danny Kendrick was a down-on-his luck performer who always struggled to find his place. He certainly never wanted to be a hero. He just hoped to earn a living doing what he loved. That all changes when he pisses off the wrong guy and gets transported to another world. Stuck in a fantasy realm straight out of a Renaissance Fair, Danny quickly discovers that there's more to life. Like magic, axe-wielding brutes, super hot elf assassins, and a talking screen that won't leave him alone. He'll need to adapt fast, turn on the charm, and get stronger if he hopes to survive this dangerous new world. But he has a knack for trouble. Gifted what seems like an innocent ancient lute after making a questionable deal with a Hag, Danny becomes the target of mysterious factions who seek to claim its power. It's up to him, Screenie, and his new barbaric friend, Curr, to uncover the truth and become the heroes nobody knew they needed. And maybe, just maybe, Danny will finally find a place where he belongs. **Don't miss the start of this isekai LitRPG Adventure filled with epic fantasy action, unforgettable characters, loveable companions, unlikely heroes, a detailed System, power progression, and plenty of laughs.** *From the minds of USA Today bestselling and Award-winning duo Rhett C Bruno & Jaime Castle,* An Expected Hero *is perfect for fans of* Dungeon Crawler Carl, Kings of the Wyld, *and* This Trilogy is Broken!

Get An Unexpected Hero now!

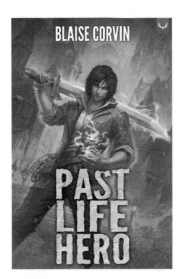

BLAISE CORVIN

PAST LIFE HERO

Reborn as a nobody, he must become a Hero again... then save everybody. *Living on Earth as a recent college graduate, Max can still perfectly recall his past life on the fantasy world of Albion before he was murdered. He'd been hailed as the "Hero of the World" after crawling his way up from poverty, eventually enjoying great fame and luxury. But reborn on mana-starved Earth, he's just a guy. However, when Earth is suddenly attacked, changing the natural laws of the world and threatening all life on the planet, Max will get a new opportunity to regain some of his lost power...and then some. He discovers an entire system of multi-dimensional colleges created for those gifted with a Path. The universe is much larger than Max had even known ever during his first life. Max is not the Hero of Albion anymore, but the drive to excel is still part of his nature. And the more power he has, the easier it should be to save his world. ...Right?* **Welcome to this unique twist on isekai fantasy in the next LitRPG Adventure by bestseller Blaise Corvin, author of Delvers LLC and Apocalypse Cultivation.**

Get Past Life Hero Now!

For all our LitRPG books, visit our website.

Made in the USA
Columbia, SC
17 October 2024